The Sleuth of Baghdad

The Inspector Chafik Stories

The SLEUTH *of* BAGHDAD

The Inspector Chafik Stories

CHARLES B. CHILD

Crippen & Landru Publishers
Norfolk, Virginia
2002

Cover painting by Carol Heyer

"Lost Classics" cover design by Deborah Miller

Crippen & Landru logo by Eric Greene

ISBN (cloth edition): 1-885941-74-9

ISBN (trade edition): 1-885941-75-7

FIRST EDITION

Crippen & Landru Publishers
P.O. Box 9315
Norfolk, VA 23505
USA

www.crippenlandru.com
CrippenL@pilot.infi.net

Contents

CHARLES B. CHILD

Charles B. Child was the pseudonym of the British writer C[laude] Vernon Frost (1903-1993). Beginning when he was 19 or 20 years old, he was a prolific contributor to the British boys' magazines, writing anonymous stories for *Hotspur* about the Red Circle School and the Wolf of Kabul for *Wizard*. Sometime during the 1920's, he "spent two romantic years tagging Abd-el-Krim in North Africa... " In 1930, he married an American newspaper woman, and for a while lived in the United States. Returning to England, he became one of the many writers of the famous Sexton Blake detective series; his book-length Blake adventure, *Crime on the Heath*, was published in 1937. According to one account, he was at this time writing about 20,000 words a week.

At the outbreak of the Second World War, Frost was living on the Côte d'Azur in France. He returned to London and was commissioned as a Flight Lieutenant in the Royal Air Force, and assigned to Military Intelligence in Iraq, where he worked both in Baghdad and in Kurdish territories in the north of the country.

In 1946, Frost moved to Connecticut and wrote stories, mostly based on his Middle Eastern experiences, for *The Saturday Evening Post* (under his own name) and *Collier's* (as Charles B. Child). His first Inspector Chafik J. Chafik story appeared in *Collier's* in 1947, and Chafik quickly became one of the most popular characters in that magazine. A total of 30 tales about the Baghdad Inspector appeared before *Collier's* ceased publication in 1957. *Ellery Queen's Mystery Magazine* published 4 more original stories between 1957 and 1969.

Frost explained that Inspector Chafik was based on Iraqi police officers he had known during the war:

> I wondered what kind of detective would fit the tricks I had in mind. Naturally I thought of my friends, and so the character of Chafik J. Chafik was born. I take no credit. Chafik just arrived quietly complete with sidarah and cigarette and introduced me to Sergeant Abudullah. Chafik is a composite of old associates. Graceful manners mean more to the Arabs than to us. They love a witty phrase, but wrap it around a hard core of truth. Their minds are agile and wind through a complicated maze, but when adapted to the problem of crime this appears to be an asset.

The most specific source was Frost's wartime interpreter, who could translate every Middle Eastern language or dialect, and who possessed the filing card memory that Frost would later attribute to Inspector Chafik.

During the latter part of his life, Frost continued to travel, and addresses are recorded for him in Connecticut, Bermuda, and Majorca. He died in San Diego at the age of 89 in 1993.

Forty-five years ago, Frederic Dannay (half of the writing team of "Ellery Queen" and editor of *Ellery Queen's Mystery Magazine*) lamented the fact that no publisher had issued a collection of the Inspector Chafik stories. We are delighted to make the best of his cases, including the first and the last, available in *The Sleuth of Baghdad*.

THE PUBLISHERS

The Inspector Is Discreet

He was a dark little man. His eyes were like brown olives; they matched the sun-colored load of desert and sluggish rivers where he had been born. They were the eyes of a people who had seen the rise and fall of the Chaldeans, the Hittites, the Assyrians and the Babylonians, and still watched curiously the coming and going of other empires.

He was nervous and carefully adjusted his tie before knocking on the door lettered boldly: H.J. ELLSWORTH, and below it, in Arabic and English: Chief Inspector, Criminal Investigation Department.

As he opened the door he speculated, as he often did, as to why the government of Iraq gave the appointment to an Englishman. "Chafik J. Chafik, sir," he announced to the chief inspector. "Inspector, C.I.D." He wondered at his own words because Ellsworth knew he was Chafik J. Chafik just as well as he knew the street outside was Al-Rashid Street, Baghdad.

The big man behind the desk looked up and said in a weary voice, "Oh, sit down, Chafik. I suppose you know about the murder last night?"

The little man repeated rapidly in precise English, "Case seven hundred and three. Miriam, daughter of Ali ibn Ali Aziz of Basra. Found at 4 A.M. on the river path outside the garden of Mr. Ronald Stewart. Dead several hours. No violation or robbery."

"It's an awkward business," Ellsworth said. "She was his mistress."

"A common possession in Baghdad," Chafik said. "I can list —"

The chief inspector interrupted hastily, "That's enough. The ambassador takes a dint view of scandal. Stewart is English, and —"

"Excuse me," Chafik said, "but only his passport is British. He is three-quarters Armenian, although he resembles his grandfather who came here in 1893. The red-haired Scotch blood is strong, but he is Armenian."

He regretted speaking when Ellsworth hit the desk and shouted, "How many times have I told you to be careful with these people? Dammit, Chafik, the man's protected by the embassy, and any complaint there comes back on my head!" The rumble of the big voice filled the room.

Chafik, perched on the edge of a chair, nervously twisted his *sidarah*, the black forage cap worn by Moslem Iraqis. He said anxiously, "Yes, yes. I should not consider Mr. Stewart's ancestry. If you will brief me concerning the death of his mistress —"

"I've interviewed Stewart," Ellsworth said, and added with the beginning of a new rumble: "It was better for me to tackle him, considering he's British." He waited a moment and then went on: "The man's story is simple. There was trouble with the girl's father who claimed he was disgraced and wanted compensation. He came up from Basra to see his daughter. Stewart gave her fifty dinars and she arranged to meet her father on the riverbank at the back of the house at eleven-thirty. Stewart went to the Alwiyah Club at ten o'clock and stayed there until two, drinking. I've checked that, and I saw him myself in the bar before midnight. His alibi is sound, except for a brief period when he says he left the bar and walked in the grounds to cool off. He doesn't remember what time it was, but when I saw him he was coming through the door —"

"Before midnight?"

"Yes," said the chief inspector. "Don't start checking on me. I'd just looked at the clock. It was 11:52. When Stewart got home the girl hadn't returned and he thought she was still with her father. He admits he was drunk and went to bed, where his butler found him when the police called." Ellsworth looked at his notes and added, "Stewart says the girl had no previous lover."

"No," Chafik said. "Stewart was the first, and last."

"You've got a mind like a card index," Ellsworth rumbled. "What do you know of the father?"

"Ali ibn Ali Aziz," recited Chafik. "Race, Arab. No occupation. A drunkard. Convicted at Basra in 1945 of doing injury by stabbing. Sentence —"

Ellsworth shrugged. "It looks like a clear case. I suppose he was full of *arak* and killed his daughter because of some twisted idea of family honor. You ought to be able to pick him up easily."

"He cannot escape, sir. That is all?" The little man stood, like a terrier straining at the leash.

"That's all, except for one thing," said Ellsworth. "The ambassador doesn't like to hear of British nationals mixed up with the Iraqi police. You're efficient, I know, but be very discreet with Mr. Stewart."

"I have heard," Chafik said, "that his temper is like his hair. I will be discreet, sir." When he was outside Ellsworth's door he murmured, "So I must be discreet with an Armenian! Oh, Merciful God!" He went to his office and touched the bell on his desk.

Inspector Chafik was talking to a tall, gaunt sergeant named Abdullah. "The little matter of the Armenian's woman which we have already discussed — is there any report yet of the father?"

"We have searched the brothels," Abdullah said, "and the other dens where men befuddle themselves with *arak*. His description is fully circulated and the gates of Baghdad are closed. But there are many ditches into which he may have fallen. Or the river," he added hopefully.

"The river is better than the scaffold," agreed Chafik. He took a case from his pocket and handed the sergeant a cigarette. They bowed over the lighted match and

Abdullah politely touched his forehead with the tips of his curved fingers. "The morgue first, sir?" he asked.

"Yes. Bodies are disgusting things, but it is God's will they exist."

Inspector Chafik followed the sergeant down the stairs and stood for a moment in the narrow doorway smelling the sourness of Al-Rashid Street, where desert Bedouins rubbed shoulders with sleek city effendis, and arabanas pulled by dying horses mingled with the taxis and fine new cars. The dirt of the street disturbed him, and for a fleeting moment he wondered how Baghdad had looked in the ancient days. It sprawled now, vast and brown and ugly, along the banks of the same Tigris, but the palaces and rose gardens were gone, and shabby modern houses smeared with the dust of sand storms crowded along the mean streets.

At the morgue he viewed the body. The girl had been very young and quite pretty. Her throat had been cut. Chafik studied the wound and said to Sergeant Abdullah, "The killer slashed from behind and she had no chance to turn. Swift and clean." He turned away. "Show me her possessions."

They brought him a handbag, some trinkets, and an expensive watch. In the bag was a bundle of dinar notes. He counted them carefully and said, "The money the Armenian gave her for her father." He picked up the watch and held it to his ear. He touched the winder and said, "It is half wound, but it is ten minutes slow. This is a fine Swiss watch and should not be slow. Take it to a watchmaker and have the mechanism checked." He stood back and wiped his fingers fastidiously. "She was with child," he said, looking again at the body on the slab. He pulled the cuffs over his thin wrists. "Abdullah, how does a father kill a daughter who has disgraced him?"

"Perhaps with a thrust in the stomach?" suggested the sergeant.

"These people have primitive passions," Chafik said. "They center their anger on the source of the disgrace. To cut a throat neatly requires coolness unconnected with passion." He sighed. "Now we will go to the scene of the crime. The mind works best by routine."

They drove out to the Jenub district. Here were the houses of the rich merchants set in gardens bright with flowers. The dark green of the date palms was a restful background and the great river embraced it all in a cool loop.

A constable was posted at the back of Stewart's house, where there was a path along the top of the embankment which held back the Tigris during the spring floods. Now the river was low with hard mud and gray sand between the water and the bank. Trees shaded the path by the gate in the garden wall.

The constable ordered away a band of children and showed Chafik where the body had been found. "Here is her blood," he said, pushing the crowding children with the butt of his carbine.

Chafik looked briefly. He took money from his pocket and threw it to the children. "Go buy sweet-meats," he said, and as they fled with shouts of joy he added softly, "A small bribe is often more effective than a threat." His dun-colored eyes searched the ground between the gate in the wall and the bank of the river. He bent to examine some dark sand scattered over the dirty white dust and gravel of the path. Rubbing a pinch of it between his fingers, he said to Sergeant Abdullah, "It is still damp. From where does it come?"

"The river, sir."

"The river," Chafik repeated. "Did the children bring it here for their play?" He looked at the constable, who answered, "I have been here since the body was found. The children did not play with sand."

Abdullah said, "If they played here yesterday the sand would be dry."

The Inspector lighted a cigarette and for some minutes remained silent while the sergeant and the constable regarded him respectfully. Finally he said, "This is a land of sand, but God willed it there should be many types, each in its proper place." He threw away the cigarette with a gesture and said, "I will go now and talk with the Armenian."

The house was large, with high, cool rooms handsomely furnished. The Inspector's feet sank into thick carpets as he followed the white-robed butler to Stewart's study. As he entered the room he touched his *sidarah* in a courteous salaam to the burly red-haired man who sat at a desk covered with papers. "Please excuse me calling, sir. But I was near by and thought —"

"What the devil can I tell you other than I've told Ellsworth?" asked Stewart. His manner was irritable and slightly contemptuous. "I can give you five minutes," he said.

As Chafik looked at him he almost doubted his own records. Stewart had the appearance of a typical Scot. He had the fair skin which burned and flaked in the sun. His big hands were freckled and the backs were matted with red-gold hairs, fine as silk. He was handsome, but there was a puffiness about his eyes which came from overindulgence. He has even inherited his grandfather's capacity for drink, thought Chafik, but unlike the old trader he lives soft. Shaking his head, he wondered at the strange race created by the phlegmatic Northerners who had settled in Iraq and married the volatile daughters of the Armenians.

"Well? What d'you want to know?" Stewart asked. He had not invited Chafik to sit down, and the little man stood, shifting from one foot to the other and smiling nervously. "Excuse me, but it is such a personal matter," the Inspector said. "The girl was pregnant —"

Stewart stood up. He was over six feet and his heavy build reminded Chafik of the water buffaloes that wallowed in the Tigris mud. His temper was equally unpredictable and the question fired it like a dynamite cap. "Damn you!" he shouted. "Is there no privacy in Baghdad?"

Chafik said, "Please, please! It is so awkward for me to have to ask questions of British people —"

"Yes," the red-haired man said. "And you'd better be careful if you want to keep your job. I've only got to complain to the embassy." He sat down and added brusquely, "Of course I knew she was pregnant. It was obvious, dammit!"

"So unfortunate —"

"What the hell d'you mean by that?" The bloodshot eyes swiveled. "It's obvious to anybody Miriam's father killed her. You Iraqis always —" He shook his head. "Haven't you caught him yet?"

Impatiently Stewart began to open and close the drawers of his desk. There was an automatic pistol in the top right drawer. He was closing the drawer when Chafik said, "We will find him, sir — but I am not sure of his guilt."

The drawer with the gun remained half open as Stewart asked, "Why?"

"The money you gave her had not been taken, sir. She wore an expensive watch and bracelets. Surely he would have taken them all? And why was the watch slow?" Chafik stopped and gave an apologetic laugh. "Excuse me. It is very bad the way I speak my thoughts, but I am puzzled about the watch. Now I will go." He went to the door and turned to say ingratiatingly, "Is it true your wife returns from England in a few weeks?"

"What's that got to do with it?"

"She was in England when the war began. It was the war that stopped her return?"

The red-haired man's anger mounted again. He shouted, "You know damn well it was the war."

Chafik bowed his sleek head meekly. "If the child had been born," he said, "I am sure Mrs. Stewart would have cared for it as her own. Such a pity!" Before Stewart could reply, Chafik was out of the house, smiling as he remembered the strong-jawed Englishwoman the man had married. To Sergeant Abdullah he said, "The Armenian is very angry."

"They are nervous people," Abdullah said. "Highly strung. Their anger comes from that."

Chafik patted his arm. "This man is like the whisky sold in the Baghdad bars," he said. "The label is Scotch, but the contents are a home brew."

He took the wheel of the police car and drove at a rapid pace down the wide boulevard. He swung left to the promenade, where riverside cafes were popular during the heat of the year. They were closed now and the promenade was deserted. Chafik stopped opposite the grounds of the Alwiyah Club, which stretched from the river to the main road. The back entrance was a flight of wooden steps leading to the tree-shaded lower garden. "Four minutes," Chafik said, looking at his watch. Abdullah nodded gravely.

"It is time for the afternoon coffee," said Chafik.

They went to the Swiss Café on Al-Rashid Street and had coffee and almond cakes dipped in honey. The noise from the crowded, narrow street was a mingling of peddlers' cries, arabana bells, klaxons, and the thwack of sticks on the hides of laden mules. Above everything grated the alien voices of celluloid actors performing at the cinema across the way, amplified to four times the normal volume. Chafik said, "It is a film of American gangsters. I will go to it. Continue the search for the father, Abdullah. We can do nothing until he is found, which will be in God's time."

When Inspector Chafik was sitting through the feature for the second time, a man came down the aisle and whispered, "We have him, sir." The Inspector sighed and got up and as they left the cinema he said, "The film had interest. I wish our police cars had sirens like in America. To sit behind such a noise must make one feel important."

At headquarters he said to Sergeant Abdullah, "How did you find him?"

The sergeant answered, "I heard he had a friend, so I brought the friend here and beat him until he told me where the man was hidden. It is a good method."

"Yes," nodded Chafik, and added, "Providing the right man is beaten — Now bring me Ali ibn Ali Aziz."

They brought in the father of the dead girl. He had a thin, weak body and his face was yellowed by the damp heat of Basra. The stale smell of *arak* made the Inspector shake orange water on a handkerchief and press it to his nose. "How you smell!" he said, and turning to Abdullah, he asked, "Did he have a knife?"

The sergeant, with the air of a maître d'hôtel presenting a choice dish, placed on the desk a narrow wafer of sharp steel attached to a bone handle. He said, "There was blood. I prepared a specimen for the laboratory, but it would appear the investigation is ended."

"Perhaps," answered Inspector Chafik. He turned to Ibn Ali Aziz and said, "You are a dog sired by a pig. You were prepared to sell your daughter to an Armenian. Why then did you kill her?"

The prisoner said in a frightened, squeaky voice, "I did not kill her. It is my knife, but I did not kill her. I went to the place where we were to meet and then the skies fell."

"What do you mean — the skies fell?"

"I stood by the wall of the man's house waiting for my daughter —"

"And the time?"

"About the half hour to midnight."

"And then?" Chafik's dun-colored eyes were suddenly alive.

"The skies fell." The prisoner's voice was sullen.

Inspector Chafik said, "Bend your head." He parted the thick, oily hair and examined the scalp. There was no mark. "Either you lie or the skies were soft," said Chafik. He went to the wash-bowl in the corner and washed his hands thoroughly before saying casually, "There is blood on your knife, and if you are innocent you would not have hidden. From me you can hide the truth, but not from God. Talk!"

"After the skies fell I slept. When I woke I was in a ditch. I thought perhaps the *arak* had made me fall there, and I went back to where I was to meet my daughter. I saw her body —"

"You had killed her," said Chafik.

"By the All-Merciful God I had not killed her!"

"Your knife killed her."

"It was by her side. I picked it up —"

"Why?" asked Chafik, and nodded when Ali ibn Ali Aziz answered, "Because it was mine and I feared it would be traced." The man coughed a tubercular cough and added, "And then I ran."

"Because you had killed your daughter."

Ali ibn Ali Aziz raised his manacled hands and let them fall in a helpless, resigned gesture. "I did not kill her," he said, tears of self-pity rolling down his yellow cheeks. "All I know is the skies fell and then I found her dead. May my body be dismembered and my soul —"

"Take him away," said Inspector Chafik in a bored voice. "Even his soul revolts me." When the man had gone, Chafik said to Sergeant Abdullah, "Yes, he revolts me, but he has told the truth."

"Sir?" said the sergeant, astonished.

"The skies fell. They fell with great force, but they were soft. Have you forgotten the sand outside the Armenian's house?" There was a sudden harshness in his voice which caused Abdullah to stiffen and say, "No, sir, but I had not seen the connection. The sand spilled from a sandbag which split when it was used."

Chafik lifted the telephone and dialed a number. As he waited for an answer he said, "It is like weaving a carpet. The little threads combine into a pattern." He took his hand from the mouthpiece and, bowing his sleek head, said ingratiatingly in English, "Mr. Stewart? Excuse the lateness of the call. This is Inspector Chafik... But it is a very small detail — Do children play in your garden?"

He held the receiver from his ear as the angry voice shouted, "A damn' silly question. Of course not. Why?"

"Because," said Chafik, "there is river sand outside your garden gate which appears to have been thrown from within. As no children played with it, there must be another reason for this curiosity. Good night, sir." He hung up and said, "How much that man hates me!"

He sat for a long time looking at nothing. The patient weaving of his mind formed a strange and ominous pattern. He said, "It is almost complete, but not quite. We have the sand, but not the bag. The chief inspector will require evidence to touch with his finger, as the wounds of the Prophet Jesus were touched by one also blind to facts. Take every man, Abdullah, and search for the bag, it may be anything. Perhaps a man's sock. Search the riverbank and the grounds of the Alwiyah Club. You understand?"

"Your wisdom embarrasses me," Abdullah murmured.

"It is not my wisdom. It comes from God — And one last thing, Abdullah: Let the men be obvious in their search so that all Baghdad knows for what they look. Let them be particularly clumsy at the Alwiyah Club." When the sergeant had gone out Chafik said to the empty room. "There is no hope of hiding it. The chief inspector will be angry with me."

In the morning he stood at Ellsworth's desk and heard the heavy voice beating about his ears. He was, as usual, nervous and fumbled with his *sidarah*. Ellsworth rumbled, "You're playing with dynamite and I ought to close the case. There's enough concrete evidence to hang Aziz. Why d'you think he's innocent?"

"Because," Chafik said, "the girl was not really mutilated. Because nothing was taken from her. Because he says he saw the body —"

"Explain that."

"Sir, the Arab mind is different from the English mind. You will excuse me if say it is not so subtle. The Arab, when guilty, does not tell a simple story, but lies badly. If Aziz had killed his daughter he would have strained his imagination to convince me he had not seen her body. He would have told me," Chafik added, smiling, "an Arabian Nights story."

Ellsworth said, "You're telling me one yourself. I want proof. I want the sandbag." He was worried because he believed the little man, but foresaw the consequences of a blunder. Finally he said, "You'll never find the bag. It's easy to hide, and all Baghdad knows about the search. The men have been damn clumsy —"

"Yes," Chafik said.

"You've got to be careful. I'll give you until the end of the day to bring me evidence. Dammit! I ought to throw you and your hunch out of my office and send Aziz up for trial!" The chief inspector hammered the desk with a sudden gust of liverish anger and roared, "Of all the damned, awkward situations. Oh, get out, Chafik! I'll have your hide if you're not discreet!"

Outside the office the little man wiped his forehead and murmured, "Discretion is a racial problem." Going to his room he called the Jenub Police Station, which Sergeant Abdullah was using as his headquarters. The sergeant's tired voice on the telephone told him there was no trace of the missing sandbag. "What now, sir?" he asked.

Inspector Chafik said, "The pattern of my carpet must not be ruined because I lack one thread of the right color. We must substitute —" He had been voicing thoughts, and smiling into the telephone. He said, "That was for your ear only, Abdullah. How is the Armenian this morning?"

"The servants say he spent the night drinking. He is now in the bar of the Regent Hotel, where it is often his custom to stay until half past twelve. His manner is dangerous."

"Yes," said Chafik, "I can imagine." Cradling the telephone in both hands he said gently, "Call off the search. We will never find the bag. And go home and rest. I do not need you any more, Sergeant Abdullah."

The Inspector sat with his head lowered and his lips moving. Finally he walked to the armory at the rear of the building and said to the man in charge, "It must be discreetly done." He did not realize he had spoken until he saw the bewilderment on the officer's face. A few minutes later Chafik left, toying with a brass cylinder hidden between forefinger and thumb. He hurried to his car parked outside and told the police driver, "Jenub. The Armenian's house." As the car passed a mosque he remembered it was the hour of the noon prayer and regretted he had no time for the ritual. Inspector Chafik was a religious man.

The white-robed butler who answered the Inspector's ring said, "Master is out. Do you wish to wait?" He was an old man and smiled toothlessly as Chafik dropped money in his hand.

"I will wait here," Chafik said, and quietly closed the door of Stewart's study behind him. He looked at the papers scattered on the desk, spilling onto the floor, his practiced eye seeing the disorder as reflecting the red-haired man's state of mind.

Slipping on a pair of gloves, he opened the top right drawer of the desk and took out the automatic pistol. He removed the clip, ejected the cartridge from the breach, and fed into the clip the blank he had brought from the armory. The slide clicked back as he reloaded the weapon. Replacing the gun in the drawer, Chafik removed his gloves and sat waiting, eyes closed, body relaxed.

He heard the car drive up half an hour later. Lighting a cigarette he murmured, "May God remember me."

Stewart burst into the room and stood looking at him. The man's red hair was disordered and his voice was shrill.

"What the devil now?" he shouted, dropping heavily into the chair behind the desk.

Chafik began, "I am afraid I give you a lot of trouble —"

"I won't be pestered this way," Stewart blustered. "I'll complain to the ambassador. You Iraqis are getting too uppish. Why the hell don't you find Miriam's father?"

"Oh, we have him, sir — but he is innocent." The Inspector watched the big hands clutch the edge of the desk and said quietly, "But a girl *was* murdered. There *was* a watch that was slow and skies that fell on the head of a father. There *was* sand from the Tigris. There *was* the fact that the girl was pregnant and the fact that Mrs. Stewart returns from England. Shall we fit the facts to a story?"

"I'm going to kick you out in just two seconds —"

Chafik flicked the ash from his cigarette and went on conversationally, "You set her watch slow so you could be first at the gate when Ali ibn Ali Aziz kept his appointment. You stunned him with a sandbag. It was necessary that it should be smooth, wet sand. The sand of the shore is mixed with gravel and would therefore mark the scalp. Also it lacks weight, so you used sand from the river. Unfortunately the bag split when you hit him. You searched for the knife such a man would carry and then you put him in a ditch — But I am tiring you, Mr. Stewart?"

The red-haired man said nothing. The knuckles of the hands gripping the desk were white.

"When the girl came to meet her father," Chafik said, "you stepped behind her and — so!" He made a slashing gesture with his finger. "Neat and clean," he said admiringly. "And you cleaned the handle of the knife and put it by the body before driving back to the club; the drive home took you four minutes. I have timed it. The entrance from the river is rarely used after dark. To all appearances you had strolled in the grounds for a little air."

The face of the man behind the desk was gray, like the river sand. An eye twitched as uncontrolled nerves contracted the muscle.

The Inspector said, "Now we will discuss the mistakes. You should, of course, have taken the money and the watch. A poor Arab such as the father would have done that. Also the method of killing was wrong. The stab should have been in the stomach.

"Once there was reason to doubt the guilt of Aziz, it was necessary to look for a man with another motive. The girl was pregnant, and all Baghdad knows your fear of the temper of Mrs. Stewart. Therefore —"

"You dirty little snooping mongrel!" said Stewart. He rose slowly to his feet, still clutching the desk.

"Therefore," went on Inspector Chafik in a tranquil voice, "I searched for one fragment of evidence that was not hypothetical. I have it here."

He took from his pocket a woolen sock tied with strong cord to make a bag. The sock was split and grains of gray sand fell from it.

"An English sock," the Inspector said. "The one you used to make the sandbag."

"You liar!" Stewart shouted. "That isn't what I —" He stopped suddenly, watching Chafik in horror.

"Now God has made you talk," answered the Inspector.

The red-haired man swayed and his bloodshot eyes searched the room anxiously.

Then he said, "you haven't got a witness, you fool! That was a plant. Fake evidence. I'll deny what I said and Ellsworth will believe an Englishman before any damned Iraqi!"

Now he is near the end, thought Chafik. His nerves have cracked — he needs just one word more. And smiling, Chafik said, "But you are Armenian!"

The blue of Stewart's eyes darkened. Warning banners flamed in his florid cheeks.

His hand flashed to the drawer of the desk and came up gripping the automatic. He mouthed incoherent insults as he aimed at the Inspector.

As yellow flame stabbed and the gun roared, Chafik ducked to avoid the stinging blast of burning powder. He felt the wad from the blank strike the side of his *sidarah* and let himself fold sideways over the chair to the floor; he fell limp and doll-like, with arms and legs flying. He kicked violently and was still. He could smell his cigarette burning the thick nap of the carpet as he thought: A detective must be many things, even a dead man...

Waiting was a lifetime. Waiting was eternity. And then he heard Stewart say, "Oh, God! God!"

The second shot was muffled, and not until the body of the red-haired man had finished floundering across the desk did Chafik get up. He was careful to squeeze out the cigarette in a tray and rub the burning carpet with the toe of his shoe. The smell of cordite made his nostrils twitch and he wasn't surprised that he was trembling; Stewart's hate might have made him fire several more times, live cartridges following the blank.

Chafik heard the servants in the hall and opened the door. "Tell the constable outside that I need him," he said curtly. "And keep out. Your master has shot himself."

He moved quickly. He picked up the case of the blank cartridge from the carpet and put it in his pocket. He looked at the powder burns on his *sidarah*. I must get a new one, he thought. The chief inspector has sharp eyes. Of course only one shot was fired. He has no reason to question the servants...

Chafik stepped around the body to reach the telephone. Ellsworth's rumble answered when he dialed the number. "Oh, it's you," the chief inspector said. "Have you got that bag?"

"No, sir," Chafik answered. "It was probably destroyed. But the evidence is no longer required, as the case would appear to be closed."

"What?" shouted Ellsworth. "Where the devil are you?"

"At the home of Mr. Stewart," Chafik replied. "We discussed the matter frankly, and —"

"My God!" the chief inspector said. "I told you —"

"To be discreet sir?" Inspector Chafik looked at the heavy body crumpled over the desk and thought: Whatever story I tell is justified, for God was the witness to what the man said...

Smiling at the telephone he said in his most ingratiating manner, "But I was, sir. After the Armenian confessed, he shot himself."

Inspector Chafik Closes the Case

The desert was an ocean of gravel and gray dust which lapped the struggling outskirts of the City of Baghdad. Spewed from the sullen waves of dead earth were hovels built partly of baked mud and partly of flattened gasoline cans, relics of the war years and the British garrison. A few goats, tethered at the doors, chewed listlessly at rinds of discarded melons, while potbellied children, dirt more than rags covering their nakedness, played in the brief shade of the railway embankment.

The sky was the open door of a furnace stoked with the Iraqi sun, and Inspector Chafik, stepping from his car and viewing the scene, said to the tall, gaunt man who followed him, "It is well we came at once. A body is always detestable, but in such heat it becomes an abomination."

Sergeant Abdullah said reprovingly, "Man's body is made by God."

"True," his superior replied, "but when the soul's breath has gone from it, the remains are only of interest to us of the police." Chafik smiled as he spoke, an unexpected softening of his dark, lean face, and a brightening of his dun-colored eyes, which were as old as the ancient land of his birth. He was a little man, with well-shaped hands and feet and a thin, wiry body. He wore a white linen suit, well tailored by Western standards, and stepped daintily over the rubbish which littered the path, careful not to soil his shoes. He was aware he was watched by people who feared him because he was Chafik J. Chafik of the Criminal Investigation Department, but he felt no pride in their fear. If the poor were all criminals I would have half Baghdad on my records, he thought, and stopped at the gate of a courtyard where two khaki-uniformed police were standing guard.

As he entered, his shadow went before him over a square of swept, clean ground. He looked at the round cakes of water-buffalo dung plastered against the walls of the hut to dry for fuel, and said, "Him we have come to see was blessed with an industrious wife. Poverty has not broken her spirit."

Sergeant Abdullah said, "Was she not always poor?"

Inspector Chafik answered with sharp reproof, "You can see for yourself. Those born in dirt die in dirt. Here is cleanliness. Furthermore, our records at headquarters should be known to you." And as rapidly as if his files and index cards were spread before him he recited the dead man's history, "Galani, Yusif. Born, Baghdad. Secondary-school education. Employment, clerical. Served as interpreter with British forces until 1945, when illness forced resignation. Brother of Hassan Galani, an official of the Finance Ministry —" Chafik shrugged and added, "It is on a white card and his life was equally as spotless. Who would kill such a man?"

When he crossed the threshold he raised his hand, touching first his forehead and then his heart with the tips of curved fingers, a salaam of respect to the dead. Although he glanced at the body stretched on a cot at the far side of the room, he did not immediately go to it, but surveyed the floor, the walls, and the clumsy thatch of date-palm fronds through which the sun slashed. He looked at the few pieces of furniture, unusual in such a hovel, and ran his finger along the back of the solitary chair. "Clean," he said. "Painfully clean." Drawing aside a curtain of sacking which covered one corner of the single room, he examined a pile of straw which had a fresh, aromatic smell. A ragged but neatly folded blanket held his attention. "Clean," he said again.

"And tidy," said Sergeant Abdullah.

"As if visitors were expected. The straw which was a bed for children has been newly shaken." Inspector Chafik made a gesture of annoyance and added, "Our records are not in order. There was no mention of children on the man's card, but two take his name."

"Sir?" said Abdullah, astonished.

"There is a food bowl by the dead man's side," Chafik explained. "You will see on the shelf three other bowls. Therefore, there are four people living here, for a poor man does not spend *fils* on what he does not need. The bed of straw is not sufficient for adults. Therefore we have children, and small children. Every fact fits as a thread in the design of a carpet. Let us see what pattern is woven here."

He went to the cot and looked carefully for the first time at the body. Galani had been a big man, but he was so wasted by disease that he now looked frail and brittle as a mummy. He lay on his back on a clean, patched sheet, his shoulders cradled by pillows. His only garment was a shirt of Egyptian cotton, fine as lawn. The comfortable appearance of the corpse was spoiled by a terrible bruise in the center of the forehead made by a heavy, blunt object which had crushed the skull. Some blood had oozed from the wound, but the main hemorrhage was inward and death must have been instantaneous.

On the floor was a towel folded three times like a bandage. There was blood on it, and Chafik, having looked from the pattern to the dead man, said to the alert sergeant, "Fetch me the policeman who was first called."

When he was alone, Chafik completed a quick search of the hut and bent to examine a heavy stone which was hollowed to form a crude mortar. The pestle, also of stone, had a wooden handle bound with cloth. There was a small sack of grain, almost empty, nearby, and as the policeman who had found the body came in, the Inspector said, "For grinding grain to make *khobis*."

He looked up with surprise when the policeman respectfully answered, "Yes, sir. It is so used."

"So I speak my thoughts aloud?" smiled Chafik. "It is indeed a bad habit. May I now hear your report?"

"Sir, I am of the suburban mounted patrol. As I rode along the railway embankment I heard shouting and came down. There were many people about this hut and I ordered them away. Inside was the dead man as you see him. He had been discovered by a woman who cares for him when his wife is away —"

"Why does she go away?"

"Sir, she washes clothes for the effendis of Baghdad —"

"Hardly a living," said Chafik. "Soap has the value of gold, and customers are few now the British have gone. The husband, of course, could not work?"

"I have been two years on this patrol," the officer answered. "He has always been too ill to leave his hut." The picture of tragic poverty was getting clearer, but at the same time it became less and less clear why Yusif Galani should have died violently.

Once again the Inspector looked at the folded towel he had found on the floor, and holding it up he asked, "Where was this when you viewed the body?"

"I touched nothing, sir — but the woman who found him said there was a cloth over his face, which she lifted."

Chafik said in a worried voice, "If the towel had been wetted to cool his brow the thing would be understandable. But it was not wetted. This is grotesque." He gently placed the cloth on the crushed head of Yusif Galani and added, "It covered his eyes." Turning to Sergeant Abdullah he said in an explanatory voice, "Obviously the pestle used for grinding grain was the weapon. It was replaced in the mortar afterward and is unstained because of the towel. You will find no fingerprints because the cloth binding of the handle presents a broken surface. I am undecided whether this is an exceptionally clever crime, or one of extreme stupidity."

"In either case you will solve it —"

"If God wills. I have no powers myself." Inspector Chafik took a final look around the room and going to the door said, "I leave you to receive the doctor, Abdullah. Medical evidence is often unintelligible to the lay mind and confuses thinking. But check on the nature of Galani's illness and ask about the drugs you will find by the bedside. It is possible that some drug made him sleep, and that he was killed when sleeping. The autopsy will give us the facts on those points."

He left, saying in a clear voice, "A comfortable corpse. A very fine shirt. Such cleanliness." Sergeant Abdullah watched him go, with affectionate amusement because he knew Inspector Chafik was unaware he was speaking thoughts.

Outside the hut in the shade of the courtyard wall a number of women were crouching, their black veils drawn to hide their faces. They waited incessantly, hennaed finger tips fluttering against their lips to produce a high, bubbling cry. Chafik stopped and said, "Is the woman of Yusif Galani here?"

One who sat silently apart from the noisy wake, nursing a small child, answered, "I am the wife."

The Inspector said to the others, "It would be better to think of the living. Go back to your cooking pots." The women fled, their black garments fluttering in the hot wind like the ragged wings of crows.

The little man lighted a cigarette. He could see only the eyes and part of the forehead of Galani's wife, for the folds of her outer robe were modestly drawn. He noted the cleanliness of the child and was pleased with the mother's dignity. Here, he thought, is one with courage, but her suffering is too great to be relieved by tears. He moved awkwardly because he did not wish to intrude on grief, but questions had to be asked and he was glad when the woman opened the conversation by saying, "My man is dead."

"He is with God."

She answered in a voice husky with tears, "He was a good man. Why does God strike a good man with sickness and leave him helpless? Is there a God?"

Chafik said, shocked, "There is a God, or you and I would not be here. What name have you?"

"Zenobia ——"

"I see only one child. There should be two."

"The other has gone for water," the Widow Zenobia said, and then lifting her head and with pride in her eyes, added, "He comes now. Truly as good a boy as his father was a good man." She was silent as a boy came up the path carrying a gourd of water, which he presently handed to her. He was a tall, thin lad, his only garment a cotton gown held at the waist with a strap. His head was wound with a ragged, but clean turban cloth and he looked at Chafik with the restless, searching look of one who, even at his age, lived by his wits. "Ahmed has ten years," the woman said. "He is a man."

Chafik said, "Then I will talk to him as a man," and turning to the son of Yusif Galani he asked, "Who killed your father?"

Ahmed answered, "I do not know, but when I find him I will take his life."

His mother clutched his hand, moaning, "Such words should not be in your mouth." To Chafik she said pleadingly, "He knows nothing, because he went early to the bazaars to earn money by carrying parcels."

"I made twenty *fils*," the boy said proudly.

"Good!" Chafik suddenly smiled. Turning to the woman he asked, "Who killed your husband?"

"I know not." A hand still slender although work-hardened reached outward and upward and then fell listlessly to the ground. "I know not," the Widow Zenobia said again. "I went to the city with wash for a customer, taking my other child with me. There was some trouble and I was late back."

"And the name of the customer?" Chafik prompted.

The woman gave the name of an English resident of Baghdad, and when the Inspector asked, "What was the trouble?" she answered, hesitatingly, "A garment was missing." Hurriedly she added, "And afterward I sat by the river and bathed the child. My man wished to be alone."

"And the reason?"

"He said he expected a visitor —"

Inspector Chafik hid his surprise. His eyes, which matched the desert, were suddenly alive. "A visitor? A man?" he asked. "What man?" But he foresaw the answer.

"A wife does not question her husband," the woman said, and repeated wearily, "He expected a man."

"Had he friends?" Chafik said. "What of his brother?"

There was a flash of fire in the reply, "Hassan Galani left him to die. He would not give one *fil* to help him."

"May God destroy my uncle," said the boy, Ahmed, in a flat, dead voice. "When I went to him and begged for help for *Baba*, he beat me. He is cruel. He —" Ahmed was silent, digging nervously at the gray dust with his bare toes. Then he asked, "Did the visitor kill my father?"

Chafik parried with a question, "Did your father tell you of the visitor?" and when the boy shook his head the Inspector beckoned one of the uniformed officers from the door and told him to inquire if a strange man had been seen. He realized the chances were slight because the hut was at the outskirts of the slum and hidden by the curve of the railway embankment. "Go with the policeman," he commanded Ahmed. "Perhaps you can help him." When the boy had gone, he said to Yusif Galani's wife, "He is very bright."

"There was never a better son. If his uncle would help so that he could have learning —"

Chafik said, "The law will make him help. You are now a destitute widow with children. Hassan Galani, as next of kin, must help. Such is the law."

The woman answered slowly, "I have heard of that law. My man spoke of it and said he wished he could die so that such a claim could be made on his brother." She repeated the hopeless gesture of her hand and finished, "Now death has come to him. Death has come to him."

The Inspector threw away his cigarette and watched the neighborhood children fight for the smoldering butt. He cleared his throat loudly and said in a harsh, rasping voice to hide his emotion, "So he wished to die? Well, it was a pity he had to leave us with so much mystery." He took a thin billfold from his pocket and found three dinars, which he dropped by the woman's side. "Go with God, Widow Zenobia. I will speak to Hassan Galani about his duties." Abruptly Chafik turned away and walked to his car.

He was stopped by the policeman he had asked to inquire about the dead man's visitor. As he expected, there was no witness, and he said, "The English have a proverb about a needle and a bundle of hay. To find a man in a desert is equally as difficult." Chafik looked back at the miserable hovels crouching breathlessly under the merciless sun and was closing the door of his car when the boy, Ahmed, who had been standing behind the policeman, darted forward. "Effendi —" the boy began, and stopped with his thin, brown hands clasped and the interlaced fingers working nervously.

"What is it, Ahmed born of Yusif?" Chafik said to him.

"The visitor killed my father?" Ahmed asked.

"The unknown man," Chafik said gently, "is a dark thread drawn through an unfinished pattern. Until the weave is complete I cannot answer."

"There was a man near the hut when I left this morning —"

The Inspector caught the boy by his thin shoulders. "What? Why did you not tell me?"

"I did not wish to speak in front of my mother —"

"Good! It is right that as a man you should not talk of these matters before women. Who was the one you saw?"

The boy said breathlessly, "My uncle!" and shaking himself free, he fled into the gray, burning wilderness behind the huts, leaving Inspector Chafik motionless by the car.

Chafik drove back to his headquarters on Al-Rashid Street and the police driver had to touch his arm to rouse him from his thoughts. The little man said, "The evil that men create returns a high interest," and went up the narrow stairs leaving the driver confused. At the top of the stairs was a door boldly lettered, H. J. ELLSWORTH, and the Inspector passed it on tiptoe because he had no desire to report to his superior, the burly, liverish Englishman appointed by the Iraqi government to head the Criminal Investigation Department.

When he was safely in his office, Chafik telephoned the home of Hassan Galani. A woman's voice answered, "My husband is at the Ministry," and Chafik said, "You are sure, Madame?" He grimaced at the instrument as the voice replied, shrill with complaint, "At least he telephoned to say he was there, but a wife does not ask questions when a husband stays away from home. Are we not chattels?"

Chafik said, "Madame, madame, I am only an acquaintance of Mr. Galani," and hung up quickly, thinking it was a pity the growing emancipation of women in Iraq had the Western weakness of emancipated tongues.

"There is danger in this," he declared, as he lifted the receiver again to dial the Ministry of Finance.

Hassan Galani was not in his office and the Inspector left a message for him, to come to headquarters. Then he opened a new packet of *Ghazi* cigarettes and sat at his desk staring at nothing and as usual thinking aloud the rambling words ending " — It is almost woven. I do not like the design." And hearing the echo of his own voice he smiled a little foolishly and was glad when Sergeant Abdullah came into the room.

Marshaling details like a parade of soldiers, the sergeant made his report of the police surgeon's examination. "The man was dying of cancer. He would perhaps have lived another six months. The drugs at the bedside were to relieve pain. He had taken a sleeping draught before he was killed and there were traces in the bowl of sour milk at his side. It is correct he was killed with the pestle of the mortar. Two blows were struck, but the first was sufficient. He knew nothing —"

"And saw nothing," said Chafik. "The cloth spread over his face is a puzzling detail."

He was silent with his thoughts but roused himself when an orderly entered and said, "Hassan Galani is here, sir."

The Inspector rose to receive the visitor, saying to Abdullah, "This will be private, but look at the man as you go out. There is the shadow of a noose around his neck —"

Hassan Galani was a middle-aged man whose dignity matched the weight of his swollen paunch. His position in the Finance Ministry was important, and he said harshly as he entered Chafik's office, "What is the meaning of leaving a message for *me* to come to *you*? I am disagreeably surprised, Inspector Chafik."

The little man answered, bowing his sleek head and smiling ingratiatingly, "I do apologize, but the matter was of importance and I feared you had left Baghdad because you were not home last night." He did not miss the quick flush which darkened the visitor's sallow, unhealthy face, nor the anxious expression. "Were you away from Baghdad?"

Hassan Galani removed his *sidarah*, the black peakless hat of the Moslem Iraqi, and mopping his almost bald head, he said, "I spent the night at my garden. Yes, at my garden up the Tigris. It was such a hot night. I have a small pavilion there and often sleep —" Abruptly he recovered his dignity and with it anger. "This is an outrage, Inspector! Why should you ask where I spent the night?"

Chafik, spreading his hands with the curved palms upward, said, "I talked innuendoes to find courage to break sad news. Your brother is dead."

"The only brother I had disgraced me with his poverty. As far as I am concerned he died long ago —"

"Poverty is not a crime, Mr. Hassan Galani."

"A man in my position must think of his reputation — but I do not care to discuss family matters with you." Hassan Galani rose heavily to his feet with the intention of leaving, but turned to ask, "How did Yusif die?"

"He was murdered," answered Chafik casually, and then in his most silky voice: "A witness has stated you were near the hut when your brother died early this morning."

"What an abominable lie!" shouted the man. "I was —" He stopped with a look of horror.

"You were at your pavilion on the river?" Chafik prompted. "Please do not trouble yourself over this foolish witness. It will, of course, be necessary to check with the servants of your *bayt*, a little matter which I will do most discreetly." He watched his visitor fumble blindly for the chair. "You see," Inspector Chafik went on, "*if* you could not prove your alibi — excuse the word, Mr. Galani — it would be very awkward. This witness hates you. He would swear before God you were there, and it might almost appear you had motive to kill your brother, because, as you told me, his poverty disgraced you."

Hassan Galani said with a pitiful attempt at dignity, "I forbid you to question the servants at the pavilion."

"Perhaps," Inspector Chafik said, "you were not there?" And leaping to his feet — with a tiger's spring he shouted, "Where were you?"

"I —"

"Circumstantial evidence can hang a man. Where were you last night? Where were you this morning? Why were you so late at your office? Why have you not been home?"

"I —" and, his face glistening with sweat, the man whispered, "I was with a woman."

"Yes," Chafik said. "You were with a woman. I thought the perfume which still clings to you did not come from the flowers of your river garden. Oh, Mr. Galani! Mr. Galani! Your dignity almost brought you to the scaffold!" He opened a drawer of the cabinet behind him and extracted a card. "My index cards are very complete. There is much on this one to interest the Minister of Finance. You appear to have expensive tastes, dangerous in a man who helps handle the nation's exchequer. There are the names of many women on this card. What name shall I now add?"

Whispering, Hassan Galani said, "Khurrem —" The name was drawn from him like a tooth from an abscessed mouth.

"Khurrem," the Inspector repeated thoughtfully. "Turkish. 'Joyous,' a notorious dancing girl at a certain cabaret in Baghdad who has already ruined several men." He wrote on the card and then said curtly to the man who was huddled on the other side of the desk, "You may go now. But remember that your brother's widow and his children are destitute, and by the law of Iraq you must support them. Be generous, Mr. Hassan Galani, particularly with the boy, Ahmed. And do not forget my records."

When the man had gone stumbling out, Sergeant Abdullah came from the other room where he had been taking down the conversation. He said with disappointment, "You have removed the shadow of the noose from Hassan Galani's neck, sir."

Chafik answered, "I have taken away that shadow, but he still lives under the shadow of my index cards."

"Both are uncomfortable, sir." Abdullah hesitated, troubled by the dead look in the eyes of his superior. He asked, in the hope of rousing Chafik from his thoughts, "Who was the witness who lied?"

"The nephew. The boy, Ahmed. His uncle planted hatred in his heart and it came back with interest. When he heard his mother say Yusif Galani expected a visitor, he saw his chance —" Inspector Chafik groped on his desk for the folder containing the reports of the case. He said, "There is medical evidence that the man took a sleeping draught. Does one do that if one expects a visitor?"

"By God, no!"

"Abdullah, it is not for you to support an opinion with the name of God — but the woman, Zenobia, she also lied, like her son lied. Obviously if she gave her man a drug to make him sleep he did not expect a visitor. Please to consider the facts. They are all there to read, and the design is complete now the false thread of Hassan has been drawn out." When Abdullah continued to look at him, his swarthy face paling, the Inspector went on, "What did we see in the hut? What was our strongest impression?"

"Cleanliness and tidiness. Exceptional cleanliness and tidiness, as if preparations had been made for a visitor —"

"Or visitors with curiosity, such as ourselves. The Widow Zenobia has great pride. We will now check on her pride." And reaching for the telephone he rang the number of the English resident for whom the Widow Zenobia did washing.

Sergeant Abdullah heard him say in his precise English, "Mr. Williamson? This is Inspector Chafik of the C.I.D. I understand you give your laundry to a poor woman and have a complaint about a missing garment —" He chuckled into the mouthpiece and said, "Oh, yes, even lost laundry concerns us! Surprising things come out in the wash... Thank you, Mr. Williamson. Thank you." And putting back the instrument he said to Abdullah, "It was a shirt. A shirt of fine Egyptian cotton."

"The corpse —" began Sergeant Abdullah.

"The corpse wore such a shirt," Chafik said. He drummed the desk for a moment and then went on, "Why does a very honest woman steal to dress her man in such a beautiful shirt? Have we not here pride, decency? Is it not the custom to bury the dead in the finest garments?" The sergeant did not reply, but his hands moved in a protesting gesture toward his ears. Inspector Chafik continued, whispering now, "And so we come to the cloth spread over the face of a man who was drugged by a draught introduced into his morning milk. Hiding his eyes. To hide his eyes."

Sergeant Abdullah said, "All-merciful God! How could one look upon the face of one who was loved, and still strike the fatal blow? Sir —"

Inspector Chafik rose to his feet. He said harshly, "You will please be silent. I do not know what you mean. Yusif Galani would in any case have died, and in agony. Furthermore, if he had lived, perhaps his sons would not have lived. Those who live in poverty must deny their children food when the man is sick." He reached for a cigarette, found one, but was blind to the match on his desk. "The Widow Zenobia," he said, "can now make a legal claim for the support of the children, and herself. A wise law obliges Hassan, as next of kin, to do his duty. That is sufficient, Sergeant Abdullah!"

He went to the window and looked down at busy Al-Rashid Street, where taxis and horse carriages were mixed in a crazy tangle. When he turned he was smiling faintly. "Don't you think," he said, "that some passing nomad entered the hut and struck the unfortunate man because he moved and was possibly going to cry out?"

Standing at attention, worship in his look, the sergeant answered, "That would appear to be the solution."

Inspector Chafik said, "Yes, it would appear to be the solution, and such a man, without motive, would be hard to find." He picked up the folder and went to the door, saying over his shoulder, "Obviously we close such a case. I will make my recommendation to our good Chief Inspector Ellsworth. Without doubt he will tell me I am a very stupid man —"

Death Had a Voice

Rumor, born as a breath in the maze of alleyways surrounding the holy mosque of Kadimain, gathered mischief as the desert wind gathers dust. It choked reason, blinded tolerance and whipped up fury in the mob that cried havoc through the shabby, dun-colored streets of the city of Baghdad.

The components of the mob were ragged, underfed men bred on the dirty body of a hate-racked world. Individually they were pitiful. Collectively they were terrible. They were armed with knives, sticks, fragments of stone: but the worst weapons of all were their brown, clawed hands. Cloaked by the darkness of an oppressively hot night, the men ran; and like all mobs, this one did not know where it was going, or why.

On the outskirts of the Bab-al-Sheik district were the police. The white tunics of the metropolitan officers were smudged chalk lines drawn across the main roads, and in the side streets lurked khaki-clad troopers of the suburban patrols, mounted on well-trained horses. Behind, were motorized squadrons of mobile police, heavily armed with rifles and machine guns, prepared to drive forward into the heart of the mob if the clubs and reversed carbines of the forward lines failed to force it back.

A dapper little man drove up in an open touring car, surveyed the preparations and nodded approval. He was dressed in a lightweight civilian suit of good cut, and wore on his sleek head the black *sidarah* of the modern Iraqi. He had a sharp chin and rather full lips; his eyes were large, mottled olive in color, and strangely flat. He was representative of a people whose beginning was veiled by the mists of history, and he looked at the mob cynically, seeing it as the rot in the timbers of a neglected civilization.

He said in Arabic to his companion, a gaunt man in the uniform of a sergeant of police, "One smells their hate. Have you not noticed, my dear Abdullah, that each human passion has a distinctive odor?"

Sergeant Abdullah replied, "Sir, I have sometimes smelled fear —"

"Fear and hatred are twins." Inspector Chafik of the Criminal Investigation Department lighted a cigarette and blew gently on the smoldering end to make it burn evenly. Looking at the mob, he went on, "I pity these foolish people whose heads we are about to crack. They are not our enemies."

The swarthy face of the sergeant darkened and he made a gesture of protest. "Permit me, sir, to observe that these men break the law, and therefore —"

"A doctor," said Chafik smoothly, "does not consider his patient an enemy. He wages his war against the cause of the complaint. And mob madness is equally a sickness." He drew on his cigarette and then went on in a voice of iron. "There is direction behind this riot. It is a cancer, and I intend to cut it out."

The little man stood up in the open car as the space between the mob and the police barrier closed. The senseless howling had died away, and it seemed for a moment that the orderly lines of uniformed men might act as a sedative, that tactful handling would disperse the crowd.

Then, somewhere in the background, a voice raised the ancient battle cry of the Jehid, "*Thibha-hum besm er rassoul!*"

The voice had the high pitch and wailing note of the fanatic, but it also carried authority. It probed to the nerves, and with that one cry destroyed the salutary effect of the massed police. When it came again, "Kill in the Prophet's name!" the mob echoed the words and launched a volley of stones.

The police came into action, but above the thud of their sticks, the cries of pain, the shouts of anger, the voice could still be heard. Sometimes it came from the front of the crowd, then again from the flanks; the darkness and confusion made it impossible to trace the source. The mob attacked with such fury that the police barrier was pushed back, and now it was the turn of the troopers. They drove wedges through the packed ranks of fanatics, and struck hammer blows with the brass heelplates of their carbines while their skillful horses backed and sidled.

But still there was the voice, "*Thibhaham besm er rassoul! Thibhaham — Thibhaham!*"

Inspector Chafik said bitterly, "Hashish would have a less maddening effect. We have now heard our enemy." He turned to a squad of mobile police. "Bring me that man who blasphemes the Prophet!" he ordered, and then beat his hands together in sharp despair as he heard the voice again, but this time from a distance.

Whoever the man was, he realized the mob was fighting a losing battle. He fled now for safety, a vampire satiated for this night, leaving behind the dead, the injured — and what was worse, the cancerous hate.

Chief Inspector Ellsworth, appointed head of the Baghdad C.I.D. by the Iraqi government, sat at his desk on the second floor of the headquarters building on Al-Rashid Street, reports of the night's events spread before him. He was a burly, red-faced Englishman, whose thick brows joined in a bar across his forehead and accentuated the sharpness of his eyes.

He said brusquely, "Fifteen dead, eighty-three injured. A lot of looting. Only thirty arrests, and those unimportant. This is a hell of a poor show, Chafik."

The little man, who was perched on the edge of a chair, moved uncomfortably. He told himself he had no reason to fear the chief inspector, but his hands were clammy. He was aware he had spoken ingratiatingly upon entering the office, and self-anger surged to his normally cool head. He began adjusting his neat polka-dot tie to hide it.

Ellsworth said irritably, "Leave that damn tie alone! …What d'you think was behind this riot, Chafik?"

"Sir, I would say that its sole purpose was to foment hatred." His English was precise.

"For political reasons?" The chief inspector's eyebrows worked vigorously.

Chafik twisted the folded *sidarah* between his slender hands and answered in the peculiar hollow voice of a man who spoke thoughts, "Hatred breeds hatred. Arabs rise against Jews, and Jews against Arabs. In India the Moslems and Hindus destroy one another. It is also this way in Europe and elsewhere. There is a plague of fear and suspicion in the world that makes each religious and political group see the other as a mad dog —"

Ellsworth interrupted, "Dammit, I don't want to hear a lecture."

The little man gave a nervous smile. "Please excuse me." Then he said with unexpected firmness, "I am a policeman and a servant of the public. In politics I must practice celibacy. Therefore I do not wish to consider the reason for the riot. But it is my duty to arrest the man who directly instigated it."

"You mean this man with the voice?" asked the chief inspector, looking at Chafik's report.

"Yes, sir. I am convinced he was paid to do what he did, in the same way an assassin is paid. The dead are his victims as surely as if he had struck them down with a knife. Perhaps we cannot touch the people who paid him — they may be outside this country — but he should hang."

The iron was back in his voice, and the Englishman looked at him curiously, thinking: He's a fanatic too. He'd give his life for the cause of law and order. Aloud, Ellsworth said, "Is there any clue to this man's identity?"

Chafik spread his hands, and the light which had briefly given color to his eyes began to fade. "The prisoners have been interrogated. Some describe the agitator as a tall man, others as a short man. He is also definitely identified as being both fat and lean —"

"In other words an average man. We might just as well try to pick one pea out of a bushel." Ellsworth rammed tobacco into his pipe with a vigorous thumb. "What about probables?"

"Investigations proceed, but I have already eliminated the majority of professional agitators on our records." Chafik paused and then added, "But a clever man would not be on our records, and this one may be a stranger."

"So you look for a man of average appearance who may or may not be Iraqi! What a hope!"

"Sir, I am not without hope. I have closed the gates of Baghdad, and am confident the man now lurks like a rat in some dark hole. I shall drive him out." Ellsworth looked skeptical, and Chafik added, "It is true I did not see his face, but I heard his voice —"

The chief inspector put his hands on the desk and looked at the little man through the smoke of his pipe. He saw him as a terrier, quivering with the excitement of the hunt, and wisely refrained from asking how Chafik expected to recognize a voice briefly heard in the confusion of a riot. Instead, he said gruffly, "Better not tell me your plans. You're so damn unorthodox... All right."

It was dismissal, and the Iraqi salaamed with the tips of curved fingers hovering near his forehead. When he had closed the door behind him he stopped and carefully adjusted his tie with a gesture of self-assertion. "Unorthodox! Unorthodox!" he repeated harshly. "What this Englishman means is that he does not wish to offend his official conscience by hearing what I may do." Chafik gratefully inhaled the acrid smoke of his Kurdish cigarette as he walked to his own office in the building.

The room was furnished with a desk and a few chairs; a row of filing cabinets stood against one wall, and on the other was a map of Baghdad. It was an excessively tidy room, but Chafik frowned and moved the telephone to an angle that squared with his "in" tray before he sat down. When he touched the bell, Sergeant Abdullah appeared with the readiness of a jinni. He said, "I have the honor to give you the final list of agents who specialize in riots —"

Chafik said, "That is not an honor. They are all sons of Judas." He read the list carefully, then threw it down and wiped his hands as though they had been contaminated. "This does not help us," he told his assistant. "There is only one way to find the man who cried, 'Kill in the Prophet's name.' Are the rioters who were arrested still in the building?"

"We have just finished interrogating, sir. But I regret to report —"

"A negative report is of no value." The little man got up and paced the room, but presently he stopped and remarked conversationally, "Of course there is a certain risk..." He flushed with anger at the sound of his voice speaking the thought, and said sharply, "Each man is to be brought to me. He will shout, '*Thibha-hum besm er rassoul*' as it was shouted last night."

Sergeant Abdullah put the palms of his hands together in a gesture of protest. "Sir, may I be permitted to express doubt that it will be possible to recognize —"

"You may not express anything."

Chafik stood at the window overlooking the yellow-brown city. The increasing heat of the day poured rivulets of sweat down his thin face, but he was unaware of discomfort.

He was absorbed by threads of thought that wove a strange and intricate pattern. But when the door opened and Sergeant Abdullah announced disapprovingly, "The first prisoner," he turned briskly.

They thrust into the room a man dressed in a dirty gown. His bare feet were caked with dust, and his oily hair straggled from under a wisp of turban. The man said in a frightened voice, "Kill in the Prophet's name —"

The Inspector lighted a cigarette. "You do not shout with enthusiasm," he said softly. "The voice that called for death to walk the streets of Baghdad did not whisper." He spoke to the escort consisting of two police officers: "Take him away and beat him so that he may learn to shout."

When the man was brought back ten minutes later, he screamed, "*Thibha-hum besm er rassoul!*" in a voice that reverberated.

Chafik said, "That is an improvement, and now I know yours was not the voice I heard last night." He nodded to Sergeant Abdullah, who waited attentively. "Let this blasphemer go. He may consider the beating just punishment — And bring the next."

The followed one another at brief intervals. Some shouted defiantly, and all loudly because they feared the instructive sticks of the police. After each shout the little Inspector said, "It is not the voice I heard. Let him go —"

At the end of two hours the door closed on the last man. The dreadful cry still seemed to echo in the room, and Chafik gently rubbed his ears as he left the window and went to his desk.

Sergeant Abdullah said sympathetically, "Your head aches, sir. It is a pity you were not rewarded. But it would indeed have been a coincidence."

"It would be even more remarkable if I could recognize the voice —"

"Sir?"

"You will now comb the brothels, the cafés, and the bazaars, and bring in every man who might have taken part in the riot to shout the same cry."

The sergeant put a brown hand to the collar of his tunic to ease its pressure around his choleric neck. He said hoarsely, "There are four hundred thousand people in Baghdad. To find the voice you may have to hear all of them. And you yourself have just said —"

Inspector Chafik opened a fresh packet of *Ghazi* cigarettes and bowed his sleek head as he offered one to his assistant. He said, "I do not intend to ask so many people to cry blasphemy in my already offended ear. That indeed would give me the madness you think afflicts me at this moment." His strange eyes became suddenly brilliant, and he added softly, "No, my dear Abdullah, I do not expect to find a voice I cannot recognize. I expect to find the man who owns it, to harass his nerves until they break."

"But, sir —"

"These men are even now telling the cafés of Baghdad that we seek a voice. And when perhaps for weeks, we continue today's test, what do you think will happen to the man who hides?"

Abdullah rapped knuckles against his head. "It is all wood up there," he said. "I had not perceived the plan. The man who shouted last night will fear that he may be brought in to face the test. Therefore, like a cornered beast, he will venture into the open to destroy that which makes him afraid —" The gaunt sergeant stopped and his swarthy cheeks paled.

Chafik said gently, "I see you are beginning to understand."

"You have made all Baghdad believe you alone can recognize the voice —"

Chafik made a sound of disapproval. "You are old-fashioned. Generals do not die in bed these days. Sometimes they even mount the scaffold. Make note, Abdullah. The man who shortly tries to kill me, or even succeeds, is the man wanted for last night's murders."

He took a manicure pad from his desk and began to polish his nails carefully.

Five days later, Inspector Chafik, seated at his favorite table in the Swiss Café on Al-Rashid Street, announced to the waiter who served him with coffee and honey cakes, "A bullet of course would be preferable to a strangler's cord —" He did not realize he had spoken until he saw the man's startled look, and then shielded his confusion behind his newspaper.

Yes, he told himself, this time silently, and it would also be an excellent thing if nerves, like false teeth, could be detached during periods of discomfort...

He lowered his newspaper and watched a stranger searching for a table. These days, Chafik acknowledged, he was suspicious of strangers, and when in a public place he always chose a chair backed by a wall. The condition of his nerves shocked him, excited him. If the hunter was affected this way, what of the hunted? The man who cried death must be near the breaking point.

The Inspector looked at his watch. The hour was seven fifteen, and this was Thursday, the day and hour when he habitually attended the early performance at the Saa'dun Picture House. Chafik was satisfied his habits were well enough known to shape the plans of an assassin; it was essential he should not change them. The feature at the Saa'dun was a detective film, his dearest form of relaxation, but he doubted he would relax this night.

When he stood up he saw one of his own men peering through the plate-glass window of the café. He had not asked for a bodyguard, and shrewdly guessed that Sergeant Abdullah had acted on his own initiative.

The plain-clothes man had disappeared by the time he reached the door, and he looked suspiciously up and down the street. All he could see was a beggar-woman crouching against one of the pillars of the arcade. She held up a baby clad in rags, shaking it for his attention until the bracelets on her arms jangled noisily. "Be merciful," she moaned. "See the belly of my child!" but the preoccupied little man let the fumbled coins fall back into his pocket and hurried to cross the road.

It was a hot and airless night. Fine sand, carried from the southern desert by recent winds, was suspended like mist above the city. It sank gradually as it absorbed moisture, and gave people and objects an unreal appearance. The Inspector, however, did not fail to see an elongated shadow in a doorway near the theater, and he said conversationally to the surprised attendant at the box office, "The gauntness of the good Abdullah cannot be effectively disguised —" Taking his ticket, he chose a corner box and lowered himself into an armchair set against the wall.

As he anticipated, he could not find his usual enjoyment in the lush screen world of corpses and clues. Nor could he relax; not only because of his taut nerves, but because he was plagued by something not done, something overlooked.

He retraced the events of the day. Then, to the annoyance of a gentleman who occupied one of the other chairs in the box, he said, "The thing is traceable to the café. Did I forget to tip the waiter?"

His chance companion said, "I think you mistake me for somebody else —"

"It was not the waiter," Chafik stared at the other man, but did not see him. "I remember now. A woman asked her alms and I did not give them to her."

"The giving of alms is blessed," said the stranger. "But so is silence in the cinema. I must request —"

"I have always given alms. The crux of the matter is undoubtedly there." He was silent for a moment and then best the arms of his chair and rose to his feet. "I have it!" he announced. "I was controlled by my subconscious —" This time he heard his voice and was grateful for the darkness as he stumbled out.

Leaving the theater by the fire exit at the rear, he walked up an alleyway to Al-Rashid Street, keeping an alert eye for Sergeant Abdullah. When the familiar figure emerged from the murk of dust, he pressed himself to the wall.

Chafik was touched by his assistant's devotion, but he thought: This sets a false value on my life... and as Abdullah stopped outside the Saa'dun and made a pretense of examining the posters, the Inspector slipped across the road.

It was the Inspector's habit on the nights when he went to the pictures to complete the evening with another visit to the café. He walked quickly, his footsteps muffled by the carpet of sand which now covered the road. The windows of the café threw a haze of bluish light. A shapeless bundle against the wall began to stir as he hurried by.

Opening the door, he said loudly to the proprietor who sat at the cash register, "I am early because the picture was not good. The hero had an inexhaustible hip flask and was still drinking when I left. I will take tea." He closed the door on the whining beggar-woman and went to his usually table.

Chafik lighted a cigarette and was annoyed because he broke the first match. When the waiter brought a glass of green tea, flavored with lemon, he sipped it carefully and wondered that the taste should be bitter. He had an uncontrollable desire to talk, but steadied himself by silently repeating the one hundred and thirteenth sura of the Koran, which begins, "I take me for refuge to the Lord of the Daybreak," after which the tea tasted sweeter.

After fifteen minutes, he looked at his watch. The program at the Saa'dun was almost over. He went to the desk and bought a telephone token and shut himself in the booth at the back of the room. Dialing the number of the theater, he called for the proprietor.

The little man said, "This is Chafik J. Chafik, C.I.D. Outside stands Sergeant Abdullah, who is known to you. Please call him." He stood waiting, drawing at his cigarette.

Abdullah said breathlessly when he came to the telephone, "Sir! I do not understand how — Where are you?"

"I will tell you presently. If I told you now you would rush to protect me, so first you will pay attention to instructions."

"I hear and obey," said the sergeant.

Chafik said, "A ship, at times, obeys its anchor, but it would be a useless object without independent motion. Listen carefully. I am arranging my departure from this place to coincide with your arrival. Something will doubtless happen when I step outside, but —"

"In the name of the Compassionate and All-Merciful, be cautious!"

"On the contrary, my dear Abdullah, it is you who must proceed with caution if this experiment is to succeed. Move quietly. Do not take action until the proper moment. Hastiness would indeed distress me." His strange eyes were bright in the gloom of the box. "I am at the café," he added, and cradled the telephone with his usual care.

Chafik waited two minutes. When he went out his step was firm, but the beating of his heart was painful. He stood in the doorway looking at Al-Rashid Street and noted that few people braved the choking sand. He saw the beggar-woman against the wall.

"Food for my son! Alms — alms!" The jangle of voice and bracelets was like a rasp on Chafik's strained nerves. She fumbled with the folds of her ragged *chadur* to expose the child.

Inspector Chafik took coins from his pocket and said gently, "The plea of a mother is not to be refused." He bent to offer the money, then released his held breath as he saw the small, snub-nosed gun partly hidden by her garment.

The beggar-woman said in a voice husky with anger, "Turn and walk. My man desires to meet you." She rose with the child clutched under her left arm and the *chadur* draped to cover the gun. "I follow you," she added grimly.

Chafik said, "Unfortunately for me it is customary for a man to walk in front of a woman." Then he said dryly, "It is done to protect her. In Western countries men are wiser and reverse the position." He made a little bow and walked slowly up the street.

They passed several people who were hurrying for shelter. The Inspector reflected that even if it were desirable to call for help, he could not escape a bullet. He had seen the gray in the woman's face; the down-dragged mouth, which twitched nervously; the hatred in her eyes. She was not unattractive, and with his usual detachment he wondered what had compelled her to become the partner of a man whose profession was death. "There is tragedy behind all this," he announced, and reached for a cigarette.

The voice behind him whispered, "Do not touch your pockets." Then the woman said, "Behind what is tragedy?"

"Behind you, Madame. You have intelligence and yet you serve murder."

"I do what my man wishes!" Chafik did not miss the defiant note, nor the catch in her voice when she said, "I do not care what I serve so long as he is with me —" He heard her bracelets rattle again and then she ordered harshly, "Enter the next passage."

"The Impasse Batshat al-Kubra? You could not have chosen a better place. It ends with a river. The English translation is 'the Great Disaster' —"

"May the dogs of Hell tear your flesh!" The woman came nearer, and he stiffened as he felt the gun prod his spine.

They came to the head of the passage. On one side was the high wall of a house, on the other a fence which enclosed waste ground. The only sound was the soft gurgle of the Tigris, which swept the bank at this spot with a strong current.

Something moved near the wall, and a man stepped in front of the Inspector. He held a knife gripped so tightly that his arm vibrated like an overstrained wire. His eyes had a jungle look. He did not speak.

Chafik said, "It would be courteous to introduce yourself. Shall I do it for you? My records are very complete. They mention a certain Syrian who specializes in agitations for foreign powers. There is no description of him, but it is known he is always accompanied by a woman, who was once an actress." He made a little bow and said in a very clear voice, "I am at your command, Mohammed Khadami. And at yours, Madame Zubayda. Those were your last aliases, I believe?"

"Kill him!" The woman drew back, into the shadows.

Chafik said sadly, "Madame your sex should be a symbol of life, not death."

"Enough, thou!" Zubayda made a choking sound.

"Your man has savage instincts," continued the Inspector conversationally. "If your love was not an obsession, you could calm him. Indeed, I believe that if you had borne him children —"

"Will you kill him, Mohammed?" demanded the woman in a fierce voice. "Has he not tortured us enough?"

Speaking for the first time, the man said, "Let him first have his wish and hear my voice." He threw back the cloak and exposed a face drawn with exhaustion and distorted with hate. He shouted, "Now hear my voice and let it echo in your ears as the fires burn you! *Thibhahum besm er rassoul! Thibhahum besm* —" With final shattering of nerves and reason, he screamed as he lunged with the knife.

Inspector Chafik's backward leap was stopped by the wall. He pressed against it, waiting, but his mind was still clear, and he thought: It was a successful experiment. The man is now quite mad. Khadami was still shouting in his dreadful voice, but as he was about to lunge again an explosion rocked the alleyway.

There were three shots in as many seconds, and the sound of bullets tearing into flesh made Chafik shudder. He saw the man who had cried death fall and clutch at his torn chest.

Sergeant Abdullah burst from the haze of dust, his heavy police pistol raised for another shot. Chafik said, "Do not waste ammunition. This man is keeping his appointment at Samarra... How rightly this is called the Place of the Great Disaster!" He turned swiftly and caught the wrist of the woman Zubayda, and with a dextrous twist made her drop her lifted gun. "Dream of vengeance later," he told her, and added not unkindly, "To soothe the last moments of your man would be an act of charity —"

Chafik reached into the darkness and picked up the bundled child, abandoned by the woman when they first entered the passage. As he rocked it gently, he heard Abdullah say, "Sir, my hand was mercifully steady. Visibility was exceptionally poor, and if you had not jumped away from him —"

"You came very quietly, Abdullah, and even I did not know you were there for certain. I sprang because I hoped." The little man felt suddenly weak and leaned against the wall. "There would have been no hope for me at all if this woman had been a better actress."

Zubayda rose. She said in an expressionless voice, "Mohammed has gone now, and as you are the hangman's procurator, that is for the best." Her mouth shaped with petulance, and when she asked, "How could I have been a better actress?" she was like a child who clung to the fantasy of a favorite doll amid the wreckage of a bombed house.

Chafik said, "This is not yours." He held out the child, which was making mewing sounds of hunger.

"Not mine, no." The woman made a movement to take it, and then drew back.

"Obviously a mummer's prop," Chafik said in a harsher voice. "Otherwise I would have walked blindly into your trap."

Zubayda said, "I do not understand you. I am a good actress." She put her hands to her face and the bracelet slid down her brown arms.

"Madame!" Inspector Chafik struggled to keep sympathy out of his voice. "I knew you played a false part when I first saw you — a mother who begs for her starving child does not wear bangles."

The Inspector Had a Wife

Chafik J. Chafik, of the Baghdad Criminal Investigation Department, sat at the dining-room table in his modest house at the corner of Nathir-al-Ni'am Street and the Karradat Miriam. He was informally clad in a wide-sleeved, ankle-length gown of brown silk, opened at the neck to catch the breezes from the Tigris. The late evening meal had been cleared, and he was engaged in his hobby of detecting philatelic forgeries.

He announced, as he lifted a stamp with a pair of tweezers, "A Bermuda 'Perot.' It would be valued at four hundred dinars if genuine. But it is an excellent copy by a Swiss craftsman, and therefore worthless." The Inspector looked at the dark woman who stood at the window intently watching the moonlit street. "You are not thrilled by this addition to my collection, Leila," he complained.

Madame Chafik said tartly, "When you find a stamp worth four hundred dinars I will be thrilled."

"My hobby is relaxing," her husband defended himself. "It is also more dignified than your pastime of observing our neighbors. You were pleased to see Madame Dejani return by boat a few minutes ago?"

His wife turned quickly. "Now you mock me. How do you know what goes on in a street you cannot see from where you sit?"

The Inspector lighted a cigarette with irritating care. "I observed you look toward the river, where there is a landing for boats. Then you retired behind the curtains, which you would not have done if the person you watched had walked on the other side of the street. Finally you contorted yourself to peer in the direction of our neighbor's front door. You had already informed me that Mr. Dejani had gone away, and that his wife had accompanied him to the train. So it was simplicity itself."

Leila said, "He must have taken the Basra train. It was after six when the taxi came. There was only one suitcase, so I knew she wasn't making the journey with him."

"Your reasoning has merit. But are you sure Madame Dejani has now returned? May I know how you penetrated the shroud of outdoor robe which makes the women of Baghdad resemble animated corpses?"

"The passenger from the boat entered the Dejani home with a key. Who else could it have been if not our neighbor? You are foolish."

"I am still not satisfied," Chafik twinkled with mischief. "The railroad station is on this side of the river, and yet this person came back across the river."

"That is strange," admitted Leila, and brightened with new curiosity. "What has she been doing all this time? It is now nearly nine thirty, and the Basra train left at seven. Where did she go? Who —"

"Give me peace," said Chafik. "Such questions remind me of my unfortunate profession —"

"It puzzles me, too, why a woman of character should be devoted to a man who neglects her for an English adventuress —"

"Wife, wife!" said the little man in a shocked voice, "How do you know about Miss Violet Shaw?"

Leila answered evasively, "But it is known to all the ladies in the neighborhood. And once when I was visiting our cousin in the Alwiyah district, I saw Mr. Dejani driving in a carriage with a shameless foreign woman. I asked our cousin who told me —"

"Enough! You hold dossiers as complete as my own at headquarters. I have now lost all interest in my hobby." The Inspector closed the stamp album and stood up, a slight figure, strangely dignified in the long robe. "I do not keep a mistress myself," he said. "If I did I would be more discreet. This Violet Shaw, who is actually a Eurasian from Bombay, is indeed an adventuress. Mr. Dejani is not a wealthy man, and her extravagances are leading him into difficulties."

"They dine almost nightly at the Zia Hotel and —"

Leila's new disclosures were interrupted by the telephone bell. Chafik's heel-less slippers made a sad shuffle on the polished floor as he went to the bedroom. He took the instrument between finger and thumb.

A familiar voice said, "Sir?"

The little man lifted an eyebrow at his wife, who had followed him. He said with resignation into telephone, "Speak." A few minutes later he said, "I come," and returned the instrument to its bedside stand. "That was, of course, my dour but admirable assistant, Sergeant Abdullah. There was a note of satisfaction in his voice. He announced a corpse."

"Murder?"

"He would not disturb me otherwise." Inspector Chafik began to dress quickly but carefully, "The corpse," he said casually as he adjusted his polka-dot tie, "is labeled 'Violet Shaw' —"

The body was in a half kneeling position on the floor: the head and shoulders and outflung arm rested across a divan, which was upholstered in black and scattered with orange-colored cushions. The woman had been wearing a canary-yellow wrapper and red slippers.

She had tried to accentuate her English features by fluffing out her straight black hair, and by using a light powder on her faintly dusky checks. But her figure, which was seductive, had been inherited from a Hindu mother and could not be disguised.

Inspector Chafik, who stood in the doorway, said, "Poor Miss Shaw! What was the cause of death?"

"Sir, she has been dealt several heavy blows on the left side of the head. The weapon, which I have not located, was a blunt instrument."

Chafik went to the body and raised the head to examine the wound. "This is indeed ugly. The object had round, beveled edge." He looked around the room and then bent over a table at the end of the divan. "There is dust," he said. "Observe, Abdullah, something with a round base, perhaps a lamp, stood here recently. Possibly the weapon we seek."

"Shall I make inquiries, sir, for a person seen leaving carrying a bulky object?"

"It is extremely unlikely the murderer was observed. The house is discreetly isolated; there are no neighbors to watch the coming and going of visitors." The Inspector placed his hand under the armpit of the corpse. "There is still warmth, but bodies do not cool quickly in the heat of Baghdad. The woman may have been dead some hours. I note she met death in an angry mood."

"Sir?"

"You can see for yourself." Chafik said sharply. "There is ash scattered over the divan and carpet. She constantly flicked her cigarette, as a person does when irritated!" He took a clean handkerchief from his pocket and wiped his hands. "Miss Violet did not keep a servant in the house. Who, then, found her body?"

Sergeant Abdullah produced a notebook and read in a harsh voice, "The following is the statement of Mr. Daoud Shuman. Quote, 'At about eight twenty tonight I was walking on the Alwiyah water front in the company of my friend, Ahmed Faris, when I saw a lady resembling Miss Violet Shaw, who is well known to me. I was surprised, because she had previously broken an appointment with me, pleading a headache— ' "

Chafik interrupted, "Briefly, what did Mr. Shuman do?"

"Sir, he went to speak to her, but she hurried away and he lost her in the crowd. Then he began to search for her. It would appear he has a suspicious nature. He went to various cafés and bars, but the woman had not been seen. He says. Quote, 'Then I went to the house. The time was about eight fifty. After knocking and getting no answer, I opened the door with a key Miss Shaw had previously given me— ' "

"This is interesting, Abdullah, for a key was also in the possession of Mr. Dejani. So Mr. Shuman demanded an explanation and was confronted by a corpse. What did he do then?"

"His action was commendable. He telephoned us. He does not appear to realize he is a top suspect."

The Inspector winced. "A detective should arrive at a conclusion only after he has collected facts. Is Mr. Shuman here?"

"I held him incommunicado, awaiting your interrogation, sir."

"Rules and regulations are engraved in letters of gold on your heart! While I talk to the gentleman, kindly inquire if my neighbor, Mr. Mohammed Dejani, was a passenger on the Basra train tonight. Secondly, I wish to see the boatman who took a lady across the river and landed her at Nathir-al-Ni'am Street shortly before nine thirty. Now bring me Mr. Shuman."

"Here, sir?" The sergeant looked meaningly at the corpse.

"We shall not disturb Miss Violet. And witnesses are less inclined to lie in the presence of the dead."

When his assistant had gone, Chafik went to the window and parted the draperies, which were closely drawn. The room was airless. He looked out on the shadowy plumes of date palms and the pink night sky of the city, and noted again the seclusion of the house. It was surrounded by uncultivated land, and a winding path led through clumps of neglected palms to Mamoun Avenue. "There are no neighbors within clear sight. The path permits secretive approaches and departures," Chafik said in a flat voice.

The drawn curtains worried him. It was the custom in Baghdad to shade windows against the fierce heat of the day, and open up everything at sundown to catch the breezes. "There is something abnormal here —" he announced in the flat voice, as the door opened and a fat young man was ushered into the room. "Did Miss Violet always keep her curtains closed, Mr. Shuman?" he asked.

"Only when the sun was strong. She often opened them before the proper time. The English like air." The young man looked with horror at the body on the divan. "I insist —"

"My position as investigating officer," said Chafik, "puts me in the unique position of doing all the insisting." His thin face suddenly hardened, and he went on in a voice like a blade, "How long had Violet Shaw been your mistress?"

Shuman flushed. "You treat me without courtesy."

"I am here to solve a crime. I have no time to be nice to you." The Inspector balanced himself on his toes like a boxer. "When did you first meet Miss Shaw?"

"Two weeks ago." The young man's moon face was now pasty.

"You knew she had been the mistress of Mohammed Dejani?"

"I knew there was another man," Shuman said. "She needed protection and turned to me."

"Such women as Miss Violet," said Chafik softly, "prefer the protection of a man who is foolish and still rich, to that or a man who is still foolish but not rich. Doubtless you insisted she should not see Mr. Dejani again."

"She gave me her promise —"

"And that was why you were suspicious when you saw her on the waterfont tonight?"

The young man interlaced his pudgy fingers. "Naturally I was surprised. I had expected to meet her tonight, but she telephoned about five o'clock to say she had a violent headache and could not go out."

"You state you saw the lady at eight twenty. Was she far from you?"

"On the opposite side of the road, near the Lido Café —"

"You recognized her face?"

Shuman hesitated. "I knew her by her dress."

"I am pleased with your answer." Chafik made a little bow. "The river promenade is poorly lighted and the moon did not rise until nine o'clock. It would have been scarcely possible to distinguish faces. Was she unusually dressed?"

"She was always distinctive. Also it would be sufficient to pick her out by reason of the absence of a robe. The English do not hide their charms in the way of our women."

Chafik said, "Let us look for the dress that Miss Violet wore." He went to the bedroom and opened the closets. There were many dresses on the hangers, but Shuman pointed unhesitatingly at one. It was a dazzling print, a pattern of huge orange and blue flowers on a white ground, fussy with cape sleeves and bows.

The Inspector winced. "This is indeed distinctive. What did she wear on her head?"

"A blue kerchief tied under her chin. I had given it to her myself."

"Then you are prepared to swear the lady you saw was Miss Shaw?"

The young man said, "I cannot deny the evidence of my eyes."

Inspector Chafik opened a packet of *Ghazi* cigarettes. "Please smoke," he said. "It steadies the nerves, and I may have to give you a shock. But first look around and tell me what is missing."

Shuman obeyed. Then he pointed to the table at the head of the divan, and said, "There was something there. A bronze nude fitted with a clock —"

"The clock was doubtless set in the navel. Such an *objet d'art* belongs here." Chafik looked at the garish room with amusement, then turned quickly on the young man. "Miss Violet argued with somebody before she died. That person may have been you."

"She was dead when I came here!"

"I am a weaver," said Chafik. "I use facts as threads. It is a fact you came to this house in a suspicious mood. It is a fact that suspicion is the seed of dissension. Anger may have caused you to seize the statuette with the novelty navel and strike the lady."

"She was already dead —"

"Mr. Shuman, you saw the lady alive at eight twenty and dead at about eight fifty. It is a ten-minute walk from the Lido Café to this house. Miss Violet took time to change from her distinctive dress to her equally distinctive wrapper. She was also embroiled in argument with the killer. This person could scarcely have left before you arrived."

"I thought I heard the back door close as I entered —"

"You did not mention this in your statement to my assistant. Amended evidence is open to doubt."

The young man made a babbling sound.

"Please sit," Chafik said, not unkindly. "The design I have shown you is ugly, but you should not be frightened by it. The weave is loose and certain threads have been discarded. As a craftsman I do not like it. I had expected a different design."

He turned to Sergeant Abdullah, who had entered. The sergeant announced, "Sir, I have completed the inquiries. The other suspect was a passenger of the train. I have telephoned the police at Hilla to remove him at that junction and return him here."

"Excellent! But it was tactless to say 'other suspect.' Mr. Shuman was already upset. It would be well for him to go home and spend what is left of the night in prayer." When the man had gone stumbling out, Chafik asked Abdullah, "What of the second inquiry?"

"Sir, I have a boatman who took a lady from the Rafidain Wharf and landed her at Nathir-al-Ni'am Street at the hour you foretold. Although she was clad in an enveloping robe, he recognized her by her voice. She was Madame Dejani."

The Inspector turned the signet ring on the little finger of his left hand. "What else did the boatman say?"

"Sir, he said Madame Dejani dropped a bulky object into the river on the way across. He condoned with her on the accident and offered to get his son to dive. She replied that the object had no value, but was obviously upset."

Chafik looked down at the ring. "How very unfortunate Mr. Shuman saw Miss Violet after the train left for Basra!" he announced in a bitter voice.

At noon on the following day. Chafik entered his house on the Street of the Scatterer of Blessings and sank into a chair in the living room. With the gesture of a man breaking lifetime habits, he pulled down his tie and opened the collar of his shirt.

His wife, who had appeared with a glass of cooling sherbet, knelt to remove his shoes and replace them with slippers. She gave no greeting, and the little man remarked, "Although you are silent your thoughts are noisy."

Leila said, "Your men come and took away Madame Dejani. The face of Sergeant Abdullah was that of a judge. She has been arrested?"

"Detained." Chafik briefly closed his eyes, and when he opened them again they were dark with shadows. "Do you think this gives me pleasure?" he asked. "I am a hunter of men. Sometimes I detest myself so much it surprises me my body does not shrivel —"

Leila said, "Please, my man, do not speak harshly of yourself. You are just. Without doubt facts forced you to detain our neighbor."

"The facts are a key, a certain bulky object, and the evidence of two witnesses. The key was in the bag of Madame Dejani and fitted the door of Miss Shaw's house. Such a key had been given to Mr. Dejani."

"His wife may have found it and kept it, not knowing what it was."

Chafik said harshly, "She used it last night. I know she took a taxi from the railroad station to Mamoun Avenue, a twenty-five-minute journey. From there it is an average fifteen-minute walk to the house. The place is secluded. There are no neighbors. It can be reached by a path across wasteland. Furthermore, the night was dark until the moon rose and a woman wearing a chuddar would have been as a shadow. But it is established by fact Mrs. Dejani was there. At approximately ten minutes past nine she appeared at the Rafidain Wharf, an easy eighteen-minute walk from Miss Shaw's house. She engaged a boatman, and on the way across the river dropped an object into the water. The boatman, who thought it an accident, offered to have it retrieved, but was refused. He remembered the spot, which is where the current swings. We dredged the thing up."

"What was it?"

Chafik raised his clasped hands to his mouth, and looked beyond her with shadowed eyes. "A heavy bronze statue with an inset clock. The base matches the wounds in Miss Shaw's head," he said. "The evidence is damning. We know that Miss Shaw was out until eight twenty. She was seen by a witness. When she returned she found Mrs. Dejani. One can understand the conversation between them was not pleasant —"

"Our neighbor is a calm person."

"When a woman becomes jealous she becomes primitive. Madame Dejani afterward fled from the house concealing the weapon under her robe. We have found stains on the inside of the robe. She left by the back door as the witness who found the body entered by the front. I am afraid she is guilty."

"Surely she did not confess?"

"She said nothing. I begged her to defend herself, but she only shook her head. She has a singularly sweet face and great strength of character. How unlike Mr. Dejani."

"He did go to Basra?"

"We took him off the train at Hula. He is a very weak man. He admits he saw Miss Shaw yesterday and was given his congé. She had taken another lover. When I confronted him with the weapon and the evidence, he wept. I had a desire to beat him."

The little man rose and began to pace the room. "I have woven a pattern with threads of facts, but two threads remain unused. They are frayed. But they are threads." He rearranged the collection of clay animals from Sulaimaniya on the mantel shelf. "Why," he demanded in hollow voice, "were the curtains drawn in Miss Shaw's room when the evening air would have refreshed it? Why did she change into a wrapper; how was there time since the two women had to talk, and Madame Dejani to commit her deed of violence? This period is barely twenty minutes."

"Why worry yourself about unimportant details?" Leila gave a sly look.

"No detail is unimportant." Her husband spoke sharply. "You should know me, that I must get everything exact." He looked at her suspiciously. "I think you know me quite well," he said dryly.

"Then I will correct you about Madame Dejani." Leila lighted a gold-tipped Egyptian cigarette. "You see her as a woman so jealous of her husband's mistress that she killed her. Yet there had been other mistresses, and they did not rouse this primitive jealous of which you so glibly speak."

"Glib — I? Chafik was shocked.

"I have noted," said his wife, looking down her long thin nose, "that men are more prone to insane jealousy than women. Our weakness is an overwillingness to sacrifice ourselves to our men. It is so with Madame Dejani. She has given everything to her husband. When he gambles away his money, she sells her jewels so that he may gamble again. She treats him as a doting mother treats an erring child."

"Almost you make me believe it is not in character for a woman to kill her husband's mistress."

Leila said, "It is not in the character of Madame Dejani." She walked gracefully to the window and rearranged the curtains to cut off a red-hot spear of sun light. She said over her shoulder, "Your unused fact about the curtains is peculiar. It was so hot last night that nobody would have left them drawn, even in a house not secluded."

The Inspector lifted a hand for silence. He was now huddled in his chair, and although the temperature of the rooms was over ninety, he shivered. Presently he announced, "It is unsatisfactory. The weave cannot be finished when there are still unused threads."

Leila said nothing.

"If Shuman had not seen Miss Violet —" Chafik began. The sentence was left dangling, and he sat up. His eyes glowed as he fixed them on his wife. "Will you be shameless for a good cause?"

"Shameless?" She was shocked and bewildered.

"I intend to make an experiment."

The announcement was made in the voice of a martinet, and Leila thought: Now he is the Inspector of the Criminal Investigation Department —

The river boardwalk leading from Saa'dun Square was a pleasant spot on a hot summer's night. The numerous cafés along the Tigris were strung with lights which twinkled like fireflies among the palms. Boats glided near the walled bank, and the music of flutes and Rababbas was added to the chatter of the young Baghdadis who crowded the walk.

Near the Lido Café, where the crowd was dense, Inspector Chafik walked with Daoud Shuman. The fat young man resembled a sleeper roused from a bad nightmare. "I still cannot believe your news," he said.

Chafik said sympathetically, "It must be a great relief. You were certainly in an unpleasant position. Circumstantial evidence is often damning, and last night I almost arrested you."

"I am sorry that Madame Dejani —"

"Let us forget the unfortunate lady." The Inspector made a sweeping gesture. "How pleasant it is after the heat of the day," he continued. "Baghdad has a certain magic at this hour. Almost one expects to meet Haroun al-Rashid. It was about here where you saw Miss Violet last night?"

"Just across the road —"

"Excuse me if I again ask you if you are certain it was she."

"Inspector. I could not be more certain. I —" Daoud Shuman came to a halt. The color which had returned to his flabby cheeks drained. His mouth opened. He clutched at his companion's arm and stuttered, "The Merciful One defend us! I see her —"

The lights of the near-by café were shaded by the fronds of the palms, which moved in the breeze and sent changing patterns of shadow across the road. A woman, colorful as a butterfly in a dress patterned with blue and orange flowers, came briefly into the light. She wore a bright blue kerchief over her head and walked with a swaying motion of shapely hips. As the shadows flickered, she appeared to dissolve into the darkness.

Shuman shouted, "But she is dead!" He put his hands to his pounding heart, and his fat body wrinkled like the fabric of a collapsing balloon. A man stepped swiftly behind him and gave the timely support of strong arms.

"Soothe him, my dear Abdullah," said Chafik. "When he recovers from his shock, bring him to my office."

The Inspector parted the gathering crowd with an imperious gesture. A sleek black car slid out of the night, and as he opened the door the woman in the bright, cheap dress scurried across the road. She huddled on the back seat of the car and Chafik heard her sob as he joined her.

"The shame of it!" came the voice of his wife. "Oh, to parade myself in that woman's dress. I feel unclean —"

He took her hand. "May I be forgiven —" he began, humbly.

Leila said, "I am all over blushes. To think I showed myself with face uncovered. The looks of the men made me feel naked." Her imprisoned hand fluttered and then was still. "It was a successful experiment?"

"The new design is complete." Her husband's voice was hard.

They brought Dejani's wife into the Inspector's office at C.I.D. headquarters on Al-Rashid Street. Madame Chafik, now decently swathed in a chuddar, went to the woman and led her to a chair. A protesting voice outside the room was heard to say, "I demand a doctor. I am ill," and Mr. Dejani entered. He was a tall man, slightly stooped with a wide, loose mouth and unstill hands. He did not look at his wife as he sat down.

Daoud Shuman came in propelled by Sergeant Abdullah. The fat young man was still trembling and looked anxiously at the two women, whose faces were hidden by the folds of their robes.

The little man behind the big desk said, "Only the corpse is absent." He saw Shuman glance quickly over his shoulder. "Yes, there are many ghosts in this room," he went on. "But they are all locked in my filing cabinets. Are you still certain it was Miss Violet you saw on the river promenade last night?"

"I am not sure of anything — now."

"With those words you destroy an alibi." Chafik paused. "Tonight you saw a familiar dress. It was worn by my wife. Last night the wearer was Madame Dejani —"

The woman said, "Oh, no, no!"

"In this case," went on Chafik, "I have learned that a devoted woman puts no limit to her sacrifice. Madame Dejani went secretly to the house of Miss Shaw, knowing she would find a corpse. She had a twofold purpose. First, to remove the statuette which was marked with incriminating fingerprints. Secondly, to create an alibi for a worthless man. She knew that the woman, Shaw, habitually walked the river front, so she dressed as that woman and paraded. She is dark as the dead woman was dark, and alike in build. The dusk and her unusual dress made it a good risk. But she did see a friend of Miss Shaw. The shock must have been severe, but she kept her head and avoided Shuman and returned immediately to the house. She arrived at eight thirty. I think she collapsed, for twenty minutes was more than ample time to replace the livid dress in the closet for me to find, and to depart with the incriminating weapon. The witness almost caught her."

Madame Dejani made a movement of protest, but the little man looked up and shook his head gently.

"It was intelligently planned. The dress was as distinctive as a uniform; as protective to the identity as a peacock's coloring. We would have found other witnesses than Mr. Shuman to tell us Miss Shaw was seen after the train left for Basra. But he so strengthened the alibi that I accepted it."

Shuman said, "I have been greatly at fault."

"The inspector was also at fault, but fortunately he had a wife." Chafik made a little bow in the direction of his lady.

"You do yourself injustice," said Madame Chafik. "You were already doubtful: two facts were left over."

"Those threads are now in the design. Miss Shaw, being dead, could not have changed into her wrapper in the presence of Madame Dejani. The curtains were not opened after the heat of the day because she died before the sun went down. She was killed by a man who was jealous because she had taken a richer lover. He acted blindly, without premeditation."

"She was a bad woman," Madam Chafik said.

"One might say he is a bad man. But justice makes allowances for the violence of passion. It is not the killing that disgraces this man, but what comes afterward. He fled in panic to his wife. He told her the sordid story. He hid like a rat while she tried to cover his crime, as she has covered so many other of his transgressions —"

Madame Dejani whispered, "He's sick. Have pity!"

"My pity is only for you." Inspector Chafik let his hands fall heavily to the desk. "I am waiting," he went on in a bitter voice. "I cannot believe this man is so degraded that he will still try to hide behind the noble woman who was ready to shoulder his crime."

Mohammed Dejani stood up with jerky movements of a puppet. His wife, rising with him, clutched with both hands, as a mother reaches for a child precariously balanced at the edge of a pit. The man said, "I confess —" but the rest of his words were lost in the terrible wailing of the woman.

The Inspector Had a Habit

$\mathfrak{B}$ aghdad had sweltered all day in a south wind, and the night brought little relief or quiet. The numerous outdoor cinemas challenged one another with a cacophony of voices, and were in turn defied by the phonographs of the cafés. At the Oasis Hotel on Al-Rashid Street, although the hour was late, a local quartet interpreted Western Dance music with lusty brass and drums.

Inspector Chafik J. Chafik of the Criminal Investigation Department, who had an appointment with a body on the second floor of the hotel, announced as he entered the room where his assistants were at work, "The dead should be respected. Let the band stop, and Baghdad will be grateful to this man for dying. Or to the one who killed him."

He noticed his reflection in the mirror, fastidiously adjusted his tie, smoothed his sleek black hair, and then glanced at the corpse slumped over a desk near the window. A bullet had been fired point-blank into the back of the head, and the Inspector wrinkled his thin nose with disgust.

"What have you, Abdullah?" he asked his senior assistant.

The tall gaunt sergeant immediately began to read from a notebook in monotone, "Sir, the deceased was a Greek from Smyrna, named Spiros. He was known to us —"

"He has used many names. We will be content with the label Spiros. May I be forgiven, but this man is better dead." The dun-colored eyes of the little Inspector were flat and fixed as he quoted from very comprehensive records: "Spiros. Details of birth unknown. Agent for an international firm of importers and exporters. His visits to Baghdad appeared legitimate. But the firm is suspect. They may export military secrets."

Abdullah continued, "The Smyrniot sat at the desk. There is a typewriter on it. The killer entered by the window which opens on a balcony extending the length of the hotel. Spiros was taken by surprise. The slumped position of the body shows he had no chance to turn before the shot was fired."

The Inspector nodded approval. "Was the shot heard?"

"No, sir. The band specializes in explosive sounds, so this one passed unnoticed. Furthermore, the rooms were empty; guests and staff sought the coolness of the terrace to escape the heat. Also, it was dance night and there were many strangers. So the unknown had perfect opportunity to visit this floor, reach, the balcony by another room, destroy his enemy, and walk out unnoticed."

Chafik nodded again. "And the last movements of Spiros?"

Sergeant Abdullah consulted his notebook. "He returned to the hotel at 17:00 hours, drank four *araks* in the bar, then took dinner. During the meat course he was called to the telephone, afterward left the hotel."

"Was it man or woman who called?"

"Sir, the operator is stupid and does not remember. To conclude, Spiros returned five hours later and retired to his room. His movements *in absentia* are being investigated."

The Inspector said, "Now we shall begin." He hitched up his sleeves and went to examine the body.

Spiros had stripped to drawers and shirt before sitting at the desk. He had a big fleshy body and, like his head, there was little hair on it. The blow of the bullet had flung him forward. The body was twisted at an odd angle.

"A man does not leave his bridgework in the keys of a typewriter unless his face has met it with force," Inspector Chafik said. "The machine interests me, Abdullah. What do you observe?"

"It is a portable of Swiss manufacturer —"

Chafik said impatiently, "Apart from the teeth of Spiros, what is in it?"

"Sir, nothing. And there are no typed papers on the desk."

"Not a scrap of anything. Yet Spiros was so absorbed he failed to sense the entrance of the killer. And why was he moved?"

With careful consideration for his immaculate clothes, the Inspector forced the body of the Smyrniot back into the chair. Death was too recent for *rigor mortis*, and the fleshy hairless arms swung free. Chafik exclaimed, then lifted the right arm.

On the underside, just below the elbow, were markings, faint yet clear, like old tattooing. The bluish stenciling crossed the forearm obliquely, in four irregular lines.

"A fragment of typewriter print. The characters are Roman, but reversed."

The sergeant said, "My deduction is: The man rested his arm, which was damp with sweat, on something freshly typed. The print was transferred. It is a common occurrence."

"Yet there is no typing here."

The wooden face of the sergeant found mobility. "Permit me to suggest it was taken by the killer —"

"Give me a mirror," Chafik said briefly.

He was given one from the dressing table and held it at an angle against the arm. The reflected lines were clear enough for reading. The words were English. The first line began with a small "*I*" and continued, "*Rahdi. The loyalty of this...*" The second line, beginning and ending with broken words, read: "*...itical insecurity of the Kurdi...*" The third line added: "*...been inflamed by sponsor...*" And the final fragment: "*...refore recommended the brigad...*"

Inspector Chafik, whose English was excellent, copied the lines into a small notebook. He said, "It begins with the name Rahdi. I know a Colonel Rahdi. He commands a mountain brigade, and the last word in this fragment is brigade. Spiros was copying a highly confidential report."

"How do you know he was copying, not composing, sir?"

"This is the cautious language of a soldier. 'Therefore recommended the brigade...' No, this is not the language of Spiros. We must continue our investigation with the military authorities."

The general was old and gray and wore heavy mustaches brushed up in the Turkish style. Chafik remembered his distinguished history. When an officer of the sultan's army, he had secretly supported the revolutionary nationalist society, Al-Ahd. This was one of the revered founders of the kingdom of Iraq, and the Inspector declined a chair and stood respectfully.

"Forgive the intrusion, Excellency," he ventured, "but you will understand my alarm. That fragment is surely from an important secret document."

The general studied it. When he looked up he said dryly, "There must be a stronger word than importance."

"Then you recognize the extract?"

"It is from an appreciation of our military situation, which I prepared at the request of the regent. Its very existence is unknown to the majority of my staff. There is a single copy."

"Then, Excellency, Spiros must have had access to the original document, since there is no copy."

"If it were not a fact, I would say impossible. It is held in our most secret archives and can only be withdrawn on my written order." The general took a release slip from his desk, entered the details, added his signature, and touched the bell. He said to the tall handsome officer who appeared, "For immediate action, Major Taimani."

The aide exchanged curious glances with Chafik, then went out. "This Taimani has access —" Chafik said in a distant voice.

"What?"

The Inspector was embarrassed. "I spoke a thought. I have the habit, a very bad one —"

"Then let me correct the thought. Major Taimani does not have access to the document. Only one man is permitted to unlock the safe, and he is more secure than the lock itself. You will now meet him."

The aide returned with a little man in a shabby civilian suit. The Inspector noted his middle years, tired eyes, and the dusty pallor of one whose life was docketed in the drawers of filing cabinets. He carried a red cardboard cover which he put down reluctantly, then stood looking at Chafik with a watchdog's distrust.

Smiling, the general said, "Thank you, Mr. Habib. Please wait outside." His nod of dismissal included Major Taimani.

When the soldier and the civilian had gone, Inspector Chafik said, "Of course I know him. Habib Hanna. Confidential clerk. Twenty years in government service. A widower. One child, a girl named Nadhilla, aged about four. He is highly respectable."

"So you know why I trust him —"

"Excellency, I am a policeman. I do not trust myself."

The general shrugged, opened the file and thumbed through the pages, handwritten in Arabic script. Presently he said, "I will read you this extract under the subheading, '12th Brigade commanded by Colonel Rahdi.' It says: 'The loyalty of this mountain brigade is questionable, due to political insecurity of the Kurdish conscripts. There is evidence they have been inflamed by sponsored hopes of a National Kurdistan. It is therefore recommended the brigade be —' " The general closed the file.

Chafik said, "The original is here. Where is the copy?"

"I expect you to find it."

"You expect. That is a command." The Inspector's voice faded. When he spoke again, his sentences were disjointed. "One could not memorize these details. Not letter-perfect. Not any man I know. The document is clean. No blood on it, yet the desk of Spiros —"

He became aware of the general. Again embarrassed by the echo of spoken thoughts, he said, "As a stream among rocks, so I babble," and excused himself with a profound salaam.

W hen he left the ministry it was late. He had interviewed all members of the general's staff, and now sat in the police car. Greedily, he inhaled the smoke of a delayed cigarette. A breath of cool air rustled the fronds of the date palms.

He said to Sergeant Abdullah, "I cannot weave without threads. The military are grudging. We of the civil services are classed as inferiors."

Abdullah dismissed the military with a sweeping gesture of contempt. But Chafik went on stubbornly. "The higher the rank, the more human becomes the soldier. Our general was helpful, his aide was not."

"Sir?"

"I have suffered the supercilious company of a Major Taimani. He escorted me through the offices, but I knew what he was thinking. His lips smiled, but his eyes said, 'You are a policeman.' Is there a leper's mark on me because I am a hunter, and not a killer, of men?"

The sergeant's reply was soothing, and presently Chafik said, "Let us forget this elegant Taimani. Tell me what you discovered."

"Sir, I have trace of the movement of Spiros after he left the Oasis Hotel in answer to the telephone call. He was seen near Ctesiphon in a hired car, which he drove himself. Still later, the same car was noticed outside the public gardens which adjoin the city water works."

"Was anybody with Spiros?" the Inspector asked.

"I have no further information, sir. It is a poor offering."

The Inspector said, "I am not a pagan god, but I appreciate offerings, and the savor of this one is exotic. I was about to visit the gardens you mention."

"Then you knew Spiros had been there?" It was a disappointment.

"No, my dear Abdullah. I am going to the gardens because of the habits of a certain man."

Chafik took the wheel of the car, drove across Faisal Square, threaded the traffic on Al-Rashid Street and accelerated on Ma'mun Avenue, before he spoke again. "Let the scientists keep their test tubes," he said. "I prefer my records. I insist on the smallest detail being noted therein — even if a man walks regularly with his child in a garden in the evening."

When they reached the place, on the inside bank of the great loop of the Tigris that embraced the city, he told Abdullah to park discreetly and wait. Then he walked under the slaty gum trees to a bench. He sat watching the river.

Chafik waited for an hour. Sunset made a painter's palette of the desert sky. As the ever-changing colors grew stronger, he became aware of brighter color near him, a small child running along the path, chasing a ball.

He picked it up and held it, smiling invitation to the little girl. He had no young of his own, but he had a way with children.

The child in the gay dress did not go to him, however. She stood shaking her head. She said in a solemn voice, "Don't know strange man."

"But I know you," Chafik said and added, "you are called Nadhilla?" The little girl nodded, and he said softly, "You have gazelle's eyes, Daughter of Habib."

He smiled at the man who came up breathing heavily.

The pallid face of Hanna Habib was lined with strain and an anxious hand went to the child's shoulder to draw her protectively against him. Then he recognized the Inspector, and the hand released the shoulder. He said, "I have not seen you here before."

"It is my loss. The garden is beautiful, and there are elves in it." Chafik smiled again at Nadhilla.

"What is lelves?" she asked.

"Tiny men with beards. No bigger than the nail of your finger, Nadhilla. They live in flowers. They prefer poppies —" He reached a hand toward a red blossom, then snatched it back hurriedly. "Ah, the rascal! He bit me. Elves do not like grownups, only little girls like you."

The child's laughter was the music of the sunset. She pressed to his knee, looked up eagerly. Habib said harshly, "She is too friendly with strangers —"

"No, no, Baba! This nice man," Nadhilla told her father. "Not nasty man, not other man —"

"We must go home." Habib hastily grasped his daughter's hand.

"Daddy very, very mad," the child confided to Chafik. "Man take me far —" A plump arm waved. "Fat, far 'way. Nasty dirty man. But horse very nice. Very funny horse."

"She has been with friends," Habib explained. "Come, little gazelle," he said, tugging a reluctant hand.

"Very, very funny horse!" Nadhilla wrenched her hand from her father's and her laughter and bracelets tinkled as she suddenly strutted up the path, throwing her chubby legs out stiffly in a miniature goose step. "How funny horse walk," she explained breathlessly. "This how we sit!" she shouted joyously, and going down on her knees, bowed her flushed face to the ground.

"Come!" Habib snatched up his daughter. "She becomes foolish. She imagines things —" He was incoherent, then found the words to say, "It is Nadhilla's bedtime —"

"Horse sit down, horse sit down," the child chanted.

"You see how excited she becomes," the father said with agitation. A small rose-hennaed hand waved as Nadhilla was carried away.

When he rejoined Abdullah in the car, Chafik's thin face was deeply lined with anger and pain.

The sergeant said anxiously, "Was the garden, or the one you met, unpleasant?"

"On the contrary, Abdullah. The garden was a miniature Eden, suitably adorned by a young Eve. But there was also the conventional snake."

"Not venomous, I trust."

Inspector Chafik flicked his cigarette. "Judge for yourself. The snake is beside you," he said bitterly.

The next day he sat at his desk and looked at a report drafted in his own neat script. His shoulders were stooped as though he carried a heavy burden.

The report was complete, except for signature. Chafik picked up his pen, then put it down. He said to Abdullah, "If I sign, God will condemn me in the next world. And if I do not sign, my superiors will condemn me in this one —"

"There is no justification for murder, sir."

"You correctly reprimand me. I am a policeman. Very well, let us look at this thing as policemen. A few more inquiries. An interrogation. We then have the killer. And more important, we discover how Spiros obtained access to a secret document and what happened to his translation. Is that sufficient?"

This tall gaunt sergeant answered, "It fulfills our duty."

"On the contrary, my dear Abdullah. We still would not know how Spiros learned of the existence of the document. The one who killed him could not have volunteered this information, otherwise there would have been no reason to kill. Somewhere lurks the real traitor, the man who gave the tip-off, as they say in English. If I sign, the smoke screen of scandal would conceal this man. Therefore, I shall not submit my report — yet."

The Inspector went to the window and stood looking out across the drab city and the broad waterway of the Tigris. Presently he said, "I should not ignore the horse."

"Sir?"

"Did I speak, Abdullah? The habit grows worse; I do not always hear myself talk. But, yes, the horse. I seek one that walks with a Prussian strut, unless he be the fantasy of a fey child. Do you know a horse that struts, that also kneels as if in prayer?"

The sergeant said, "I suggest, sir, the military should be consulted. Cavalry mounts are trained for strange things."

"The military. I am reminded of my bruised ego." Chafik shrugged. "I will take this problem to them."

He was delayed by routine work and it was late afternoon when he went to the ministry. As usual, when he imagined inferiority, he was ingratiating; a hand hovered to his *sidarah* in half salute and half salaam. He asked to see the general's aide, hesitating to go to the great man with nebulous questions. A bored orderly escorted him to Taimani's office, and told him the major was in conference and would see him later.

Perched on the edge of a chair, the Inspector looked around the office. He noted the handsome rug, the good furniture, the many maps. But there was only one filing cabinet. The walls of his own austere office at headquarters were lined with cabinets; remembrance was refreshing rain to a parched ego. Chafik thought: *This man is more decorative than useful. I shall tolerate no more rudeness.* He lighted a cigarette and moved to a more comfortable chair.

From here, his eyes were drawn to photographs above the desk. They were all of Taimani at various stages in his military career. Chafik, with a tolerant smile, admitted the major made an effective figure in uniform, especially when on horseback.

The Inspector was impelled from the chair. He stood before three unusual pictures of a fine horse. His absorbed eyes went from one in which the horse pawed the air, to the second where it strutted with stiff forelegs, to the last where the horse knelt, Major Taimani proudly posed beside the bowed head.

Excitement made a din in Chafik's ears. He did not hear himself say breathlessly, "So the horse was not fantasy. If Habib's daughter saw these photographs —" But his policeman's ears picked up the click of the closing door, and he turned quickly.

Taimani was leaning nonchalantly against the wall. Chafik thought he saw something in the major's face that denied nonchalance. Then there was only the familiar boredom, and he wasn't sure of the something which might have been fear.

"Well, here I am. What do you want?" Taimani demanded.

"I wish to see the general —"

"He's gone."

"A pity. Such a courteous man." The little Inspector permitted himself brief satisfaction when Taimani flushed, then said quickly, "I was admiring your horse. An astonishing animal."

"It is a high school horse — but not mine."

"That is to be regretted, you are obviously attached to him. Who, then, is the owner?"

"An Englishman. He is no longer in Baghdad." Taimani spoke curtly. "What did you want with the general?"

"A confidential matter. I will call on him in the morning. How you must envy the Englishman. I hope," Chafik said, "you enjoy the horse in his absence? Do you keep it with your own? I believe you have several?"

Taimani said impatiently, "Yes. Now if you will excuse me —"

"A thousand pardons." The Inspector went to the door, but stopped on the threshold to say, "No doubt you keep them on the estate you recently inherited?"

"Yes," the major said irritably.

Closing the door behind him, Chafik thought: *Yes, the estate you inherited near Ctesiphon, Major.* His manner was now authoritative, but he was too preoccupied to notice the sentry's salute to authority as he drove away.

Alone in the car, he wove a pattern with the new and abundant threads. Presently he stopped near the river where the sunset was reflected in the sluggish water. Blood red predominated, and Chafik announced, "This ominous color also predominates my design —" He heard himself and angrily clattered the gears as he turned the car.

He had gone less than a block when the fear came to him.

Shock took color from his face. He pulled up by the officer on traffic duty at the intersection of Bank Street and said with a tremor in his voice, "Did I? Was I so excited I did not hear myself? Did I say —"

"Sir?"

Chafik said harshly, "Give me your gun."

He dropped it on the seat and drove off rapidly. Al-Rashid Street was cluttered with traffic, but he wove through it recklessly, crossed the Saa'dun Square at a diagonal, and fled up the broad avenue behind his screaming siren.

He reached the quiet garden where Hanna Habib usually walked with his daughter in the cool of the evening. Already the sunset was beginning to fade. He snatched up the gun, jumped from the car, and ran.

The main path was hedged by clumps of oleander and tamarisk. Chafik stopped in the shadow of a tree. He heard the pealing laughter of a child and ran again.

He turned a bend and saw Nadhilla skipping toward him, her bright eager face turned up to her flying ball. Hanna Habib walked with his eyes down, unaware of danger.

To the right of the path, where dark green foliage mingled with the coral blossom, Chafik saw something move. A hand, gripping a revolver, parted the screen of oleanders.

Chafik fired.

He heard the bullet cut through the tangled bushes, telling him he had missed, and threw himself flat as death passed. Fear was paralyzing. Then he thought: *I must not lie here. God, the Compassionate, give me courage. The child —*

Chafik pulled his knees up under him and rose as another bullet scorched his cheek. And he fired in return, the hammer blow of one explosion crashing upon another as he walked steadily in on the man hidden behind the oleanders.

When he was halfway across the seeming infinity of the path, Chafik saw the man pitch forward. He heard the harsh laboring of torn lungs. He was without pity and fired his last shot coldly and deliberately into the bent head. With a final convulsion the body rolled over at his feet.

His hands trembled as he reached for a cigarette. Inspector Chafik had never known Kurdish tobacco to taste so sweet. And looking at the once handsome face of the dead man, he said, "You do not wear death as decoratively as you once worse your uniform, Major Taimani."

The general said to the little man perched uncomfortably on the edge of the chair, "I can hardly credit it. Taimani a traitor, and Hanna Habib —"

"It is the way they work, Excellency. I mean the people who employed Spiros. They exploit weakness. This Taimani was a candle burning in daytime, gutted by his extravagances. So they sent Spiros with a tempting offer. So safe. So undefiling to the hands. He only had to say the document was in existence and name the watchdog who guarded it. They paid him well. But Spiros knew he could not tempt Habib. So he stole Habib's only treasure —"

"What greater treasure than a child?" The general sighed, remembering the years. "Go on," he said harshly.

"Spiros hid the kidnapped Nadhilla on Taimani's estate. Did Taimani know? Perhaps. But he was in the Smyrniot's power. Spiros then named the ransom to Habib. Access to the document. In the way of kidnapers, he surely warned the father he would never see the child again if he came to us. What could he do?" Chafik turned to conceal emotion. Then he spoke again as a policeman should speak. "Habib fulfilled the terms. One wonders why, after Nadhilla was safe, he did not ask our help —"

The general said compassionately, "Fear would always remain for the tortured father."

"This one was also your faithful watchdog, Excellency. When his daughter was returned he went to the hotel. He entered the room, snatched up the document, shot Spiros, and left. He took all that was on the desk. The original document was returned unsoiled to the archives. All this became clear to me when I talked to the child in that, then, pleasant garden. She also gave me the clue to the real traitor."

"But I am mystified why Taimani rushed to kill her."

"Because of my habit —"

"What?"

"You have heard me speak my thoughts. I cannot break the habit. I was searching for the performing horse which Nadhilla had seen in the place where she was confined. When I saw the photographs in Taimani's office, I had found the animal, and exclaimed the fact aloud. And in my excitement I failed to hear myself." The Inspector made no attempt this time to hide anguish. "My carelessness put the life of the little Nadhilla in jeopardy. Overhearing, Taimani was in a panic. If it were proved that the child was hidden on his estate, it might hang him. So he went to destroy the witness. God warned me."

Inspector Chafik rose. It was easier to say what he had to say standing erect like a soldier. "I killed Taimani, Excellency!"

"A traitor's death is unimportant —"

"But I killed him deliberately. To silence him."

The general raised his shaggy eyebrows. "Explain."

"I have not yet submitted a report on Hanna Habib. Only you and I know he took the document, and why. Only you and I know he killed Spiros. A tortured father, as you yourself have said, Excellency. But also a very faithful watchdog. Now to be trusted doubly? Do you want to lose him? And shall we take happiness from the bright face of a child?"

The questions were left suspended in a long silence. While Chafik waited, the general fitted a cigarette into his amber holder. When he looked up, his hard face softened, and he said, "Surely, it is sufficient the report has been made to God."

He Had a Little Shadow

The boy was a waif who frequented the great bazaar of Baghdad. He was small for his years, which were perhaps eight, very slim and high-waisted, with delicate hands and feet, a bright elfin face and large, dark eyes. He wore a ragged gown girdled with a piece of rope, his turban was a wisp, he had never owned shoes; his only possession was a basket which he used to carry the purchases of shoppers for a few pennies.

Chafik J. Chafik, an inspector of the Criminal Investigation Department, stood on the steps of the Imperial Bank and idly watched the child who flitted through a patchwork of evening sunlight and shadow with the basket balanced on his head. The boy sang in a thin treble, sometimes skipped and clapped his hands, and the Inspector, troubled by end-of-the-month bills, had a moment of envy. He was turning away when he saw a man lurch from the crowd.

The man wore the tribal dress of a minor chieftain of the Muntafiq. His magnificent build was typical of the marsh Arab, and so was the hair-trigger temper that made him turn on the boy, with whom he had collided, and strike him in the face.

It was a brutal blow and the youngster dropped the basket and clasped his arms over his head, but they made a frail barrier. When the man raised a heavy brassbound stick with intent to continue the senseless beating, Inspector Chafik ran down the steps, wrenched it away, and threw it behind him.

He said mildly, "Temper is as intoxicating as alcohol."

The man turned. He had pale lips, flattened to his teeth, dilated eyes staring with madness. Normally authority was Chafik's protection, and he was suddenly and painfully aware of muscular inadequacy; but he drove his elbow against the man's nose, bringing a bright gush of blood. Then, rising on his toes in an effort to increase his stature, he used his forearms as clubs.

A constable intervened opportunely with a swinging gun. Inspector Chafik said, "Two blows are enough. This head is not a nut, there is no sweetness in it. But I advise handcuffs. We have madness here."

There was blood on his sleeve and he looked at it with disgust, for he was a meticulously neat man. Irritably he took out a pocket mirror, examined his thin face, gently touched a bruise on his swarthy cheek, and straightened his polka-dot tie. Then, recovering his *sidarah* which had fallen in the dirt, he brushed it and adjusted it to the correct angle on his long head.

"As an angry cockbird ruffles its feathers, so I have ruffled my clothes," he said to the boy.

The face that turned up to him was white and frightened. Tears welled in the big eyes, but the boy held them back with courage, even with dignity, a quality engaging in a waif who begged his daily subsistence. There were too many fatherless children in Baghdad; lack of organized welfare made boys like this grow up with minds sharpened by animal cunning, and in time most of their names were added to police records. Chafik sighed and took money from his pocket.

"Go fill your belly," he said as he thrust the coins at the boy.

A grubby little hand touched his own, clung to it. "Sahib," the boy said. "You are my father, sahib —"

It was a pleading, not a wheedling, voice. Chafik smiled, but was startled when he saw how worshipfully the boy looked at him. "How are you named?" he asked.

"They call me Faisal."

"That is the name of our young king. Who named you so royally?"

Faisal shook his head. "There was once a woman who called me Faisal. Very long ago when I was small. She died," he added vaguely.

"And now you are a man?" Chafik asked gravely.

"A man, sahib. I work. Truly I do not steal much." The big eyes glowed with gratitude and adoration. "That one would have killed me. I saw it in his face. You are my father, sahib. I will go with you."

The Inspector was embarrassed. He had been married many years and was childless, a circumstance which could be adjusted by polygamy under Moslem law. But he was devoted to his wife; although he knew she was distressed by lack of children, he had convinced himself they would have disorganized his well-regulated home.

"Take the money and eat," he said, and turned his back.

The constable had secured the man, and Chafik bent and rolled back an eyelid, then announced, "One sees the reason for madness."

"He has eaten the forbidden fruit, sir," said the officer.

"Yes — hashish —"

The Inspector clasped his slender hands with unexpected emotion. For several months he had been trying to stop a flow of narcotics responsible for a crime wave in Baghdad. In spite of his efforts hashish continued to enter the city and in its wake came violence and death. The attack on the boy was typical.

Chafik said harshly, "Let God pardon me, for I wish death, and not an easy one, for those who peddle this evil."

He shrugged, lighted a cigarette, and looked with loathing at the hashish eater, who struggled against the handcuffs. When a police ambulance arrived the Inspector walked away.

The cigarette had a bitter taste and he dropped it, but could not discard the bitter thoughts. He threaded a path between the benches that overflowed from the cafés, turned right at the intersection of Samawal and Al-Rashid Streets, and walked under the shabby arcade to his headquarters. He had the sensation of being followed as he entered the narrow doorway, and turned swiftly.

He saw an elfin face and appealing eyes. "Sahib!" Faisal pleaded. "You are my father, sahib —"

"Away with you!" Chafik said, and losing dignity he ran up the worn steps to his office.

Inspector Chafik was received by his assistant, tall gaunt unemotional Sergeant Abdullah, who was sufficiently stirred by sight of his superior's bruised cheek and ruffled clothes to say in a solemn voice, "Sir, I trust the individual who assaulted you is detained."

"In the hospital, my dear Abdullah. But I did not put him there. He is the victim of hashish."

"Sir, we have many hashish victims today. I bring you the reports. Two killings. Five assaults with intent to kill —"

"The menu is unappetizing and unvaried," said Chafik. "There is always a list of crimes over the week end." The Inspector took a manicure set from a drawer and began to clean his nails. After a moment he said, "My conclusion is no hashish is stored in Baghdad; if it were, it would be distributed more evenly throughout the week. It is smuggled in. But when? And how? I am a policeman, not a seer. What is the source of the drug? Does it come from Syria? From Turkey, Saudi Arabia, Kuwait or Persia? Or is it brought by sea from India?"

The sergeant said gloomily, "So many places, sir."

"And so many routes. There are highways, a railroad, the transdesert autobus, aircraft and innumerable camel caravans."

"We watch them all. The frontier checks are severe —"

Inspector Chafik interrupted, "Can we guard every mountain path? One man with the legs of a goat can carry enough hashish to poison half Baghdad." He put away the manicure set, breathed on his nails and gave them a final rub with a silk handkerchief. "Our records show crime increases with the waning of the week and in this is a clue. But like a photographic negative the image does not appear until developer is applied. If we had the formula —"

He went to the window and looked over the vast dun-colored city. Here and there the cubist pattern of flat roofs was relieved by the blue dome of a mosque, and in the distance the Tigris made a tawny highway through groves of date palms. It was a noisy city. Harsh sounds always jarred the Inspector, and when a car pulled up with a screech of brakes in the street below, he winced and looked down.

A boy had darted across the street and now squatted on the other side with his feet in the gutter.

"Am I to be haunted?" Chafik asked indignantly.

"Sir?"

"You have three daughters, Abdullah. Do they follow you about and regard you with admiration?"

"They do, sir."

"You find it embarrassing?"

"Sometimes, sir. But it also gives me a warm feeling here." The sergeant struck his breast.

"Then the emotion is normal," said Chafik. His voice had the hollow sound of one who speaks a thought unintentionally; hearing himself, he flushed, irritated by his incurable habit. "We must find the means of developing the image hidden in our records," he said hastily. "But enough for the day."

He was too preoccupied to see the boy who lurked under the arcade, but when he reached his car parked on the city square, he was roused by a light touch. An eager voice began, "Sahib! My father —"

It pulled a trigger of temper and the Inspector shouted, "Out, Pestilence!" and slammed the door of the car.

He drove over the great steel bridge that spanned the river. His home was on the Street of the Scatterer of Blessings, off Mansour Avenue. The yellow brick house, which was small and typically suburban, was cooled by breezes from the Tigris. Chafik latched the street gate, carefully wiped his shoes, and let himself into the softly lighted hall.

His wife, a dark, slim little woman, was there to make him welcome. Her face was freshly powdered and she wore an attractive dress. After fifteen years, Leila knew the wisdom of working at marriage. She was a woman of considerable intelligence and combined a Westernized appearance with a degree of meekness expected of an Eastern wife. She said, anxiously, "You are late, my man."

"It was a question of a formula for extracting from our records what is surely hidden there. You would not understand."

"No," said Leila. "But I understand you are tired."

She maneuvered him into a chair, removed his shoes and brought his slippers. He sniffed the appetizing odor of the waiting meal, sighed and said, "Yes, I am tired. Also hungry. One cannot eat records."

After eating it was possible to relax. The only sound in the house was the ticking of the clock, and he was grateful for the quiet and closed his eyes.

Leila stood at the window, hidden by the curtains, watching the street. She liked to speculate about those who passed; her interest in the foibles of the humanity filled gaps in her day, times of idleness inevitable in a childless household.

Suddenly she said, "The house is watched —"

Chafik sat up. "What?"

"There is a boy outside. He has been there for some time."

Her husband joined her and saw Faisal leaning against the gate. The elfin face was white and pinched in the light of the street lamp. Chafik reacted with confusion. He felt compassion, as for a lost a woebegone puppy, then anger came and he went to the door, but changed his mind and came back. "This foolishness must end," he said to Leila, and explained what had happened. "He follows me everywhere," he complained.

"Such a little boy, and he has such charm," Leila said wistfully.

"A waif. He doubtlessly has lice."

"He has a hungry look —"

"I gave him money for food. That was my mistake."

"Many give him money," Leila said wisely. "His hunger is not only for food. He walked far to be near you. Oh, pitiful! He makes his bed on our doorstep. Could he not sleep in the shed in the garden?"

Chafik heard the tenderness in his wife's voice and felt a twinge of an old pain. "I forbid," he said angrily. "Once you brought a cat into the house and I was inundated with kittens. You are too impulsive."

"Such a little boy —" said Leila, sighing.

Her husband realized she had not heard a word. Irritably he announced, "I am going to bed," and left her still at the window.

He slept heavily, but not well. In the morning, when he went out, the familiar small figure was waiting. He noticed crumbs on the mouth that curved to greet him and had a dark thought for his wife as he brushed past the boy.

During the day he caught glimpses of Faisal and continued to ignore him. When he came home in the evening, the boy appeared so quickly outside the house, Chafik guessed he had stolen a ride on the back of a car, perhaps even his own. He felt helpless and his wife gave no comfort; she was suddenly withdrawn.

Estrangement was rare between them. He was aware of the reasons, and at any other time would have used tenderness to relieve the futile longing that happened sometimes to Leila, like the aching of a tooth which is really sound. But the problem of the drug smuggling was a leech in his mind and he could think of little else as midweek approached and, with it, the dreaded increase in hashish crimes.

He was tormented because he was certain the answer of when and how the drug entered the country was in his records. These records were amazingly detailed, and included files on all regular travelers to and from Baghdad, and on all known criminals in the city. But to attempt to unearth the answer in his crammed filing cabinets without a key would be as difficult as finding the proverbial needle in a haystack.

On Thursday morning, when Chafik found Faisal waiting as usual, he got into his car and recited a few calming verses from the Koran, then reopened the car door. "Come, Pestilence," the Inspector said. He remembered Leila in the window and was embarrassed by his odd impulse toward the boy.

Faisal began to chatter gaily. The pleasant young voice disturbed thinking, but when the boy said, "Sahib, today I shall make money," Chafik came out of preoccupation and wondered a little irritably what could be done for the persistent child.

"How will you make money?" he asked, slowing the car.

"A train comes. There are things to carry. People tired with travel pay well," Faisal added wisely.

"So today you will eat. But what of tomorrow?"

"Tomorrow does not matter if I eat well today, sahib."

"I envy your philosophy," Chafik said. "Myself, I would be distressed by such ups and downs. The graph of my life follows an even line; if yours were plotted it would soar to a zenith, then plunge into the nadir. And again to the zenith and so on, indefinitely. Such a graph would be untidy, but the pattern would reveal the fluctuations of your belly, the days when —"

His voice died and he forgot the boy. He was fascinated by his hand which had left the wheel to trace a wavy line in the air. "A graph!" he shouted. "The key — the formula —" The car shot ahead through traffic lights and was parked hastily. For the second time in these few days the sedate little Inspector astonished the guard outside headquarters by running up the stairs.

Sergeant Abdullah was waiting with a pile of reports, but Chafik said, "I have no time for routine. I have found the key."

"Sir?"

"The hashish matter," Chafik explained impatiently. "Abdullah, if we could fix the day when the crimes begin to mount, the exact day every week, perhaps the same day, would it not aid our investigation?"

"Indubitably. A fixed day recurring weekly over a period of several months would permit the narrowing down of means of entry. It would be possible to eliminate certain routes of transportation. For example, sir, highways are sometimes closed by sandstorms —"

"Then bring me squared paper."

"Sir?"

"Paper marked with squares. I am going to make a graph. We will plot all crimes committed by hashish addicts during the past three months. Thus the data from our records will emerge visually."

When Abdullah brought the paper, Inspector Chafik prepared the frame of the graph and indicated weeks and days of each week along the bottom line. He explained, "I shall count one vertical square for each incident. You will now read me the daily hashish reports from the files."

The sergeant read in a courtroom voice that reduced crime to its proper level, unglamorous and monstrous. Chafik's pencil moved up and down marking the level of crime for each day. When he reached the end of the week he linked the daily tallies with a red line.

It was tedious work. The sergeant opened the collar of his tunic and permitted his ramrod back to ease against the chair. The clock over the Mustansiriyah buildings had struck ten before he closed the last file.

He said with feeling, "Police work is sometimes unexciting."

Chafik showed his assistant the completed graph. It resembled a mountain range.

"Here is a genuine picture of a crime wave," the little Inspector said, smiling. The joke was lost on his sergeant and he demanded brusquely, "What do you observe?"

"Sir, I observe the parabola of crime begins to rise each Thursday. Then there is a variable peak period of about three days, then a decline."

"What does that mean to you?"

"It proves supplies of hashish are released on that day."

"By what means, Abdullah?"

The sergeant ventured sarcasm. "Perhaps the graph shows how."

"It does," Chafik said. "Today is Thursday. What transport arrives from foreign parts this day?"

"Sir, solely the international train from Turkey, the Taurus Express. But it is a semiweekly train. There is another on Sunday."

"Where are your wits?" Chafik asked. "The crimes begin Thursday, their peak declines on Sunday. Therefore this man who smuggles the hashish travels only on Thursdays. Storms interfere with the desert autobus, with aircraft and the camel caravans, but they rarely stop a train. It is the means of entry." He made it a statement of fact.

Sergeant Abdullah was critical. "But we search the train."

Chafik again gave attention to the graph. "He has a means of tricking us," he said. He put his finger on the red line where it oddly flattened for a two-week period before leaping to a new high. "What happened here?" he asked.

"Apparently no hashish was available, sir. I remember the period. Many people went to hospital sick through lack of the drug."

The Inspector lighted a cigarette, took a few puffs, then stubbed it. He was shaking with excitement, and said, "This graph is clairvoyant. Bring me our lists of Taurus Express passengers for the past three months. Fortunately it is a short train."

These lists were always taken at the border and copies were sent to the Inspector's office. They checked the names of regular passengers against the police records, but their work was unrewarded.

Abdullah said, "Your thought was admirable, sir, but —"

"I object to 'but.' It is a sly conjunctive that conceals a dagger. You do not think my thought admirable." Chafik shrugged. "We have eliminated the passengers, but there are others. The Taurus Express is an international train. True, the engine, its crew and the conductors are changed at the frontier, but the day coaches continue to

Baghdad. Also one sleeping car and a diner. Read me the names of the staff attendants."

Six men made the midweek run from Istanbul to Baghdad, all were regulars. There was a *chef de train*, a sleeping-car attendant, two cooks and two waiters.

While his assistant read the names, the Inspector followed the dates on the graph. Suddenly he looked up. "That was a new name," he said.

"Yes, sir. It would appear that Najar Helmy, a waiter, was replaced for the week in question."

"Does Helmy ride the train the following week?"

"No, sir, but he is back the third week —"

There was a dry snapping sound. Sergeant Abdullah looked at the Inspector, who was huddled over the desk. A broken pencil fell from Chafik's hand and he said in a choked voice, "By God and by God!"

"Sir?"

"Have you forgotten the two-week period when the graph flattens, when no hashish came to Baghdad? Najar Helmy's absence coincides. But is it coincidence that all other Thursdays when Helmy worked the run the telltale line of my graph mounts?"

The sergeant was inarticulate. When he found voice he exclaimed, "Without leaving your office! Sir, without leaving your office you have solved it, even to the name. Let us go seize this Helmy —"

"He who seizes a scorpion in haste repents with haste." Chafik looked at the clock, saw it was nearly train time, and said briskly, "But I confess I am curious to meet this man."

They went to the Baghdad North Station and waited in the office of the railroad police, which commanded a view of the platform. The train had arrived and the scene was bedlam. Kurdish porters, clad in rags, cursed and fought over the baggage. A merciless sun beat on the iron roof and dust blew across the platform.

Chafik pressed his face to the window, but drew back when a familiar pair of eager eyes met his own. He had forgotten Faisal. They boy's presence was natural, for he had said he would make money from the arrival of the train, but the Inspector was annoyed and ignored Faisal's salute.

He waited patiently as the passengers streamed through the exit gate. A detective of the railroad police was at his side and presently said, "There is Helmy. He stands on the steps of the restaurant car, sir."

Najar Helmy was a Turk, short, stocky and olive-skinned. He stood bowing to a belated passenger, the picture of the perfect attendant who earns his tips.

"You know him?" Chafik asked the detective.

"We are acquainted, sir. He always stays overnight at the Parliament Hotel on Hasan Pasha Street."

The station became quiet, a field after battle, littered with cigarette stubs and torn paper. The attendants bustled in and out of the diner and sleeping car, putting everything in order for the next day. The attendant of the sleeper dragged a hamper of dirty linen to a locker room, and then Helmy appeared with a garbage can.

The Turk held one handle; the other was clutched by Faisal, who used both hands as he strained under the weight of the can.

Chafik said in a worried voice, "The boy is at ease with this man. He knows him."

Helmy and Faisal disappeared into the yard at the back of the station. When they returned, Helmy the Turk gave the boy money and dismissed him. Soon, the Turk again left the train, submitted a suitcase for inspection and went up the platform toward the yard and the employees' exit.

Sergeant Abdullah said, "This time he is without hashish."

Chafik was puzzled. "But why should he change his routine?"

"Perhaps he was forewarned, sir."

The Inspector exclaimed and abruptly left the office. Faisal was squatting on the platform, and Chafik took his arm and pulled him roughly to his feet.

"The man who gave you money," he said harshly. "You know him?"

"Sahib, my arm," the boy said plaintively, trying to break free. "I did nothing wrong, only helped to carry rubbish, as I often do. The man gave me twenty *fils*. A lot of money —"

"What did you say to him? What did you tell him?"

"Nothing, sahib! Nothing — you hurt —" Faisal squirmed away, looked up reproachfully and then fled.

The Inspector's anger cooled but his face remained grim. He said to Abdullah, "We have been tricked. I think I know how he took out the hashish." He ran up the platform to the station yard.

A garbage can stood upside down behind a stack of rusting oil drums. Flies swarmed over the scattered rubbish.

Abdullah began, "Sir —"

Chafik said, "Our heads are of the same density. Who would think of searching that filth? When Helmy went out a few minutes ago, he merely upturned the can and took what was concealed there. That is his regular method — and the boy helped him carry the can —"

"If Helmy went directly to his hotel he has the supply with him, sir. We can take him."

"Not yet. I wish to learn how he distributes the hashish."

The Inspector called headquarters, ordered a check, and soon learned Helmy was at his usual hotel. Arrangements were made for a man to register there, for others to be placed strategically throughout the quarter where the hotel was located. Chafik installed himself in a near-by café, ordered coffee and his favorite honey cakes, and waited. But the coffee grew old and the cakes were untouched; even honey could not sweeten his thoughts.

"A policeman should not have emotions," he announced.

Sergeant Abdullah began, "Sir, you think this boy —"

"It does not matter what I think," answered Chafik discouragingly. He looked up and down the street and was silent for some time. Then he said, "There he is!"

"The Turk? I do not observe —"

"The boy." Chafik darted across the street to an alleyway.

Soon he returned and said harshly to Abdullah, "He escaped me. But how long has he been spying? Has he gone to report to the Turk? Call our man at the hotel."

The sergeant came back to say Faisal had not been seen. "But he is small, he has the ways of a mouse," he added.

"Or the ways of a rat," Chafik said bitterly.

They remained at the café all afternoon. Reports were relayed from the detective in the hotel; Helmy had taken a meal, received no visitors, and was now in his room.

Shortly after sunset the signal came that the man was leaving, and presently they saw him, strolling in the cool of the evening.

Chafik said, "Keep away from me, Abdullah. You are too obvious in uniform." He got up and followed Helmy to another café.

The place was crowded and the Inspector sat beside a portly sheik, using the man's bulk to screen his slight figure. Helmy was alone at a table, reading a newspaper.

Presently a man came in and greeted the Turk effusively. Helmy offered a cigarette and after a few puffs his companion made a gesture of pleasure. The Turk smiled expansively and took a box from his pocket and passed it across the table; his pantomime seemed to say, "You like my cigarettes? Then take this as a gift." At that moment the bulky sheik engaged Chafik in conversation and when the Inspector looked again Helmy was gone.

During the next hour the incident was repeated, another stranger received, as a close friend, a gift made of two boxes. Watching without interruption this time, Chafik saw something pass in return for the cigarettes. When the second man had gone the Turk also left the café.

He went to a cabaret in the Bab-el-Sheik district. Once again Chafik saw the play of a stranger, a cigarette and a gift. When the stranger left, the Inspector signaled an assistant to watch Helmy and then joined Sergeant Abdullah outside.

The stranger was still in view and Chafik said briefly, "He has a box of cigarettes I wish to examine."

Abdullah glided into the shadows. Chafik followed slowly; he heard nothing, but when the sergeant reappeared he had the box. Unemotionally he said, "Sir, I took the precaution of silencing him. His skull was thin and the wall hard."

"That may not be a misfortune," Chafik said.

The small oblong box was inscribed with the name of a famous brand of Turkish cigarettes, but inside the scaled foil was a block of brownish-green resinous substance. It had a faint and peculiar odor and Chafik looked at it with loathing. "This is where the graph led us," he said.

"Hashish, sir?"

"The essence of the crude bhang." His thin shoulders expressed what he thought. "Helmy is a very clever man," he went on. "He is the wholesaler. Agents meet him at the various cafés. They buy the hashish cash down, as I observed, then distribute it to their own customers. Helmy takes the lion's profit and avoids the danger of dealing directly with addicts. He has virtue rare among criminals — he works alone and does not let his business become too big."

They returned to the cabaret. Outside was the man Chafik had left to watch the Turk. He said in a worried voice, "Sir, I have lost him."

"What!"

"A man came shortly after you left. He spoke to Helmy and they both went to the cloakroom. When they did not return I investigated and found an open window... "

Chafik's face darkened. "Did a boy speak to Helmy or to this other man?"

"I did not notice, sir."

The Inspector put aside suspicion for the moment. "This man was obviously a bodyguard," he said. "When he saw me follow the agent, he warned Helmy. It is a pity, but not too important. We now know how hashish enters Baghdad and this beast who battens on human weakness is trapped within our city. His arrest is certain."

He called headquarters and ordered a general alarm, then went with Abdullah to Helmy's hotel. The man had not returned. They searched the room and found many boxes of hashish. Chafik said, "He takes only a few with him when he goes to meet the agents. Such a cautious man."

They left men to watch and returned to headquarters. The general alarm was in operation; every officer in Baghdad was alerted, mounted patrols had sectioned off the city, motorized squads stopped all cars on the highways. In the middle of this web, Chafik sat at his desk, a patient spider.

But he had troublesome thoughts. Once he announced, "It could be coincidence. Faisal carried the garbage, but why was he hidden near the café?" Later he said, "I dealt roughly with him; he may have been afraid to show himself. I am naturally suspicious when followed." This time he heard himself and pounded the desk with vexation.

"My habit becomes intolerable," he told Abdullah. "I shall go home and rest. Helmy has a good hide-out." As he left he said in the familiar hollow voice, "Must I tell Leila about the boy? What can I tell her that will not give pain?"

He walked to his car parked on the landscaped square near a clump of rhododendron. He had a feeling of letdown and was not his usual alert self.

As Chafik opened the door of the car, a man rose from the bushes and struck a shrewd blow with a blackjack. Then he bundled the inert Inspector into the front seat, got in, and drove away.

Two policemen coming up Al-Rashid Street saluted as the familiar car passed.

Chafik was in a room, lying on the floor. The first thing he saw was a vaulted ceiling decorated with arabesque in gilt paint. He announced, "Turkish influence. This is an old house." He tried to sit up, but pain stabbed his head and he closed his eyes again.

The next time he opened them he saw a man astride a chair, arms folded on the back. The man said, "A very old house and a convenient neighborhood. Your police will search for days."

Chafik blinked against pain. His head was clearing and he stared at the man, thinking: *This is what I hunted. An ordinary man, one who might have been my neighbor.* Aloud he said, "Nevertheless, you cannot hide here indefinitely. Arrest is inevitable."

Another man came within vision, a squat barrel-chested man who was doubtlessly the bodyguard. The man held a leather blackjack.

Helmy said, "Restrain yourself, Ali." And to Chafik he said, almost with apology, "He is like a mastiff."

"I, too, have a faithful henchman." Chafik thought of Sergeant Abdullah, the comfort of those broad shoulders and accurate gun; then he had another thought that was not comforting, and asked, "Is the boy also faithful to you?"

Helmy was puzzled. "What boy?"

"The one who helped with the garbage."

"I always use a brat to help me, it disarms suspicion. But I don't use any particular boy."

Chafik smiled in relief. "My mind is clear of an unjust suspicion," he said.

Helmy pulled the chair close to the Inspector. At near view the Turk's mouth and eyes warned Chafik that this was not a neighbor who lived within society, and the laws protecting it. Here was one who coldly calculated chances, made crime a business. Such a man would know no pity.

"I have a proposition," Helmy said conversationally. "You will write a note to cancel my arrest. I will leave on the train tomorrow."

"A simple proposition, I agree. But not practical. Such an order would be questioned by my superiors."

"You will say in the note you use me to bait to catch others."

Inspector Chafik thought: *He is clever. There is a chance such a request might be approved.* But he said, "It is known you work alone. Furthermore, I am not in the mood to write such a note."

Ali struck him with the blackjack. Helmy kicked him, then pulled him to his feet. They had him between them, knocking him from side to side; when he fell down they lifted him again and beat him again. He heard screams, recognized his own voice, thought: *How demeaning that I should evidence pain!* The next time he went down they left him.

"Well?" Helmy asked.

The Inspector tasted blood, screwed up his face in disgust and said, "This does not help. Your arrest is inevitable."

They did it over again. All Chafik said was, "My work is finished and I am now expendable." He began to recite from the Koran in a high thin voice which gradually became unclear, then incoherent. Unconsciousness released him from the agony of waiting for the next treatment.

He did not hear the sound of feet on the stairs, but he revived with the crash of the door. He heard Helmy's oath and the violence of gunfire and somebody familiar who shouted, "Dogs! Devils!" The guns talked once again; then there was silence and the Inspector dared raise his head.

Near him was the body of the Turk. The other man crouched against the wall, coughing blood. The room was filled with police, among them Sergeant Abdullah.

Chafik said, "Did I rub a magic lamp?" He laughed hysterically, but managed to check himself when Abdullah raised him.

"Praise to the Merciful One!" exclaimed the sergeant. "If it had not been for the boy —"

"The boy?"

"Sir, I refer to the waif. He was in the back of your car, apparently waiting for you, hidden on the floor. He saw you struck. With commendable restraint he remained silent while you were driven to this place. Then he ran back, found me at headquarters, and so —"

"Faisal!"

"That is his name, sir. I detained him in your office."

Chafik said humbly, "God works in strange ways." Then he added urgently, "Let us go there quickly." Moving, he was reminded of pain and was glad to lean on Abdullah.

In his office he stood and looked at Faisal. The boy was asleep in a chair, cheek on his arm, his face smeared with recent tears. In sleep his little hands were clenched into fists and he stirred restlessly and once murmured, "My father... "

The Inspector said, "May I be forgiven!" Then he quoted in excellent English, "I have a little shadow, he goes in and out with me —" After a pause he added, "But the use of him I *do* see."

He went to the telephone and was again reminded of a dozen pains. He dialed the number and, waiting for his wife to answer, his eyes were tender, but hearing her voice he said casually, "I will be with you soon, Leila. I fear I am a little bruised and have ruined good clothes, but it is not important. And I have to announce a decision." He drew himself up and said very firmly, "I have decided to make an adoption."

There was no answer. He rattled the telephone and shouted, "Leila! You hear me, Leila? I am adopting a boy."

The voice of his wife came mildly. "I hear you, my man. All Baghdad hears you. Please come very quickly. I have had Faisal's room waiting for him these three days, now."

All the Birds of the Air

They found Hadji Hussain huddled on a chair in the summer room of his house on the banks of the Tigris. He had a bruise above the forehead and died from a brain hemorrhage shortly after they carried him out.

The room was actually a deep windowless cellar with a single entrance at the foot of an outside flight of steps. An air shaft led to the roof and trapped the river breezes, making the *surdab* a pleasant retreat from the excessive heat.

Inspector Chafik of the Criminal Investigation Department of the Baghdad police appreciated the coolness. Outside, the white light of noon glared on the tiles of the courtyard. The Inspector's shirt stuck to his thin body and disturbed him; he was fastidious about his clothes. Wiping his swarthy face with a handkerchief sprinkled with orange water, he announced, "I consider it unreasonable for people to die on such a hot day."

His assistant, a tall unemotional sergeant, understood why the Inspector was worried about Hussain's death. The Hadji, who was loved and venerated in Baghdad, was head of the courts where ecclesiastical matters such as divorce, questions of Moslem theology, and disputes concerning religious institutions were brought for settlement.

Recently the old man had handed down a decision that concerned a property willed to the Shafiite shrine at Zagros. He had favored the relatives who had brought a complaint of coercion against the shrine. In consequence the Shafiites, a small but fanatic sect, had threatened reprisals, and a police guard had been placed at the Hadji's house.

This affected Sergeant Abdullah personally because the detail had been in his charge, so he began anxiously, "Permit me to report —"

Chafik said, "Later, I have not yet digested the medical report. It is always an unappetizing dish. They tell me the violence of the blow might have killed a younger man. The Hadji was old, frail. If he fell and struck something —"

"Sir, there is nothing to indicate it," said the sergeant. "And what was he doing in the chair?"

"It is possible that after the first impact of the blow he recovered sufficiently to find his feet and stumble to the chair. He may have retained consciousness until the clot formed."

The Inspector had strange dun-colored eyes, flat and expressionless except when he was worried. He looked around trying to visualize what had happened. The room was very simply furnished. There were a cot, a few chairs, straw mats on the tiled floor, a bedside lamp; near the lamp was an open copy of the Koran which had been put down so hurriedly the edges of the pages were folded. A light blanket was flung back from the foot of the bed.

Chafik said, "There is the impression of a head on the pillow; the Hadji was reposed. And the position of the Koran, the blanket, tells us he was rudely disturbed. The interruption occurred shortly after he came to rest, otherwise he would not have been reading. The aged do not have to woo sleep."

He folded his slender hands and glanced at the sergeant, who knew what was expected and immediately began to quote from memorized notes, "Sir, the Hadji entered the *surdab* after the noon prayer. He was escorted by a retainer named Murad, who closed the door behind his master and then proceeded to other duties. Murad is the house watchman."

"Where were you stationed, Abdullah?"

"I was in the courtyard, sir, where I could observe all the people of the house. I now list them. First, there is Mr. Romani, the deceased's nephew, visiting from Amara —"

"A lawyer, I know of him," Chafik said.

"Then there is Mr. Sadir, a young man who lives here."

"His father died two months ago and was a close friend of the Hadji, who was appointed guardian to the youth. I find it strange," Chafik added, "that an adult should require a guardian, but there are rumors Sadir preferred Cairo to Baghdad. Life there is gay."

"A sinful city," said the sergeant.

"The mole," remarked Chafik, thinking of his own city of the dusty plains, "without doubt calls the lark sinful. But continue."

"Sir, Mr. Sadir and Mr. Romani also retired because of the heat. Their rooms are on the second floor. The servants, too, were in their quarters. Only the watchman Murad remained active. He stood at the main gate within my view." The sergeant cleared his throat, then stood rigidly at attention and said without inflection, "It is now necessary to make confession —"

"You slept?"

"Because of the heat, I dozed, sir. Briefly, only a few minutes, but I deserve reprimand. When I opened my eyes I saw Murad running toward the *surdab*. I halted him. He said he had heard the door open and thought his master had called out. We both proceeded to the spot. The door was indeed open and we saw the Hadji collapsed on the chair. I sent Murad for Mr. Romani, who came at once. Over my protests, he carried his uncle to an upper room."

"It was unwise to move a dying man, but in this case, it probably made little difference. You searched the room after the Hadji was taken out?"

"Diligently. There was nothing that resembled a weapon here."

"And where was Mr. Sadir?"

"In his room, sir. He is a heavy sleeper and had to be roused."

The Inspector looked at the bare walls of the *surdab*. The only break in the smooth brickwork was the air shaft; it resembled a narrow chimney and ended about six feet above the floor in an open vent. Chafik could see a small square of sunlight far above. The twittering of many birds echoed down the shaft and reminded him that the old man had loved birds and given them sanctuary in his garden.

"This place may be cool," the Inspector said, "but I do not find it restful. The birds are noisy."

Sergeant Abdullah interrupted, "Now what a knucklehead I am! I forgot to tell you about the bird."

"A bird?"

"Dead, sir —"

"Here in the *surdab*. It lay on the Hadji's lap, in his hand. I have labeled it as an exhibit."

He produced a pathetic bundle of black and white feathers. The bird had a forked tail and rakish wings; there was a chick's down on the breast.

Chafik said, "A swift." He touched the dangling head. "The neck is broken, it has not been dead long. A lazy, fledgling that refused to fly until it was pushed from the nest. Possibly it tumbled down the air shaft, a not uncommon occurrence. Or perhaps it fell against the door. The thud might have disturbed the Hadji, made him leave his cot and open the door —"

He stopped and gave Abdullah a sharp look; the sergeant's rare expressions were easy to read and Chafik said with sudden wrath, "So you think somebody was waiting outside the door?"

"Sir, it did enter my mind."

"Was this person invisible that he wasn't seen by the watchman at the gate? Was he foolhardy enough to stand there while you were briefly dozing a few yards away? What fiction have you been reading?"

As he left the room, the Inspector added indignantly. "Must everybody die murdered to please you, Abdullah?"

The house was a relic of old Baghdad. Rooms opened on an inner courtyard tiled with honey-colored brick. An archway led to a terrace that faced the river. There was a garden bright with flowers and shaded by ancient trees, all enclosed within a high wall.

Chafik joined two men who were waiting on the terrace. One was the Hadji's nephew, a middle-aged man with the sallow hungry look of a sufferer from a stomach ailment. Romani, who practiced law in the southern town of Amara, came to Baghdad several times a year to visit his uncle.

His companion was much younger, little more than a youth, and had a downy mustache. He looked bored. The cut of his clothes and the way he wore them gave Chafik a twinge of envy and he hoped that one day he, too, might visit a Cairo tailor.

Reluctantly, he looked away from the dapper Sadir and waited for the older man to speak.

Romani asked, "Have you formed a conclusion?"

"I let facts form their own conclusions."

The Hadji's nephew nodded approval. "It is a definite fact," he said in his thin clear voice, "that my uncle was threatened. The Shafiites are a lawless people."

"In the past they have not stopped at assassination," the Inspector said.

"On the other hand," Romani said, "it is wrong to use the history of yesterday as evidence of violence done today."

Chafik made a little bow. "How justly you correct me! But I can say what I think about them because you alone took serious view of their threats. Your uncle did not."

"In point of fact I agreed with him. But I advised him to ask for police protection as a precautionary measure, and when he refused, I took the step myself. Naturally."

Chafik thought he knew why Romani's law practice was small. The man was too cautious. He had a good reputation, always refused doubtful cases, but such legal ethics did not appeal to minds nurtured by the labyrinth of bazaars where business was conducted in Iraq.

The Inspector turned for relief to Sadir. "What did you think of the threats?" he asked the young man.

Sadir was polishing his manicured nails. He looked up languidly and said, "I am used to the civilized life in Egypt. I confess I paid little attention to this talk of threats and violence." He mopped his face with a handkerchief. "Such heat!" he complained.

"You miss Cairo?" Chafik asked.

Surprised and pleased that somebody should understand him, Sadir became confidential. "This place destroys me," he said. "There is no beauty here. Life is so crude, so lacking in urbanity —"

Romani interrupted, "Do not take our time with your foolish problems, Sadir. I know you wish to return to Cairo. It matters little to me personally, but the legal aspect of your case must be carefully considered. You were made my uncle's ward for two years. But we will discuss this later."

The young man flushed and moved away up the terrace. Romani shook his head and said sternly, "He has no sense of responsibility. Have you any more questions, Inspector?"

"I was going to ask if you entirely rule out the possibility of an intruder."

The Hadji's nephew looked down at the river, at a fisherman who stood in the shallows, his brown arm lifted to throw a weighted casting net. "I rule out nothing," he said finally. "But how could an intruder pass the police guard? Observe, for example, the height of the wall on the river side. The Tigris is at its lowest, there is a drop of thirty feet to where that fisherman stands. The door at the top of the steps that lead down to the water is always locked."

Chafik interrupted, "What do you know about Murad, your uncle's watchman?"

"I believe he is able and trustworthy."

"He has a Kurdish name. The Shafiites are a Kurdish sect —"

Romani said, "I close my ears. What you say is slanderous, even defaming, and as a lawyer I advise you to be more cautious."

The Inspector permitted himself the thought that this man probably tested the temperature of his bath water before he put a toe in it. Venturing another question, he asked, "Did you know your uncle was nursing a dead bird when he was found?"

Romani was startled. "A dead bird? No."

"It may have fallen down the air shaft or against the door. Your uncle loved birds. Something disturbed him in the *surdab*. If it was the bird he would have jumped up to succor it, and then —"

"In his haste he slipped, struck something —"

"Conjecture," Chafik said, smiling at his mild triumph. "But you may be right." He stopped, almost deafened by a shrill outcry from the many birds perched on the roof. "How noisy they are!" the Inspector said.

"I do not share my uncle's affection for birds. He would not allow a single nest to be destroyed." The thin voice trailed and Chafik looked at the man curiously.

Meeting the Inspector's eyes, the lawyer explained, "I had a thought. I reprimanded you for an unjust suspicion; now I find I have one myself."

"Concerning whom?"

"Murad. On previous visits I noted his sober habits. He rarely left my uncle's side. But lately I have seen him in cafés frequented by people of his class. I thought it odd because he is careful with money."

"What do you suggest?"

"I suggest nothing. I merely present facts." The lawyer turned away as a solemn procession began to file through the house gate. "The corpse washers and mourners are here," he said. "Excuse me, Inspector, I have my sad duties."

He went away, carefully choosing the middle of the tiles that flagged the terrace. The Inspector shrugged and turned to Sergeant Abdullah, who stood at his elbow.

"You wish to interrogate the watchman, sir?" asked Abdullah.

He indicated Murad, who stood in the background at attention and holding a heavy brassbound staff at his side in the position of a grounded rifle. The man had a soldier's straight carriage. His hair and mustache were grizzled; he was quite old.

Chafik said, "Sometimes discreet inquiries are more fruitful than interrogation. I am told this man has changed his habits and become a frequenter of cafés. You will check this information,"

"At once, sir."

When Abdullah left, Chafik completed his inspection of the house. He climbed high steps to the gallery surrounding the upper floor. Here had been the quarters of the harem women, but it was many years since bright eyes had peeped through the iron latticework of the windows.

One door was open. The Inspector glanced inside and nodded approval of the neatness. This must be Romani's room, he thought.

More steps led to the flat roof which had served as a promenade for the women in the cool of the day. At this hour it was exposed to the glare of the sun and Chafik covered the nape of his neck before venturing out.

He was greeted by a scolding chorus from the gathering of birds and was puzzled by their behavior until he looked up and saw a hawk poised in the sky. The birds were swifts, a gregarious species that banded together against an enemy. They commonly nested in old buildings.

Chafik loitered to watch a pair perched on an air shaft. The cock picked up a wisp of straw and offered it to the hen, who chirped plaintively and ruffled her feathers. Such obvious dejection roused the Inspector's sympathy and he said, "The fledgling that fell, was it yours?" He heard himself and was embarrassed because it was an old habit, this talking to himself.

Briefly he looked at the air shaft which rose a few feet above the parapet of the roof. The small vent in the side faced up-river to catch the prevailing summer breeze. Possibly this was the shaft which fed the *surdab*. There were traces of a nest in the vent, and Chafik wondered who had destroyed it. The Hadji would not have sanctioned it, but a servant might have taken unauthorized action.

"Was it your nest?" Chafik asked the unhappy pair, who had made shrill complaint at his approach.

He was again embarrassed by the sound of his voice making foolish conversation with birds. Walking to the far side of the roof, which overlooked the river, he glanced over the parapet. The fisherman he had noticed earlier was still standing motionless in the shallows.

The Inspector watched idly and then called down, "What fortune?"

The man looked up. "Fortune will come if Allah wills," he answered.

"Do you expect fish to rise in this heat?"

"Who can be certain of the ways of fish and men?" the man said, shrugging. "But I know there is a fish. It jumped and roused me when I was sleeping after the noon prayer. A very big fish, it made a big splash. I will get half a dinar for it in the bazaar."

"You are patient. It is three hours since the noon prayer."

The man said stubbornly, "He will rise when the sun goes down."

"May you be rewarded," Chafik said.

He went down the steps and passed the ground-floor room where the Hadji lay on the funeral bier, surrounded by chanting mourners. In the garden Chafik found Abdullah, who announced, "Sir, I have made the inquiries you requested. It is true about Murad."

"He frequents cafés?"

"Yes, sir. And I am informed he chooses places that have a Kurdish clientele. The Shafiites are a Kurdish —"

"Yes," said Chafik, twisting the signet ring on the little finger of his left hand. "I trust you made your inquiries discreetly?"

"I am your disciple, sir. I picked one of the lesser servants as a likely informant. When he talked, I arrested him on suspicion of theft so that no gossip of what I asked might reach Murad."

"You are as cautious as Mr. Romani. And now it would be tactful to remove ourselves from this house of mourning," the Inspector said. "My head whirls and I am going home to rest."

Entering his home on the Street of the Scatterer of Blessings, Inspector Chafik removed his jacket, loosened his tie, and announced to Leila, his wife, "I shall forgo food. Food causes a body to perspire. A perspiring body is as unpleasant as a dead one." He dropped into a chair under the ceiling fain.

There was an illusion of coolness; shutters had been closed at an early hour and the tiled floor was sprinkled with water to sweeten the air. The fan, rapidly drying Chafik's dank hair, chilled him, and he said irritably, "Wife, cover my head. You know I am susceptible to colds." He looked at the small boy who waited to greet him and added on a severe note, "A son should help his mother. Remove my shoes, Faisal."

The boy squatted on his heels. Then, looking up at the tired man in the chair, he asked, "Was it a very bloody murder? Was his throat cut?"

Chafik forgot the heat. He said, "Such words from such tender lips! But the error is mine; I forgot you had ears."

The ears of the eight-year-old boy who had been a waif in the bazaars of Baghdad, and adopted as the son of a childless marriage were small and pointed, and he had enormous eyes. The father tweaked an ear and smiled, then looked at his wife who took Faisal away.

She returned to cover her husband's head with a shawl and when he took her hand and held it to his cheek, she knew he was troubled. "Let me share the burden," she said softly.

"Did I speak? Voice a thought? It is such a disturbing habit, this talking to myself."

"You were silent, but a wife reads her man's thoughts," said the small dark woman.

Chafik sat up and lighted cigarette. "Yes, I am troubled," he admitted, and told her of the death of Hadji Hussain.

Leila exclaimed, "Oh, the poor old man! He was so saintly, so beloved."

"His death is a reflection upon my department."

"So it was murder?"

"An accident," Chafik said shortly.

"Then, my man, there can be no blame!"

"Women and ostriches," said her husband, "both seek sand piles for their heads when faced by an unwelcome fact. The Hadji died surrounded by men. Therefore I am responsible, accident or not."

"But it was an accident," Leila insisted.

He said impatiently, "Yes, yes, an accident. It could not be otherwise since the house was so carefully guarded. I do not believe an enemy entered invisibly, struck him and vanished. But —" Chafik looked for an ash tray for his cigarette and Leila hurried to bring one, "The watchman, Murad, changed his habits," he finished.

"That worries you?" She did not understand but let him talk to ease his mind.

"Everything would seem to indicate that Hadji Hussain's death was accidental. But the behavior of Murad is not clear. And then there is the dead bird. Did it fall inside or outside the *surdab*? And the open door. Did the Hadji open it? Before or after his fatal fall? I must satisfy myself on these points before I make my report," Chafik added as he settled back to rest.

Leila left him and presently he was lulled by the swish of the ceiling fan. He slept perhaps for half an hour, restlessly, muttering to himself. Then something disturbed him and he was abruptly wide awake.

A rhythmic tapping came from the hall adjoining the room and a voice timed to it chanted in a whisper, "Wunna two, abbookel my shoe, three, four, shutter door —"

Inspector Chafik rose and drew back the bead curtain from the doorway. His small son was bouncing a hard ball against the floor; the ball was attached to an elastic looped to Faisal's finger, which made it snap back into his hand.

"Fwife six, piccup six —"

Chafik said, "Macbeth murdered sleep; you murder sleep and the English language. They do not teach you well at school. Say, 'Five, six, pickup sticks.' " The father instructed with the precision that characterized his second tongue. "Six is a numeral. Sticks are instruments of chastisement. I am tempted to use one on you."

He took the ball, looped the elastic over a finger, and idly bounced it. "When you can clearly say, 'One, two, buckle my shoe,' you may have this back," he told Faisal.

Chafik turned away so that he should not see the tears in the boy's eyes; the man who had brought punishment to so many found it hard to punish his own child.

"But, my Father, already I speak English well," Faisal pleaded for approval. "Today I learned, 'Hookilt cockerobbin.' "

"You learned what?"

"Hookilt —"

Chafik put his hand to his ears. "The word is neither Arabic nor English. Surely you mean, 'Who killed — ' and it goes on about a bird. A pity I cannot remember the rhyme exactly, to school you in it. I believe there is something about a sparrow."

The boy interrupted eagerly, "I sedder sparrow wit' my bowen narrow."

"Then," said Chafik, still trying to remember, "there was a fly. And Cock Robin's funeral was quite a social affair. All the birds of the air gathered —"

He stopped and looked blankly at his son and repeated, "All the birds gathered because one died. Yes, they do. Particularly gregarious birds such as swifts and sparrows." He opened his hands in a groping gesture and Faisal's ball fell and dangled unnoticed on its elastic. "I had assumed the hawk had alarmed them," Chafik went on. "A wrong assumption; they gathered to keen the end of the fledgling. And the dead bird in the Hadji's lap, when was it killed, how long before?"

Faisal was bewildered, angry and tearful. "A bird, Father? Who has murdered a bird?"

"Who has murdered, and how?" Chafik repeated softly. Absently he began pulling up the dangling ball by its elastic, then suddenly let it fall and once more pulled it up, watching with growing excitement.

He announced, "There was a fish. It jumped. And a fisherman, a fisherman with his net."

"A net, Father?" Faisal repeated.

"The threads weave a pattern. But who was Death? Who —"

Chafik ran from the house, hatless, into the sun of late afternoon. He was halfway up the road when the wail of his son's voice penetrated the fog of his thoughts.

"Father, my Father, you have forgotten your shoes!"

The Inspector hired a boat at the top of his street and dropped downstream to the river house of Hadji Hussain. He urged the boatman to make speed; he was afraid the fisherman might have gone away.

But the man was still there and looked up reproachfully as the boat floated under the high wall. "You scare my fish," he grumbled.

Chafik said, "It has not risen? Then cast your net. Here is a dinar; let me see your skill. Cast where you saw the splash."

The fisherman whirled the circular net and released it. Opening in mid-air, skimming the water like a giant bat, it struck the spot where he had seen the splash five hours earlier. Weights carried it down and with a leap the man was on it, feeling with his toes for what he had caught.

"There is something, but not a fish," he said with disappointment.

He ducked under and gathered the net around his prize. Shaking out the sand and gravel, he untangled an object from the mesh and brought it to the boat.

"A stone wrapped in a cloth," he said with disgust. "My fish!"

Chafik silenced him and examined the catch. Double folds of cloth were fashioned into a small stout bag. Inside was a smooth rock or lump of metal; the weight was about three kilos, the Inspector judged. The neck of the bag was tied by strong twine which had been cut short and left a dangling end.

When Chafik looked up he had the face of a hanging judge and he said to the fisherman, "This day you have netted a man's head." Then he ordered his boat to the shore.

He was admitted to the Hadji's house by the watchmen.

Chafik said, "Oh, man of the hills, why did you change your habits and go to cafés? To places frequented by Shafiites?"

Murad answered directly, "I have eaten my master's salt these many years. I went to look for his enemies among those who had threatened him. I would have killed them. Was that not proper?"

The Inspector looked at the man and saw tears in his eyes. He patted Murad's arm and said, "Forgive me, my mind follows tortuous paths. I did not perceive such a simple explanation. Go with God, faithful servant."

He ran up the steps to the roof. Swifts were darting to and fro in the golden light of early evening, but the disconsolate pair he had noticed on his previous visit were still perched on the *surdab* air shaft.

Chafik said, "Be comforted, you who witnessed this thing. Your evidence is now very clear."

He put the weighted bag by the shaft and went down to the gallery on the second floor. The mourners were still chanting below and there was an odor of incense.

The Inspector entered Romani's room and made a careful search of closets and drawers. His task was simplified by the lawyer's tidiness and he was soon finished. Empty-handed and troubled, Chafik announced in a flat voice, "Of course, one so cautious might have destroyed it."

He went out and tried several of the other rooms. Left of the steps leading to the roof he found another that was tenanted and when he saw the clothing scattered around, the cluttered drawers, he had censorious thoughts for youth. But he searched methodically and disregarded the impulse to tidy the shambles.

With long, sensitive fingers he probed the confusion in the drawers of the dressing table. Then, from the jumble of odds and ends, he took out a tangled ball of strong cord. He put it in his pocket and continued the search.

There were letters with Cairo postmarks. He skimmed through them unaware that the chanting below had stopped, that the ceremony of preparing the corpse of Hadji Hussain was over. He was still reading, oblivious to his surroundings, when instinct warned him and he looked up.

Sadir stood in the doorway, and behind him was the gaunt figure of Romani. Sadir said petulantly, "What are you doing in my room reading my letters?"

"You will explain, Inspector," interposed Romani sternly. "I strongly disapprove of this irregular action. As a lawyer —"

"The hyena," said Chafik, "normally follows in the wake of the lion. I have not yet made the kill."

"I shall complain —"

"Complainants, some of them, await on the roof. Let us join them." The Inspector made his little bow.

He escorted the two men from the room and up the steps. Sadir had a dazed look and he stumbled. Romani's thin body was stooped. No one spoke.

When they were on the roof, Chafik said, "The open door of the *surdab* led me astray, but now I know who opened it. The Hadji received a fatal blow, and when he was able, he stumbled to the door for help. But already it was too late, and he collapsed after he opened it."

"An accident," insisted Romani. "My uncle tripped and fell."

"It was murder."

"He was alone in the room."

"Yes," said Chafik. "He was alone, yet he was attacked. I will show you how it was done. But we lack a dead bird, a fledgling. There was one in a nest here." The Inspector pointed to the vent of the air shaft. "Your uncle did not permit nests to be destroyed, but it was necessary to remove this one to clear the shaft. The marks on the stone prove it was done recently. Even more conclusive is the agitation of the birds. Have you noticed how many swifts have gathered, a whole community rallying to a bereaved family?"

Romani said, "Come to the point. I know nothing about birds."

Chafik said, "Fortunately I have a son who remembered an English nursery rhyme. But to continue. The nest was destroyed, the neck of the fledgling was twisted, and as bait for the old man who loved birds it was dropped down the shaft."

He looked from one man to the other. The lawyer was tense, his forehead furrowed as though he concentrated on a difficult brief. Sadir's dazed eyes stared and he chewed his underlip.

"The Hadji was reading," continued Inspector Chafik. "He was disturbed by the fall of the bird and rose to succor it. He picked it up, wondered what had caused the fatality, and naturally looked up the air shaft. Then this happened."

Chafik produced the weighted bag found in the river and knotted to the neck the ball of twine from Sadir's drawer. He said conversationally, "This is how a man was killed," and dropped the weight down the shaft, retaining the end of the line in one hand.

Nothing in forty feet of smooth brick work impeded the fall. When the bag struck the floor of the *surdab* the sound echoed back.

"Not a perfect test," Chafik apologized. "It was not so noisy when it struck the Hadji's head. The force of a three-kilo weight falling forty feet can be calculated. It was not necessary to practice marksmanship — the opening is small and the target was large. Even a glancing blow would have been fatal to a frail old man."

He stopped and for the first time looked directly at Sadir. The young man's mouth opened, but no sound came from it.

"And then," the Inspector said pitilessly, "you hauled up your weapon, cut the line short and threw the bag into the river. Did you fear the line would float? But how careless of you to leave it in your room! Otherwise you planned well, took nice advantage of foolish threats made against your victim by quite harmless people. You reasoned that with a police guard around the house the death of a man in a closed room would be considered an accident. And you would have been right if parent birds had not keened the cruel death of a fledgling, if my son had not played with a toy which I found very suggestive. And if there had not been a patient fisherman."

Romani shook his head and said in his thin voice, "This case has a weakness. What was the motive for the alleged crime?"

"You yourself told us this wretched young decadent preferred Cairo to Baghdad. Also there are letters from a woman which suggest a powerful motive. Sadir was desperate to get back to her, but the Hadji had been appointed his guardian and controlled his money and his freedom. Young, spoiled, ruthless — I trust you are convinced, Mr. Romani?"

Lulled by the cadence of his own voice, the Inspector was unprepared when the lawyer turned with unexpected speed and caught Sadir by the throat. "You killed my uncle! You killed my uncle!" he screamed as he forced the young man to his knees.

Chafik broke the death grip. "Restrain yourself!" he said sharply, and then with a smile he added, "Such depth of emotion, Mr. Romani! How admirable — and how unexpected in one so cautious!"

There Is a Man in Hiding

Chafik J. Chafik, of the Baghdad police, took his place at the breakfast table in his house on the Street of the Scatterer of Blessings. The swarthy, neat little man, dressed for the heat of the day in immaculate whites, accepted the homage of his family with the indulgence of a Babylonian king. He glanced at his watch, announced, "I am four minutes late," and dipped his spoon into the bowl of *liben* and honey-colored dates.

Leila, his wife, a serene and graceful woman, asked, "My man, you did not sleep well?"

She glanced at her son, a wide-eyed elf of a boy, and saw that his effervescence was precariously corked. Her look constrained him.

Chafik said, "The Compassionate One willed me a bad night. There were comings and goings and voices, and the most objectionable voice was the voice of a cat." He put down his spoon and looked at his son reprovingly.

Faisal began, "My father —"

Leila interrupted: "Faisal's cat had kittens."

"Five," the boy said proudly. "May I keep them? May I, my father?''

It was difficult for Chafik to deny his son anything, but he was incensed by his sleepless night. He sighed. "Ah, what base ingratitude!" he said. "I took this animal into my house as a homeless waif and —"

He stopped, for he suddenly remembered that Faisal had seen a waif, too. It was less than two years since the boy, then an eight-year-old orphan, had been one of the pack of homeless urchins who frequented the Baghdad bazaars. Chafik had taken him from that life to fill the gap in a childless, but otherwise happy, marriage, and had never regretted the impulse which had given him a fine son. So, shocked by his unfortunate remark, the little man looked beseechingly at his wife.

Leila's head was lowered; she said nothing.

Chafik took refuge in attack. "Does not my sleepless night suffice?" he demanded. "Am I now denied the brightness of conversation? And must I have kittens underfoot, too?"

The telephone rang, and the Inspector padded on stocking feet to answer it. The caller was Sergeant Abdullah of the homicide squad.

Abdullah said in a voice of doom, "Sir, I trust you have enjoyed breakfast?"

"My stomach," Chafik answered, "is delicate this morning, and judging by your ill-omened croak it is well I left it unfilled. What horror have you to show me?"

"I regret, sir, a corpse." The sergeant went on to give details.

When Abdullah had finished, Chafik got his shoes from under the hall table, for Arab-fashion he did not wear them in the house. He picked up the shoes and returned to his family.

"The evil continues," he said. "Now I have a corpse. They found one on the premises of Mr. Topalian, the jeweler and antique dealer of the bazaars. And Mr. Topalian has vanished. Enough, therefore, of ungrateful cats and pestilential kittens. Respect my wishes and cast them out."

Faisal's wail followed Chafik to the street. The Inspector sought comfort in the wisdom of the Koran, and prayerfully hoped his thoughtless remark, which had distressed his wife, had escaped the notice of their adopted son. Knowing the sharpness of those faunlike ears, he was not sure.

"If the Devil had not given us speech, there would be less misunderstanding in the world," the little man said, as he drove away.

The establishment of David Topalian was in one of the far reaches of the great bazaar. Inspector Chafik, who had left his car outside the Imperial Bank, where the labyrinth of covered ways began, arrived on foot, and was received by the tall police officer who had telephoned.

Abdullah said, "Sir, the corpse is that of a man named Esiah Constantine. He —"

Chafik gestured for silence, extracted a record card from his tidy train, and quoted: "Constantine, Esiah. Aged fifty-seven. Resident of Basra. Educated. Assisted in the archeological excavations at Ur in the nineteen-twenties." He paused and then added, "Believed to be in possession of valuable antiques — allegedly he stole them from the excavations. I will now face his corpse."

They went down a short passage into a vaulted room, cool and shadowy, and brightened by silk prayer rugs on the walls. There were many treasures in the place, which was an exotic setting for the colorful Armenian dealer who normally presided over it in a velvet gown and embroidered skullcap. But Topalian did not preside today, and the corpse of Esiah Constantine was not exotic.

The body was sprawled in a low chair with its head bowed on an ebony coffee table. Two cups, which had been used, were overturned, and drunken flies crawled over the pool of sugary coffee. The back of the dead man's skull was crushed; on the floor was a bronze club shaped like a lion's paw.

Inspector Chafik looked at the club and said, "Ancient Assyrian — a warrior's weapon. Mr. Topalian has a large collection of such relics."

He examined the body, touched the mashed head, noticed splinters of protruding bone, and announced, "The killer stood on the right, possibly after pouring coffee to honor — and disarm — the guest. Three blows were struck. Wasteful energy: one was enough."

Sergeant Abdullah said, "Sir, the man has been dead some nine hours. It fits the time of Topalian's departure. He —"

Chafik wiped his hands on the coattails of the corpse. "Let us begin at the end, as detective stories are written," he said. "Who found Constantine?"

"The missing man's cousin, sir. George Topalian. I will produce him."

The sergeant brought in a handsome young man whose heavy-lidded eyes suggested that he kept late hours. He was nervous, and the ash of many cigarettes was spilled on his expensive, but crumpled, clothes.

"A candle that burns at both ends should at least gut itself neatly," Chafik said. "However, that is not my affair. Your name is George Topalian. You are twenty-three, unmarried, but not inexperienced. You work for your cousin, who is thirty years your senior. You discovered the unfortunate gentleman who lies here. Inform me of the circumstances."

The young man would not look at the body as he answered, "My cousin expects me to open the shop at seven thirty, but I was perhaps half an hour late this morning. The door was still locked —"

Chafik interrupted: "Your cousin has a residence in the Jenub district; he also has a sleeping room above these premises. You feared he had stayed the night and would reprimand you for lateness?"

George Topalian's handsome face became sullen. He nodded.

"So you knocked?"

"There are witnesses. Our neighbors —"

"They will talk later. With diffidence toward an elder, you knocked, and there was no answer. Then?"

"I unlocked the door and went in. I saw Constantine."

"You knew him?"

"I knew of him — that he was coming from Basra to sell something."

"What?"

"A chalice. The funeral cup of a Sumerian noble."

Chafik thought: *So my records are correct. Constantine did steal treasures on that expedition years ago. Now he tries to sell them. And to what better dealer could he go than David Topalian?*

Aloud, the Inspector said, "The killer apparently took the chalice away. I need a description."

The young man shrugged and answered disdainfully, "I can't help you. I care little about antiques; I like modern things. But any collector can describe the chalice; they all knew Constantine had it."

Chafik was disturbed because his record had missed this important fact, but he said, "So when you found the body, you ran for help?"

"First I went to see if my cousin was upstairs."

"Thereby establishing that nobody was hiding on the premises. Excellently done! Chafik took out a packet of *Ghazi* cigarettes and offered one to the witness. "Now, your cousin's disappearance. When did you last see him?"

Topalian lighted the cigarette from the Inspector's match and answered, "Last night, about eight o'clock. We were closing. He told me to get porters for a customer's purchase."

"Several porters means a bulky object," Chafik said. "Was it the object that formerly stood outside in the entrance passage? I noticed a portion of lighter-colored floor. Observation is the fetish of my trade," he added apologetically.

"You observed correctly. It was a Meccan bridal chest. I found porters, escorted them to the purchaser's home, saw delivery made, left —"

"Wait," Chafik said. "I cannot stand on the curve of time and see all dimensions at once. Had the customer departed before you went for the porters?"

"Yes."

"And your cousin was here when you returned?"

"He had gone upstairs to rest and to wait for Constantine. I did not disturb him. Furthermore, I was in a hurry."

Chafik detected evasion in the young man's reply, so he asked with deceptive mildness, "You had an engagement, perhaps?"

Topalian stared down at his cigarette; his heavy lids concealed the expression in his eyes. "I was to meet a friend," he said.

"For the sake of tidy records, give me his name."

"We — he — we were to meet at the Shahrazade Cabaret. No, it was the Roxy. But he didn't turn up. I —" He stopped abruptly.

The Inspector would not let his confusion pass. "The sequence of events may refresh your memory," he said. "To whom did you take the chest?"

"To Dr. Ghaffari."

"Ghaffari, Mohammed," Chafik quoted. "Aged sixty-two. Ph.D. from London University. He buys antiques rather than food." The little man smiled, then asked, "At what time did you make the delivery?"

"I — I don't remember."

"Be at ease, the doctor will remember. You see, I try to help you," Chafik said kindly.

"Ghaffari wasn't at home. He had an appointment, too. Before he left my cousin's shop he gave me a key,"

"You were in the doctor's house alone after you dismissed the porters?"

"For a few minutes. Why the Devil do you ask so many questions?" the young man asked angrily.

"How timely to mention the Devil! He was busy here, directing Constantine's murder, the disappearance of the chalice, the disappearance of your cousin —"

George Topalian interrupted vehemently, "Now you implicate my cousin!"

"I have made no accusation, yet. How much was he to pay for the chalice?"

"I don't know. He complained that the price was high, but he hoped to get it lowered. Besides, he had a buyer, an American — they are all foolish about antiques. So why should he kill?"

"An eloquent defense," Chafik said. "Let us, however, be factual and consider only the facts of his disappearance. Who saw Mr. Topalian last?"

The inquiry was addressed to the Inspector's assistant, who brought in a very old man clad in tattered battle dress.

Sergeant Abdullah said, "The next witness, sir. Shah Murad, the bazaar *charkachi*. Formerly of the Levies."

Chafik noticed with pity how the watchman strained to come to attention. "Did he see Constantine arrive?" he asked Abdullah.

"His evidence is that he saw the deceased admitted to these premises. Half an hour later, he states, Topalian left in a great hurry. Murad claims he saw him turn the corner into the Street of the Coppersmiths. Since then so far as I can ascertain, no eyes have beheld the Armenian."

"What was Topalian wearing?"

"The robe he favors, sir. Also a hat with a brim, such as Christians wear."

Chafik said dryly, "An odd costume for a man who planned to disappear."

The Inspector went outside. The bazaar was roofed by straw mats which were rotted by the weather; sunlight and shadow made an intricate pattern over the unpaved way. The Street of the Coppersmiths was entered through a narrow arch a few yards from Topalian's shop.

The street was a place of thunderous noise and of sudden, leaping flames that brushed the workers at their forges with glowing color. Numerous passages, barely wide enough for a man on foot, led into mysterious reaches. Chafik shrugged, knowing the hopelessness of searching such a maze.

"Human tigers prowl this jungle at night," Chafik said. "If it were known that Topalian carried an object of value —" He finished the thought with a finger across his throat.

"A body," the sergeant said thoughtfully, "is difficult to hide."

"Its presence," the Inspector agreed, "would become evident in this heat in two days. In three days," he amended, flinching from the odors of the open drains. "You will instruct the police to alert their noses."

"That will be done, sir. But what of Constantine?"

"Yes. Constantine. The discovery of a dead Topalian would not answer the questions raised by the corpse he left behind."

The little man stopped, stared at the corner of the Street of the Coppersmiths and ran. He was blocked by the crowd that had been attracted by rumors of murder.

"I swear I saw him!" Chafik exclaimed to Abdullah.

"Mr. Topalian, sir?"

"No. Faisal — my son. He should be at school."

"Boys look very much alike, sir, and there are many in the bazaar. They rush this way and that with great energy. It is the way of boys. I have daughters," the sergeant added smugly.

"Daughters undulate," Chafik said. And then, unhappily, he remembered the episode of the cat and kittens and his unfortunate remark at the breakfast table. He hurried back to the antique shop to call his wife.

"Leila," he began.

"Oh, my man!" There was relief in her voice. "You got my message?" his wife went on.

"What message? I am closeted with an uncommunicative corpse."

"I called your office to inform you that Faisal's school —"

"Yes? Yes? What, my wife?"

"They have reported he did not attend this morning."

Chafik was shocked and silent. He wanted to rush home, but duty restrained him and it was necessary to reassure Leila.

"A childish prank, my wife. I shall discipline Faisal," he added sternly. "Inform him, when he comes home, that his father will not speak to him for twenty-four hours." And with fond words for Leila, the Inspector hung up.

Then he beat his fists together and exclaimed, "All because of the cat. That monster and her kittens!"

"Sir?" Abdullah asked.

"Nothing, nothing." The Inspector sought escape in action. "I am going to Dr. Ghaffari, who perhaps can describe the object Constantine brought to Topalian. I assume he, like all collectors, knows about it," Chafik added. "As for yourself, check on the cousin. That young man's alibi was unsatisfactory. And, Abdullah —"

"Sir?"

"If you should see my son, reprimand him severely and send him home. He does not belong here, not in the bazaars, not now."

The man the Inspector wished to see lived at the back of the bazaars, in a house that thrust its ancient foundations into the river's slime. It was once a Turkish palace but now housed many families; Ghaffari had rooms on the first floor.

As Chafik picked his way through the refuse of the streets, he had a feeling that he was being followed, and he looked around. He saw nobody suspicious, and was distracted by a boy who resembled Faisal.

The urchin wore a ragged gown and a wisp of turban. He skipped blithely on naked feet, balancing a basket on his head; light portering was the precarious livelihood of these waifs, and they could be hired for a few *fils*.

They grow up to become entries in my criminal records, Chafik thought sadly. *This might have been Faisal.*

The youngster passed, then twirled, like a ballet dancer, across the Inspector's path. He had a sharp, bright face, too-wise eyes, and an engaging smile. "Sahib?" he said.

"I am not shopping," Chafik said. "And I have nothing to carry." He reached into his pocket for a coin.

The urchin ran backward before him. "Policeman Sahib, I am not to take money. I have a message."

Chafik stopped.

"I am to say that yesterday the Armenian merchant, Topalian, and his cousin, quarreled. About women. The young one has many women. The elder threatened to banish the younger from Baghdad, unless —"

"Who sent you?" Chafik demanded. "How do you know I am a policeman?"

The boy did a pirouette, kicked up his heels, laughed, and disappeared.

"Was it Abdullah?" Chafik wondered, as he walked on. "No, he would never send such a message by a seedling! So who?"

At Dr. Ghaffari's house, he rattled the heavy knocker.

The doctor was a tall, stooped man who peered at the Inspector with tired, sunken eyes. His clothes were threadbare, but he had gracious manners and bowed as he recognized his visitor.

"I am honored, Inspector! Come in, come in! If I had known of your visit I would have prepared coffee."

"I am on duty, Doctor." Chafik was well aware Ghaffari had no coffee in the house. To save money for antiques, the doctor bought the dross that merchants scraped from their sacks.

Ghaffari lived in three large rooms which opened off the entrance hall. Light came grayly through barred windows and touched the treasures that crowded every corner. The man had once been wealthy, but now his dinars were interred in this magnificent collection.

Chafik said, "I have come for help. You know about Topalian?"

"Yes. I heard. It's incredible. I saw him yesterday and he was in fine spirits and happy about an important deal. I can not believe —"

The Inspector was in a hurry and stopped Ghaffari. "I am informed the deal concerned an antique which Constantine brought from Basra. It has vanished. Did you know of it? Can you describe it?"

"Can a man describe Paradise?" Ghaffari's eyes shone, and color touched his sallow cheeks. He went to a cabinet and reverently lifted a crystal cup which filled his two hands like a bowl of light.

"This," he said, "is Sumerian craftsmanship, but compared with the chalice you ask about, it is clay. The chalice is of this size and shape and made from a block of lapis lazuli worked so fine it shames eggshell. Yet it is strong; gold is fused with the lapis. And the color! The sun-flecked blue of the canopy of God's Throne!"

"It would appear you have seen the cup," Chafik said.

"Constantine showed it to me in Basra years ago."

"So it is true then that he hid it from his superiors when they excavated the death pits at Ur?"

Ghaffari shrugged. "Who can blame him? But permit me to continue. The chalice is a funeral cup. When a Sumerian noble was buried, they put a cup filled with rare wine in his hands. And round about him were guards and attendants —"

"Slaughtered," said Chafik, "to attend their master's afterworld comforts. It is well I was not a policeman in those days. What value do you put on the chalice?"

"Value? You mean money? Inspector, one does not estimate such a treasure in dinars! I was shocked when Topalian said Constantine was going to sell. I had thought better of him."

Chafik was puzzled. The chalice was so rare that a warning circulated among the police of all countries would frighten away all prospective buyers. "And so," the Inspector said, "Constantine's murderer must be aware that if he tries to sell, he will be paid by the hangman."

The doctor insisted on showing his collection and Chafik went politely from room to room. He was overwhelmed by the beauty he saw, and he felt pity for the man, living in poverty amid such wealth.

When they returned to the hall, the Inspector examined a large chest and asked Ghaffari if he had bought it from Topalian. The doctor nodded, raised the heavy lid, and launched into a discourse.

"I believe this dates to Sheba," he said. "The painted designs are Meccan, but there are traces of others underneath. However, the years have taken their toll, and perhaps I did not get a good bargain."

He pointed to cracks in the side of the chest and then let the lid fall. It closed like a slammed door and wafted odors of myrrh and frankincense into the room.

"I am told," Chafik said, "that young Topalian delivered this in your absence. You considered it safe to trust him with the key to your house?"

Ghaffari said, "I know the young man well and have always found him exemplary, except for —"

"Women?" Chafik suggested. They both smiled.

As he prepared to go, the Inspector asked, "Doctor, when you returned, did you find the chest open?"

"Open? Let me think." Ghaffari turned and looked at it. "Yes — yes, I am sure I found it open."

The little man salaamed and left. On the doorstep he threw down the stub of his cigarette, and, looking back a moment later, saw Ghaffari pick it up.

So he also denies himself the comfort tobacco, thought Chafik. *Surely the Compassionate One has afflicted him.*

Anxious to telephone his wife for news of Faisal, he walked rapidly, and it was some time before he realized that a bazaar boy was running after him. He stopped, turned quickly, and the boy just as quickly backed away.

"Sahib! A message!"

"Another?" Chafik asked.

"Sahib, Hassan Ali, the beggar of the Street of the Leatherworkers, yesterday boasted he would rob the Armenian, Topalian."

The Inspector reached for the boy, and clutched air. The boy was as elusive as smoke. Bewildered, Chafik continued on his way.

"There is organization behind this," he told himself. "Only the All-Merciful knows if the intention is to hinder or help."

As if he had been sent in answer, a third boy appeared from nowhere with the same breathless "Sahib?"

"Deliver your message," Chafik said with resignation.

"I am to tell you to forget about Hassan Ali. After he boasted, he fell down drunk from drinking much arrack, and slept all night."

"I thank you," Chafik said. "The original rumor would have reached me on a police report and would have caused tribulation for both Hassan Ali and myself until the truth was known. Therefore I am grateful to whoever directs you, fleet-footed Father of Long Ears."

And courteously saluting the grinning urchin, he turned and left.

There was no news of Faisal. Inspector Chafik stood at the window of his office overlooking Al Rashid Street, and saw in the ugly, brown city the reflection of his mood. Somewhere among those half million people of all races and creeds was his son.

He reproached himself bitterly. Now he was sure Faisal had misunderstood the remark about the stray cat, had remembered that he had once been a homeless waif and, believing himself unwanted, had run away.

But I cannot divert men to find him, Chafik thought despairingly. *I am a police man. There is murder.*

Sergeant Abdullah came in. He was as emotional as the stone image he resembled, and was excellent therapy for the distracted father.

In his usual ominous voice, Abdullah said, "Sir, I have checked the alibi of the younger Topalian. He lied. He was not at any cabaret. Nor did he go home last night. And, sir, by careful inquiry I have learned that yesterday he —"

"Quarreled with his cousin about a woman," Chafik said.

"A fierce and wordy argument. But, sir, how did you know?"

"I have ears, many little ears. You re-examined Topalian?"

"He is stubbornly silent and refuses to detail his movements after he delivered the chest. I have detained him."

"Did you establish how long he stayed alone in Dr. Ghaffari's house?"

"There are no witnesses, sir. The porters departed immediately."

Chafik looked down at the signet ring on his left hand. "What else, Abdullah?" he asked, absently.

"One of those miserable urchins who frequent the bazaars —"

"I adopted one," Chafik said softly.

Abdullah went on, flushing. "The waif commanded me to tell you that four days ago Dr. Ghaffari purchased a chain and iron collar, suitable for a large dog. I could not detain my informant."

"It would be easier to catch a gazelle. These young messengers are bombarding me with wild rumors. Ghaffari has no dog. Yet, I wonder — I wonder."

The Inspector looked at his watch. "So late? I am going home. Continue to press the search for the elder Topalian. If his body does not appear within a few days, it will mean the man has left this city. Although why an honored citizen should turn murderer and thief is beyond me."

When Inspector Chafik reached home, he found his wife in tears; Faisal had not returned and it was already night.

The stillness in the house was heartbreaking. Chafik remembered the busy feet, the treble voice, the uproar of a lively boy, and he repented moments of anger when meditations had been disturbed. He held Leila and tried to comfort her with passages from the Koran, but grief overcame him and he joined her in tears.

"How fortunate that we are not English and do not find it necessary to inhibit emotion," he declared.

Presently he gave Leila a sedative, arranged for a neighbor to sit with her, and went out into the dark streets. He wandered, searching, and questioning the police patrols; duty would not permit him to assign men solely to the quest for his son.

At dawn Chafik went to his office and fell asleep in a chair. And it was there that Abdullah, arriving early, found him. The sergeant, too, was red-eyed and weary.

"Sir," he said with pity, "I regret I have no news of Faisal."

"You, too, have been searching?"

"I took the liberty, sir."

"Keep to your duty. We must both remember our duty," Chafik said, and added less harshly, "but thank you, Abdullah. Is there news of Topalian?"

"None. Today, perhaps, the noses of the police will discover —" the sergeant stopped suddenly, remembering the missing Faisal. Hurriedly he said, "I have to report a singular incident. There was another of the bazaar waifs outside as I came in."

"Yes? Yes?"

"He told me to tell you that Dr. Ghaffari has made large purchases of food. I held the child briefly, but his teeth were sharp." Abdullah tenderly nursed a wrist.

Chafik reached for a cigarette. "So the little ears are still busy. Could it be?"

No, it was too fantastic. "Yet, it is strange," he went on, "that a man who has never squandered more than fifty *fils* a day on his stomach these many years should suddenly indulge his appetite."

With little heart, but still pursuing this elusive notion, he began a busy day. Other things than the Topalian case required his attention, and the Inspector occupied himself with these until the call to prayer reminded him that the day was ending.

Chafik thought: *Another night. Darkness, and all it shrouds. My son —*

Violently, he swept the papers from his desk and shouted, "To the Pit with duty! To the Pit with Constantine and Topalian! I will divert every man. I —"

Sergeant Abdullah appeared at the door. "Sir," he said, "a boy wishes to speak with you."

The boy was frightened. His bare toes curled and uncurled on the cheap carpet.

"What now?" Chafik asked.

"Sahib," the boy said breathlessly. "I am to say there is a man in hiding. The proof is his stomach's demands. He who sends me has found a way into the hiding place and has entered it to seek final proof."

The Inspector, with a tiger's leap, reached the boy, seized the slack of his gown, and shouted, "Who sent you?"

"I will not talk! I am Faisal's man!"

There was a ripping sound as the thread-bare garment tore. Brown buttocks vanished through the door and disappeared down the gloomy corridor, as the boy outran the police.

"Imbecile!" Inspector Chafik exclaimed. "Imbecile!"

"I could not stop him," Abdullah said defensively.

"I am the imbecile! How could I doubt that Faisal was behind all this? He is of the bazaars. He mobilized his old friends and directed their inquisitive ears to help me. And I was too stupid to understand his messages."

The moment of revelation passed. "Faisal! Where has he gone? Into what danger? I must find my son, Abdullah!"

Chafik calmed himself and forced himself to sit at his desk and light a cigarette. "A man in hiding — misered *fils* spent suddenly on food. Oh, Merciful One! A chain and an iron collar but no dog! Abdullah, get the young Topalian from the detention room."

When the sergeant returned with George Topalian, Chafik stood on tiptoe in an effort to match the young man's stature.

"You are foolish and stubborn," he said, pointing his chin accusingly. "You gave me a lying alibi for the night your cousin disappeared, because you went with a woman, probably a married one since you protect her with your silence. You quarreled with your cousin about her because he had stern morals. So, enough. Tell me, when Dr. Ghaffari left the shop after purchasing the chest, did he slam the door?"

Topalian stammered, "Yes — yes, I think I heard it slam."

"Neither you nor your cousin actually saw Ghaffari reach the street?"

"No, the passage leading to the door is at an angle."

"And when you returned with the porters, the chest was locked?"

"It had been padlocked."

Inspector Chafik's face was a mask. He reached into a drawer, grabbed his gun, and ran.

The crowds that filled the bazaar parted for the madman with a gun. He shouted, "Compassionate One, grant me time!" He was hatless, his pomaded hair was in disarray, and he had torn open his collar.

When Chafik reached the old house by the river, he hammered on the door and his voice cracked as he demanded admission. There was no answer, and he butted the door with his shoulder.

At that moment it opened, and he fell into the dark hall.

He lost the gun on the tiled floor and scrabbled with bleeding fingers to find it. A figure materialized from the shadows and Chafik saw an arm raised to deliver a blow. He rolled clear and was shocked by pain as his shoulder hit the gun.

He seized it and rose to one knee.

In the smoky light from an oil lamp in an adjoining room, he saw the dull gleam of metal — an ancient battle-ax poised for another blow. He steadied his wrist and fired twice.

The shots echoed in the vaulted hall. Inspector Chafik rose and looked down at the still form of Dr. Ghaffari, and said in prayer, "God forgive me." He turned quickly away.

He searched the rooms until he found a door hidden by a wall hanging. It was locked. He blew out the lock with his gun and did not feel the splinters that lacerated his face. He went down winding steps into the cellar of Ghaffari's house.

Ghaffari's prisoners were in an alcove strewn with straw. The man had an iron collar around his neck and was fastened to the wall by a chain. The boy was bound with rope and both were gagged with tape.

Chafik released Faisal, saying over and over, "My son, my son." He took the boy in his arms and wept.

Faisal's lips were torn by the tape and he whimpered, "Father, it hurts. But, my father, there is the man."

Inspector Chalk used the barrel of his gun to force a link in the chain. He said, "Later we will remove the collar. It does not exactly adorn you, Mr. Topalian."

The antique dealer was unharmed, but shock had left its mark. He shook his head and said, "Ghaffari is a madman. Why did he keep me chained and feed me so lavishly? How did I get here?"

Chafik said, "After you sold Ghaffari the chest and he asked to have it delivered, he gave his house key to your cousin. Then he went out and slammed the door. But it was not the door he slammed. It was the lid of the chest. He was inside it."

"Then Ghaffari attacked me after George had gone for the porters!" Topalian exclaimed. "I remember that now, and a nightmare of suffocation."

"You had been bound, gagged, and probably chloroformed. And you journeyed, sir, in the chest, escorted in all innocence by your cousin, who was in too much of a hurry to heed the porters' grumbles about excessive weight. Your suffocation was real; you survived because there were cracks in the chest and because Ghaffari did not want you to die. Only one murder was planned for that night — Constantine's."

"Murdered?"

"For the chalice. Ghaffari admitted him to the shop, posed as your friend, and then killed him. Afterward, he put on your robe and hat and walked out boldly. He had correctly calculated the fading eyesight of the bazaar's ancient watchman. After vanishing into the maze of streets, he removed the robe and went home without exciting suspicion. He had the chalice, and he had his alibi."

Topalian shook his head. "But why didn't he kill me?"

"Because, sir, he couldn't dispose of your body. In this heat and in a house where there are other families —" Chafik raised his thumb and forefinger to his nose. "He had to keep you alive until the search for you as the murderer had died down. And if my son and his friends had not noticed the change in Ghaffari's shopping habits —"

The Inspector heard a noise upstairs. He checked his gun and ran. The doctor's body was gone from the hall and a trail of blood led to one of the rooms.

Chafik followed it. The dying man was in a chair by the moonlit window. He had taken the chalice from its hiding place and sat holding it with both hands. The beauty of the lapis and gold transfigured his waxen face. In his last moments, Dr. Ghaffari forgot pain.

He slowly raised his head, recognized the Inspector, and whispered, "I did not take it for money. I could not let it go — into alien hands — far from our land."

The deep-set eyes became brilliant. "This," Ghaffari said in a suddenly strong voice, "is how the Sumerian was buried, holding his funeral cup. Where is my escort to the next world? The slaughtered ones — the —"

He bowed his head over the chalice; even in death he embraced it...

When Inspector Chafik was able to leave with his son, Faisal looked up anxiously and asked, "My father, did I do well?"

"My son," replied the little man, "it was not well to distress your tender mother, and me, and I do not think it was wisdom to enter a murderer's house. But, my son, yes, you did most well, you and your army of little ears!"

"Then, if I did well, am I to be rewarded?"

"Ask, my son, ask!" Chafik said, embracing the boy.

Too late he saw the calculating look in those large eyes. Too late he remembered that Faisal had been whetted on the stone of the bazaars.

"My father," Faisal said innocently, "it is sad to be homeless, as I know. And have you not shown me that one must have compassion for a waif as the cat and her five kittens? I did what I did because of them. So, may I keep them?"

Death in the Fourth Dimension

On a day that had ended prematurely for the city of Baghdad in the bloody twilight of a dust storm, a boy burst into a neat house on the Street of the Scatterer of Blessings and announced, "Father, my father, I have seen a murdered corpse!"

"You have doubtless seen many corpses," Chafik J. Chafik said. "Your good mother unwisely permits you to go to the cinema."

Then the little man squared his thin shoulders, remembering the parental duty which had brought him home from the homicide bureau, and commenced, "Faisal, I am told you take to school imaginary tales of my exploits as a policeman."

The innocence of the boy's wide-set eyes made him look like a fawn, and Inspector Chafik had to resist an impulse to take him in his arms. *My son*, he thought. *Not flesh of my flesh, nor my wife's, a waif found in the bazaar's of Baghdad, but still our son.*

Chafik went on, "I never fought and subdued three armed men of alarming proportions. Nor did I encounter a society of assassins whose main activity was to gather at midnight and swear oaths on a bloody dagger. Yet these things you have related. Both are untrue."

"Father! Listen!" the boy said urgently. "The murder was at the Bayt Kamil Hadi, and I saw them bury the man and —"

"Eh? What?" exclaimed Chafik.

"Father, you know the house. There is a garden behind a big wall and I heard a woman scream and I climbed a tree and looked and she was there, the lady of the house, El Sitt Rejina, and one of her brothers held her — the bearded one, Jamil — and the drunk one, Ibrahim, had a spade and there was the dead one on the ground. I know he was dead because his head was twisted — so —" Faisal put his head on one side.

"God the Merciful!" exclaimed Inspector Chafik's wife, who had just come into the room. "A boy — to see such horror —"

She was a woman whose sweetness leavened her husband's grim profession.

The Inspector had to force himself to his duty. "Be silent, Leila. Let the witness complete his lies."

"Stories, yes, not necessarily lies. Have understanding, my man! Children live in a world of make-believe."

"Yes, of trolls and jinn. But he sees crooks and corpses!" the Inspector said indignantly.

Tears gathered in Faisal's eyes, and he cried, "I did so see what I said I saw! And I know the dead one. Zaki Attala —"

Chafik rarely had to consult a citizen's dossier. He referred to the filing cabinet of his memory and quoted, "Attala, Zaki. Related to Rejina and her brothers. A third cousin. Age, twenty-six. Married. Recently here from Basra. Suspected of irregularities —"

Faisal interrupted eagerly, "The old woman, his cousin, is rich, and all Baghdad knows Zaki was going to get a divorce and marry her."

"Enough!" shouted Chafik.

He, too, had heard the scandal, for the gossips of Baghdad never tired of discussing Rejina and her brothers. They were the children of a rich merchant who had expressed his displeasure with the sons by willing his estate to the daughter. And so, for twenty years, this matriarch had ruled with her father's rod. She had never married, nor permitted her brothers to marry.

"But, my father," Faisal insisted, "I am sure it was because he might have married this Zaki that her brothers killed him." The boy read disbelief in Chafik's swarthy face and stamped his foot. "They did kill him! And they saw me and if you don't put them in prison they will come and kill me, too, and you'll be sorry!"

The mother silenced the boy and turned to her husband. "He doesn't mean to be naughty," she pleaded.

Chafik pronounced judgment: "The seat of our son's naughtiness is the mind. It would be unjust to apply the rod to his other seat, which is innocent. Therefore, I have decided to use psychology and confront him with his nebulous evidence. Wife, get me my shoes."

Leila had a smile as she hurried to obey. The little man took Faisal in a policeman's grip and went out into the storm.

At the door of the Bayt Kamil Hadi, Chafik rang again and again. Finally the gray-bearded Jamil Hadi came and asked indignantly, "Do you think us all dead?"

Chafik remembered he had a delicate mission, and his salaam was profound as he introduced himself. "I come not as a policeman, but as a father."

He was not sure, but thought Jamil Hadi was relieved. Chafik went on to relate Faisal's tale of a nightmare and was careful not to name names.

The other brother had come to the door. This one, Ibrahim, had the face of an alcoholic. At first he was inattentive; then he pressed the palms of his hands together and exclaimed, "The boy said it happened here? Oh, Compassionate One! If our sister should hear!"

He drew close to Jamil, and the two middle-aged men stood in a conspiracy of fear, peering back into the courtyard of the old house.

The Bayt Kamil Hadi had two stories, and the rooms were built around a central courtyard. On the water side was a broad terrace, and on the land side the wall of the house was extended to enclose a garden of shade trees and neglected flower beds.

Inspector Chafik tightened his arm around his son and joined the conspiracy of the brothers. "She rests?" he asked.

Jamil put a finger to his lips. "It would be a kindness not to disturb our sister. But if you must —"

"I am not here as a policeman," Chafik reminded him. "Where is Zaki Attala? He was my son's vision of a corpse."

It shocked him that Ibrahim should laugh. The man clapped a hand to his mouth, then said, "Pardon — I lack manners —"

Jamil said, "Now this is ridiculous!"

He left his brother to guard the door and went away. Baghdad gossips said Rejina did not tolerate servants, and it seemed to be true. Presently he came back with a young man, at whose appearance Faisal cried out and buried his face in his father's coat.

"The same man," Faisal said in a muffled voice. "He was dead. They were burying him."

"Enough!" commanded Chafik. The gentleness of his hands as they caressed the trembling boy atoned for the harsh voice.

He turned to Zaki. The man was very handsome, very conceited. Reckless, too, thought the Inspector, noting the swagger.

Zaki said mockingly, "Take a dead man's word for it, it's all true about paradise. Black-eyed houris, flowing wine —"

Chafik remembered his position and checked a retort. Humbly he asked permission to take Faisal into the garden. "I must convince him there is no grave," he explained.

They went through a cloister, then turned into the garden path. Faisal snatched his hand from his father's and ran ahead. "Here! Here they buried him!" He stamped on a spot beneath a fig tree crucified against the garden wall.

The sandy ground had been long unspaded.

"He has visions," Ibrahim said. "I, too, sometimes have them." He put a hand to his mouth to stop a giggle.

The Inspector struggled with his pride, and, at the house door again, he humbled himself. "Be merciful and forgive," he begged. "My son does not really tell lies. It is his imagination. He —"

Zaki was amused and Ibrahim laughed nervously, but Jamil said unpleasantly, "I advise you take a stick to that boy."

He slammed the door. Chafik stared at it, his face choleric. Then he vented his anger on the violence of the dust storm.

He wrapped his coat around his son and they started along the riverbank. But after a few paces, the Inspector whipped around, assailed by fear. In the brief life of a brilliant lightning flash, he saw a man sheltering in a grove of date palms opposite the doorway of the Bayt Kamil Hadi.

The image was fixed as on a photographic plate: portrait of an ordinary, middle-aged man, with a fringe of beard. Yet not ordinary; the fury of the storm was in his face.

Chafik commanded Faisal, "Stay!" and went running.

He found nobody, and, returning to his son, he shook his head and said, "Imagination. Yet I'd swear I saw —"

They went on and at last reached the house on the Street of the Scatterer of Blessings.

"Well," Chafik said to Leila, "the corpse was walking, and furthermore, it mocked me. However, Faisal has learned a lesson." He looked at his son.

The boy said, "The man was alive and there was no grave." Then he burst out, "I saw him dead. They were burying him! I did so see! I did!"

Chafik found his slippers; he picked up one of them.

"Oh, no, my man!" Leila cried. "No!"

"If it were willed," shouted Chafik, "that a delinquent boy should not receive corporal punishment, the All-Merciful would not have designed him with a bottom."

The storm and Chafik's anger passed; but whereas Baghdad forgot its ordeal in the sparkle of a perfect day, the Inspector had no such dawn to win forgiveness.

It was a silent breakfast table. The subdued boy avoided him, and Leila never looked up from her plate. He was glad when the car arrived to take him to his office.

"You would think I was the transgressor!" the Inspector said to his assistant, Sergeant Abdullah, who was at the wheel.

"Sir?"

The sergeant was a big man, an image carved in mahogany, but there was warmth in the dark eyes he fixed on his superior. Chafik said, as they drove away, "Abdullah, inform me how you discipline your three young daughters."

"They discipline me."

"You never raise an angry hand?"

"Retaliation would be triple-pronged."

The Inspector told his assistant of Faisal's story and then turned his attention to the street scene. In and out of the crowd shuttled small, ragged boys who begged pennies and skipped and laughed in the sunlight.

Chafik was reminded that Faisal had once lived on his wits as did these waifs. "Such lies these boys tell," he said sadly.

"Ah, how blessed I am with daughters!" exclaimed the sergeant. "They do not climb trees and suffer hallucinations!"

Chafik said defensively, "Imagination, not hallucination. Furthermore, from the top of a date palm, at that height —"

He stopped. "That's it!" he exclaimed. "To understand his illusion I must view the scene from Faisal's perch. Turn the car, Abdullah."

The sergeant made a turn, and they drove back down Mansoor Avenue. Another turn brought the Bayt Kamil Hadi into sight at the end of a dirt road. On the fringe of the grove was a tree overlooking the garden. Chafik took a bearing and decided his son had climbed it to look into the garden. He took off his jacket, folded it and gave it to Abdullah.

The slant of the tree helped climbing, but halfway up Chafik paused for breath; he was sticky with sweat and told himself a man past forty should not climb trees.

He went on and at last reached the feathery crown. In the foreground he saw the spot in the garden where he had stood with Faisal. He rubbed his eyes and looked again. All at once he was cold in the sun.

Where there had been nothing yesterday there was now a long narrow mound.

In haste he got down and went running toward the house. The door was ajar, and Chafik did not wait to ring. He stumbled through flower beds and bushes, followed by Abdullah, and prayed that what he had seen would prove a mirage. The prayer was not answered.

He fell to his knees and began to dig feverishly. The soil was light and sandy, and caved back in as he dug. Lower down, where moisture had not yet evaporated and the soil had more consistency, his task was easier, and a cold face was exposed.

Zaki Attala mocked him from the grave.

He pushed the sand back quickly.

A pleasant voice asked anxiously, "Zaki is there?"

"Yes," Chafik answered absently.

"I am relieved."

Awareness came, and the Inspector got up hastily; a woman stood at the graveside. She was tall and angular and old, and dressed for youth. Her hair was brightly hennaed under a black silk scarf, worn as concession to custom, although it was not drawn to veil her face in the presence of a stranger.

Chafik had never met the matriarch of the House of Hadi, but Rejina had been aptly described by Baghdad gossips. He was fascinated. Beneath her rouge were many wrinkles, but the woman was still handsome. The features were strongly boned. The large brown eyes, which had a life of their own in the decay of the face, shone softly.

The Inspector remembered that Baghdad said this woman was haunted by strange spirits. "Madame," he said, "why are you relieved that Zaki should be in this grave?" He added sharply, "I am the police."

Rejina answered, "Of course. I sent Jamil for you. And surely it is natural to be relieved that the poor young man has not left his grave? The dead should stay dead." Her voice was quiet and her eyes were calm.

Chafik sent Sergeant Abdullah to telephone and then returned to Rejina. She had picked some arum lilies. The flowers were nursed in the crook of her arm and she caressed them with her rouged cheek, like a mother a child.

"The boy was charming," she said. "You must bring him to me."

He asked, "What boy, Madame?"

She said, obviously surprised by his stupidity, "You brought him here yesterday. I saw from my window. Such a pretty boy! I would have given him honey cakes —"

A flame flickered in the mirrors of her eyes, and when it passed they were warm with tenderness.

Chafik felt compassion and looked away. "You mean my son?"

"Bring him to me," Rejina pleaded.

Her smile was sweet, and the Inspector resisted an impulse to bow over her hand. He was a policeman, so he asked, "Why does my son interest you? Did you overhear my conversation with your brothers? Did you know —"

"I do not eavesdrop," Rejina said coldly. And then she went on, "The boy came twice. The first time he climbed a tree to look into my garden. That was naughty. Suppose he —" Suddenly she let the flowers fall and cried out: "Oh, he saw! What horror! His innocent mind!"

The Inspector shuddered. "He saw what?" he demanded.

"That they were burying our cousin."

"They? Who?" He took Rejina by the shoulders.

She freed herself with dignity. "My brothers," she said; and then added with faint surprise, "Surely you knew they killed Zaki?"

He tried to reassure himself: *I deal in facts*, he told himself. *I will not let a boy and a moon-mad woman confound the evidence of my eyes. I saw Zaki alive.*

He lighted a cigarette and asked casually, "Why did they kill him?"

"Like so many others, he fell in love with me." The woman's destroyed face lighted with pleasure and childlike credulity. "He wanted to marry me."

A delusion, Chafik thought, and asked, "You refused him?"

"What else? I was flattered, but he had a wife, Naomi. A child, very simple and desperately in love with this deceiver." Rejina added with a frank laugh, "Besides, whatever my charms, I was a little old for him. Perhaps he deceived me, too," she added, with shrewdness. Suddenly the rouged face was beautiful. The woman said, "This Naomi, Zaki's wife, has greater riches than I. She has a child in her womb." And then she added briskly, "I will have her live with me — the least I can do, considering her man was killed because of me."

Chafik was lost. It was difficult to deal with a mind that one moment winged in the clouds and the next was earth-bound. He said brusquely, "I am a policeman. I want facts."

"A policeman, yes, but gracious until now!" Rejina said, reproving him. "As for facts, it was simple enough. They quarreled with Zaki about me. They forced me to my room and killed him — I heard the shot — and I broke out and found them about to bury him. Jamil took me back to my room and locked me in. I do not know which one killed Zaki, but surely it was Jamil. Ibrahim is not a violent man."

"Where is Ibrahim?"

"Poor foolish one! He has taken refuge in the bottle."

Rejina led Chafik into the house and along a corridor to a bedroom.

Ibrahim lay on a rumpled bed. He was fully dressed, and his clothes were damp and there was yellow mud on his shoes. His breathing was heavy and he could not be wakened; he smelled strongly of *arak*. Chafik opened a window and went out.

"Madame," he said to Rejina. "You said Jamil has gone to the police. To confess?"

"That one will confess to nothing! He had the temerity, this morning, to deny he had killed Zaki or buried him. He was so convincing that I — I —" She stopped, her luminous eyes wide.

Chafik was moved by pity, for he knew she was afraid, and why. "And so you were relieved when I found Zaki?" he asked gently.

"It proved that what I saw, I saw. Otherwise..." The woman left her thought unfinished.

Hastily Chafik led her to safer ground: "When was Zaki killed?"

"When I heard the shot, my clock had just chimed five."

Now it was the Inspector's turn to doubt his sanity, for nearly an hour later he had come to the Bayt Kamil Hadi with Faisal and seen Zaki alive. He shouted, "Impossible!"

"You will remember your place," Rejina said in the voice of a great lady. "I have been very patient with you. The hour was five."

She veiled herself and went away. At the top of the stairs, she stopped, and Chafik saw she had had another mercurial change of mood.

"Do not forget to bring the pretty boy," she said.

The Inspector heard with relief the sirens of police cars in the distance.

They dug up the body, and, later, Sergeant Abdullah came and said in his business voice, "Sir, the corpse is identified as Zaki Attala. He has a bullet between the eyes. The gun was of small caliber and is missing. It rained when he was buried, his clothes are wet, and it ceased to rain at midnight. Therefore, he was buried —"

"Yesterday," Chafik said. "Always I am haunted by yesterday. Until now, murders have been three-dimensional. This one appears to have been activated on a fourth plane." He shrugged. "Did they bring Jamil Hadi?"

"Yes, sir. He was at headquarters."

They brought Jamil to the salon which Chafik had requisitioned for the inquiry. The man looked as though he had slept in his clothes.

"Tell me what happened after I left last night," Chafik said.

Jamil used his sleeve to wipe his forehead. "After you left, Zaki said he had to go home."

"What was the time?"

"Nearly seven."

"And why did Zaki risk the storm?"

Jamil hesitated. "He was concerned about his wife."

"Concerned? And yet he was prepared to divorce her?" The Inspector's smile was unpleasant. "Continue please, Mr. Hadi."

Jamil fingered his beard. "The story is delicate. Ibrahim was drunk, lying here in the salon, and my sister was in her room. Storms disturb her. I had gone to the kitchen and I heard a shot. I found Zaki in the cloister near the house door. He was dead. The door was open and outside I saw —"

"A man," Chafik said, "with the fury of the storm in his face."

Jamil turned up the palms of his hands. "All things are known to you," he said.

"That should be said only of God." The Inspector was, nevertheless, glad to have confirmation he had actually seen a man.

"Who was he?"

"Aziz Chelebi of Basra, Zaki's father-in-law. He is a small merchant. Zaki married beneath himself."

"Scarcely an excuse to divorce a pregnant wife," Chafik said. "A father, however humble, would have justification for anger."

"A murderous anger? Zaki told me Aziz threatened him —"

"A threat is not a deed. Let us return to the facts. What did the man do when you saw him?"

"He cried out — I think it was, 'No, no!' — and he ran."

"And?"

"I followed and lost him. Then I went to find a telephone and report to you, but our line was down. Then I was worried about my sister perhaps finding the body, so I came back." Jamil's round eyes reflected horror. "There was no body," he whispered.

Chafik was incredulous. "Eh? Zaki buried himself?"

"I told you Ibrahim was very drunk. He must have found Zaki and somehow acted on your son's fantastic story. I found my brother in the garden — and a grave exactly where —"

Chafik remembered the mud on Ibrahim's shoes and clothes. "I suppose your brother will remember nothing."

"That is always so the next day." Jamil hesitated and then said, "I regret my delay in coming to you after the storm. I — I was afraid — of the situation, of the boy's tale, of you."

The little man recalled yesterday's indignity and grew taller. He said, "Your story appears to hold together, but your sister says you killed Zaki."

Jamil said, "Now it has happened, and a brother must talk. Surely, Inspector, you observed my sister has a strange mind?"

"She is strange, certainly," Chafik said, "but I have never met a woman so serene."

And then he remembered something long forgotten. The will, which had given Rejina everything, had been unsuccessfully contested on grounds of her mental incapacity. The case had happened many years ago, and the Inspector looked curiously at the man who had contested the will. Jamil was embarrassed.

"Can you explain," the Inspector asked plaintively, "how is it that she corroborates the fantasy of my son?"

Jamil Hadi moved in his chair. He answered, "I cannot. You met Zaki alive. You know —"

"Yes," Chafik said. "I am your witness..."

The Inspector continued his investigation. Near the house door, he detected a stain where Jamil claimed Zaki Attala had died.

The he walked down the cloister to the river wall and there he found a chip in the masonry. Something, he decided, had struck with the authority of a bullet and made its mark very recently. But where he stood was at least twenty yards from the house door and stained pavement. He looked up and saw that Rejina's rooms were above.

Chafik said to Sergeant Abdullah, "Possibly of no importance, but note it. And now express your opinion on the case. I do confess to bewilderment."

"Sir?"

The Inspector looked at his assistant. Then he said, "Listen to me, Abdullah. Here is the situation. On the one hand, we have the evidence of an afflicted woman and an imaginative boy. They saw a man being buried just after five o'clock. On the other, we have Jamil's evidence. Although his evidence is not confirmed, let us admit Zaki was alive when I met him — and at that time he should have been dead."

The pious sergeant exclaimed, "God and by God!"

The little man sighed, "But why should the stories coincide? Did Faisal's fantasy wing its way into the clouded mind of Rejina? Telepathy? Is such a thing possible?"

The Inspector was interrupted by an officer who said, "Sir, there is a band of boys at the door. One says he is your son."

Faisal came in, dragging a reluctant boy. Other urchins, uniformed alike in ragged gowns and wisps of turban, waited outside the door.

Faisal said, "Here is Malek and he has something to tell you about the murder done here and —"

"Wait!" Chafik said hastily. "Tell me first how you knew a murder had been committed here."

"All Baghdad knows," Faisal replied.

"I am a detective in a fish bowl!" exclaimed the Inspector. The horde of ragged boys still hovered cautiously in the background.

"Bazaar waifs, sir," Sergeant Abdullah said in the Inspector's ear. "Scavengers, thieves."

Chafik was stung into defense. "My son was once one of them," he whispered fiercely. "These are his men. The wild boys of Baghdad recognize Faisal as paramount and call him 'sheik.'" He realized he was talking too much. "Well?" he demanded. "What has Malek got to tell me?"

"Malek will not talk to policemen," Faisal said. "What he has to tell is that last night he took shelter from the storm outside there among the date palms." He pointed through the doorway. "He heard a shot and then the gun came, thrown by somebody, and he looked and saw a woman and —"

"A man, not a woman," Chafik said absently. "But a gun? Thrown!"

"This one," said his son.

He reached into his blouse and gave his father a pistol of old pattern. The butt was chased with silver, and there was engraving on the guard and along the barrel. The weapon had been fired.

"The fingerprints have got all rubbed off," Faisal said. "And, my father, Malek was honest to bring it to me because he could have got perhaps two dinars for a gun and he should be rewarded."

"Truly you are Sheik of the Waifs!" Chafik said dryly.

"Yes, my father. And so when Malek told me his story, and I heard you found the body here — just where I said it was —"

The Inspector said hastily, "At what time did the incidents you have described happen to the witness?"

Faisal shook his head. "Malek does not know time. But his belly said it needed filling, and it is always empty at the seventh hour and —"

"Ah, hearsay!" exclaimed Chafik.

"My father, I have come to help you — I and my men. If there is somebody you wish to find, he cannot hide from them; they know all Baghdad. You said there was a man —"

"Aziz Chelebi, the father-in-law of Zaki," Chafik said absently.

Immediately Faisal said, "My men will find you Aziz."

"Enough!" commanded the Inspector. "What manner of thing is this? I have a police force, and you offer me your ragged Baker Street runners! Go home and stay home!" He slapped the seat of the boy's shorts.

Faisal went away crying.

Chafik became aware that somebody stood behind him, and turned quickly. It was Jamil Hadi.

"That is not a pleasant boy," Jamil said, his eyes fixed on Faisal's departing back.

Chafik said warningly, "You speak of my son!"

And then he remembered the gun Faisal had given him. "Can you identify this?" he asked.

Jamil stared at it. He turned it over and over. Finally he said, "No, I cannot identify it." He gave the gun back and averted his face.

"Did it kill Zaki?" Jamil asked after a long pause.

"That is for ballistics to prove — but a small-caliber gun was used —"

The Inspector stopped.

The lady of the Bayt Kamil Hadi came into the room, and her face reddened with anger as she cried, "Beast! You struck the boy! You —"

He tried to placate her and said, "Madame, my son is inquisitive. If the murderer thought Faisal knew —"

"But you struck him! A child!"

"I disciplined him," Chafik protested, as she turned from him.

"Oh, no, no!" she cried. "Let the dead stay dead!"

He watched her run through the splashes of sunlight and shadow. He was shocked that one so habitually calm should sob so wildly. Then he remembered the gun in his hand.

Poor woman! he reproached himself. *How clumsy of me, I should have concealed it! Even if Zaki is only her lover in her dreams...*

He called after her, "Lady, I —"

But she had gone into the house.

Only Jamil remained. "You see how it is with her," he said.

Chafik went to call on Zaki Attala's widow, Naomi, the daughter of Aziz Chelebi. He found her in two cluttered rooms in the Nassah Quarter. She was heavy with Zaki's child.

The woman was veiled, for she was old-fashioned, although she was young.

He said, "The compassion of God embraces you."

Naomi said, "My man is dead. I loved him."

Chafik wondered how a good woman could love one like Zaki, who would have deserted her, but it often happened that a woman's emotions were wasted on an engaging rascal.

The Inspector had not come to deliver a homily. "Where is your father?"

Naomi's hands, worn by service for her man, clasped tightly. "I do not know where my father is."

"Do not hide things from me. He came from Basra yesterday, at your insistence. He went to many cafés looking for Zaki; he made many threats."

Chafik added, "And in the end he traced Zaki to the House of Hadi and went there. I saw him."

The woman said in a surprisingly firm voice, "I know. I followed him. I was afraid for Zaki. My father's temper —"

Chafik got up and paced the room and noted the many absurd gadgets Zaki had bought to please his wife. And to ease his conscience, thought the Inspector.

He turned and asked, "What made you send for your father if you feared his violence towards your husband?"

"I — I was overwrought. I did not think. When one is with child —"

"All the worlds knows," Chafik said. "When you heard that Zaki might divorce you to marry his cousin, what did you —"

"I hated him! I hated them both!"

"Do not hate Rejina," Chafik begged. "She refused him. But what of her brothers?" he asked.

"Jamil was friendly; he came here often. Jamil and my husband talked a great deal together. I do not know what they talked about, because they whispered as people do when they plot something." Naomi added, "Zaki had many ideas about becoming rich."

Somebody knocked, and the Inspector went to the door and found an old man who carried a giant basket of fruits. In an ancient voice, the messenger said, "Bless the sender! A gift from the Lady Rejina to the Lady Naomi!" Chafik tipped him and sent him away.

The woman and the police inspector stared at the basket.

Then Naomi said, "That woman sent it? *That* woman?"

Chafik said, "The human mind cannot probe the depths of Rejina's heart." He remembered that the matriarch of the House of Hadi had spoken of taking Naomi into her home.

"People say she is mad."

"People are unkind. She is very gracious but eccentric."

Zaki's wife hesitated and then took an apple from the basket. The Inspector went to find a plate and a knife.

He found a knife in a rack above the kitchen sink. It was a novel rack; instead of slots, a bar magnet held the implements, and Chafik thought: Another of Zaki's gadgets … He returned to the widow.

Carefully he peeled the apple and offered it, then he became the policeman again. "Do you recognize this?" He brought out the gun that Malek, his son's man, had injected into the case.

Naomi let her head covering fall, and for the first time he saw her. Briefly she was beautiful, and then she was hysterical.

"No, no, no!" she screamed. And she seized the basket of fruits and threw it with shocking violence on the floor. "I will take nothing! Nothing from that woman! She enticed my man. She —"

The Inspector backed to the door, hands raised defensively.

"For God's sake!" he said to the policewoman who was in attendance. "Calm her! She is with child!"

Later, in his office, Inspector Chafik read the laboratory reports. Ballistics proved that the bullet taken out of Zaki matched the gun; both the gun and the ammunition were old-fashioned. Furthermore, the gun belonged to an era when registration was not required.

Then there were the surgeon's findings; the suggested time of Zaki's death covered a period of two hours either side of five o'clock.

"A crystal-gazer would have been as accurate," Chafik announced.

He looked at other reports. The police still had not found Aziz Chelebi, the father of Naomi. He wondered how a man like Aziz, who had no criminal cunning, could elude the dragnet.

And then the small voice of Faisal boasted in his ear, "My men will find you, Aziz." He reached for the telephone and called his wife.

"With reference to my just chastisement of our son —"

"Faisal has refused dinner," were Leila's first words to him this difficult day. "He tells me you railed against him when he sought to help you."

"He also boasted!" Chafik cried into the telephone. "In front of my men, he boasted that his wretched urchins —"

"Wretched urchins?" echoed Leila. "Have you forgotten he was one?"

Chafik shouted, "They taught him how to lie! They —" He jiggled the switch. "Leila! Listen carefully. I insist you keep Faisal at home. He must see no more of those boys; he must keep his nose out of this case — Leila? You are there?"

She answered, "I am here, but my husband is not there. Not the man I know. But we obey your edict." She hung up, too late to cut off a sob.

The Inspector wanted to rush home, but pride held him back and he became angry. He swept the papers from his desk, set his hat on his head at a reckless angle and went out, saying, "Well, there's only one way to forget!"

Inspector Chafik marched an assertive track to his favorite café and went to a table on the dais at the back of the room. He said to the waiter, "A honey cake!" and as the man turned away, added recklessly, "Make that two!"

A day passed and nothing was changed. There was still no trace of Aziz Chelebi, and Chafik again sat at the table in the café. It was late, and he was satiated with honey cakes, but reluctant to go home. He had slept the night on the sofa because he felt unwelcome in the connubial bed.

Chafik hid behind a copy of *Al-Hawedith* and only put the newspaper down when his assistant arrived.

One look at Abdullah's face, and Chafik paid his bill and got up.

"We have found the suspect, Aziz Chelebi." Abdullah said.

"You speak of him as if he were an inanimate object."

"Yes, sir. He is. Stabbed, sir."

The father of Naomi lay in an alleyway not far from his daughter's house. There were many knife wounds in his back, and he had not been dead long. The patrolman who had found the body had seen nobody suspicious and had nothing to add to the meager facts.

Abdullah said, "A curious item, sir. He has not been robbed. May I venture to suggest he was killed in anger?"

"The suggestion deserves consideration, but I think it was panic, not anger," said Inspector Chafik.

He turned the corpse over and looked at the face, and it was the one he had seen in the storm. Now it had no expression.

Chafik said, "Poor father!" Then he added, "Poor daughter, twice bereaved in three days!"

While he talked, he went through Aziz's pockets. Suddenly he exclaimed, then held up for Abdullah's inspection a few rounds of revolver ammunition.

"Caliber .32. You'd need an old-fashioned gun to fire it. It's dated ammunition. And it would fit the gun that killed Zaki. But why was Aziz killed?"

Chafik came home to the Street of the Scatterer of Blessings as the stars were going out. He walked wearily up the garden path, wondering why there were lights on in the house.

Leila was in the hallway. She was wearing a wrap over her nightdress, and her dark hair was unbraided. He went to her eagerly, then noticed her pallor, then saw with alarm she was trying to conceal a pistol.

"What happened?" he asked sharply.

"Faisal saw something. He cried out. He shouted that somebody was at the window, and I ran to look. I saw —"

"You saw his nightmare?"

"I saw a shadow." Leila shivered and drew her wrap around her. "I took your spare pistol," she said. "I went out —"

He beat his hands. "Courageous but foolish!"

"Faisal's nightmare dropped this," Leila said. She showed him a knife which she had wrapped in newspaper. "I thought to preserve fingerprints," she explained.

He was too overcome to commend her police methods, and his hands shook as he took the knife. It had a good steel blade set in the wooden haft; there were thousands of knives like it in the kitchens of Baghdad. Somebody had used electrician's tape to make a better grip, and the Inspector's hope of fingerprints faded. He slanted the blade to the light and saw particles embedded in the imprint of the manufacturer's name. His face said what he thought.

"Blood?" Leila asked, losing control.

He nodded. "I will send it to the laboratory for analysis," he said tiredly.

Then he heard his son's voice calling, and he ran to the boy's room.

Faisal was sitting up in bed, and his enormous eyes seemed to fill his face. He had learned the meaning of fear this night. He asked his mother, who had followed Chafik, "You told him?"

"I told him," Leila said.

They talked as if Chafik were not there, and the little man wondered if ever again he would have their confidence. Finally he went and sat timidly on the edge of the bed. "Now you've got a real adventure to tell your friends," Chafik said with false cheerfulness.

"But, my father, it was real the other time."

The Inspector listened with half an ear. He remembered the Koran, for the prayer call now sounded from all the mosques in Baghdad, and he sought in it, as always, guidance for the day. He found it in the seventeenth sura, the thirty-eighth verse: *And follow not that which thou hast no knowledge; because the hearing and sight and the heart, each shall be enquired of.*

He clapped his hands and cried to his son, "This is truly a revelation! I have no knowledge, so must inquire! Exactly what did you hear and see when you climbed the tree to look into the garden?"

Faisal answered, "I heard nothing after the lady screamed."

"You didn't hear the spade digging?"

"The trees sighed, and the river throwed itself about, and I could not hear the spade because Ibrahim had not started to dig. It was like the cinema when the sound goes off. You know what I mean?" he finished, anxiously.

Chafik grasped the small shoulders, and, as he looked into his son's puzzled eyes, his own began to glow. "Buskin and grease paint make a piquant sauce, but — yes! I know what you mean!"

The boy had put his finger on it, he decided. All that had happened at the Bayt Kamil Hadi had been a three-act play. The second act, staged when he called with Faisal, had been impromptu, but the first had been carefully rehearsed and would have gone off smoothly if Faisal had not unexpectedly joined the audience.

"A play intended for an audience of one," Chafik told his son.

Faisal was bewildered. "But, my father —"

"Where is your intelligence?" shouted the little man, and he harangued the boy as he would have an assistant: "Consider that chip in the masonry under Rejina's window. That was obviously made by a bullet — the bullet she heard fired at five o'clock. But it did not kill Zaki."

"No, my father," agreed Faisal, diplomatically.

"Zaki was killed in the third act. I don't know how, for certain, although the evidence points to Aziz. But was there a fourth act? Could Aziz have been innocent, and was he killed because he saw something he shouldn't?"

"Like I did?" the boy asked.

Chafik remembered he was talking to a child, and the bewilderment in his son's eyes matched his own. "Well, I talk to you like a man, and you like that, don't you?" he said gruffly to cover his embarrassment.

"Yes, my father." Faisal snuggled down, and the bright eyes warned Chafik he had said too much. "So what I saw I should not have seen," the boy knew no more than he had told, and panic was too often the reason for murder.

Chafik commanded himself to be calm. He asked the question: *If my theory is correct, how did this individual trace Aziz?* He thought a moment and then had the answer, and went to sit on the bed again.

"My son, with reference to the edict I issued against seeing your men, it is rescinded. I mean you may see them," he clarified hastily. "And, Faisal, when a sheik has been in exile he may find, on return, that his wise laws have been disobeyed. This is particularly so when a sheik has had a boastful moment —"

"My father, then you think —" Faisal began.

Chafik nodded and went and told his wife to go to the boy; then he stealthily telephoned Sergeant Abdullah and routed the big man out of bed. The sergeant expressed neither annoyance nor drowsiness.

Chafik said, "Abdullah, my friend. Clothe yourself and come and watch my son. Duty has compelled me to put an idea in his head, and I fear his rashness. But with your discreet protection —" All at once he broke down. "I put Faisal in your care," he announced tearfully.

It was a very hot day, and the Inspector dressed in a crisp white linen suit. He was no longer tired, his brain had rarely been so active, and as he rode toward his office, he concentrated on the obscurity of the knife dropped by the intruder. The laboratory had already checked it and reported it could have made the wounds in Aziz's body, and, as Chafik had suspected, there was human blood congealed on the blade.

"And they tell me the knife's magnetized," he grumbled. "Now why should that fact needle me?"

The car stopped for traffic opposite Hasso's Department Store, and the Inspector noticed a display of hardware in the window. It gave him the key to memory, and he startled his driver by striking his hands together. He cursed his profession and the malignancy of his thoughts, and finally told the driver to take him to the house of Zaki Attala's wife.

The widow was sitting at the window. Despite the heat, she was wearing a heavy robe. The eyes that peered at the Inspector through the head folds were without luster; he hands lay motionless in her lap.

He glanced at the policewoman, whose nod informed him her charge was out of shock. "Again," Chafik told Naomi in a heavy voice, "you are with God."

"Is there a God?"

The blasphemy distressed him, and so did her voice; it was dead, like her eyes. He made a hasty excuse and went to the kitchen to draw a glass of water.

The malignant thought that had brought him here made him examine the knife rack on the wall. There was a space where a knife was missing. He detached another and touched it to an iron pot, and, as he had feared, there was weak, but definite magnetism in the blade, created by the novelty rack.

"There are few like it in Baghdad," Chafik said. "May I be forgiven for what I think, but —"

He went back to Naomi and said abruptly, "Have you considered the possibility that your father, in his anger, might —"

Naomi cried, "That lie is a dagger in your heart!"

"By custom," continued Chafik, "a father arranges a daughter's marriage. If the marriage is a mistake, and he is a fond father, he —"

"It was not his will I married Zaki. I asked for Zaki! My father was too proud to refuse, but he warned me; he said Zaki was mixed in strange affairs with Jamil —"

"So you knew more of that than you told me when I questioned you," he said sternly. "Open your mouth, woman! Confess!" He detested himself for his police methods.

She protested, "But I am not sure what they talked about. I think it was about Rejina. Jamil said she was insane. If it could be proved —"

"He could take the estate!" Chafik interrupted.

And he went on, forgetful of his audience. "Now we have the theme of the play. They put on an act, those precious brothers and your man. They staged a quarrel and pretended to kill Zaki — that was the shot Rejina heard — and then they pretended to bury him. If Faisal had not seen it, all would have gone according to plan. Rejina would have told her tale, and then Zaki would have been produced alive. What better proof of her insanity, and her unfitness to handle her father's estate?"

He pulled himself together and asked Naomi, "If you knew all this, why did you believe Zaki was going to divorce you?"

"I was in despair. I feared he would desert me. And I hated Rejina. I did not know her, or her kindness. I had not met her. When she came here yesterday with her brothers, it was as if my mother lived again."

"What?" Chafik shouted. "Rejina came here? And Jamil and Ibrahim? Why was I not informed?"

Naomi said, "Yes, they came. Rejina is strange, but God gave her her heart." She added painfully, "I was blasphemous just now. I denied God — but surely God made Rejina ask me to live with her."

Inspector Chafik thought of the knife and how another person could have taken it from the magnetic rack. He took the young woman's hands and bowed over them. "Oh, God the Merciful!" he cried. "Forgive a policeman his suspicions! And forgive me, too, Naomi, daughter of Aziz!"

The Inspector ran from the house.

The windows of his office were screened with camel's-thorn kept green by a sprinkler, and the filtered air was fresh, but the Inspector came in from the furnace of Baghdad, and the familiar haven brought no comfort.

He was worried about his son. He told himself that his fear was neurotic, that Abdullah was protecting the boy. But even the fortress of Abdullah could be breached. So he went on worrying and waiting.

It was long after the call to the midday prayer when the door opened and Abdullah came in with Faisal. The sergeant said, "Sir, I bring you a disturber of the peace. It was a very good fight while it lasted." The big man smiled.

Faisal had a swelling under one eye and was licking his knuckles.

"What was it all about?"

"It was about what you told me last night, my father. One of my men had cheated. You know, I make them put the money they earn in an old hat at the end of the day, and they share out —"

Chafik interrupted, "How much did this boy hold out?"

"It was five dinars. So much money is —"

"How did he earn five dinars?"

Faisal's unbruised eye widened. "Now this is strange. It concerns Aziz Chelebi —"

Chafik said, "Somebody gave him five dinars to find out where Aziz was hiding."

The light went out in Faisal's heart-shaped face. "You know everything before I begin!" he complained. Then he rushed on, "It was a man; he smelled of *arak* —"

"*Arak!*" exclaimed the Inspector.

He looked at Sergeant Abdullah, who said, "The drunken brother. I had hoped it would be the other one, sir."

Chafik went to the boy. "Go home and put on your best clothes," he said. "We are going to call on a lady. There will be nice things to eat."

"Ice cream, my father?" Faisal asked eagerly.

"And honey cakes," the father said hopefully.

The Inspector had sent Rejina a note and received a courteous invitation. *And now I come as a snake into her garden*, he thought.

Faisal said, "I think I see police among the palms."

Chafik put a finger to his lips and then rang the bell.

Rejina wore a soft blue dress and a chiffon stole, and on her hennaed hair was a chaplet of artificial flowers.

She exclaimed, "Oh, the pretty boy!" and held Faisal with an ardor that frightened him.

Rejina turned to Ibrahim, who was acting as butler, and said, "Brother, go bring the good things. Our young guest has an eager stomach." When he had gone, she confided, "He is a good man in many ways — not like Jamil."

"Where is Jamil?" Chafik asked casually.

"He has been resting in his room all day. He was out all night."

The Inspector held back an exclamation. The woman was engrossed in Faisal, and Chafik slipped out to the kitchen to interrogate Ibrahim.

Chafik said softly, "Did you take the knife from Naomi's house?"

"A knife? What use would I have for a knife?" asked Ibrahim.

"Did you bribe a boy to look for Aziz Chelebi?"

"I do not remember. When the wine flows, I forget, and —"

"Aziz was killed last night," Chafik said brutally. "He was followed from his hiding place. He was on his way to his daughter's house, I think."

The alcoholic shuddered. "There has been too much killing."

"Who killed Zaki?"

Ibrahim drew himself up. "Do not inquire into that!" He said fiercely. "If you do, there might be — another —" He stopped and glanced toward the salon, whence came the treble of Faisal's voice and Rejina's laughter. "I am happy for her," the man said emotionally. He picked up a laden tray, and they went out.

Faisal was sitting enthroned, and on his dark head was Rejina's chaplet of flowers. The boy exclaimed, "Father! The nice lady says it is true there are sprites in the river and they tease the fish and —"

The Eden snake was a saint compared with me, Chafik thought. He found a chiding voice and said, "Too many fairy stories! The next thing, you'll be telling the lady about what you imagined you saw on the day of the storm."

Faisal jiggled on the sofa and shouted, "I did so see it! There was Ibrahim, and there was the other one who had the beard, and there was a dead man and —"

Rejina turned to the boy's father and said fiercely, "Enough!"

"Lady," the Inspector said — and he did not like himself — "what happened after your brothers killed Zaki, as you told me they did?"

"They buried him, and he got up and walked again."

Chafik looked across the room. Ibrahim stood rooted in the doorway; he could not speak, and he could not move to go to his sister.

Rejina put a honey cake on Faisal's plate. When she was sure the boy's attention was distracted, she went on calmly, "Yes, Zaki walked again. Probably he came to look for me, since he loved me. Poor restless spirit! The dead should stay dead."

"Sister!" Speech burst at last from Ibrahim.

"It was indeed a visitation," she said, not heeding him. "I saw Zaki's poor spirit wandering near the house door. I even heard Zaki poor, dead voice!"

Faisal looked up with interest, and she hastily piled food on his plate.

"So I took my father's old pistol," Rejina told Chafik, "and returned to the house door. It took only a moment to give him rest. That was proper, don't you think?"

"Surely, Lady," Chafik said, and tasted dust.

"And then I threw the gun away. I do not like guns." A gentle smile came. "I know Zaki is at peace, because his poor ghost has not come to haunt me again."

The clouds passed. She turned to Faisal and said indulgently, "Shall I tell you another fairy story, pretty boy?"

Watching her, Chafik knew she had already forgotten, and he envied her; he could not forget, ever.

It unrolled like a mat, and he saw the whole design; Jamil's plan to prove his sister's insanity, the failure of the plan because of the unexpected audience, Faisal. None of the three plotters had guessed how fragile Rejina's mind was, and probably Jamil did not care. The thread of her reason had snapped, and she had taken the gun and gone to Zaki, as a mother goes with soothing medicine for a sick child.

Aziz, waiting outside, had seen his son-in-law fall in the open doorway, and because of his threats to kill Zaki he had run in panic.

Jamil, seeing him run, at first thought him guilty. Then, when the familiar gun was found, he had guessed the truth and shared the horror with his befuddled accomplice, the weak Ibrahim.

Here was proof of Rejina's insanity, and ironically, it could not be used; the evidence would inevitably bring the conspiracy to light, and involve the brothers as accomplices. Now, they were certain Aziz had witnessed the killing and would talk when the police found him.

"So he became a menace to be removed," Chafik announced. "Panic! And the one who panicked was —"

Instinctively, he swung around. He saw Ibrahim, who still stood helpless in the doorway. He saw him thrust violently aside. He saw Jamil, the beard and hair wild, gun in hand.

"That hell-brat!" the man shouted.

Chafik said carefully, "*I* am your nemesis, not Faisal."

He braced his feet. The distance was too great, and he had to wait until Jamil came nearer.

Jamil said, "You made her talk! You used the boy and made her talk! Always the boy! If he hadn't come nosing around, if one of his guttersnipes hadn't found the gun, if —"

"You and I," Chafik said, "have the real quarrel. I traced the knife that will hang you."

The man's round eyes switched to Chafik, but the gun was still on Faisal. *Give me time*, Chafik prayed.

"And I do not admire your cunning," he went on. "You hoped when you took the knife from Naomi's house that she would appear guilty of patricide."

He willed Jamil to come nearer, and said, "You put cartridges in Aziz's pocket to make it look as if he had killed Zaki with that gun. And you used your brother as go-between with the bazaar boys, so that if one plan failed, the other might succeed. You knew Ibrahim would be too drunk to know if he'd killed or not!"

Jamil forgot Faisal and turned the gun on the little man who goaded him. Chafik hurled himself forward as the wildly fired shot resounded in the room.

Falling short, he scrambled to hands and knees. He saw Jamil level the gun again. He saw Ibrahim throw himself at his brother, and heard him shout, "No more killing! No more —"

There was a second shot and Ibrahim fell away.

The impact of Chafik's body carried Jamil to the floor. He put his knee into him and used his forearms like clubs. He thought of Aziz Chelebi, of the widowed Naomi, of Rejina's fragile mind; he struck Jamil again and again for each of them. He was still striking when strong hands dragged him from the helpless man.

"Leave him for the hangman, sir!" said a familiar voice.

The fog lifted, and Chafik recognized Abdullah; the police had rushed in with the first shot.

He looked first for Faisal. The boy was sitting on the sofa, staring. His mouth and his hands were sticky with honey cake. Chafik said to one of his men, "Take him out," and went quickly to where Ibrahim lay, his head pillowed on his sister's lap.

Rejina said, "Poor brother!" She rocked him like a child.

Ibrahim whispered, "Sister, little sister whom I wronged! I beg you — forget — never remember that night —"

"What night?" Rejina asked in surprise, bending to hear the answer.

But he did not answer. He had gone into the shadows.

Inspector Chafik sat in his office. He was alone with his son. Presently he looked up from the report he was writing.

"Faisal, you are a man, are you not?"

"Yes, my father, I am nine years —"

"Then you will understand it is sometimes merciful to make a little twist in the truth. It would, for example, be nice to forget something a lady said, particularly since that lady has herself forgotten."

"Yes, my father," Faisal said blankly.

Chafik took his pen and wrote: *With reference to the death of Zaki Attala, I submit the evidence is clear that he was killed in a quarrel with Jamil Hadi. I respectfully suggest that as Jamil Hadi already stands accused of the murder of Aziz Chelebi, and the death of Ibrahim Hadi, a full investigation of the case is unnecessary. However, I append the names of two witnesses who observed Zaki Attala's burial, by the two Hadi brothers, at, or about, the evening hour of five on the day in question...*

The Inspector hesitated and then wrote firmly: *Rejina of the House of Hadi, and Faisal, my son.* He signed the report, looked at the solemn boy, and winked. "So what you saw that day you really saw," he announced.

"Yes, my father. Truly I saw it."

"Ah, you are truly a man, Faisal!"

Inspector Chafik took his son by the hand, and they went out together into a carnival Baghdad, lighted by the lanterns of the stars.

Death Had a Birthday

Chafik J. Chafik, a senior officer of the Criminal Investigation Division of the Baghdad police, a neat little man, sat at breakfast and gently chided his adopted son, Faisal, saying, "When the mouth is stuffed with words it is improper to put food therein."

The boy submissively put down his spoon and looked up with soft brown, hopeful eyes. The Inspector, whose own eyes were drab and cynical, was touched by his ten-year-old son's innocence, and smiled warmly. Yet the glance that passed between foster father and son was tempered with caution; Faisal knew that a sleek cat, purring, must not be stroked the wrong way, and Inspector Chafik was aware that simplicity often camouflages a trip wire.

He had found Faisal in the great bazaars of Baghdad, a ragged waif, one of the pack that hunted there. Chafik was childless and the boy had appealed to him, so he had taken him into his home, an impulse that neither he nor his wife Leila had ever regretted.

The Inspector bowed toward the chair where his wife normally sat. Leila was away on a visit and he missed her. *Wives become a habit after nineteen years*, the little man told himself. Then he added: *Such happy years!* Tenderness made him drop his guard and he said to Faisal, "Speak, my son. Surely words were put into your mouth to please me."

The boy immediately began, "I want —"

"Eh?" Chafik said, becoming alert.

"It is because of tomorrow, my father, and I cannot tell you what it is, but I only have a fifty *fil* piece and it costs a dinar and you can take it out of my allowance and so you will not be pockets down and please, therefore, give me the money and —"

The Inspector covered his ears. "Beware of the rhapsody of words!" he said in a somber voice.

"But a dinar is only a piece of paper and anybody can make one and —"

Faisal was silenced by Chafik's expression; the swarthy face had become gaunter, the shadows under the high cheekbones darkened, and lines appeared at the sides of the thin nose. Slowly, deliberately, the Inspector reached to the inside pocket of his white linen jacket and took out a wallet.

The currency of his country was based on the English pound, and the well-engraved bill he put on the table was of the same value and the same olive-green color. He tapped it with a polished fingernail and announced, "Here is money —"

"Give me, my father! Give me —"

Inspector Chafik restrained Faisal's reaching hand. "Learn," he said sternly, "to respect this token; call it not paper, for the pure silver of man's toil is in it. And speak not of counterfeit, or you will live hereafter in the shadow of prison bars!"

As he returned the money to his wallet, a car's horn sounded at the street door. "Abdullah has come," he said, and went to get his shoes from under the hall table. A Moslem, he respected the sanctity of his home and walked stocking-footed on Leila's waxed floors, as in a mosque.

Faisal followed him, crying, "Father, my father! A dinar! Just one! For tomorrow — tomorrow —"

"Tomorrow," Chafik said, "is another day." He embraced the boy and went out to the car. A towering police sergeant greeted him with a salute, a dour smile, and a murmured blessing. The Inspector affectionately patted the big man's arm and, the sun being strong, stood in his shadow as he lighted a cigarette. Faisal's appeal puzzled him and he asked, "What urgency has tomorrow?" and was immediately embarrassed because he had not intended to broadcast the thought. "What *day* is tomorrow?" Chafik demanded to cover the slip.

Abdullah answered, "The fifth, sir."

"It has significance?"

"Days, being granted by God, all have significance."

The Inspector accepted the rebuke and got into the waiting car. The sky was a blue arc, but the groves of date palms along the way were still dark with morning shadow. Pumps sounded up and down the river, water glittered in irrigation ditches, and perpetually courting doves cooed under the eaves of the houses.

"And from this," Chafik complained, "you take me without doubt to some disgusting corpse."

His assistant replied soothingly, "It was not a very violent night, sir, but a man named Khalib —"

"Is he the petty criminal?"

"Yes, sir, the same one. He was beaten to death in an alleyway of the old town. No witnesses. An unimportant crime, sir; such a —"

"Nevertheless, his soul cries out for vengeance and we must heed. Has anything else of note happened?"

Abdullah eased the car into the traffic of the great bridge that spanned the Tigris. "Sir," he said, his mahogany face showing astonishment, "there were two more denouncements this morning — detailed and lawyerproof. We only have to make the arrests."

The Inspector raised his eyebrows. At intervals, for some months now, his office had received anonymous reports on the Baghdad underworld. The identity of the informer could not be traced; no Judas reward was asked; no shabby spy ingratiated himself.

"Surely this accuser will share the fate of the unlamented Khalib!" exclaimed Chafik. Bewildered, he shook his head. "Is that all then, Abdullah?"

"A report from the Ankara police, sir. They have taken a counterfeiter and found plates for our currency. Series 'Y,' commencing with the number thirty-eight, sir, and one-dinar denomination only."

The Inspector forgot Khalib and the mystery of the benevolent informer; he was back at the breakfast table lecturing Faisal, seeing the pleading eyes, the practiced begging gesture of the curved palm. "This day is under the influence of a mercenary planet," he said gloomily ...

They went to the Suq-al-Jedid police station to see the remains of Khalib. The man had been viciously clubbed by a gang, and then he had been stripped and his clothes abandoned and his possessions scattered. Sergeant Abdullah said, "They either searched for something or put him to the question."

"If they questioned him they didn't get an answer," Chafik said and showed his assistant the medical report. "An abnormally thin skull. The first blow or two caused a hemorrhage. Dead before they ceased beating him. Such a waste of energy! What were Khalib's prior movements?"

"I understand, sir, that he toured the cafés, begging for money —"

"I am sympathetic," said Chafik, remembering pressing bills.

"Yes, sir. But I am informed Khalib was desperate. Eventually he went to the Café of the Abundant Fruits —"

"Iskander's place?" The Inspector's drab eyes were as barren as the desert. "That den of iniquity!" he exclaimed.

"Khalib then improved the company he kept, sir; his last witnessed contact was with Madam Aliya —"

"Eh? *Binti Ma'mum?* The Lady of Good Deeds?"

She who was called the Lady of Good Deeds was a strange and much-loved character; she moved among the poor of Baghdad, begged for them, and gave all to them. The old woman was a member of a noble family, and Chafik knew what she had sacrificed for her charity. He salaamed, curving the fingers of his right hand to his forehead. "Good old woman," he said. "Do not let us name her in the same breath as Khalib or Iskander!"

"Khalib raised his voice to the lady —" Abdullah continued.

"Then he deserved to die," the Inspector said and went to look at the dead man's possessions, which were arranged on a table. He picked up a pen, then a watch, shrugged, and announced, "Smuggled goods. That was trifles. I am puzzled that anybody should bother to kill him."

He tossed aside the dead man's identity papers, paused to read a letter, and said, "So the animal had a wife in Basra!" Then he became absorbed in a document that had been typed on an old, but curiously familiar, Arabic keyboard. Chafik startled Sergeant Abdullah by exclaiming, "Merciful One! Another denouncement!"

"Sir?"

"And so unique! It is an imprisonment warrant for the man who carried it! What are our criminals coming to when they go around Baghdad with their dossiers in their pockets?"

Abdullah took the document. It was typed on cheap paper, so spongy that the faded ribbon often left a smudge instead of a character, and it was typical of all the anonymous denouncements they had received at headquarters. Detailed in it was Khalib's illegal trade; his sources, his customers, and when and where he had met them. The police, to prepare such a case, would have had to switch men from serious investigations and expend limited funds in extensive bribes.

The sergeant returned the paper and said, "Sir, I, too, am surprised." The repose of his impassive face was flawed by a twitch.

Chafik shouted, "God the Compassionate! So my sergeant is surprised!" In an excess of emotion he tugged at his tie. "Khalib is interesting and deserves my personal inquiry," the Inspector said in a calmer voice. "Shall we begin with that Father of Humbug, Joseph Iskander? Shall we descend into the depths to talk with him? Come, Abdullah!"

They walked through airless and narrow streets, between high walls. Windows, shuttered against the sun, were secretive and hostile; a shutter would open, and then be immediately closed against the glances of the uniformed police sergeant and the little man in the white suit.

Iskander's Café of the Abundant Fruits was a tall old building with a tawdry façade facing the busy street and a rear exit opening onto the brown waters of the Tigris. There were green benches outside where robed Arabs sprawled; within, the café was a den infested by flies and secretive men.

The proprietor came toward the two men. He had a round jovial face marked with the blotchy scar of a Baghdad boil. The waistband of his trousers strained over an enormous stomach and when he extended short arms in greetings, patches of sweat showed on his once white shirt.

He cried, "My friend!" and clapped his pudgy hands to summon a waiter. "Honey cakes for the Inspector!"

Chafik pressed a handkerchief sprinkled with orange water to his nose. "Not even honey cakes, Joseph," he said. Out of the corner of his eye he saw men get up and slink from the café. "I am not good for business," he added dryly.

"You have business?" asked Iskander in a confidential whisper.

"Concerning Khalib —"

"A bad man!"

"He was killed last night."

"So?"

"He was here before he was killed."

The café proprietor lost his jovial expression. "Yes, Khalib was here," he admitted.

"Did he ask you for money?"

A bead of sweat ran down Iskander's cheek. "You talk of money!" he shouted. "Listen, last night that Khalib ate my good pilaf and drank a carafe of my Syrian *arak*, then left without paying — and now you tell me he will never pay me!"

"Was he alone? Did anybody follow him when he left?"

"I did not see. I was busy. There was a little trouble, a fight, and I had to put people out. You know what a good place I run here," Iskander said, and was jovial again.

The Inspector selected a cigarette and, as an afterthought, offered it to Iskander. "A very special brand," he said as he struck a match. "Have you recently seen that good lady, Madam Aliya?" he added casually.

"The old one?" Iskander muttered under his breath. Then he said, "Such a nice lady! We all love her! Put a finger on *Binti Ma'amum* and the mobs of Baghdad will be after you — and me, too!" The fat man laughed. "What do you want with her?" he asked.

"Khalib was with her before he was killed."

"So?" Iskander said and studied his cigarette.

Chafik waited expectantly, but then the café proprietor gave an almost imperceptible shrug. It was always the same; nobody would talk about the Lady of Good Deeds.

"Devils are supposed to materialize when one mentions them," said Iskander. "You, Inspector, talk of angels, and — lo — one appears." He nodded in the direction of the door.

The street was a stage, the sun a spotlight. A frail, bowed woman stood against the flaked whitewash of the wall across the way. She wore a chuddar, the shroudlike outdoor robe of the Middle East. A bulging oilcloth reticule dangled from one hand and in the other was a *khubis*, a piece of unleavened bread, folded over meat; she gave it to a beggar who came whining up to her.

"So kind," said Iskander, tearfully.

Chafik said nothing, but the sergeant said softly, "May the Great Architect of the Universe shower His abundant blessings upon her — apples of silver, caskets of gold —"

"You prate as a bazaar letter writer writes," grumbled the Inspector. He crossed the road to talk to the old lady. She was unveiled and the headfolds of the rusty dark robe were arranged to frame her nut-brown, wrinkled face, to which the years had given serenity after beauty. The woman's mouth was gentle, and her kindly eyes sparkled with a hint of mischief that reminded Chafik of his son. He noticed that she gave her hair careful attention, even used henna. Coquetry in one so old pleased the Inspector and he performed his most gallant salaam.

"Of course I know you!" said the Lady of the Good Deeds when he had introduced himself. "And I know your son; once he was one of my waifs — such a rascal!"

"A touch of that sauce improves the flavor of small boys."

Madam Aliya's laughter was like the tinkle of bells on the toes of a dancing girl. "I wondered at the time why the face was so familiar," she said thoughtfully. "They all look much alike when smeared with dirt."

"What is this about Faisal?" asked Chafik suspiciously.

"Nothing, oh, nothing!" the old woman said and her delicate hand, bare of rings fluttered like a hummingbird.

The Inspector decided the old lady was senile. "I have a query," he said, speaking carefully, as to a child. "Did you meet a man named Khalib last night?"

"He is a bad man."

"Yes, madam —"

"And sometimes bad men repent."

Chafik decided the Lady of the Good Deeds was being evasive and he said with a touch of brusqueness, "You did meet him!"

She nodded. "He gave me money for my poor; I think it was ten dinars —" Madame Aliya fumbled among the greasy packages of food in her reticule and brought out a small notebook. "Yes, ten," she said as she consulted it. "And I have given it all away — the last dinar only a few minutes ago to —" The laughter of a dancing girl's bells again rang in the street.

A tidy man in person and thoughts, Chafik was shocked by the present disorder of his mind. One part of it was puzzled by the woman's gentle mockery, while another asked why Khalib, who had gone around the cafés begging money from acquaintances, should have given with such munificence to Madam Aliya's poor.

He said, angered because he couldn't reason it out, "So Khalib gave you money, eh?"

The old lady closed the notebook and put it away but not before the Inspector had noticed a list of names, some followed by figures, others not — the latter were struck out. "You are rude," Madam Aliya said.

"I am a policeman!" he said.

"Did he —" the Lady of Good Deeds started to ask and hesitated. "Did Khalib steal that money?" she said.

"I am not concerned about his ten miserable dinars!" Chafik said, still angry. "Madam, Khalib was killed last night! You were his last witnessed contact, and I want to know, I must know, if anybody was with him — if you saw —"

He was bewildered by the woman's suddenly lifting the folds of her robes over her face, and he was reminded of his son. Faisal had the same baffling trick; he hid under the bedclothes when he was questioned about a misdemeanor. There was even the eye, the one anxious eye, that always peeped out from under the covers.

"Madam," Chafik said, anxious to placate her, and then he heard the murmur and was aware of the mob.

There were beggars on crutches, bedraggled women nursing naked children, and there were workmen armed with tools, and shifty men who blinked in unaccustomed light. Suddenly they had come, out of nowhere, and Inspector Chafik knew the reality of Iskander's warning that the poor of Baghdad would protect their benefactress.

If I take her for questioning there will be a city-wide riot, he thought. So be discreet. You can always go to her later if you want her ... He smiled at the old lady, said, "Madam, I leave you to your friends," and reproved himself for being afraid when he turned his back on the mob.

In the wide and orderly streets beyond the bazaar, the Inspector began to breathe more easily. "That was not good, my temper was tried," he admitted to Sergeant Abdullah.

He stopped to admire a haberdasher's display. Often, when on his rounds of the city, the little man took time out for this shop window; he was attracted by ties and socks as a woman is by novelties and hats. "An imported foulard," Chafik said, as he rubbed the dust of a recent storm off the window, the better to see a certain tie. "One dinar," he added and fingered his thin wallet. "Abdullah, remove me from temptation," he said, and walked on.

Then he went back and pressed his nose to the glass. There was a boy in the shop, a small olive-complexioned boy, who proudly displayed a dinar bill as he waited to be served.

"Faisal!" exclaimed Chafik. He went in and in his best policeman's manner put his hand on his son's shoulder. "Where did you get that money?" he demanded.

The eyes that were lifted to his own turned blank with fear. "But, my son!" cried the Inspector, troubled by the reaction. Then he saw the patches of dirt on the boy's face, leftovers from a recent and hasty cleaning. He remembered Madam Aliya's allusion to Faisal, "They all look much alike when smeared with dirt!" and how she had mocked him with her laughter. Chafik's suspicions were confirmed.

"You have been begging!" he accused his son.

"Father, I — it was for tomorrow — you wouldn't give me the money — I had to have money!" Faisal's sobs made him incoherent.

"Enough about tomorrow!" the Inspector said, his thin face darkened with anger. "I know what you did! You borrowed rags from one of your unsanitary friends of the bazaars, dirtied yourself, and went honey-voiced to the Lady of Good Deeds! She thought you one of her waifs! Ah, you Thief of Baghdad!" shouted Chafik.

Sergeant Abdullah soothed him, saying, "Sir, the mischief of small boys and puppies is not delinquency. The hand that has an urge to apply itself to them should be restrained —"

"Nevertheless, that hand, like night, must inevitably fall," Chafik said, but controlled himself; a Moslem father did not strike a son in public. "I do not understand," he went on sadly, "you are not a deceitful boy, Faisal, and you have all I can give you, yet you impose on a good old lady whose bountiful charity —" The embarrassed Inspector looked at the dinar which he had been folding and unfolding. All at once he smoothed it out. "You got this from Madam Aliya?" he demanded in a terrible voice.

"Really, truly, my father, I had to do it because — because —"

Inspector Chafik ignored his son. "Abdullah," he said. "With reference to the report of the Ankara police on the subject of counterfeit currency. Was the series Y-thirty-eight?"

"Yes, sir."

"Then here is one of the bills! My son had it and he got it from Madam Aliya! Without doubt it is part of the gift the worthless Khalib gave her last night."

It was Chafik's habit to wander through Baghdad when faced with a difficult problem, and he did so now. He had sent his assistant to headquarters to organize a search for the counterfeit money. He expected that the dinars given away by the Lady of Good Deeds would be easily recovered, since he doubted that the counterfeiters had flooded the city. It took time to mastermind such an operation as that, and the warning of the Ankara police had been prompt; so the immediate problem was Khalib — his part in the conspiracy and why he had been killed. And why the man had carried a denouncement of himself!

Twilight and cooling air encouraged Chafik to extend his walk and he went almost to the village of Hinaidi, then crossed the river by the old bridge of boats. He watched some water buffaloes being driven to their night quarters by a group of small boys. He went up the right bank of the Tigris, through rustling palm groves, and so came to the houses of the Karradat Miriam. The lights of Baghdad beckoned in the distance.

Every detail, Chafik thought, must fit into place. It is like weaving a fine carpet. Colors must blend and harmonize with the pattern; and there can be no loose threads.

He dismissed the possibility of Khalib's being the major criminal, for a vendor of smuggled watches lacked both the skill and ambition. Furthermore, if the man had had access to all the counterfeit money, he would not have made such a desperate round of the cafés, seeking a loan.

Somewhere in the period between bilking Iskander and meeting the Lady of Good Deeds, he had found the counterfeit money. "But where?" Chafik asked the equestrian statue of King Faisal the First, which he was passing. The monarch who had tried to unite the Arab world continued his perpetual ride out of Baghdad towards Damascus. The Inspector made an obeisance and went to a nearby police station to telephone headquarters.

Sergeant Abdullah told him nine of the ten bills distributed by Madam Aliya had been recovered. "Sir, you have the tenth in your pocket," the sergeant said, reproaching him. "The one you took from your son, sir."

"I hope I do not spend it in my wanderings," Chafik said.

He was satisfied now that there had been no general issue. It was as he had expected; Khalib's passing of the forgeries had been an isolated incident. The Inspector continued his walk. There was no moon and the streets were dark. He crossed to the left bank by the upper bridge and so came to the old town and the neighborhood of the bazaars. Pedestrians avoided the little man in the white suit who made gestures and talked to himself.

"Would even Khalib dare to cheat God by giving charity with counterfeit coin?" Chafik demanded. "No!" he announced, and stopped in the middle of the sidewalk. "The creature didn't know it was bad money! He found it or stole it, and its owners followed him to get it back, and —"

He heard his voice, cursed the unbreakable habit that made him broadcast his thoughts, and took refuge in a shop where he habitually bought cigarettes. *Chafik J. Chafik, you should be the city crier, not a policeman!* he reprimanded himself. And then he said to the shopkeeper, "Khalib's skull was thin; he died before they could make him tell what he had done with the cash! How fortunate for the Lady of Good Deeds! But why did he give her the money in the first place? Eh?"

The tobacconist, an old man, said, "I'm not answering questions." His name was Setty; he had a criminal record and disliked the police.

"Is she as innocent as she looks?" the Inspector added, striking the counter with the flat of his hand, shocked by the thought.

"I don't want to hear anything," Setty told him. "I'll not talk, least of all about *Binti Ma'mum*." He took a pack of Chafik's special brand from a drawer and looked up with softened expression at a cage where a bird fluttered. "Your noisy voice disturbs my Abdu," he complained.

Chafik was suddenly aware of the man, the cage and the cigarettes. He fumbled for money and tried to remember what he had said to annoy Setty. Always diplomatic, he admired the man's bird: "How unusual," he said, "to see one so plump and happy behind bars! He sings?"

"Once Abdu sang like a muezzin, now not at all." The tobacconist shook his head sadly, took Chafik's money, then threw it down and shouted, "Father of Guile! You send your police to warn me of counterfeit, then give me worthless paper, hoping I will change it so you can arrest me!"

The Inspector saw he had given the man the bill he had taken from Faisal. "A thousand apologies!" he said. "I did not intend ..." He wanted to placate the man and had the inspiration to whistle at the silent bird. Abdu cocked his small head, wiped his beak on the perch, chirped, and then sang.

"Truly," exclaimed Setty, clasping his hands. "Abdu has the voice of an angel! And you, Inspector, must be the friend of angels to have inspired him after such long silence!"

Chafik murmured his gratitude to Abdu and praised God for the miracle of song. "You will co-operate and immediately report bad money?" he asked Setty as he replaced the counterfeit with the last bill in his wallet.

Setty promised. "Kindness deserves a kindness," he said and listened contentedly to the trilling of the bird, and then muttered, imitating the Inspector's habit of talking to himself, "I'll not tell him a thing about *Binti Ma'mum's* little black book!"

In his haste, Chafik left the cigarette on the counter, and he was running before he reached the end of the street. The significance of Madam Aliya's notebook and why some of the names listed in it were struck out had come home to him. "Oh, Mother of Rascals!" he cried. "I put a weapon in your frail and mischievous hands! It is double-edged — may the Merciful One protect your nice old throat!"

The Inspector doubled through the alleyways of the bazaar and arrived at the rooming house where the Lady of good Deeds lived the life of one of her own poor. There was a light in her window and Chafik took cover in a doorway. A cautious man, he wished a police patrol would come around, for he had no desire to use the gun in his shoulder holster.

He waited nearly half an hour, afraid to go to a telephone because Madam Aliya might be gone when he got back; then the light went out and the woman appeared. She was no more than a shadow in the dark street. Her body seemed formless in the bat-winged folds of the dark-colored chuddar. He recognized her by the oilcloth reticule that dangled from one hand, and by the way she hopped over ruts and piles of garbage, intent on some mission.

He followed. Her knowledge of this part of Baghdad was better than his own and he knew he must not frighten her with some unusual sound. He went quietly, staying close to the rough walls of unfriendly buildings, aware of the silence, afraid of the silence.

Madam Aliya stopped at a corner and, with an anxious gesture, opened her bag and began to rummage in it. Chafik was afraid that she had forgotten something and he backed into the shadows before she could turn.

A small dark man came up behind him and struck him. The Inspector was in a whirling spiral of shadow and light, and at the top, waiting, was the old lady. The reticule she carried was huge. Then he was inside it and heard the catch snap.

The room was cluttered; there was an ornate table, a confusion of chairs, an old-fashioned roll-top desk overflowing with papers, and, in a corner, a modern safe. It was an airless room but from somewhere came the odor of spices, heated oil and savory food.

Chafik's first movements told him he was lying on a divan and was not bound in any way, but they had taken his gun. His head throbbed and the light hurt his eyes. "It was more restful in that bag," he said, then raised himself and saw the Lady of Good Deeds sitting at his side.

She said, "Poor man," and touched him with a cooling hand.

He winced as he tried to raise his head. "Madam," the Inspector said. "I expected you to lead me to Khalib's killer. I know how you strive to encourage bad men to do charitable acts, but the violence that has been done to me confuses me. Could it be that my reasoning was wrong? Are you responsible —"

A voice from the door interrupted, saying, "For shame, my friend! How could you have any doubts about our *Binti Ma'mum* — that blackmailing old hag!" Anger choked the speaker.

It was, thought Chafik, quite logical when Joseph Iskander came into his range of vision: it experienced the cooking odors — the room was above the Café of the Abundant Fruits. "I should have worked the thread into the pattern earlier," the little man said.

"Pattern?" repeated Joseph Iksander, puzzled.

"Ah, that habit of speaking thoughts! I was, Joseph, merely reprimanding myself. Obviously Khalib — the man that you had killed — was without funds when he came here, yet when he left, he went straight to Madam Aliya and gave her ten dinars — counterfeit —"

"Khalib, that thief!" exclaimed Iskander. "He robbed me! Last night — you remember? — he ate my food and drank my wine and went away without paying, but what he also did was to come into this office when I was busy with a fight downstairs —"

"I remember," Chafik said. "You told me you had to put men out of your nicely run kitchen of thieves."

Iskander nodded at the roll top. "I had the money on the desk," he went on. "The good counterfeit hills, Inspector! I had taken one sample from each of the packages that had arrived on the Taurus Express, and I was looking at them under the glass to make sure all had come from the same plate, then —"

"So careless to leave them on the desk," Chafik said.

"I slapped my face! The entire amount — fifty thousand dinars — all of it gone, all gone! — because a thief takes ten — just ten! — worthless pieces of paper!" The fat man swore.

Chafik said reprovingly, "There is a lady present, Joseph." He looked at the old lady huddled under the dark robe, and then he shook a finger at her and said, "You naughty one! How many years have you fed the poor of Baghdad by blackmailing Iskander?"

She lowered her eyes and there was a touch of laughter in her voice as she confessed, "One year, perhaps two."

"But the denouncements you wrote of various individuals are recent."

"One must sometimes apply unusual pressure to squeeze blood from a stone," said the old lady.

"So there was revolt against your gentle touch!" the Inspector said, and then went on: "You had to make examples of certain individuals, whose names you then removed from your notebook! I do congratulate you on your presentation of these cases, madam. I presume your poor filled in the details?"

A snarl from Iskander frightened the old lady and she lifted the folds of her chuddar over her face. Chafik once again was reminded of his son's retreat under the bedclothes. "For shame, Joseph!" he chided.

"But she makes me so angry!" complained the café proprietor. "The people tell her everything, and she goes around with her notebook and bag of denouncements and we have to pay. Look at what she wished to sell me" — he showed the Inspector three typewritten sheets — "for five thousand dinars!"

"A small sum for your neck. But I am shocked that madam should have offered to keep silent about murder."

"My poor," said the old lady with spirit, "might have benefited. The law, hanging a bad man, helps neither the living nor the dead."

"You see, Inspector?" said Iskander. "She has no respect for either of us! What is truly troublesome is that we have been unable to cut her throat because of her mob," he went on confidentially.

Chafik frowned; he remembered the empty streets. "I did not see her friends tonight," he said.

"I expected her this evening," Iskander told him. "I sent my men out to beat the heads of those who watch over her and then alert the mob. I regret that they also beat your head —"

Chafik touched the sore spot and then fumbled for cigarettes; he had none and exclaimed, "I must smoke!"

The fat man made a contented sound. "So I have *Binti Ma'mum* and I have you, and neither her mob nor your police know where you are."

"I need cigarettes," Chafik said in the complaining voice of a small boy.

"My café has plenty —"

"Not my brand!"

"A condemned man is permitted small luxuries; we will get your brand." Iskander beckoned to one of his followers. "Wait! Who sells your cigarettes?" he asked suspiciously.

"A shop near the old bridge. Setty's place."

"Setty?" Iskander laughed. "No friend of the police, that one! Get the Inspector what he wants," he told the waiting man.

Chafik called the man back. "I desire to buy my own," he said with dignity and took a folded bill from his wallet. "I take nothing from murderers, nothing!" he added with a reproachful look at the Lady of Good Deeds. The old woman made a protesting gesture and the Inspector took her hand and patted it gently, forgivingly.

When the messenger returned with the cigarettes and the change from the dinar, Chafik returned the change, saying, "A fee for the executioner!"

So they sat, the old lady with her hands clasped, Iskander nursing his stomach, and the Inspector moving only to put the butt of a cigarette in an ash tray. Eventually, Chafik asked, "What do you propose, Joseph?"

"The river," Iskander told him. "But let us wait until Baghdad sleeps, my friend."

Chafik added another butt to the tray — he had stacked them like logs — then he looked at his watch and said, "It is already tomorrow." He remembered the breakfast-table conversation with Faisal, and now he said with the wistfulness of remembrance, "What *was* the significance of tomorrow?"

"With two such valuable presents, it must be Death's birthday!" said Iskander. He watched Chafik add another butt to the pile. "So symmetrical!" he exclaimed.

A man came in and announced, "It's all quiet now and the boat is waiting."

The Inspector put out his last cigarette and reached for the tray. Iskander, rising, took it away and said, "Such a tidy man! All Baghdad knows how you pull the butts of your cigarettes!" He shook a reproving finger and added, "No clues! All this goes into the river with you."

The knuckles of Chafik's left hand touched his forehead in the Moslem's gesture of accepting his fate. "Let us go," he said to Madam Aliya and offered her his arm.

As they went out the old lady spoke from behind her robe, saying, "My poor might have won so much money, had they but abandoned me to this man."

The rear door of the Café of the Abundant Fruits opened on the mud flats of the Tigris. There was no moon, only the stars lighted the night, and it was so quiet that the sound of water rippling against the poles that marked the main channel seemed unnecessarily loud.

Iskander struck a match to guide the escort and prisoners. "Death's birthday," he said, pleased with his earlier jest. "Come, now! We cannot keep Death waiting!"

A beam of light came from the middle of the river, swept the bank, and found the boat where it was being steadied by a waiting oarsman. A yellow flame stabbed from the dark and was followed by the sound of a gun.

Joseph Iskander put his hand to his stomach and pitched forward into the mud. Chafik grasped the old lady and threw her down and lay beside her, saying,

"Madam, please be still! You will do much for your poor in the future — with certain reservations as to method."

There was more shooting, and then somebody shouted, "Sir? Sir?" The searchlight of the police boat moored in the middle of the stream continued to search the mud flat.

The Inspector got up and called, "All is well, Abdullah. Kindly do not bleat at me, and put your gun away. *Binti Ma'mum* had given one of them to my son, from whom I recovered it — and it was that one I gave to your man to buy me cigarettes! Setty —"

"No friend of the police is that one! Why did he warn —" Iskander bit his lips in sudden pain.

"There was a prior incident with a bird —" Chafik commenced to tell the fat man, but the explanation came too late. "Such a waste!" said the Inspector, as he took the cigarette, which had fallen from the dying man's lips, and threw it away.

When he came home to the house on the Street of the Scatterer of Blessings, it was dawn, and his wife Leila had returned from her visit. The small dark woman, who wore an expression of acquiescence that was to be expected of the wife of Chafik J. Chafik, extended her arms to him. "I did not expect to find you in such disorder," she said, with reference to his muddied clothes.

"That can be remedied," he said, embracing her. "What needs immediate attention," he added, pausing in enjoyment of his wife's perfumed hair, "is to understand the significance of today —"

"Today?" Leila repeated. She held the little man at arm's length to look at him.

"Yes, today! It was tomorrow, yesterday — so confusing! But today is what I ask you about. Why, for example, did our son need a dinar for the tomorrow today? His persistence eventually produced the clue that enabled me —"

Leila said, "As a detective you may be reasonable, but you are unreasonable as a father with a son. Faisal — and it is my fault. I forgot before I went away — needed money to buy you something for the tomorrow which is now today."

"Eh?" shouted the little man.

"I should not tell you, but he has a tie for you," whispered the small dark woman. "A beautiful foulard tie, my man! We — Faisal and I — know how you have admired it in that shop window. So go to Faisal; he awaits with the gift."

She took his ears and pulled his head down and kissed him. "Fool!" she said. "Don't you understand that this tomorrow, which has gloriously become today, is your birthday?"

Death Was a Wedding Guest

The telephone rang at midnight, waking Inspector Chafik of the Baghdad police from a pleasant dream. "The tongues of women, and other clamorous instruments, should be stilled at this hour," he complained as he reached over his wife to the bedside table.

A man with a pleasant voice said, "Inspector Chafik, I fear I disturb you."

"Sleep is not for the fathers of teething babes, nor for policemen," Chafik answered, regarding himself sympathetically in the mirror on the wall. He was small and dark and had a large head, high cheekbones, and a thin face. With subconscious vanity he studied his proud features.

"The dead will keep you awake tonight," said the stranger.

"A poor jest —"

"I do not jest. Go to the house of Ursule, she who was once wife to Sheik Majid, the exile. There is an arbor in the lady's garden. You will there find —" The voice stopped, then went on, hushed and urgent. "Come, please come!" and then the connection was broken.

The Inspector knew he could not trace the call — the city had an automatic exchange — and, grumbling, he began to dress.

"Possibly a hoax; you may expect me back in a snarling mood," he said to his meek-looking wife.

"Must you go then?" asked Leila, with the deference an Arab woman shows her husband.

"Sheik Majid was mentioned. You would know nothing about him, but fifteen years ago he encouraged the tribes to revolt and had to flee the country. There was a report today that he had left his place of exile and might cross the frontier."

"Does he not have a daughter?"

"Yes, the sheik has a daughter by his first wife, the one who died," Chafik said, using this conversation to brief himself. "Her name is Noemi. She was given into the care of his second wife, the Lady Ursule, who divorced him after his disloyalty. Tomorrow, Noemi is to wed —"

"Is to be sacrificed!"

Chafik turned and looked at Leila in astonishment. "She weds her cousin, Tarik," he said indignantly.

"Tarik is a monster!"

"Madame!"

"God," said Chafik's wife, "sometimes touches a man and thereafter he converses with the birds. In the case of Tarik, as all Baghdad knows, the Devil touched him at birth; he creeps with the reptiles. Furthermore, Tarik is not Noemi's cousin, not really. He is the nephew of her stepmother, Ursule, and like Noemi he is a ward of that woman. Ah what a schemer she is!"

"The Lady Ursule is a matriarch —"

"A schemer, my man! Sheik Majid forfeited his estates when he fled the country, they have been held in trust by the Keeper of Properties as his daughter's dowry, and now they will go to the husband. But as Tarik is Ursule's creature, she —"

"Enough!"

"Poor little Noemi is really in love with that nice Lieutenant Risa of the army, whose father is a parliamentary deputy —"

"Why do I keep records?" shouted Chafik. "All I have to do is listen to you coffee-cup gossips!"

"Then the facts are correct?"

"More than twenty years we have been married, still I walk into your parlor like a witless fly! Yes, it is all probably true — the Lady Ursule will be the real benefactress of Noemi's dowry, and it's none of my business. I'm a policeman, not a marriage broker!"

Leila brushed back the cloud of blue-black hair from her smooth shoulders. "It is dreadful. I hope Sheik Majid is here to stop it."

"How can he? The man is an outlaw and has no civil rights."

"A loving father might be forgiven if an accident happened to the bridegroom."

Inspector Chafik threw up his hands. "Woman!" he said in a terrible voice, and then he saw Leila's smile. "An improper jest," he went on sternly. "Furthermore, your proposition is impractical. Our laws demand financial retribution from a murderer's family, besides his neck. If the sheik did what you foolishly suggest, his daughter would forfeit her dowry in blood money to Tarik's next of kin. And do you know who that relative is?"

"His aunt, the scheming Ursule," Leila answered in a subdued voice. "I had not thought of that. My solution was hastily conceived."

"Women are always hasty," Chafik told her.

He adjusted a black *sidarah* on his sleek head, lighted a cigarette and went out. He was in the street before he realized how completely he had been briefed, and his thin face darkened as, from the bedroom window, he heard a soft laugh.

Sheik Majid's former wife lived on the outskirts of Baghdad, in a district of gardens and fine villas. A breeze from the river rustled the palms, the air was sweet, the sky was brilliant with stars, and Inspector Chafik was almost amiable.

"No siren, Abdullah," he said to the police sergeant who drove the car. "This may be a sleeveless errand and I do not want to disturb a household needing rest for tomorrow's ceremony."

Sergeant Abdullah, a vast and shadowy man, said with the privilege of long association, "Sir, this marriage should not take place."

"You, too?" exclaimed Chafik.

"I have daughters —"

"Ah, yes — three... " Chafik shrugged and there was a glint of mischief in his eyes when, in the superior voice of the father of a son, he said, "Daughters are very nice, but it is inconceivable a man would risk everything, including his neck, to save one from an unpleasant union —"

"I would make such a sacrifice!" shouted Abdullah.

The Inspector said, "Your pardon, old friend, it was only a test. I wanted to make sure fathers of daughters truly love them. Now I know."

When they had gone a little farther and Abdullah was calm, Chafik said, "I trust the report about Majid is incorrect. He is still politically dangerous and would find sympathizers if he came to Baghdad."

"Also enemies —"

"His implacable enemy is his former wife. She betrayed him once and would betray him again. I am concerned for her, particularly after what you have just taught me about the fathers of daughters. She almost invites vengeance ..."

The thought made him fidget, and he looked around anxiously. They were going up an avenue lined with oleanders. The great dark river was ahead, and the lights of the train ferry crossing it were like swimming stars. There was no other sign of life.

Then from somewhere came a fusillade of gunshots, starting up the cacophony of hysterical dogs that too often made Baghdad nights hideous.

Sergeant Abdullah spoke professionally, "An automatic, sir. Small caliber, short barrel. It jammed after the third shot. They often do. A revolver is more reliable."

Alertness pleased the Inspector, but he was worried. "My midnight telephone call becomes a nightmare," he said, and leaned forward to peer into the darkness.

At that moment the car came to a sudden stop, and he was thrown against the windscreen. And then he saw the sergeant running to a man who had fallen in the path of the car.

The Inspector got out and went to join the sergeant. The man on the ground was young, good-looking and well-dressed; blood from a head wound was smeared over his face, but it was not a serious injury.

"Struck with a blunt instrument," Sergeant Abdullah said.

"Help him up." When the dazed victim was on his feet, the Inspector said, "Your name, please. I am the police."

"Risa. Ali Risa."

Chafik remembered his wife's gossip about the young army lieutenant who was loved by Sheik Majid's daughter, and so he knew this was the man. "I detest coincidence," he said aloud, but speaking to himself — an unbreakable habit. When he realized he had spoken, he was embarrassed and therefore angry. "What happened?"

"I was struck from behind; that is all I remember."

"Where were you?"

Lieutenant Risa hesitated and then pointed to a grove of citrus trees near the brick wall of a house. "I was walking there," he said.

"An odd place to walk at such an hour. Did you hear shooting?"

"I heard nothing. I was stunned — shooting? Where?" asked the young man, suddenly aware of the import of the question.

Chafik turned to a police patrol which had just arrived from another direction. "Have you traced it?" he asked the senior constable.

"The shooting was somewhere in this quarter, sir. There are lights in that villa, and I was going to inquire there," the officer said, and pointed his carbine toward the nearest wall.

"Whose house is it?"

"Madame Ursule's, sir."

The Inspector spun around and began to run toward the wall. There was a gate and the hinges creaked when he touched it. His surprise was echoed in the sergeant's gasp; gates are not left open in Baghdad at midnight. They looked into a garden thick with trees.

Chafik saw lights in the house but went down a path to the rear of the garden. "Surely one coincidence is enough for one night," he said.

"Sir?" asked Abdullah, following close behind him, gun drawn.

"There is an arbor in the lady's garden," Chafik said, repeating what the stranger had told him in the midnight telephone call.

They came to the pool, and nearby was a trellis covered with vines. Chafik took the sergeant's flashlight and went to look into it.

A man sat sprawled at a table under the vines, head resting on one outflung arm, back turned. One leg was twisted under the chair as by a violent and suddenly arrested contortion. A stick was on the floor at his side.

There were three bullet wounds, all in the back; it had been a frenzied killing. The Inspector touched the body and found it warm. He thought: *If I had not been delayed by meeting that young man, Risa, I would have found the lion crouching over its kill.* He wondered if that had been the hope of the person who had telephoned him.

He knelt and lifted the lolling head. The face was trimly bearded, otherwise very much like his own. An odd twist of the lips suggested a smile, as if the corpse said: *Well, what do you make of me?*

Chafik stood up and turned to the sergeant, "Abdullah," he said.

"Sir?"

"A daughter has lost her father — here is Sheik Majid."

Fifteen years of exile had changed the sheik; once a heavy-set man, he was now gaunt to the point of emaciation and so changed that he had been able to move about in Baghdad without being challenged. "Even his friends would not recognize him," said Sergeant Abdullah.

"But an enemy did."

Chafik picked up the stick that lay beside the dead man's hand. It was the sort a watchman carries and had a lead load and brass rings, which made it a formidable weapon. On it there was a smear of blood mingled with a few hairs, and the Inspector said, "Not Majid's blood. This has almost dried. Blows were struck tonight —"

Abdullah's face showed unusual animation. "Suppose —" he began.

The Inspector stopped him. "We are both leaping to a conclusion. Supposition is a policeman's major sin."

"Yes, sir, and you have also taught me to frown on coincidence. Yet a young man with a bloodied head and a blunt instrument —"

"Enough, enough," Chafik said bitterly. He admitted to himself that the circumstances made a case against Lieutenant Risa; and he looked at the corpse reproachfully, wondering why Sheik Majid should have come out of exile to add this final horror to the misery of his daughter's wedding eve. It was inexplicable, and so was the telephone call that had announced the imminent tragedy.

Chafik remembered the voice, casual, slightly mocking, and tinged with sadness. And then there had been urgency: "Come, please come!" the man had pleaded before the connection was broken.

"Too many threads and all broken," grumbled the Inspector. He lighted a cigarette and then stood forgetful of the flaming match held in his hand.

Somebody was running down the path from the house — a dim white figure with dark flowing hair. The light of the match showed huge frightened eyes and a young, graceful body, as she ran to the man slumped over the table. "Ali! Ali!" she cried. "They've killed you! Ali —"

Chafik dropped the match as it burned his fingers; Abdullah's flashlight came on. "Not Ali!" the girl said, looking up at them, too dazed by relief to wonder who they were. "But this man!" she went on. "This kind man with the sad eyes who gave me Ali's message —"

"What message?" asked Chafik.

"Ali could not meet me tonight. The man, the one who lies here, stopped my carriage when I was coming back from visiting friends and told me — Oh!" cried the girl, suddenly aware that the man was dead and turning to flee.

Chafik grabbed her arm. "You are Noemi," he said.

"Yes."

"Then you do not know who that is there?" He prayed that she had not recognized her father so changed by all these years.

Noemi said, "He looked at me strangely when we met, just as if we were acquaintances, but I did not know him." The daughter of Sheik Majid shuddered, then wrenched free, and instinctively ran to Abdullah, who held her gently.

"You father of daughters!" said Chafik. Angry because duty compelled him to restrain compassion, he shouted. "Her tears are overgenerous, like monsoon rains!"

"Sir! I protest —"

"Abdullah, she had a rendezvous here; a wayward child trysting on her wedding eve." He tossed away his cigarette. *Had the father known about the tryst?* he asked himself. *Had he tried to stop it and had there been a fatal quarrel with Risa?* Chafik went to the girl and forced her to look at him. "You love Ali Risa?" he asked harshly.

With all the defiance of a seventeen-year-old, she said, "Let all the world know!"

"Tomorrow you wed another —"

"What choice have I? An Arab woman has no rights! Yes, I marry the creature of Ursule's choosing, but I hate him, and I hate her! I love Ali and shall always love Ali. And she knows it!" shouted Noemi, pointing behind the Inspector.

He turned. A woman stood in the path, watching and listening, a woman of medium build and years, and comfortably fleshed. A chuddar, the outdoor robe of the Middle East, was draped around her shoulders, but the folds that should have veiled her face were thrown back. She was carefully groomed, handsome, her manner commanding.

Inspector Chafik recognized her and salaamed. "Lady Ursule," he said, and formally announced, "I am Chafik J. Chafik of the police —"

Sheik Majid's former wife raised her hand and sent the girl running.

"Madame —" the Inspector began.

"You will attend to your own affairs, policeman," Ursule said coldly. "There has been an unseemly disturbance — shooting — in my garden."

"I regret it, but death is no respecter of property."

"You will go about your work decently," Ursule went on in her insolent voice. "There is to be no scandal." She looked into the arbor and shuddered. "It was suicide, of course."

"What makes you say that?" asked the Inspector.

"Young lovers are foolish. This Risa, he —"

"Madame, that is not Risa there."

Ursule was visibly upset. "Not Risa?" she said. "Of course it is Risa. Who else would be so vulgarly romantic as to come here and shoot himself on Noemi's wedding eve?"

"One you know, madame, and he did not kill himself." Angered by the woman's manner, Chafik raised the dead face and brutally turned it toward her.

"Majid!" she cried. "Oh, fool, fool!" She drew the folds of the chuddar over her head and fled, shrieking.

When the Inspector saw her again it was in the house and his men were everywhere, engaged in routine duties. The dawn was spreading over the desert, and the chant of the prayer callers came from the towers of Baghdad's many mosques.

Ursule had recovered by now and said, "I regret my weakness. It was the shock."

"So understandable," he said sympathetically. "Divorce is never a successful operation; there is always a trace of memory left —"

She looked at him coldly. "You are mistaken, policeman. I have no lingering affection for Majid. He was a traitor, and it is right that he should be dead. I was shocked that it should have been done in my garden."

The Inspector abandoned compassion. "Why were you so sure that it was Risa?" he demanded. "Did you hear something, see something? Why were you dressed for the day instead of the night? Were you expecting a visitor?"

"You are insolent!"

"And you, madame, are evasive."

"I was dressed," Ursule said, "because I awaited my nephew —"

"Ah, yes, the bridegroom. Here it is the dawn of his wedding day, and he has not yet found his bed!"

"Tarik went to a party —"

"Given by Mr. Rinaldi, a friend," the Inspector said, and absently quoted a police record: "Rinaldi, Hussein. Age: thirty-one. Inherited fortune from his father. Two wives, three mistresses. Entertains lavishly... There were at least a hundred guests invited last night," Chafik added, remembering a routine report.

Ursule lost her poise and cried, "You police! You know everything!"

"Duty, madame —"

"Spying, always spying! Yes, it is true I was disturbed tonight! I saw a man in the garden —"

The Inspector was astonished by this sudden co-operation, but he looked at Ursule calmly.

"It was just before the shooting," she went on. "I was looking out of my window, waiting for Tarik, and saw a man run down the path toward the pool."

"Why did you not call the servants?"

"This was not a matter for servants; I thought I recognized Risa. I knew my stepdaughter had been having secret meetings with him! I was about to go and send him away when the shots came. That is why I thought it was his body in the arbor, that he had committed suicide —"

"And you saw nobody else?" Chafik's fingers began to move nervously.

Ursule stared at them and cried, "Will you stop that? I will not stay here to be tormented!"

She turned to leave, but at that moment a door at the back of the room opened, and a shambling, heavily built youth came in, escorted by a constable. "He was found entering the house by a window, sir," the officer told Chafik.

The youth had an overlarge head, a flat, vacant face and thick lips: his animal-like eyes were small and sly, and they stared with panic. Seeing Ursule, he wrenched himself free and ran to her. "Aunt! Aunt! Who are these people?" He spoke in the thin treble of a child.

Ursule turned and shouted at Chafik, "How dare your men touch him! Tarik has a right to be here!" And then she said to her nephew, soothing him, "You are late, so late. Was that why you entered by the window? You were afraid I would scold you? Poor Tarik —"

"I — I —" Tarik began, his lips trembling.

"Yes, yes, Tarik, you were naughty, but I forgive you. This is your wedding eve. Your party kept you; it is understandable. You had trouble finding a carriage? Where did you leave it? Why didn't you drive to the door? Why —"

Chafik said sharply, "Madame, let me do the questioning."

"You would frighten him. You can see how timid he is. And what has poor Tarik done except come home late from his wedding-eve party?"

The Inspector shrugged and looked as the constable, who said, "He did come in a carriage, sir. He left it a short distance away."

"He saw the house lighted up and was afraid I was waiting up to scold him," Ursule said hastily. "Isn't that so, Tarik?"

"It was lighted up and I was afraid you would scold me," repeated the youth.

At that moment his shifting gaze stopped and brightened, and he went across the room to a table where there was a bowl of fruit and sweetmeats. His sliding gait reminded Chafik of Leila's description of Tarik: he creeps with the reptiles.

Tarik greedily filled his mouth. His thick lips smacked with coarse delight, and wiping his sticky hands on his clothes he reached toward the bowl again.

Ursule said, "Enough! Go to your room and rest. Today you wed —"

"Today I wed," repeated Tarik. "Noemi ..." He mouthed the name as though it were another candy, and his hand darted to the bowl again. He went out smiling.

The Inspector could not hide his disgust. "Why tell him he is to wed?" he asked Ursule. "How can there be a wedding with the bride's father dead in your garden?"

"That makes no difference!"

"But —"

"Majid was a stateless man, a rebel; there is no mourning period for him. Noemi has no father. She marries Tarik!" Ursule said, and left the room.

Chafik stood motionless, shocked into silence. But when Sergeant Abdullah entered, the Inspector said, "Surely dogs howl in Baghdad when the Lady Ursule walks the streets!"

Abdullah had news. "We have found the gun, sir; it was in the pool. An automatic, short barrel. When we heard the shooting I said —"

"Only a contortionist pats himself on the back," Chafik said absently.

The Inspector walked over to the table and the bowl of sweetmeats. "Halva," he said, identifying the pink-and-white confection, and then he surrendered to temptation. "Almond flavored," he announced, as he took another piece and followed his sergeant into the garden.

He looked at the gun his men had dredged out of the pool and congratulated them on their thoroughness. There would not be much chance of finding finger prints; mud and water would have smudged them. He had the weapon sent to ballistics.

They had found the two ejected shells — the third had jammed the mechanism. There was nothing else. The ground was too hard for defined footprints, although there was the faint imprint of a man's shoe near the wall that enclosed the garden.

Beyond the wall was the citrus grove where Lieutenant Risa had walked and had been attacked, according to his story. Chafik was unhappy and said, "Well, the stick that Majid bloodied on somebody's head will have to tell us about that."

He stood in the street for a final survey before leaving for headquarters. It was dawn of the new day — Noemi's wedding day, thought Chafik, and felt compassion and disgust and anger.

He crossed the road to a public telephone box, and something clicked and hummed in his mind. "An excellent view from here, Abdullah," he said.

"Yes, sir."

"One can see both the garden and the adjoining grove. Have this instrument dusted for prints."

"And whose am I to find, air?"

"That depends. If my midnight caller was human, you will find his. Or you may be rewarded with the prints of the individual responsible for the death of Sheik Majid."

The Inspector got into his car. His fingers were sticky from the filched sweet meat — halva clung like glue — and he licked his fingers reflectively.

His office was on Rashid Street, the main thoroughfare of Baghdad. The shutters were closed against the sun, and as the day wore on, the small room became filled with smoke; a pyramid of cigarette butts bore witness to Chafik's concentration.

He was a tidy man and liked everything sorted out before he began to weave his solution, but in this case there were broken threads and he was distressed.

The reports that came in about Risa made an ugly case: the pathologist stated that the hairs mingled with the blood on Sheik Majid's stick came from the young man's head. The Inspector had Risa brought to him.

He was a sullen witness and said, "I know nothing except what I told you." He refused to admit to a rendezvous with Noemi. The evasion was clumsy.

"It is curious," Chafik said wearily, "how the process of breeding an officer and a gentleman destroys the more human instinct for preservation. Take this gentleman away!"

He added another butt to the neat pile in the ashtray. A vision of Noemi's face with its huge frightened eyes drifted in the smoke of a fresh cigarette. In a few hours she would become Tarik's bride, and the Inspector, not a profane man, swore.

Abdullah came into the room as silently as if he had materialized. "You are bursting with news," Chafik said, looking up.

"Yes, sir." The sergeant placed the automatic found in the pool on the Inspector's desk. "Nothing," he said. "It did kill Sheik Majid, but as we feared, there are no defined prints. Nothing, sir, except a foreign substance on the butt which is being analyzed."

Chafik could see a whitish smear in the corrugations, and be picked at it with a penknife as he listened.

"No possibility of tracing the serial number," Abdullah went on. "Illegal entry of lethal weapons into this country, sir. All that. Possibly purchased abroad. Possibly."

"Abdullah, your real news, please," Chafik said.

"Sir, it is about the telephone box near the house of Madame Ursule. There *were* fingerprints —"

"Ah! So my midnight caller did have a body!"

"Yes, sir, a dead body. The fingerprints were Sheik Majid's." The sergeant dropped his news like a bombshell, but the Inspector went on picking at the substance on the butt of the gun.

"He had a nice voice," Chafik said mildly. "He wasn't a bad man, you know. Too ambitious. Politics." He shrugged. "I have a medical report here somewhere which says the sheik was fatally sick, so the gun anticipated the inevitable ..."

The Inspector thoughtfully looked at the point of his penknife and the substance that adhered to it. Then he carefully tasted the substance scraped from the gun. He announced, "Almond-flavored —"

Suddenly he struck the desk with his fist; his sallow face looked like a bronze mask and his eyes reflected the fire of the stone set in his signet ring. He said: "Let us go and stop this unholy marriage!"

Noemi's marriage was being held in her stepmother's house. The big room where Inspector Chafik had interviewed Ursule was now divided by a curtain. On one side waited the bride and her womenfolk, hidden from the eyes of men; on the other side sat the bridegroom and his attendants, with a white-robed mullah who inspected documents.

The bridegroom slyly took sweetmeats from his pocket and chewed steadily: his eyes were on the curtain that hid Noemi.

The official finally put away the documents. "All is in order, the contract is correct," he said. He looked at Tarik, sighed, shook his head, and then turned to the curtain behind which the bride waited. "Noemi, daughter of Majid," he said. "Do you accept or oppose this union?"

"It is opposed!" said voice from the door, and Inspector Chafik burst into the room. "A thousand pardons for this melodrama; there was no time to send in my card —"

He crossed the big room, his shoes silent on the fine Bokhara rug; his white suit was crumpled, his polka-dot tie askew. "Reverend sir," he said, stopping before the mullah, "the curtain that discreetly hides the bride also hides the pinches that force her submission —"

"Explain," said the dignitary.

Chafik bowed and turned to Tarik, who was fumbling in his pocket for the only comfort he knew. "You went to a party last night," Chafik said, "a party given for you by your friend Hussein Rinaldi. There were many guests and you were confused."

"So many guests —" mumbled the bridegroom, chewing.

"And one came to you and took you aside?" The Inspector spoke gently as to a child. "You remember a stranger, a man with a beard, who told you distressing news about Noemi?"

Tarik's round face grew pale. "The man with the beard!" he wailed. "He told me Noemi had a lover. He told me I was not a man unless — unless ... Aunt! Aunt!" cried the youth his eyes searching wildly.

Ursule flung back the curtains, saying. "Silence, you fool!" but Sergeant Abdullah was waiting and his dark hand gagged her.

Chafik ignored the interruption. "The stranger told you to come here at midnight," he told Tarik. "And he gave you a gun and warned you not to tell anybody what you were going to do —"

"He gave me a gun —"

"Then he went away."

"He went away. I looked for him but could not find him again. So many guests. He went away —"

"And what did you do then, Tarik?" Chafik asked.

"I came here at midnight and there was a man waiting for Noemi and I shot him and —"

"Aunt came?" asked Chafik.

"Aunt came. She took the gun and threw it away. She told me to go away and come back in a carriage and not know anything — Aunt! Aunt! This man looks at me! He makes me talk!" Tarik cried.

Ursule made throttled noises; she was helpless in Abdullah's grip.

"Your fingers were sticky from sweetmeats," the Inspector said to Tarik. "They always are," he added gently. "They left their trace on the gun — halva clings, and it hardens in water. But you have talked enough and eaten enough," Chafik added with compassion for the creature.

He looked at the mullah. "Reverend sir, tear up the contract. The law forbids this union."

"That is true," agreed the old man. "There is blood between these people, although it would appear that the sheik arranged his own death."

"He could do nothing else, sir. He was a stateless man and a dying one, and his only thought was to save his daughter. So he arranged that he should be killed by the bridegroom and then he called me to bring me to the scene of his death, to capture Tarik red-handed. The plan almost failed. My arrival was delayed by Risa."

Chafik fumbled with a cigarette. "First the sheik stopped his daughter from keeping her rendezvous with Risa; she did not know it was her father who brought her that false message canceling the rendezvous. And then, fearing Risa would frighten Tarik away, he ambushed Risa and struck him down when he was about to climb the wall to go to the arbor. Risa recovered too soon, sidetracked me, and gave Ursule time to get Tarik away —"

For the first time, the Inspector looked at the woman. "Lies come smoothly to your lips," he said. "It was Tarik you saw in the garden, not Risa as you told me. You just had time to get your nephew away after the shooting, no time at all to examine the body, which you were so sure was Risa's. What a shock, madame, when I turned the dead face of Noemi's father to ward you! Did it mock? Did those lips seem to say, *This is my victory*? The law will be kind to Tarik, not quite a man, but the law will be harsh with you, madame."

Chafik went quietly from the room. He stopped in the garden to look at the evening sky. He thought how pleased Leila would be with the romantic conclusion, and smiled with indulgence.

Even the gossip of a woman, ground in God's mill, makes a fine, white flour, he thought, and as he lighted a cigarette, he said, "I, of course, am a reliable millstone."

Invisible Killer

The police sergeant and the Inspector knelt beside the first corpse. The sergeant said, "Sir, this one has been dead four thousand years, but in its back there is a modern knife." It was cool here in the vaulted chamber, but outside, the sun beat down on the treeless plains of Iraq and on the dun-colored remains of Akkar, an ancient city recently uncovered by archaeologists.

The Inspector flicked ash from his cigarette. "My Dear Abdullah," he answered the sergeant. "We of the Baghdad police should concern ourselves solely with corpses of our era. The recent stabbing of this long-dead one is desecration, not murder. However, I am intrigued and you did right to serve up this gentleman as appetizer."

He touched his forehead in a salaam to the figure between them; it had the substance of leather and was blackened by the bituminous soil that had preserved it. Burial had been made in a squatting position with arms wrapped around the legs. Elaborate ornaments of lapis lazuli, crystal and carnelian were scattered around, and fragments of a robe, stiff with gold embroidery, still clung to the remains.

The knife between the shoulder blades, incongruously, had a cheap wooden handle.

"English manufacture," said Sergeant Abdullah. "Imported for the bazaar trade, sir, and sold mainly to tribesmen."

He was interrupted by an exclamation from his superior, who had focused a powerful reflector lamp on the body.

"Observe the small strong bones, the delicately shaped hands and feet!" cried the little man. "Note the head, overlarge for his otherwise perfect proportions! The wide brow, the hollow checks, the pointed chin, the sharp high-bridged nose! He was a handsome man; his height about five feet five and his weight possibly one hundred and thirty pounds. Whom do you see, Abdullah?"

The sergeant said in a shocked voice, "I see you, sir!"

"Yes! Myself! Chafik J. Chafik as he would be if miraculously preserved after death. But this is really of passing interest," he said, and the flush faded from his swarthy checks. "This man begat my race yesterday and is as forgotten as I will be tomorrow."

He passed a cigarette to his assistant and then chose one for himself. The flame of the match made dancing points of light in his flat, neutral-colored eyes. The sergeant, who was massive, sat and waited as patiently as the dead man beside them.

"Well?" the Inspector asked.

"Sir, I will brief you concerning the other corpse. It is that of Mr. Jamil Goury."

Chafik said impatiently, "That information was given me before I left Baghdad." He went on to quote from his memory of records: "Goury, Jamil. Age thirty-three. Unmarried. Educated at the Oriental Institute, Beirut. Formerly an assistant curator at The Iraq Museum. Appointed field representative to the Department of Antiquities in nineteen fifty-two. Brilliant. High-strung and inclined to nervousness. Yes, yes! I know all about Mr. Goury, except how he died."

"He was strangled."

"And where did it happen?"

"Here, sir, in the passageway to the tomb." Sergeant Abdullah indicated the shaft the excavators had dug into the tomb. It was narrow, and one section could be passed only by crawling. "It was there that he died," Abdullah went on. "The bruises on the throat resemble those made by powerful hands. Yet there was nobody in the tomb to strangle him except this dead gentleman."

"Do you accuse my ancestor?" Chafik asked mischievously.

Abdullah looked at the Inspector reproachfully.

"Who else was present when Goury died?" Chafik asked.

"There was Dr. Anton, sir; he is head of the expedition. And there was Mr. Garwith, a New Zealander who is his assistant. Also the doctor's wife. Gisela Anton, and Mahomet Kubba, the foreman. Many workers, sir, at least fifty."

"A surfeit of witnesses is as bad as none at all," complained the Inspector. He leaned forward to look at the knife in the back of his ancestor. "And the hand that did this was not seen either?"

"Nobody knows how it got there."

They sat in silence. The body that had sat for four thousand years threw a shadow on the brick wall of the tomb; and the shadow was shaped like a question mark.

"I find it cold here," Inspector Chafik said to Abdullah at last. "Let us go seek the sun."

"Yes, sir, I also find it cold, yet I perspire," the sergeant said.

They crawled out. The Inspector, who was leading, stopped in the narrowest part of the shaft and examined a forked twig partly covered by sand. It had been broken recently and he recognized it as peach wood, yet no peaches grew at Akkar these days, and the gardens of Baghdad were thirty miles away.

He said, "This is as old a relic as the other, and even better preserved — it is greener."

Still lying in the narrow shaft, he picked up a lead pellet the size of a small bead and wondered for what purpose it had been cut with a groove. Then, crawling on, the back of his jacket caught on something and ripped. Freeing himself, Chafik damned the unknown relations of the unknown man who had long ago driven a bronze hook into the brick that formed the roof of the tunnel.

Light blinded the Inspector as he crawled out into the sun. He brushed his clothes and was soothed by the familiar scene. Columns of dust, raised by the wind, danced over the drab, empty plains. On the horizon, date palms stood along the winding course of the Euphrates. And above was the copper shield of the sky.

He was a devout Moslem, and half aloud he chanted to himself from the Koran: "By the noonday brightness and by the night when it darkeneth, the Lord has not forsaken thee!"

Dr. Julius Anton, who headed the expedition, was a big blond man of vigorous middle years. He had a short beard streaked with gray, and tufted eyebrows shaded his blue eyes. His hands were strong and square and grimed by the rubble of the city he had resurrected. The streets of Akkar and the foundations of buildings were all around him, monumental evidence of his patience and enthusiasm.

The archaeologist was an Austrian who had dug in various parts of the Middle East before the second World War. Politically, as Inspector Chafik knew, Anton had been a neutral.

Anton spoke brusquely in English. "I trust you have not touched anything down there. We have not yet catalogued the finds."

Chafik answered precisely: "I prefer to let sleeping ancestors lie."

The archaeologist stared, then turned to his wife and said, "Do you not see the likeness, Gisela? The Inspector is a throwback to another age!"

Mrs. Anton had a fair and gentle beauty. She was small, a figurine in porcelain, and considerably younger than her husband. The Inspector wondered at her lack of vivacity as he bowed over her hand: her touch was as timid as the brush of a moth's wing.

He said. "Madame!" ardently, and was rewarded with a smile.

"My husband is very rude," Gisela Anton said.

"To call me a throwback? But I am! Oh, I assure you, Madame, I also see myself as a curiosity walking."

Her hand was withdrawn, and the life that had been kindled by his gallantry flickered out. "So, another scientific mind?" she asked wearily.

Dr. Anton said, "Please, Gisela! Enough! The Inspector does not make a social visit." He turned as a man came up the ramp from the excavations, and then he said, "My assistant, Mr. Garwith."

The New Zealander was dwarfed by his chief. He had a sun-dried face, deep-set gray eyes and an oddly twisted mouth. The thumb of his left hand had been amputated and a scar on his arm suggested a war wound. Garwith greeted Chafik with an indifferent nod, and then his manner softened as he turned to Gisela Anton and said, "I've uncovered some pre-Amorite pottery, might be Sumerian, we're getting down to that level. Wish you'd go take a look." When she hesitated, he added, "Please?" and she turned to go.

Richard Garwith's expression as he watched her walk away was gentle, and he said, "We don't want her here when we talk about Jamil Goury."

Dr. Anton said, "Foolishness, Richard! Inspector Chafik wishes to question her."

"What d'you want to know about the Rabbit?" Garwith asked Chafik.

"Rabbit? I do not quite comprehend."

"Goury was a timid bloke, so are rabbits," Garwith explained.

"My records say he was high-strung —" Garwith gave a short laugh and the Inspector asked authoritatively: "High-strung or timid, how did he die?"

Garwith said, "We were all going in. Goury was leading, he didn't as a rule, but I'd teased him —"

Dr. Anton interrupted. "You were inconsiderate, Richard. Goury was frightened of the mummy. It is not a true mummy, of course, Inspector — your people, the ancient people, had no cult of the dead, as had the Egyptians. The preservation of the one the tomb was accidental —"

Inspector Chafik said impatiently, "The soil of my country is productive of more history than crops. Kindly tell me how Goury died."

Anton shrugged and said, "We were crawling through the narrow part the shaft: I was behind Goury. The lights went out —"

"Somebody stumbled over the power cable and unplugged it from the generator," Garwith explained, interrupting. "There were a dozen of us in the shaft at the time: the doctor in front of me, Gisela in back, then Mahomet Kubba and a party of workers. All a sudden, it was blacker than hell down there."

"The horror has begun," Julius Anton said, his command of English giving way as he recalled the horror. "Goury has cried, 'Let go!' Never have I such fear heard! And then he has pulled hack, and then has thrown himself forward."

"Why forward?" asked Chafik.

The archaeologist threw up his hands. "Perhaps to grasp the enemy. But then Goury has jerked; his legs have thrashed, like he is being choked. Awful!"

Garwith was calmer and took over the story: "Goury fought something down there; I'm sure of that. But the shaft was so narrow we couldn't see what held him. Dr. Anton tried to haul him out —"

"By the legs, hopeless," said Anton, calmer now. "I could not move him, someone — something held him fast. And then his body became limp. I reached over him to grapple with whatever was holding him. Nothing was there! And then all at once he was free and I got his body out."

"There is no other way into the tomb?"

"Positively none, Inspector! Furthermore, my foolhardy assistant, Richard, went in —"

"Nothing there except the blasted mummy!" Garwith said.

"Had my ancestor been stabbed?" asked Chafik.

Garwith rubbed his jaw with his mutilated left hand. "No," he said.

"Yet the knife was there an hour later," Anton said. He became angry and stared about at the ruins. "As if I did not have enough trouble!"

"Ah, yes," Chafik said. "Rumor — always an unreliable witness — has informed me you are stopping work here, Doctor."

Anton's expression was angry. "What can I do! The foundation that was financing my dig has withdrawn funds. They claim I spend too much. My life's work!"

The Inspector was familiar with the shrill voice of fanaticism and thought: *If only this man saved some of his emotion for his wife.* Aloud he said sympathetically, "Indeed, much money is needed for an army of workers. Have any of your men deserted since the murder?"

"Only one, a man we call El Chukar," Anton said.

"Chukar is the name for our Middle Eastern partridge," the Inspector said, frowning.

Dr. Anton laughed. "Exactly, this man has the scuttling run of the partridge. Not quite right in the head, 'touched by God' you call it in your Arabic. He was Goury's servant."

Garwith said, "Whatever El Chukar was, he was devoted to Goury. He probably took to the ruins to be alone with his grief."

Chafik said dryly, "We of the Middle East enjoy grief, Mr. Garwith. Therefore I find this man's disappearance odd, and a chukar hunt is in order. And now excuse me, I have an appointment with the recently dead. I am always at the beck of somebody's corpse," he added plaintively and applied a handkerchief saturated with orange water to his fastidious nose.

The dead man lay on a canvas cot in one of the tents. The Inspector, who was not easily shocked, exclaimed when he saw the body, "This was not a tidy killing!"

"No, sir. I, too, was disturbed," Sergeant Abdullah said.

"He looks like one badly hanged," the Inspector said. "The throat is discolored and lacerated. What opinion did you form?"

"Sir, the hands that strangled him were of exceptional hardness, one might almost say they were fleshless —"

The Inspector, who had been bending over the corpse, abruptly straightened and seized his assistant by the throat. "What do you feel?" he demanded.

"Chiefly, sir, I feel — your thumbs," gasped Abdullah.

Chafik released him. "The grip used in strangulation relies upon the thumbs; the bruises they make are deeper than those left by fingers," he said. "With this in mind I suggest you look again at Mr. Goury."

The sergeant obeyed. "I do not observe the contusions that you described, sir, and that doubtlessly appear on my own throat. Pressure on the dead man's throat was equal at all points of contact, so it would appear that the strangler lacked thumbs."

"I am of that opinion, too, Abdullah," Inspector Chafik said and stepped out of the tent.

Akkar was dominated by a ziggurat, a vast pyramid of moldering brick which had once been topped by a shrine. There the sacrificial fire had burned for the twofold purpose of propitiating the gods and guiding caravans that voyaged on the vast plains. Now there were no gods and no travelers. Inspector Chafik stood atop the ziggurat and stared down at the unearthed city below.

"An eerie place," complained the sergeant, climbing up to join the Inspector.

"A graveyard at dusk always is, but here we are free from those who might eavesdrop. Was the chukar hunt successful?"

"No, sir, a dozen men searched diligently, but they did not find Mr. Goury's servant."

"We must widen the search; he may have fled to a village. Did you inquire into the marital relationship of Dr. Anton and his charming wife?"

"Yes, sir, most discreetly. The doctor is cold toward her."

"Wine and women, when left standing, become sour, although in this case another man appreciates the vintage and would sip."

"Yet the husband, this time, seems quite disinterested," Abdullah said, a note of surprise in his voice. "On the other hand, Mr. Garwith only recently fought with the deceased —"

"Do you suggest Mr. Garwith was jealous?" the Inspector said sharply. "I am sure that Mrs. Anton did nothing to bring about a quarrel between rival lovers."

"I confess to inaccuracy, sir. It is true she spurned the attentions of Jamil Goury, whose reputation with women is public gossip."

"Let him keep his reputation, he no longer has his life. The essential fact is that Gisela Anton is a virtuous little moth." And then he added harshly, "Ah, you fool!"

"Sir!" the sergeant said indignantly.

Chafik patted his arm. "I addressed the husband who has taken this lost city as mistress."

He sat with his arms folded around his knees, in the pose of his ancestor in the nearby tomb. He rocked as he sat, and noted that the dusk had created a mirage: Out of the desert sprang a forest of enormous trees.

"What happened at Akkar?" he asked his assistant.

The sergeant said, "Sir, my knowledge of history is insufficient to —"

Inspector Chafik broke in impatiently, "My question referred to today's yesterday, Abdullah, not to yesterday's yesterday."

Abdullah nodded. "You refer to eleven years ago, a date in the second of the World Wars, when enemy units dropped from the skies and landed near here."

"They were saboteurs," Chafik said, taking over the story. "They had excellent geographical knowledge of our land, but they were not well informed about our people. They thought they could bribe our tribal princes with gold. Although they failed and were arrested, nobody ever found their gold."

"No, sir," the sergeant said. "I remember well the parachuted containers of their supplies which fell into our hands. But no gold, sir."

Preoccupied, Chafik got up and started to climb down the ruins of the ziggurat, stepping carefully in the darkness. When he had gone a little way he stopped, rooted by fear, as a grotesque shadow reared before him.

In shape it was human, but the way it moved was not. Chafik, who was unarmed, cursed the darkness and his imagination; then he told himself, fear is an expression of disbelief in God's hereafter, and he closed in for attack.

The shadow had substance, and the Inspector was encouraged until he realized the inequality of his strength. Sinewy hands gripped his throat; he broke the hold, shouted, "Abdullah!" and felt the hands seize his throat once again. There was a roaring in his ears, the stars above him seemed to leap like flames of wind-blown torches, and then suddenly there was peace.

When he came back from the place of peace and darkness, Chafik was aware of pain in his throat. He opened his eyes and saw the soft glow of a lamp, not the flames of the stars: the anxious face of a woman, not the shadowy form that had attacked him.

"Madame Gisela!" The exclamation tortured his raw throat. He looked about and saw that he was in his tent in Anton's camp. "I did not die here: my corpse should not have been moved," he said.

The laugh that answered him was a caress, as was the voice that said, "Now I know you have recovered!"

Chafik's senses cleared. "The illusion of death was pardonable. I thought angels administered," he said gallantly, and his hand went to his neck where something rested lightly.

"That compress will soon take away the bruises," Gisela said.

"So cool," Chafik said, closing his eyes.

"They think it was Goury's servant who attacked you out there, the one we call El Chukar —" She stopped and then asked in a frightened voice, "What is it, Inspector?"

"Throats, bruises, compresses, interference with evidence!" he rasped, as he threw away the cloth. "Who did this? Bring me a mirror!"

Rudely, he snatched the compact the woman brought and tilted the small glass to examine his neck. "Thumbs!" he said.

"What?"

"Thumbs, thumbs! I looked for a thumbless man!" Chafik shouted.

The violence of his own voice startled him, and he stammered, "Madame I —" He saw her face grow pale at she stared beyond him toward the tent door. He turned his head and saw the canvas flap being raised by a maimed hand.

"Richard," whispered Gisela Anton.

And then Julius Anton came into the tent, saying, "Such a shocking event to have happen in *my* Akkar!" He was followed by Abdullah and Richard Garwith.

"Sir," the sergeant said to Chafik, "your alleged attacker escaped but —"

"Let me rest!" Chafik shouted, turning to the tent wall. "Let me rest," he begged tearfully.

The sergeant ushered the others out and showed no surprise when he returned and found the Inspector sitting cross-legged on the cot, nursing the inevitable cigarette.

"I had to get rid of them and I have always admired myself as an actor," Chafik said, without looking up.

He was very tense and the sergeant recognized the symptoms and waited at attention. Presently the Inspector looked up from the objects laid out before him: a broken twig from a peach tree, the coat that he had ripped on the bronze hook in the tomb of his ancestors, and a bead of lead, deeply grooved.

"These are threads with which I must weave," he said, "and this is another" — he touched his lacerated throat.

"There is, of course, a thread that I shall have to reproduce. Also, we must add the psychology of these people, their passions and ambitions —" He stopped, and then said harshly, "The pattern I weave is hideous, but it is so with all murder. And the solution will be equally terrible." The rasp of command was in his voice as he went on, "Find me a length of wire, Abdullah. Thin and very strong. Find it discreetly. One of our drivers should have what I want in his tool kit."

"Yes, sir."

"Send a man to the nearest orchard and cut me a forked switch from a peach tree. A fast car should take him to the gardens of Baghdad and back in as hour.

"Finally, there is to be an alarm at dawn, Abdullah. The men should fire carbines and run shouting to the tomb of the man who died so long ago. Let them stop there; let nobody enter."

Six hours later, Inspector Chafik stubbed out his final cigarette, adjusted the knot of his tie, combed his smooth black hair, put on his *sidarah*, and went out. The flap of the tent closed behind him and he stood for a moment looking at the ruins of Akkar, tinted pink by the sunrise.

The sharp crackle of police carbines stirred the Inspector and he hurried to join his men, who stood guarding the entrance to the tomb. Watchdogs barked in Anton's camp and the archaeologist hurried out from his tent, a coat thrown over pajamas.

"What has happened?" Anton called, running toward the tomb. Garwith followed close behind him.

Chafik said, "Somebody, something, went down into the tomb."

"There are devils in my Akkar!" Anton said. "Richard, the generator! Give us light! Come," he said to Chafik. "The one you call your ancestor is to me the crown of my Akkar, and already he is damaged with a knife."

The generator started and the lights came on. Dr. Anton went into the tomb, followed by the Inspector. Garwith, who ran to join them, was crowded aside by

Abdullah; as always the sergeant was officious when his natural place was challenged. A file of policemen and workers formed the afterguard.

And then Gisela Anton appeared and was ordered back by a corporal, who said, "Madame, I have orders to escort you to your tent and guard you." He was deaf to her protests and led her away.

Inside the shaft, the men began to crawl forward. As the passage narrowed, Anton called back, "Careful."

Behind him, Chafik said softly, "Here Jamil Goury died." He felt for the cable along the wall, yanked on it, and the lights flickered. Impatiently he signaled again, and this time the generator coughed and died, and the tunnel was plunged into darkness.

"*Gott!*" Anton cried out and tried to draw back. His legs thrashed and he cried again, "*Gott, lieber Gott!*" And then he scrambled forward to fight what was there in the darkness. The sounds he made were those of a man who was strangling.

Chafik seized the thrashing legs. Reaching over the Inspector, Abdullah gripped Anton's ankles, and said, "I have him, sir."

The Inspector said urgently, "Release the pressure! Do not kill him!" And then he said to the strangling man, "Jamil Goury was called a rabbit, but there are other animals that kick and thrash when caught in the hunter's noose. Tell me why you killed him!"

Anton gasped and Garwith shouted, "Let him go, you devil!"

Chafik said grimly, "The devil and I have much in common. But you, Mr. Garwith, should be thinking of the lady. She will need you more than ever when our work here is finished," he added sadly.

Once again he spoke to Anton, saying, "You will tell me how Jamil Goury died; confession is essential to our law." The doctor did not answer and Chafik said to Abdullah, "Encourage him to speak."

"Enough," Anton gasped; "he died like this."

"Why was his death essential?"

"Because — because —"

"Because you found the gold brought here by the Nazi parachutists so many years ago?" asked Chafik.

"*Ja, ja,*" Anton choked, "Let me go. I will tell you."

The Inspector said, "So you found the gold in the tomb, where the parachutists had hidden it. You needed this gold for your mistress Akkar, and Jamil Goury knew you had found it. So he had to die. Perhaps you had prior knowledge the gold was here, perhaps the Nazis used you during the war — but it is of no importance, that war is forgotten.

"But what is not forgotten is how you killed a man with a rabbit's snare, how you hauled on his legs to 'save' him," Chafik went on. "Like this —" Savagely he pulled on the doctor's legs and the harsh sound of choking filled the tunnel.

"A rabbit's snare," the Inspector repeated, "a noose of wire weighted with lead beads — possibly bullets from a gun — carefully spaced like the fingers of a hand, a hand without thumbs. Such a neat way to conceal an obvious imprint of a wire. And then you used a twig of peach to trigger this contraption, so that the rabbit, entering, would blunder against it and drop the noose around his own neck. You prepared for him such a horror here in the darkness as I prepared for you. But I am merciful, I shall not wait for you to die, Dr. Anton. Turn on the lights!" he ordered.

When the lights came on, Chafik reached over the feebly struggling man and loosened the wire noose. Then he unfastened it from the bronze hook on which he had once torn his jacket. "I shall not hide my noose as you concealed yours when you so lovingly removed Jamil Goury's body. But I wonder at your carelessness in not salvaging the broken peach twig, and the lead bead that became detached from the wire."

They took Anton out into the early-morning light. Through the streets of the ruined city came a small patrol of police, escorting a man who moved with the scuttle of a running partridge.

Chafik said, "Ah, so the chukar hunt is ended."

He went to them and said, "Be gentle. This poor man, befuddled with grief and superstition, went into the tomb after the crime and stabbed my ancestor. His poor brain thought that the hands of a man dead four thousand years had taken his master's life."

Wearily Inspector Chafik turned to Richard Garwith and said gently, "Go to the lady. When this cloud of horror has lifted, may she find a silver lining."

Royal Theft

Inspector Chafik of the Baghdad police, a sleek man in a cool white suit, stood near the gateway of the al-Waqi'ah Mosque in the old part of the city, tapping his foot impatiently. It was the hour of *zuhr*, the day was Friday — the Moslem Sabbath — and the Inspector had an appointment with his son to attend the noon service.

"If I had made *my* father so wait, the application of a slipper would have justly rewarded me!" Chafik announced to the holy man who squatted in the shade of the temple wall.

Chafik had a thin, swarthy face, prominent cheekbones, and a long narrow head on which a black *sidarah* was set precisely. He was a proud man; his upper lip, below his neat mustache, curved arrogantly, and he had a trick, when speaking, of rising on his toes to give an illusion of stature.

Thought led to thought as the Inspector considered the punishment due his son; and, as was his habit when agitated, he began to talk to himself. "The metaphorical chastisement I received this day from my director was not justified," he said aloud. "Am I the only policeman in Baghdad? Are there not others to prevent this series of holy-day crimes? Why…"

His voice became shrill. He heard it and was embarrassed by the presence of the ragged holy man, who raised astonished eyes from his work of molding beads of clay, mixed with dust from a saint's tomb, which were sold as charms. The holy man had a wisp of hennaed beard, the badge of one who had been to Mecca, and the sunken cheeks of a fanatic.

"Heed me not," Chafik said. "Anger has loosened my mischievous tongue. Nothing, alas, can loosen yours, Husain the Voiceless."

He patted the dumb man's shoulder and watched him engrave on the finished bead the Arabic characters for "the Pardoner," one of the many names of God given in the Koran. Husain set the amulet in the sun to bake and immediately started another. He was a permanent part of the street scene, familiar as its cobblestones. The chanting of the worshipers disturbed the doves that nested on the blue dome of the mosque, and Chafik looked up as they rose in a swirling cloud. There, where the birds flew, was peace; below, in the tortuous streets of the drab city, stalked a menace that had outwitted the best efforts of the police.

The crimes had begun five weeks before, and all had taken place on Friday, when business premises and cafés were closed and the mosques were thronged. Robbery was the motive and the victims were the gold- and silversmiths who traded in Baghdad's ancient bazaars. There had been terrorism, brutal clubbings, and no witness had dared come forward.

Chafik checked over precautions he had taken this Friday. He had divided into small areas the warrens of covered ways that extended along the left bank of the Tigris River, and he had assigned plain-clothes men to patrol them. A mobile squad to picked officers under the charge of his personal assistant, Sergeant Abdullah, was strategically located to cordon off any sector where trouble arose.

Secrecy was essential, and to explain his own presence in the old part of the city, Chafik had arranged to meet his son for the *zuhr* service; he was known in Baghdad as a devout man, so it was natural he should attend a mosque. *Chafik J. Chafik, what a hypocrite you are!* he reproved himself; *but God has loving-kindness and will surely understand.* Nervously he toyed with the heavy signet ring on his left hand and looked up and down the street, aware that the underworld would destroy him if the lash of his authority lost its sting.

The neighborhood policeman, Officer Yusif, went by and Chafik made a mental note to chide the man for so elaborately pretending not to see him. Impatiently he looked at his watch and raised the dividend of punishment due his tardy son.

There was the clatter of feet in the empty street. A small boy, running, turned the corner and the Inspector sighed with relief. Forgotten was anger and the thought of corporeal reprimand; fondly he looked at the boy who came to him with head hanging.

Faisal was an adopted son, and in a flashback Chafik saw the ragged urchin, a waif of the bazaars, whom he had taken into his childless home. He had never regretted the impulse, nor had Leila, his wife of twenty happy years. Little Faisal had filled the only gap in their lives.

Alarmed by the boy's unusual humility, the doting father said, "Fear time, my son, do not fear me. We are both slaves to the hours."

Faisal continued to hang his head and Chafik said in a sharper voice, "Look up! Eye should meet eye when men talk!"

"My father, it is because of the eye I do not look up."

Chafik put a hand under his son's chin and raised the heart-shaped face. One of Faisal's eyes was brimming over with tears. The other, closed to a slit, was encircled by a darkening bruise.

"So! You fight on the holy day!"

"It was not that I wanted to fight, my father — truly, I was very meek and took their insults. But when they said you could not catch a crook even if he was under your nose, and that your nose was a big one, then I —"

"Who are 'they'?"

"My men, my father."

The Inspector knew that Faisal referred to the pack of waifs who infested the bazaar. The boy had kept in touch with his old friends, and, inspired by Leila, encouraged them to become respectful citizens. Now, the threatened prestige of his father had lost him face, and his leadership of the gutter children was at stake.

And so it begins, Chafik thought. The jackal pups yap at my heels and soon their sires will come to feast on me ...

Faisal, wound up, was saying, "And it was George, the red-haired one, who said that about your nose, my father, and you know George, his father was an English soldier in the war and his mother one of the women who —"

"Enough!"

"He hit me and I hit him and he blacked my eye and I hurt my hand on his teeth and we fell to the ground and — and he got up and kicked me and I punched him until he cried and —"

"You and I," Chafik interrupted, "suffer alike. My director reprimands me, your 'men' challenge you. Truly we need prayer's comfort!"

He stopped in the gateway of the mosque to look back and saw the local patrolman pass again. Husain the Voiceless had removed his ragged gown and now squatted in his loincloth as he searched for the unwelcome guests that lodged on his emaciated person.

"Do you see what he is doing, my father?" exclaimed Faisal with the embarrassing clarity of youth. "All my years I have never seen the like! Holy men *never* destroy the little things that bite. They say they were sent to keep us awake to recite the Koran, and —"

"Come, Faisal," said Chafik, "let us put our minds to sweeter subjects."

He knelt to remove his shoes and then, hand in hand with his son, walked humbly into the cool, whitewashed interior of the temple.

An hour passed. They had listened to the imam's sermon and commenced the ritual that followed. Inspector Chafik, at peace for the first time in days, stood with hands to his ears to pray. His glowing eyes were fixed on the fault of the dome, where crystal chandeliers vibrated to the chant of the worshipers.

The little man's spiritual concentration was interrupted by Faisal, who tugged at his father's coat, pointed to the courtyard, and whispered excitedly, "Sergeant Abdullah is here, my father!"

A massive man, dark as a mahogany carving, was outside, walking toward the temple. The buttons of his uniform flashed the fire of the sun, and the holster of his gun, polished by wear, was no less bright. His shadow moved ominously before him, and the man stopped at the threshold of the holy place to signify he was here for other duty than prayer.

Chafik said, "Alas! I am not to gain a merit in heaven this day!" He told Faisal to stay until the service ended and then go home. He stepped over the prostrate worshipers and joined his assistant.

One glance at the gaunt, expressionless face of Sergeant Abdullah was enough, and the Inspector put on his shoes, and followed the man to the gate. "Are you as voiceless as Husain here?" he demanded when they were in the street.

"No, sir, but I could not talk on a secular subject within those sacred precincts —"

"You croak like a bird of ill omen!"

"Yes, sir, I regret to —"

"Another raid?" Chafik suddenly felt cold in the sun.

"On the premises of Elias Samoon, the jeweler, sir. So far as I can ascertain, they took only certain pearls entrusted to Samoon, who was to prepare a necklace for one of the royal princesses. And that is not all ..."

Abdullah's dark eyes filled with compassion for his superior as he finished: "This time it is murder, sir!"

They went at once to the jeweler's shop not far from the mosque. Inspector Chafik curved his fingers to his forehead, completed the salaam, and said to the corpse, "Elias Samoon, we are both victims of my failure. The club that killed you destroyed me too."

Sergeant Abdullah interrupted: "Sir, you did all that was possible!"

"When a cracked pitcher returns empty from a well it goes on the rubbish heap," was the Inspector's bitter reply.

He raised the head of the old jeweler. Samoon's thin skull had been crushed by the first blow, yet the intruder had continued the beating — to make sure, Chafik decided. Samoon must have recognized the man, who therefore had to kill him. Chafik looked at the safe, expertly blown, at the still-crowded trays of bracelets and rings; there was a gap in the otherwise untouched display and he questioned his assistant.

"The pearls were there earlier, sir," Abdullah answered positively. "You may remember I was personally entrusted with their delivery to the deceased."

Chafik nodded. He wondered how the presence of the royal pearls here had become known, and thought perhaps the jeweler, Samoon, had boasted of his appointment to the court — so natural when an artist, and an old one, had arrived at his zenith.

The pearls were rare black ones, perfectly matched, incredibly valuable. The raider had wisely avoided the temptation to take any of the bulkier pieces, which would have been difficult to hide. "So he curbed his appetite; he has admirable discipline," said Chafik. "Such a man will go a thousand miles and wait years before he disposes of his loot. What action have you taken, Abdullah?"

"I have closed the bazaars, sir. Nobody can go in or out."

"There are so many ratholes, and we have no description of the particular rat that was here. What about the patrolling officer?"

"The thief incapacitated him, sir. We found him in a doorway and he is still unconscious. The alarm was given by the man in the next sector."

"When did you arrive?"

Sergeant Abdullah frowned. "There was a delay," he confessed. "I had deployed my squad to the goldsmiths' bazaar to seize an unsavory individual. One named Abu Nahabi, sir. I detained him for loitering."

"Abu Nahabi, Father of Thieves," said Chafik. "An underworld character of note. He has the brains to stage these raids but I am doubtful of his patience. I will interrogate him later; he may have served as decoy."

The little man lighted a cigarette and drew gently on it to make it burn evenly. He noticed fragments of dried mud on the floor, possibly brought in on the killer's feet, and bent to sweep them up.

"No witnesses?" he asked Abdullah.

"Like yourself, sir, the devout of Baghdad were at prayer and the bazaar was deserted. The deceased, of course, was not of our faith; so unfortunate — otherwise he might be alive. However, there is a woman who claims she saw a man running, a man wearing a cloth over his head."

"How does she describe him?"

Sergeant Abdullah expressed contempt for civilian witnesses: "Tall, short, lean and fat, the usual confusion. But she insists he ran down the Street of the Weavers, which leads to the mosque, sir."

"Perhaps the policeman who patrols there saw him." The Inspector put the fragments of dried mud he had found into an envelope, slipped it into his pocket, and went out.

The al-Waqi'ah Mosque was five minutes away and he found Yusif, the local officer, standing at the gate watching the holy man, who was still absorbed in his devout work. Yusif shook his head when Chafik questioned him. "I saw nobody, sir."

"Then we deal with an invisible man! Did nothing untoward happen on your patrol? Nothing?"

Yusif hesitated; he was a good officer, but dull and factual. "I — I imagined something ..." he said.

"We are informed by learned doctors of psychiatry that imagination is the picturing power of the human mind, triggered by an actual event. Therefore, my dear Yusif, do not blush; kindly tell me your experience."

"Sir, it is absurd," Yusif said; "but after you entered the mosque and I returned on patrol, I had the illusion — I — it was as if a house was missing from the street, sir!"

Chafik was disgusted. "A house had disappeared, eh? Doubtlessly you have sunstroke!" he said dryly. He turned to question Husain the Voiceless.

The holy man answered by inscribing in the dust with his forefinger the word meaning "nothing," and returned to his task of bead making. There was a pile of freshly molded amulets in front of him, and on each one he engraved the Koranic name for "the Protector."

"Apparently sacred charms, like secular merchandise, come in popular lines," said Chafik.

He lighted a cigarette and over the flame saw a redheaded urchin dart from an alleyway. The boy's freckled face was bruised and, when he opened his mouth and shouted, "Yah, Father of Noses!" he exposed a gap where a tooth had recently been knocked out.

Dirt, flung with deadly aim, spattered the Inspector's jacket; the boy was gone before Sergeant Abdullah, outraged, could move.

Chafik stopped his assistant's pursuit, saying, "It is true my nose is over-large and I cannot see the evil under it. Moreover, Abdullah, my son has already punished George."

He walked away, head high, his eyes alive with shadows, like the warning shadows of vultures gathered to a desert kill.

They were holding Abu Nahabi, the Father of Thieves, in a nearby police station, and Chafik interviewed him in a bare, whitewashed room. The man, arrested on suspicion, was truculent and leaned over the Inspector's desk and shook his manacled fists.

"Can a citizen not walk in the bazaar?" he shouted. "I demand my rights!"

Inspector Chafik put a box of cigarettes at his left elbow, an ash tray to his right. He sat and smoked and was silent until the first butt was discarded; then he said softly, "You shall have your rights."

"That's more like it!"

"The right to pray before they hang you," the Inspector added.

"What? What?" Abu Nahabi's choleric face went gray.

"The right to cleanse your soul with confession before it stands before God for judgment," Chafik continued. "Elias Samoon is dead. Even if you did not do it, the diversion created by your presence in the goldsmiths' bazaar confused my men — made it possible for another ruthless individual to go to Samoon — so at the least you are an accomplice. And an accomplice to murder is hanged."

The little man tidily arranged the discarded butts in the ash tray. "I commend you to the hangman," he went on conversationally. "Fear him not, he is experienced. He will strap you and take you to the scaffold and stand you on the trap; he will put a white hood over your head, lodge a noose under your chin, and drop you fluttering into eternity. The snap of your overlong neck will be the last sound you will hear."

The Father of Thieves went to his knees. "Sir, sir! Not I! I did not kill Samoon!"

"Then who?" Chafik demanded, his voice calm.

"The hooded one, the leader —"

Chafik remembered the woman who had seen a hooded man running in the bazaar, "So there is such a man!" he exclaimed. "Name him, thief! — perhaps I can save you from the scaffold."

Abu Nahabi cried, "He calls himself Ali Rafah and he lives at the house of Zeinab on the Street of the Fountain. He did this killing — not I!"

"Describe Mr. Rafah."

"A man of medium build, thin. I never saw his face; he keeps it covered. A disease has eaten it —"

"And his soul! How long have you been his lieutenant?"

"Six months."

"Oh, faithful servant! How well you served the Devil! And what have been your wages?"

"Nothing yet. He said we must wait, that things taken must be passed cautiously."

The Inspector considered this, then chattered aloud to himself: "Just as I thought — patience. Also a persuasive personality and the ability to command authority. What a man!" He toyed with his signet ring, looked casually at the Father of Thieves, and said in a monotone to Sergeant Abdullah, "Remove him; I am reminded of creatures that live under stones."

When the sergeant had taken the man out and then returned, Chafik said, "H'm! It's curious."

"Sir?"

"The Street of the Fountain, where this Rafah fellow lives, is in the neighborhood of the al-Waqi'ah Mosque. I was so close to him and didn't know!"

They went to make their call on Ali Rafah. The house was built around a court where a dusty palm tree struggled for life, like the people who lodged in sordid rooms.

Chafik said to the woman, Zeinab, who owned the place, "O mother of Cockroaches, where hides Ali Rafah?"

"Respect my sex, thou Father of Noses!" shrilled the hag, and Sergeant Abdullah inserted his foot before she could slam the door. "All right!" Zeinab grumbled. "But why do you want Rafah, that quiet one?"

"You admire quietness?"

"I do not like voices that hiss like snakes, such as yours."

The Inspector held his tongue and followed the woman up the stairs. When they passed a dark cave in the wall, he asked, "What lives there?"

"One who has more merit than you," Zeinab answered tartly. "I give it as a godly gift to that holy man who sits at the mosque gate."

"You mean the amulet maker?" Chafik looked in; there was a straw pallet, a tattered blanket, a bowl for food, foulness and the scampering of rats. "Truly your charity will be rewarded in heaven, Mother!" he said ironically.

They went to the top floor, where Zeinab stopped and drummed on a locked door. "He lodges here, the quiet one."

"Why do you call him 'quiet'?"

"Rafah gives no trouble. He goes out when it is dark. During the day he stays soundless in his room."

"Admirable tenant! When did he come?"

Zeinab considered. "Some seven months ago, I remember it was a month after I took in the holy man, Husain." She beat on the door again. "Strange! Rafah must be there; I did not see him go out."

The Inspector looked at the sergeant; Abdullah applied his shoulder and pushed the door in, deaf to the screeching of the woman. "Empty, sir," he intoned.

Nobody had lived in this room for a long time. The air was stale and the floor carpeted with dust. Chafik's shoulders drooped with defeat, and then straightened as he turned to the landlady.

"Did you lie to me, old woman?" he asked in a deadly calm voice.

She stared blankly into the room. "Rafah lives here! Every week he comes to me and pays the rent. He lives here! Would you have me doubt my eyes?"

"Surely those inquisitive eyes see everything. Or almost," Chafik added thoughtfully. "Did you perchance see his face?"

"It is covered. He said he had had an illness, and —"

The Inspector shrugged. "The same story, a faceless man; he lived here yet did not live here. Alas, old woman! You gave lodging to a jinni!"

Zeinab fled in terror, and Chafik, amused, pulled up a chair to the rickety table. He sat with elbows propped on the table, his chin in his hands. Sergeant Abdullah leaned against the wall, resignation on his dark face.

Time was measured by the pyramid of cigarette butts piled in a saucer. After a while Chafik said conversationally to himself: "Rafah went to her and paid his rent; she never had to come to this room. Now that's important, and so is his quietness. Oh, he was here, all right. She saw him go in and out and she sees everything. But what did he do all day? And how did he get out on Fridays in daylight without her seeing him?"

Chafik pulled at his tie and shouted, "The fellow's a Houdini! Look at that unimaginative cluck, Yusif, I had posted at the mosque: he had a tale about a house disappearing when Rafah was about!"

The Inspector's thoughts were diverted and he scratched himself, grumbling, "Bah! There are lice here in this filthy hole!" His thin face lighted up with humor and he said, mimicking the falsetto of his son: "They were sent to keep us awake so we can recite the Koran, my father."

Suddenly he stood up, so abruptly the chair fell over. "Abdullah!" he called. "Sir?"

"Reprimand me — I had forgotten something."

Chafik took an envelope from his pocket and carefully poured onto the table the fragments of dried mud he had swept from the floor of the murdered jeweler's shop. "Clay," he murmured, and he carefully picked out the larger pieces and fitted them together. Finally he had enough and turned wordlessly to his assistant.

The sergeant said, "Sir, I observe it is a beadlike object and there is an inscription on it: one of the names of God, sir."

" 'The Just,' " said Chafik. "And I remember another name — 'the Protector,' " he added.

Abdullah, now excited, exclaimed, "This is one of the amulets made by the holy man who sits at the mosque! The killer of Elias Samoon must have carried it as a talisman. Therefore at some recent time he must have bought it from Husain. Therefore Husain may remember him. Therefore —"

"Therefore do not put the untrained horse so eagerly to the fence!" Chafik interrupted. "However, I am encouraged by your reasoning. Kindly go to the jail where we hold Abu Nahabi, the Father of Thieves, and —"

"He is to hang?" the sergeant added hopefully.

"In due course, without a doubt. Meantime, release him and warn him by his neck to attend at the al-Waqi'ah Mosque with his fellow jackals. And, old friend —"

"Sir?"

"Telephone my home. Tell my son to gather his 'men' and bring them to the same place. Particularly I require the presence of a boy called George; he criticized my nose."

The sunset prayer had yet to be called when Inspector Chafik drove up in an open car and made a characteristic entrance; his shoulders were squared, the white jacket was perfectly set, and he was careful to turn his fine profile to the audience as he lighted a cigarette.

They were all there, the mob that Abu Nahabi had obediently gathered under the whip of fear. A group of urchins of assorted sizes and ages had been marshaled in the background by Faisal, who basked in his father's rediscovered authority.

Chafik made an ironic salaam and went to stand on the mosque steps near Husain the Voiceless. The holy man, disturbed by the gathering, pouched his amulets and shuffled away. The inspector gave a prearranged signal, and Sergeant Abdullah, master of ceremonies, ushered in the neighborhood policeman, who obviously disapproved of the performance in his street.

"Ah, Yusif, how your light runs before you!" Chafik said with gentle sarcasm. "Look about, faithful one, and tell me if the house has disappeared again."

Yusif ignored the audience and examined the street brick by brick. He frowned and then cried, "Indeed a house has disappeared! What a woodenhead I am, sir! The holy man isn't here; it was his absence I noticed the other time!"

Two plain-clothes men escorted Husain the Voiceless back to the mosque steps. The dirty and emaciated man clung to his hennaed beard and kept his eyes humbly lowered.

"I need all on my stage, and you went out on the wrong cue — for you," said the Inspector. "And you went so quietly, just as you always do, Husain the Voiceless, Rafah the Quiet ..."

The silence in the street made it unnecessary for Chafik to raise his voice as he went on: "I know by my records there was a maker of amulets named Husain who lived in the holy city of Kerbela. Perhaps he died, perhaps he was murdered, but a man who resembled him came to Baghdad eight months ago and was given lodging by the virtuous Zeinab. A month later one who called himself Ali Rafah, and who hid his face because he said it was ugly, came to the same house; yet he never occupied the room he rented. I submit this was the same man, holy by day and a hooded thief by night.

"This man is clever, very clever," continued Chafik. "Least of all was he suspected by the policeman who patrols this street. Yusif is too familiar with the scene; he did not see when Husain went away to do murder — he thought a house had disappeared!"

Then the Inspector said with pride, "It was a boy — my son — who noticed the major error. Holy men do not destroy the little things that bite them; they believe them to be blessed, sent to keep them awake to recite the Koran." He turned to Husain and reproachfully shook his head.

Husain still fingered his beard, but his eyes were watchful and on the mob.

"You fear them? Did you plan to cheat them?" Chafik asked, deliberately raising his voice. "Were you going to go away with the loot and leave them to hunt the sewers of Baghdad for their faceless leader? And where is all that loot, where are the pearls? What have you here, Husain the Voiceless, Rafah the Quiet?"

Chafik snatched the leather pouch the man wore at his side and opened it. He took out a clay bead and held it up: "This is one of many inscribed 'the Protector,'" he announced. "A jest he played with me when he rolled them in my presence, but not a nice jest to play thus with a name of God."

Between strong fingers the clay crumbled as Abu Nahabi and his friends pushed forward, their feet shuffling on the cobblestones. Inspector Chafik showed them the black pearl hidden in the amulet.

"Find your voice and confess, murderer!" he said to the silent man. "Or shall I leave you to them?" He got into the police car, and as it moved slowly away, the mob surged in on the criminal like a tide.

Clubs and knives came from under tattered robes. They were a jackal pack, the gutter sweepings of Baghdad, blind with hate and wanting blood. "Kill!" came the cry. "Kill! Kill!" And stones began to fly.

Husain ran after the police car. He clutched at the rear but could not hold it and fell; he got up and ran again. Stones battered him, and he shrieked: "Mercy! By the Compassionate One! Mercy!"

Chafik looked back and smiled. "God has so many names," he said. "One is 'the Just,' which was on the amulet you left by accident with Samoon's body!"

"Mercy! They'll kill me! They —"

"Confess!"

"I killed Samoon! I didn't intend — he came on me and knocked the cloth from my face and recognized me as Husain. I had to kill him then!"

The Inspector ordered the car to stop, and Sergeant Abdullah dragged the man to safety just in time. As they picked up speed, Chafik stood and called over the mob to his son, who ran with other whooping urchins in the rear.

"Faisal!"

"Yes, my father!"

"Tell George he is quite right, I do have a big nose — the better to smell criminals with, my son!"

Inspector Chafik, ego repaired, lighted a cigarette.

Death Starts a Rumor

One day in Baghdad, a small boy who carried his shoes dodged through the ferment of traffic on Rashid Street and arrived, miraculously unscathed, outside the drab headquarters of the security police. He ducked under the arm of the guard, threw open a door lettered *Chafik J. Chafik, Chief Inspector, Department of Criminal Investigation*, and cried, "My father! There is a man who will kill himself and it is not proper to do away with the life that has been given us and —" His breath gave out.

Inspector Chafik got up from his desk, which was walled in by filing cabinets, and angrily reprimanded the guard. "An assassin, instead of my son, might have made this unceremonious entry!" he said.

Chafik, immaculate in a well-tailored white suit appropriate for the hot summer of Baghdad, was a light, small-boned man whose swarthy face was sharpened by high cheekbones and a prominent nose. The profile he turned was as arrogant as that of a Babylonian king, but his face and voice softened as he said to the guard, "I do wrong to blame you. Nobody can stop my son when he is running. He is of the bazaars."

Chafik dismissed the guard and turned to the boy, gazing tenderly down at the elfin face and huge dark eyes. This was his adopted son. Chafik had chosen him from the many waifs who lived by their wits in the great bazaars of Baghdad, and taken him into a childless home. Polygamy, permitted by Islamic law if the first wife proves barren, was unacceptable to Chafik. He loved Leila, his lady of many happy years, very dearly, and they both loved the boy they had taken to be their son.

With effort the Inspector hardened his heart and said sternly, "Faisal! Why do you not wear the shoes your mother bought you?"

"My father, I do not wear shoes because I had to run faster than fast to tell you about the man who will murder himself, and shoes do not help the feet to go fast, and —"

"I have a slipper at home that goes very fast!"

Faisal looked pleadingly at his father. "Please do not spank me because I bring news Mr. Shaddock is going to cut his throat!"

"Eh? You say Shaddock?" exclaimed Chafik. He began talking to himself in a singsong voice: "*Shaddock, Ali. Age, fifty. Profession, import merchant. Recently suspected of smuggling activities, no previous conviction. Married. Name of wife —*" The Inspector heard himself quoting from the official dossier and stopped; thinking aloud was an old and unbreakable habit, but it never failed to annoy him.

"The wife is named Anina!" Faisal said quickly, eager to placate. "All Baghdad knows he is going to do it because of her, and because she left him, and because he must forfeit the dowry he gave her when they got married, and because he's pockets-down with debts, and —"

Chafik paced the carpet of his office, deep in thought and forgetful of the boy. "Nonsense!" he said sharply, as if to an adult. "The religious courts, which deal with matters concerning the dowry given by the husband to the wife, and with divorce, will decide in his favor. I am informed that there is another man in the story, that it is *she* who seeks the divorce."

"Everybody knows she had pulled him around by the nose these many years!" Faisal said.

Chafik became ruefully aware of his son. "Rumor shouts from the housetops!" he said. "You have been with the bazaar boys, that Army of Little Ears that infests keyholes!"

"It is true I had the report from my men, my father, but the tale is told every-where."

The Inspector sighed and gently drew Faisal to him. "About this matter of rumor," he began. "Listen! There was once a respected chicken, and she lost a feather searching for fleas with her beak. A second chicken told a third chicken about seeing the feather fall, but the gossiping chicken made it two feathers. So the news went around the coop, and each time *another* feather fell — until it was said the original chicken had plucked out all her feathers and was running about undressed. So they pounced on her, beat her, clucked, 'You're a disgrace!' and threw her out."

The Inspector raised an admonishing forefinger as he finished his parable: "Before you help spread rumor, my son, always remember how softly fell that first feather! Remember —"

The telephone interrupted. "Chafik J. Chafik!" he said curtly. Then, hearing a deep warm voice, he added hastily, "Never am I too busy to talk to you, Wife!"

"My man! Faisal has not yet returned from school, and I wondered if —"

"He is here and has no immediate desire to return home. A rendezvous has been made between a certain part of his anatomy and my slipper!"

The wife of the Inspector Chafik laughed. "Ah, so you say now!" she mocked. "Without doubt you will feed him honey cakes in a café somewhere and forget the matter of delinquency ... My man, I was at our sister's just now, and there was a lot of talk, and everybody wondered what you would do about Mr. Shaddock. He —"

"Wait!" Chafik broke in. "I have just narrated a parable on that subject to our son."

"So he knew too?"

"You both have unrivaled sources of rumor," Chafik said dryly and closed the conversation.

There had been a discreet knock on the door, and now a large man entered. He wore a sergeant's stripes, and the holster at his belt was as worn as his mahogany-colored face. "Sir!" he said and saluted.

The Inspector studied his door assistant and said, "Abdullah, you are the shadow of a kite hawk that circles over a desert kill!"

"Yes, sir," answered Sergeant Abdullah, and glanced disapprovingly at the Inspector's son.

"To send Faisal from us," said Chafik, "would only encourage his curiosity and leave him with the nasty answers of an uninstructed boy. You would not understand, Abdullah — you only have daughters."

"Three, sir. They curb their curiosity," the sergeant added smugly.

Chafik reddened. "Report!" he said gruffly.

"Sir," Abdullah announced, "the individual named Ali Shaddock, who is of interest to us, has apparently drowned himself. His body awaits you across the river, near the place where his estranged wife lives. I venture to point out that all this was anticipated. Everybody knew that Shaddock intended —"

"Enough!" Chafik's face flamed. He drove his fist into his palm and shouted, "Sons of jinn and evil spirits! All Baghdad knew he would kill himself — except me!" But his anger quickly passed, and he touched curved fingers to his forehead in a salaam to his sergeant. "Forgive me, Abdullah, as I hope the All Merciful will forgive me," the Inspector said humbly.

The brassy sun had set and silver stars were lighting up one by one when Inspector Chafik and his assistant arrived at the Karradat Miriam, a residential district on the other side of the Tigris. Here there were date palms, small farms and mellow old houses built on the embankment.

"This is the place," Abdullah said, and stopped the car on a parapet high above the river, which was very low at this time of the year. Chafik followed the sergeant down the steps to a boat landing.

Gentle ripples lapped against a dark bulk that had been dragged halfway up on the beach. Nearby waited a constable and a civilian. "This gentleman found the body," the constable told the Inspector. "He hailed me as I passed on patrol. He was trying to drag it out."

"So commendable!" said Chafik, glancing briefly at the civilian. "Your evidence will be required. I am sure the constable has all particulars. You are a stranger in Baghdad?"

"I am of Basra. Oh, what a dreadful experience! If only I had arrived sooner — just a few minutes — I might have saved this pitiable one who has damned his soul!" The man who spoke with such agitation was middle-aged, square and strong but a little soft with sedentary living. The expression in his olive-brown eyes was strained as he went on: "I was on my way to a café named the Pleasant Hours. So ironical —"

"No pleasant hour here for you," agreed Chafik.

"Such a thing to happen! Never in my life! I was walking, and I ..." The man went on to tell again how he had found the body.

The Inspector thought with tedium: Bah, these civilians, always the same — meet their first corpse, think it's never happened to anyone before, talk their heads off. His eyes fixed cynically on the man from Basra. "So the deceased was unconscious when you found him?"

"Oh, yes! I assure you I took action at once. I —"

"As you have told me," Chafik interrupted curtly. Then he made an effort at politeness: "But I have kept you too long. You are wet and the night is chilly after the day. My care is at your disposal." The Inspector salaamed, and the man turned away with obvious reluctance. "You didn't know the poor fool who drowned himself?" Chafik asked, and quickly berated himself when the man turned back.

"I do not even know his name. If I might be told why he —"

This time the Inspector's salaam was dismissal. Abdullah escorted the man to the car and instructed the driver to return.

Inspector Chafik glanced at the body and said dryly to the constable, "Of course, *you* know the name of this unfortunate one?"

"Ali Shaddock, sir! All Baghdad said he would —"

"— do away with himself." Chafik finished the sentence in a dangerously quiet voice. "I suppose you babbled all this to the gentleman, eh?"

The constable's look was reproachful. Chafik patted his arm. "Of course you wouldn't! And you got all his particulars?"

"He is named Mohammed Fahay, an official of the Port of Basra."

"I'll want a full report later. Meanwhile I'll interview this gentleman." The Inspector indicated the body at his feet.

When he finished the examination, Chafik took off his shoes and socks, pulled up his trousers and waded into the river. He went a long way out before the water reached his knees. "Where was the corpse found?" he called back.

The constable replied, "Nearer the bank than you now are, sir, according to Mr. Fahay. When I saw him he had it very near shore. He said he dragged it about ten meters, perhaps more."

"Fortunately, the gentleman is strong and Shaddock was slight." Chafik continued to wade out, but presently gave it up. "One can wade almost to the middle at this time of the year," he said when he came back. "The deep water is off the other bank; if *I* doubted the compassion of God, I would drown myself there."

He used a handkerchief to dry his feet, put on socks and shoes, and said to Sergeant Abdullah, "Well, let's go and tell Ali Shaddock's woman that Death has settled her divorce."

They walked along a path flanked by date palms. Packs of pariah dogs came to snarl at their heels and were driven off by Abdullah, who had filled his pockets with rocks.

"One never walks in these parts without provision," he said.

"You will doubtlessly present yourself at the gates of Paradise thoughtfully provided with equipment for the Other Place," Chafik said, smiling, and Abdullah grinned appreciatively.

Presently the sergeant said, "With reference to Shaddock's drowning, sir, I have the impression you are not satisfied it is suicide."

"I am puzzled," the Inspector admitted. "The water was so shallow. It takes a lot of courage to keep your head in a puddle to take your life."

"Yet he may have been desperate."

"We'll find out how desperate when we talk to his wife. Did you notice what was ejected from his lungs and stomach when you tried resuscitation?"

"Sand and mud, sir. Also specimens of the organisms that populate the river bed."

"In other words, he bit the muck down there. Isn't that the action of a man who struggled against a force more aggressive than his will power?" Chafik asked. Then he added thoughtfully: "And there's that mark on the neck — it could be a bruise."

"Do you suggest he was *held* under?" exclaimed Abdullah.

"At this stage I suggest nothing. I am not yet ready to weave, I still gather threads. Among other things, Abdullah, I want a careful check of that man, Fahay, who found the body."

"But he is a stranger to Baghdad, sir —"

"Precisely. Yet he spoke of Shaddock's damned soul. He didn't see the drowning, and if he didn't know Shaddock, why would he associate him with that wretched tale of suicide?"

"It would not take unusual powers of deduction, sir," said the sergeant. "He heard a man intended taking his life and then found a man drowned."

Chafik laughed. "Splendid, my dear Abdullah! I told you we are not ready for the weaving! Ah, well, let's give our knock and break the news to the lady here." He rapped his knuckles on the gate they had come to.

The path had led them to a fertile plantation where there was a small, neat house. This was the property Ali Shaddock had given his wife as a marriage gift, the disposition of which the divorce courts had questioned.

"I wouldn't have to be a policeman if I owned this," said Chafik.

There were lights in the house but nobody came, and the Inspector repeated his knock with authority. An old woman, a servant, finally opened the gate and said in a frightened voice, "What do you police want? My lady has retired. She —"

"You sound instructed," Inspector Chafik said.

He walked through the gate and stood a moment in the well-kept patio, drinking in the fragrance of night-blooming flowers. "There is much beauty behind the barred doors of Baghdad," he said with pleasure. "Also mystery," he added and indicated a shadow flattened to a wall.

Abdullah dragged into the light a young man, who wailed, "I'm only a visitor! I was leaving!" He had a sullen mouth, narrow eyes that would never come to meeting with another's and the dark grace of a panther.

The Inspector stood tiptoe and patted the youth's cheek. "Shaving is no problem," he said, and with distaste: "Can this be the delight of women with middle-aged husbands? I know you, Mr. Maqsud Majib. Because of you, the divorce courts question Mrs. Shaddock's right to this property."

"Such unfairness!" protested Majib, struggling in the sergeant's grip. "I only help work the estate. I —"

"A woman's marriage gift is a trust," Chafik said sternly. "I refer you to the excellent Koran: 'Give women their dowries as free gift; but if they of themselves be pleased to give you a portion of it back, then eat it with enjoyment.' "

The Inspector added, "You would eat it like a locust, Mr. Majib."

A shadow loomed over him and Chafik turned and made a salaam to an unveiled lady who stood as tall as Juno. She was of an age when a woman has the startling beauty of the fall somberly edged with regret for the spring. "What is this talk about locusts?" she demanded in a strong voice.

"Madame, my nimble tongue is shamed by your quick ears."

"Let your face show shame also. Majib spoke the truth. He works this land as my overseer, yet the courts have decided against me!"

"But the news is not yet public. I heard it only a little time ago. Who told you, lady?" Chafik's voice was softer than the purring of a cat.

"My husband."

"He was here?"

"You know that. You came to arrest him!" The strong voice rang with rage. "*You* sent the false message telling Ali I wished to see him! A trap!"

The Inspector was startled. Forgetful of manners, he lighted a cigarette without asking the lady's permission. "Why should I want to arrest your husband?" he asked.

"Ali said he had done something; he did not explain, but he said he was going to confess. The fool babbled some nonsense about prison being cleansing!" the wife of Ali Shaddock added with contempt.

Chafik thought: Yet rumor would have it that he damned himself by taking his life. He said, "What else did he tell you?"

"The decision of the courts. He said, too, that he would make me an allowance." The woman added grudgingly, "In many ways he was a just man."

"I hear regret in your voice, Madame — possible remorse."

"I hear a snake's hiss in yours!"

"They always say that about me." Chafik watched the woman carefully. "When did Mr. Shaddock leave you?"

"Perhaps an hour ago."

"And was your overseer hidden on the premises at the time?"

The woman towered dangerously and the Inspector retreated a step. "Majib came later!" she cried. "Later!"

"I was at a café!" the youth insisted. "The Pleasant Hours, up the river —"

"The place recently mentioned by somebody else," Chafik said thoughtfully. He crushed his cigarette under his heel and then stooped, with instinctive tidiness, to pick up the stub. Still crouched, he saw the legs of Majib's trousers; they were oddly crumpled for a young fop. The Inspector reached out, touched the fabric and announced, "Wet!" in the voice of an accuser.

"I stumbled into an irrigation ditch," Majib said quickly. "It was dark —"

"Strange you should not know the pitfalls of the land you work!"

The Inspector straightened up, and this time he did not retreat when the imposing Madame Shaddock came between him and Majib. "Your questions, like fishhooks, are barbed," she said. "Why are you here?"

He waited a moment before he replied, "Madame, do you not know a detestable individual like myself always walks at Death's heels? Your husband drowned himself after he left you."

The wife of Ali Shaddock shrieked, put hands to her piled hair, tore it down and was constrained by the Inspector when she sought to beat her head against the wall. The excessive grief did not surprise him; he was wise to the women of the country who employed histrionics and the purdah veil to hide their true emotions.

Chafik gave Madame Shaddock into the keeping of the old servant woman. "You don't seem very keen to comfort your lady," he said to the young man.

"I didn't know her husband was here," Majib protested. "I was in the café. Besides, all Baghdad knew he was going to do away with himself."

"Did I say he *didn't*?" asked Chafik. He kept his eyes on Madame Shaddock, who was staring at Majib with horror — and perhaps fear.

"You fool!" she said harshly, "did you not hear him say Ali drowned himself!" All at once she crumpled, and the servant led her away.

Watching, Chafik felt compassion born of sudden understanding. She had come to a place in life where she stood on the crest of the hill and felt panic at the descent. It is a moment women encounter, Chafik thought, and men too. She was a woman who had no children to compensate for the lost vanities of youth. No children, and now no husband, and she knew her lover to be craven. Whatever her guilt, she had paid dearly.

Chafik sighed and turned to the young man and said, "Go to your Café of the Pleasant Hours; you will find no more of them here!" He turned to his assistant. "Come, Abdullah," he said and the two men walked back to the car and drove away.

The sergeant stopped the car outside the small house in the Street of the Scatterer of Blessings. "The detestable young man was eager to establish an alibi," he said.

"You will check it, Abdullah."

Chafik opened the gate to the forecourt of his house, and the squeaking hinges reminded him they needed oiling. "All that talk about Shaddock's doing away with himself — as noisy as this gate," he complained. "Too well publicized, that suicide. Somebody was very anxious to make us believe it."

"We must discover how the rumor started, sir," Abdullah said.

"Yes, but booted policemen with blunt questions, or furtive agents with oily insinuations, will get us nowhere. Rumor is a sly, night-living thing; the trail it leaves is tenuous, as fragile as a spider's thread. We will begin where the trail ended — with my son."

"But, sir!" the sergeant exclaimed.

"Faisal heard the story from his friends, the bazaar boys. I'll get him to trace it back through them." The Inspector closed his ears to objection, said good night and went into the house. At the door, Faisal took his father's shoes and placed them under the hall table, and then humbly presented a slipper. "By your command, my father! It is for that spanking I'm to get for breaking in on you with the news about Mr. Shaddock."

Chafik, who had forgotten the incident, said fondly, "Honey cakes!" and gave Faisal a package. "And there is important business to discuss with you, my small Captain of the Most Irregular Army of Little Ears!"

Inspector Chafik sat in his office overlooking Rashid Street, talking to himself. The ash tray at his elbow was neatly stacked into with butts and, adding another to the pile, he said, "You are as well smoked as an Englishman's kipper, Chafik!" He lighted a fresh cigarette and stared at the reports on his desk.

There was proof that the bruise on Shaddock's neck had been made by a weighty object. Medical opinion said he had been partially stunned, then dragged into the river. "They drowned him like a helpless kitten!" Chafik said.

Abdullah, entering unobtrusively, asked, "Who are 'they,' sir?"

"The prize for that question is a hangman's noose. But we have no clues, nothing that points to anyone," the Inspector said plaintively. "There is Majib. He was obviously planning to marry the lady for her property; he had every reason to get rid of Shaddock before the divorce was final."

"But the courts had decided, sir —"

"Majib had not heard the decision." Chafik added reluctantly, "Madame Shaddock could have been a party to the deed."

"It is not without precedent," agreed the sergeant.

"Worse, she might have done it herself. She is strong enough, was infatuated enough. If that evil youth induced her to ... Ah, what an ugly pattern I weave!" The little man sighed. "And then there's Fahay."

"The gentleman who discovered the body, sir?"

"A report from Basra states he is a minor port official," Chafik said. "He checks goods coming into port against the importer's license. Therefore —"

"Shaddock dealt in contraband!" Abdullah said excitedly. "Fahay could have forged documents to release goods from bond!"

"You leap on a theory with the frenzy of a honey-drunk bee in a clump of honeysuckle, Abdullah. True, Shaddock had an illegal trade. Poor man." Chafik continued with regret, "he was tempted when he thought he had to pay the dowry. Then the courts decided in his favor and his worries were over. But God had given him a conscience, so he decided to confess."

"And was killed to silence his tongue!" exclaimed the sergeant.

"There you go again," Chafik said peevishly. "We have nothing against Mr. Fahay. The Port Directorate where he works is a department heavy with paper work, and with bottomless filing cabinets. It would take a lifetime to uncover evidence — if there is any!"

He added wearily, "My hopes hang on the fragile thread of the suicide rumor. If I knew who started it, if my son would only bring news!"

Abdullah said briskly, "Faisal has had his chance. Permit me to —"

The Inspector put a finger to his lips. "Sh-sh! I think news arrives."

There was an uproar in the corridor, the thump of boots, the shrill voice of a boy and the gruff one of a man. And then Faisal came in, firmly held by the guard, who said with satisfaction, "He did not pass me this time!"

"This time," Chafik said dryly, "I expected my son. Release him."

When the crestfallen officer left, Chafik sat back in his chair, closed his eyes and said, "Report!"

Faisal began: "The story that Mr. Shaddock would kill himself was told me by George, one of my men, the one that's got red hair. George's father was an English soldier, and —"

"Confine yourself to the rumor."

"Yes, my father. George heard from Ali of the One Eye, who was told by Haik the Armenian, who had it from Yusif. Yusif got it from Habib of the Clubfoot, who overheard Ibrahim the Coppersmith telling Hamid the Carpetweaver. And Mr. Ibrahim, when I asked him, remembered he'd been told by Murad the Porter, who said he heard it from Ishak —"

"Do you bring all the population of Baghdad into this?"

"I near the end," said Faisal. "Ishak brought the tale from across the river. He heard it in a café, but doesn't remember who told him, and —"

"What is the name of the café?"

"It is called the Pleasant Hours, my father."

The Inspector's eyes opened; they glowed like the stone in the signet ring on the small finger of his left hand. "I hear that café mentioned a third time!" he cried, and then was silent.

Faisal and Sergeant Abdullah waited side by side; the boy stood like his giant companion, hands behind his back, legs apart, the military position of "at ease." The clock on the wall ticked noisily.

When the Inspector finally looked up, he said, "My little Captain of the Army of the Ears, do you recall the parable I told you about the chicken?"

Faisal came to attention. "Yes, my father. There was a chicken and it plucked out one feather, and all the other chickens said it had lost many, and —"

"Go," said Chafik, "and drop a feather very softly to your man George, who will tell Ali, who will tell Hassan, who ... Oh, just let it be known that Mr. Shaddock did *not* take his life — he was murdered!"

"His throat was cut? There was blood?" Faisal asked breathlessly.

"Go!" said the Inspector.

He sat at his desk, deep in thought, until it was dark. His sergeant eventually took him home ...

The next day Chafik went to the office, greeted nobody, and sat in thought as before. Abdullah brought him reports. He said, "Sir, it is rumored all over Baghdad now that Mr. Shaddock was murdered."

"He was," Chafik said. He was silent for another hour, and then he said, "Bring me the Captain of Little Ears."

Faisal, schooled by Abdullah, came and saluted. Chafik gazed at him. "Go," he ordered, "and drop another feather. Let all Baghdad know that at precisely six o'clock tomorrow evening I shall arrive at the Café of the Pleasant Hours to arrest the killer of Mr. Shaddock!"

Faisal forgot discipline, clapped his hands and asked, "Can I come too?"

"Go!" his father said.

When Faisal went, Sergeant Abdullah risked reprimand. "Sir! I am ignorant of your intentions, but I believe that the murderer will be alarmed by this latest rumor, that he will become dangerous."

"Murder," announced the Inspector, "is not the prerogative of the male sex. Danger, however, is the prerogative of the police."

The third day Chafik was early at his desk. He sat and stared at the wall. He did not eat; he did not smoke. He thought about the feather of rumor, and he hoped and feared that somewhere, someone who dealt in death would accept the appointment he had made. He knew himself to be afraid.

The sergeant came to him at the hour of 'Asr, the late-afternoon prayer. "Majib is drinking heavily," he announced.

"It will corrode his liver," Chafik said. "Then he will die. Good!"

"The man Fahay canceled his flight to Basra this morning."

"Doubtlessly he finds the fleshpots of Baghdad hard to leave."

"The woman, Madame Shaddock," said Abdullah, "has been seen walking in the date grove, as one obsessed."

"She mourns either her husband or her lover," said the Inspector.

"And the lady, your wife, is on the wire, sir."

Chafik took the telephone, and hearing the voice of his Leila, peace came to him. "The music of Paradise could not be sweeter," he told her.

"My man, I am frightened! I hear you are going to the café to arrest the murderer of Mr. Shaddock. Madame Bassmachi brought me the news, and she heard it from Madame —"

The Inspector said, "I've heard something like that before! Do not worry, my Leila." He hung up the telephone.

He reached for his *sidarah* and set the black cap squarely on his head. He adjusted his polka-dot tie, passed a finger over his thin mustache and said to Sergeant Abdullah, "Let us go!"

The Inspector refused a car, and walked to the Café of the Pleasant Hours in the twilight. A policeman on traffic duty saluted and called, "Good fortune, sir!" and a beggar at the foot of the great bridge that crossed the Tigris cupped a hand for alms and mumbled, "A thousand sons! May you take the evil one who killed Shaddock!"

Out of nowhere darted a small boy, redheaded and freckled, who touched the Inspector's hand, gave a toothless smile and announced, "We will be there to help you!" He hitched up ragged trousers, his only garment, and ran ahead.

"Without doubt that is Faisal's man George," said Chafik.

He stopped in the middle of the bridge and wiped his forehead. Sergeant Abdullah looked at him with understanding and said in a strained voice, "An abnormally hot night, sir."

"On the contrary, it is abnormally cool. I perspire because I am frightened. Even the shrilling of the birds becomes the whistle of an assassin's bullets. I am a coward."

"You go *to* the rendezvous, sir, not away from it."

"Thank you, Abdullah. You are right; fear is not a synonym for cowardice."

"You expect the murderer to be there?" asked the sergeant.

"I have used a powerful magnet," said Chafik. "The murderer will have to know if identification has really been made, if clues have been discovered. Killers have often been known to attend the funerals of their victims."

Beyond the bridge was a broad way lined with cafés. The Inspector walked slowly and watchfully; at his side loomed Abdullah, the flap of this holster open and his hand ready, like the inflated hood of a cobra raised for a strike. "Walk well behind me," Chafik said sharply. "Even the innocent would swoon at the sight of you!"

He increased his pace and came to a great arch, a monument to past glory; opposite was a café. The green benches set out under dusty locust trees were crowded, and the sound of excited conversations filled the night. As the Inspector crossed the road, the noise stopped.

He came to a group of women, alike in shapeless black robes worn with a fold over the head to hide the face. One tall, stately woman stood apart, and Chafik thought: There could be a gun under that chuddar! He walked quickly by Madame Shaddock.

Then he was stopped by a man he hardly recognized, the once-handsome face was so distraught. The man shrieked, "I didn't! I didn't!"

"Didn't what?" asked Chafik.

"I didn't kill Shaddock! *She* killed him!" Majib cried. "She knew I wouldn't marry her unless she had title to the estate. These old women! What they'll do —"

The Inspector stood tiptoe and, using the inside of his forearms, hit Majib, right, then left, on the side of the head. It was a merciless battering and, when the youth collapsed, Chafik said with disgust, "The thing you've murdered is your manhood."

Beyond, Mr. Fahay sat alone at a table. The man from Basra looked very old, and his olive-brown eyes stared into space.

The Inspector said, "You and I, Mr. Fahay, both perspire on a cool night; we are equally afraid." He went and stood at the table and his hands pressed the marble top for support. "You were very courteous to keep the appointment. However, I thought you would. You were very curious when we first met; you wanted to stay and watch me. I had to dismiss you."

The man from Basra said nothing.

"I admire your quick thinking," continued Chafik. "The constable on patrol almost caught you drowning Shaddock, so you pretended you were making a rescue. And that rumor you spread in advance about suicide was excellently planned, although overdone. Of course, you knew Shaddock's confession would give you away?"

"He — he confessed?" The olive-brown eyes were dazed. "I — I don't understand. He wrote me he was going to, but said he'd wait — to give me a chance to get out of the country. I was sure I was in time to —" The bewildered mumbling stopped, and the man's eyes widened with knowledge of what he had admitted.

"How unthankful of you to kill such a thoughtful partner!"

"I had a fortune at stake!" cried the man from Basra. "You devil! Satan's son!" he shouted and brought his hand out from under the table.

The Inspector looked into the eye of an automatic. His slight body blocked the marksmanship of Sergeant Abdullah, who by order had stopped at the café entrance. Chafik thought of Leila, of Faisal, of the long years behind him and the brief seconds before him.

He told Mr. Fahay, "The hangman can stretch your neck only once; therefore, secularly speaking, you lose nothing if you kill me."

Chafik watched the trigger finger tighten; there was a lump in his throat. He continued in a strong voice, "But your soul, soon to go to God, is more complex than your neck. The Compassionate One might cleanse it of one killing, never of two. If you kill me, then for all Eternity your soul will suffer the Pit, sulphurous fires ..."

The Inspector leaned heavily on the table; his legs no longer gave support, but he did not collapse until Mohammed Fahay turned the gun on himself.

When Chafik left the café, Madame Shaddock came to him and timidly touched his arm. Her face was hidden by the fold of the chuddar and she spoke in a humble voice. "You avenged my man —"

"Only God is vengeance," the Inspector told her.

"I drove him to his death with my foolish infatuation for Majib. What shall I do now?" she asked like a child.

"Pray," said Inspector Chafik. "I too am going to pray for your husband, and for the one who killed him." He smiled in compassion and turned and walked away into the night.

The Man Who Wasn't There

Abdul Rahim, a fledgling constable of the City of Baghdad police, halted a department car at the intersection of Rustan Higidar and the New Bund Road. The sergeant driver, a dour veteran, growled, "Debase yourself, you fool!" — and jerked his chin to indicate the passenger.

The passenger, a small man neatly dressed in a lightweight civilian suit, said, "Abdullah, suffer the officer to approach me."

He eased himself from the low slung car and stood tiptoe, an unconscious habit that gave him more stature. He wore on his sleek head the black *sidarah* of the modern Iraqi. His face was thin, his large eyes were the drab color of desert sands where shadows drifted darkly like the shadows of kite gathering to a kill. "I am Chafik J. Chafik, Chief Inspector," he announced.

The constable, Chafik noted as he looked up into the tall young man's gaping mouth, needed dental care. I must reprimand the medical department, he said to himself. "Speak up!" he went on in a kindly voice. "Fear only God — the punishment I inflict is brief, His is eternal."

"Sir — I — it's about the man who isn't there —" stammered Constable Abdul Rahim.

"If he isn't there, why does be concern us?"

"But — but he *is* there, sir! He goes up the stairs. Mr. Faris has seen him. I keep constant watch, but —"

An ominous sound came from Sergeant Abdullah, whose bulk dwarfed the constable. "Permit me to discipline him," he said to Inspector Chafik, then turned his carved mahogany face to the hapless constable and roared, "Hup, you! What did they teach you at the Academy, hey? To give evidence clearly, concisely, chronologically, hey? Then do so, Father of Imbeciles!"

"Enough, Abdullah," the Inspector intervened.

Constable Rahim stood at attention, closed his eyes, and stated, "Sir, I was on duty patrolling Rustan Gardens when I was called to house number 12/4 New Bund Road occupied by the complainant, Zakir Faris. Mr. Faris said his premises had been entered by an unauthorized person. At his request I entered the premises and conducted a search. I did not find the alleged intruder, but there were alien footprints on the stairs to an unoccupied upper floor —"

"The front door to the house was closed?"

"Yes, sir, and secured by a heavy bar —"

"Yet the intruder passed the barrier and left footprints? Curious. Either a *jinni* or a creature of Mr. Faris' imagination."

"Imagination!" snorted Sergeant Abdullah.

"But I was called to the house three times this week!" protested the constable. "On each occasion I found footprints on the stairs — and the complainant states he has seen the intruder —"

"And very properly you went for reinforcements," interrupted Inspector Chafik. "We are at your disposal." He patted the officer's arm, a habit he had to comfort one distressed.

Sergeant Abdullah said, "Sir, may I remind you of your appointment with the Director?"

"He is a civilian. We are policemen. The Director can wait."

They drove to the address, a narrow-fronted house isolated by a highway in process of construction. It had been built in the Turkish era of Baghdad and had an old-world, but shabby, elegance. The house was also a fortress: iron grilles protected all the windows and those on the upper and lower unoccupied floors were also heavily shuttered. The man who lived here was obsessively fearful, for it was a quiet neighborhood. Nearby was the Soldiers' Garden, Iraq's Arlington, and the villas of wealthy Baghdadis. A neighborhood, thought Chafik, where a fledgling constable could try out his wings with few bruises. He smiled at the troubled young man.

"Inform me about Mr. Faris," he commanded.

"An Egyptian, sir. A recluse — no friends or visitors, no servants. A learned man. He has many books.

"And that is all you know?" The Inspector twisted the signet ring on the small finger of his left hand and his eyes reflected the ruddy glow of the stone as he recited: "Faris, Zakir. Born, Cairo, 1910. Profession, journalist. Editor of the defunct newspaper, Al Ra'ad. Exiled for political activities, escaped severe sentence due to influence of his elder brother, who recently died. Only remaining relative, a nephew, Gamal Faris, from whom he receives a monthly pittance."

Chafik returned the dossier to the filing cabinet of his brain and said sternly to the discomforted constable, "You must memorize the records of everybody who lives in your area, with special attention to political misfits."

He squared his thin shoulders with the dignity of a Babylonian god-king, and entered the house.

Stone steps mounted to a landing, then continued to the upper floor. Here the stairway narrowed and they mounted in single file with Abdullah, as always, close behind the Inspector. The stairs were carpeted with dust which filtered from the moonscape of desert that surrounded the city. There was a confusion of footprints in which the square toes of police boots were prominent.

"I was very careful to avoid the tracks of the intruder, but Mr. Faris smudged them," explained the constable.

"Mr. Faris wears slippers?"

"Yes, sir."

"He favors the left leg. The other individual wore new shoes. One asks, why are the soles unblemished? Small shoes, possibly a small man, a lightweight — but he stamps when he marches." The Inspector fingered the line of his mustache and added, "A disembodied being should not have feet."

The tracks led to the upper floor and ended at a closed door.

"What is beyond?" asked Inspector Chafik.

"An empty room, so I understand, sir. I hesitated to force an entrance." The constable was nervous and eased the high collar of his tunic; then, alerted by a shuffling on the stairway, he wheeled and drew his gun with a speed which brought a grunt of approval from Sergeant Abdullah, in whose cobra-hooded hand a Mauser materialized.

The man who was now climbing the stairs wore a gray robe and flapping slippers. He was troubled by his left leg and eased it carefully on the high treads. A tall man, light-boned, narrow-chested, possibly consumptive, Chafik judged by the occasional racking cough. And, yes, frightened, he thought, noting the wide staring eyes. Or alarmed, perhaps by me? He corrected his first impression and stored the thread of thought or later weaving.

Zakir Faris recovered his breath. "I demand protection," he said.

"You have it. *I* am here." Chafik introduced himself.

The corners of the man's wide mouth turned down. "I am grateful. But this — this intrusion — should not concern your Excellency —"

"My stomach is flat, therefore I am not an Excellency." Chafik tapped the door of the closed room with a manicured fingernail. "There is a key?"

Zakir Faris shook his head.

"Lovers and policemen laugh at locksmiths," said Inspector Chafik, and nodded to Abdullah.

The sergeant braced, raised a foot, flexed his knee, and drove an ironshod heel against the lock. The door crashed back on rusty hinges.

They looked into an attic-smelling room.

Nothing.

Sunshine slanted through weathered shutters and made a prison pattern on the dusty floor.

But no footprints.

"I heard him walk!" exclaimed Zakir Faris. "So did the constable," he added, turning to the young man.

Chafik also looked at the officer.

"Sir! — on the second occasion Mr. Faris called me I heard the intruder. I was in the apartment below this room and Mr. Faris called my attention —"

"How did the intruder walk? Lightly? Heavily?"

Officer Rahim's forehead creased. "Walked," he said. "Just footsteps —"

"In future pay attention to the sound of footsteps. Footsteps can be firm — an honest man going assured to his destination. Or hesitant — a man doubtful, unwilling, or guilty. Or dancing and gay — a man going to his mistress. Footsteps, Constable, are talkative, but the footsteps of this intruder apparently failed even to whisper. Seal the door, Abdullah," Chafik added to the sergeant.

He went down to Zakir Faris' apartment. The rooms were small, stuffy, and cluttered. In the main room were many books, as the constable had noted, and Chafik lingered, browsed, then said in precise English, "You have a very interesting library, Mr. Faris. All your books are from Foyle's of London."

"I attended the University of London — I took my degree in literature," Faris said proudly.

"I envy you. My English is of local vintage. No color. Robot talk, suitable for my profession. Ah, poetry!" Chafik exclaimed as he took out a book which was pushed to the back of a shelf.

It opened at a dog-eared page; he shook his head disapprovingly as he smoothed out the corner, then read aloud: "'The Psychoed' — what an odd title! 'Hugh Means, 1875'..." His voice trailed, he muttered in Arabic, then came back to English as he quoted from the text: "'As I was going up the stair, I met a man who wasn't there'... How very appropriate, Mr. Faris!" The Inspector's thin nose twitched.

"Yes, that is why I marked the page —"

"It goes on: 'He wasn't there again today, I wish, I wish he'd go away,' " Chafik completed the couplet.

"My wish, too! But he was there, Inspector — I saw him clearly, a small dark man with a scar on his left cheek, prominent eyes, pointed ears almost like horns. He stood where the stair turns, bowed, went up — and vanished!"

Constable Rahim interrupted, "Sir, I did not actually see him, but there was a shadow on the stair —"

"You had just entered?"

"Yes —"

"The sunshine outside was bright?"

"High noon, sir."

Sergeant Abdullah laughed and said, "His stomach was empty!"

The Inspector disapproved. "Empty stomachs rumble, they do not see," was his sharp comment, and the sergeant accepted the reproof with a salaam.

Chafik toured the apartment, looked at clothing, and rooted out a pair of dusty shoes from a closet. "New?" he asked.

"I hope to wear them one day." Zakir Paris indicated his slippered feet. "Gout," he explained.

"I sympathize. We of the police also suffer from swollen feet. But these shoes look too small for you." The Inspector glanced at his watch and said to Sergeant Abdullah, "We have kept the Director too long. He will be bleating for his shepherd. There is nothing more to do here. I leave it to the officer."

He patted the constable's arm. "That man on the stair who isn't there would make an interesting trophy. Bring him to me — when you see him."

"Yes, sir!" The young man touched his holstered gun.

On the way back to the city Inspector Chafik confided to his assistant, "I don't like it. I don't like it at all. On the surface, so silly — and yet ..." His voice trailed; then lost in thought he announced, "I gave bad advice —"

"To whom, sir?" asked the patient sergeant.

"That young man — our rookie —"

"Permit me to express an opinion, sir. Constable Rahim has the makings of a good policeman —"

The Inspector looked at Abdullah with astonishment. "You, too?" he said. Then he went on in his mixture of thinking and talking. "But he is so inexperienced. We should not leave him with this problem — so inexperienced, and I smell evil somewhere —"

"There are roses in your garden — the Constable is a very fast gun," Sergeant Abdullah said comfortingly.

The following day, shortly before *Zuhr*, the midday prayer, Inspector Chafik was in his office on the second floor of a building on upper al-Rashid Street, when Sergeant Abdullah made silent entry. The Inspector, tied up with detested paper work, was annoyed.

"From where do you ooze?" he asked sharply. Then, recognizing the look that cracked the veneer of the big man's mahogany face, he pushed aside the papers. "Who? Where? What?" he asked.

"Sir, the man who wasn't there — in the house of Zakir Faris — shot, by Constable Abdul Rahim —"

"A dead ghost cannot be classified as a corpse."

"The corpse," said Sergeant Abdullah, "is that of Mr. Faris' nephew, Gamal Faris, who made an unexpected visit to his uncle. He closely resembles the alleged intruder. The constable challenged him — the deceased ignored the order. I have ascertained the deceased suffered with deafness —"

"And the constable is a fast gun."

"Yes, sir."

"That budding rose in my garden has pricked my finger," Inspector Chafik said bitterly.

Long after *Isha*, the late prayer, the sergeant again intruded on his superior. Chafik had not moved from his desk; he sat crouched under a fog of cigarette smoke, and the ashtray at his elbow had grown a *ziggurat* of neatly stacked butts. "Do not tell my wife, Leila. She warns me of my smoking — she insists I set a bad example for our son, Faisal," said the Inspector as he opened a new pack of *Ghazis*.

"I do not have that trouble. I have daughters," Abdullah said smugly.

"Four," said Inspector Chafik, and added absently, "Sons such as mine may be your trouble later, my friend."

His long fingers flexed like the legs of a spider spinning a web; sometimes he plucked an invisible thread from the air and added it to his weaving. He muttered. Then he said aloud, "What a devil!" Then he went back to silence and his fingers moved faster, twisting and knotting. The understanding sergeant waited.

"A complicated and dark pattern," Chafik announced in a clear voice.

"So I observe, sir."

"Dark and ugly."

"Yes, sir. Dark and ugly for the constable," said Abdullah, "who has been suspended. Dark and ugly for ourselves. Mr. Faris has been to the Director, crying and complaining that you left an inexperienced officer in charge —"

"The complaint is justified. I am at fault."

The sergeant raised his hands in protest, palms outward, like shields.

"I need no defense," Chafik said sternly. "When I told the constable to bring me the man who wasn't there as a trophy, my humor was misplaced. He obeyed literally. All this is part of a pattern, the device of a remarkable, but sick, brain. Abdullah, do you believe that an individual entered Mr. Faris' house through a barred door, walked up the stairs, bowed to him, and then vanished in a locked room?"

"Without a precedent, sir."

"There is always a precedent!" The Inspector rearranged scattered papers, marshaled the pencils on his desk, removed specks of dust with a crisp white handkerchief. When he spoke again, it was with the uninflected intonation of self-talk, an incurable habit. "Footprints," he said. "New shoes — flat-footed impressions — too clear — stamped, no weight of body above them." Shadows swirled and shaped in the radar screens of his eyes and with an abrupt return to normal communication he asked his assistant, "Where were there new shoes?"

"In Mr. Faris' closet, sir."

"Mr. Faris said they were unworn because of his gout. An unsatisfactory explanation, since the shoes were too small for him. Yes, new — yet there was dust on the soles. The shoes could have been manipulated by a man's hands as he cautiously crawled up the stairs —"

Sergeant Abdullah exclaimed, "God and by God!"

"The constable heard footsteps in the upper room. Who drew his attention to them?" asked Inspector Chafik.

"Faris! — the complainant."

"And when blinded by the midday sun the constable entered the house and saw a shadow on the stair — *'I wish, I wish he'd go away'*— who?"

"Faris!"

"And who described the intruder? A small dark man, with a scar on his left cheek, pointed ears, prominent eyes? — and forgot to add that his nephew was deaf?"

"Faris!"

"And who had a book of poetry — this Hugh Mearns who wrote *The Psychoed*, all about a man who wasn't there, on a stair?"

"Faris! — I remember the book was pushed to the back of a shelf and had a dog-eared page. Did this give him the idea, sir?" Sergeant Abdullah looked down at the neat little man sitting at the tidy desk. "But — motive?"

"Oh, Father of Policemen, that I have, too!" Inspector Chafik took forms pasted with teletype from his in-tray. "My flying carpet is the telephone — and there is Interpol," he said, and then sat back and defiantly lit another cigarette.

The agent of the Cairo police had reported that Gamal Ahmed Faris had applied for permission to visit Baghdad to discuss family business, and had submitted pleading letters from his uncle, Zakir Faris, to support the application. Travel restrictions fixed the date of his departure. "So Mr. Faris had prior knowledge of his nephew's arrival," commented Abdullah.

"Conceivably —"

"Then he lied when he said the visit was unexpected! I smell a sulphurous devil!" shouted the sergeant.

"Abdullah, please. I have a headache — and you have yet to read the final enlightenment." He produced a flimsy with a conjurer's flourish.

"... *Interpol, Cairo. Pers. Chafik CID Baghdad. Ref. estate Faris, deceased. Further ref. death nephew. Gamal Ahmed Faris. Uncle Zakir Faris inherits...*

Sergeant Abdullah forgot himself and struck the Inspector's desk. He swore, then disciplined himself — he was a religious man, a Shia'a by persuasion. "May I be forgiven my oaths," he said, bowing over his folded hands. Then he shouted, "May that Father of Devils rot in the Pit! He tricked the constable — he made him his gun! — and there is no way to bring him to the scaffold!"

Inspector Chafik tidied the cigarette butts scattered by his assistant's hammering fists. "There is way," he said softly.

"He will never confess!"

"When we sin, Abdullah, we confess to God. This man knows his guilt, and his earthly punishment is prescribed in the second chapter, verse one hundred and seventy-eight, of the Book. Recite it," he added sharply.

The tall dark sergeant bowed his head. " '*Retaliation is prescribed for you in the matter of the slain*'," he quoted in the sonorous voice of a prayer-caller. "'*Free for the free, slave for a slave, female for female . . . and whoever exceeds the limit —*' "

"My limit," interrupted Inspector Chafik, as he lit a cigarette, "is not excessive. That man on the stair who wasn't there, but caused Constable Abdul Rahim to kill the nephew of Zakir Faris, can do it again."

He outlined his plan ...

"But it is not Law!" protested Abdullah.

"Law is a code of public order, a man-made deterrent demanding facts. Law is an ass," Chafik added in his precise English.

"Sir! — but what you suggest — I beg you to reconsider — sir!"

Inspector Chafik turned a face cast from bronze — in profile a plaque from the death-pits of Ur, the likeness of an ancestor who had lived before Noah. His drab eyes, cynical with the knowledge of centuries, stared down the Arab. "You will do what I command. God is Justice — and sometimes we of the police are His instrument," he said.

He stood, a small man with high shoulders, and went to the window. The city was dark, but somewhere in the acres of flat-roofed houses and drab streets, there was awakening. Stars in the vaulted sky went out one by one; then, beginning far away in the direction of the shrine of Kademein, echoed the first wailing call to prayer, the muezzin's nightingale song. Chafik turned to his assistant.

"Morning," he said. "Let us go and say *Fajr* together."

Sergeant Abdullah drove him from the mosque to the house on the Street of the Scatterer of Blessings where Chafik lived. The Inspector said to his assistant, "Tell the Director I am unwell — a virus is a suitable lie."

He went in and said to his dark-haired wife, Leila, "I am going to bed. Bring me a crying towel — I have much to weep about."

And he said to his son, Faisal, a boy with large eyes and faunlike ears, who came sleepily from his room to kiss his father's hand, "Do well at the lyceum, my son — you may have to support your mother."

Then he removed his clothes, tidily folded them, cleaned his teeth, and took sanctuary in the bed perfumed by his wife.

On the first day of Inspector Chafik's retirement a constable — not Abdul Rahim who had been removed from duty — hammered on the door of Zakir Faris' house and called, "Sir, did somebody enter? I thought I saw a man —"

"You have visions," Zakir said, and slammed shut the window.

On the second day the same officer disturbed the noon rest hour with his whistle. "Is your door secured, sir?" he asked urgently.

"Locked and barred —"

"Keep it so, sir — there are strangers about."

On the third day, near sunset, when the house-martins dived in the cooling air and fluted to their mates, another officer knocked and cried, "Open, sir! — I have seen a small, dark man —"

"Go away!" said Zakir Faris.

On the fourth day, near midnight, a police car roared to a halt and a sergeant flourishing a gun shouted, "Stop! Stop!" He then kicked the door. "Somebody entered your house, sir," he said to the gray-faced man at the window.

"Impossible," Zakir said.

"But we saw him! I must search the premises — I have orders to protection."

"Go away!" screamed Zakir.

On the fifth day a mobile searchlight unit, stationed at the intersection of the Higidar and the New Bund road, blazed into action. Zakir Faris rushed out, slippers flapping, and yelled at the junior inspector in charge, "How can I sleep? Have I not enough trouble? Go away — go away!"

"But, sir, we have to make it safe for you to sleep," explained the officer. "A small man with a scarred face and pointed ears has been seen in the neighborhood — he might be in this house —"

Zakir Faris slammed the door.

On the sixth day, which had been exceptionally hot, when the predawn breeze from the Tigris gave breath to the city, the police hit with a commando raid, swarmed over rooftops, trampled through gardens, shot at shadows, dragged people from their beds. And Inspector Chafik, recovered from his virus, accompanied by Sergeant Abdullah, called on Zakir Faris.

"I do regret this intrusion, but it is for your safety — that man is about," the Inspector said unctuously.

"You are insane! I have already complained to your Director —" Faris had a fit of coughing.

"How rightly you complained!" Chafik salaamed. "All my efforts," he went on, "are to make amends. The constable shot the wrong man — your nephew — but the other one, that one on the stair who bowed to you endangers you, sir."

Zakir Faris spat phlegm into his handkerchief.

"Bronchial. I trust you take medication?" commiserated the Inspector. When the man had recovered, he said, "Our protection is feeble, sir. That man with the pointed ears and scarred face comes and goes as he pleases. You must have means to defend yourself — I bring you a gun."

He put a Beretta automatic on the table, then went to the bookshelf and found the book by Hugh Mearns, "What an extraordinary poet!" he said in his precise English. "I wonder if he *did* meet that man on the stair who wasn't there?" The Inspector salaamed again and left Zakir Faris with the gun and the open book.

When he was in the car, sitting straight-backed to give himself stature, he said to Abdullah, who was at the wheel, "Sergeant, did you see me give Faris a gun?"

"No, sir," answered the sergeant, and drove off calmly and deliberately.

On the seventh day, which was Friday, the sabbath, Inspector Chafik attended the mosque, listened attentively to the imam's sermon, and returned to his office through a howling sandstorm. Dust filtered through the closed windows and the oppressive heat made him loosen his tie. "Does God will this discomfort?" he asked his assistant.

"All things have a purpose," Sergeant Abdullah said piously. "The storm grievously disturbs Mr. Faris, who, after the third visit by an officer today, is now ranting —"

"Then may I be forgiven for questioning the storm. Is our subject ripe?"

"A breath will shake him from the tree."

"Then I will go blow at him."

The sergeant was disturbed. He stood, a giant shadow on the yellow-green wall, and said in a voice choked with emotion, "Sir, this man is not a fruit, he is an unexploded bomb! Permit me to deal with him."

Inspector Chafik reached into the bottom drawer of the desk, took out a manicure set, and began to clean his nails.

"I am the trigger," he said softly.

The storm was an umbrella spread over the city; the sun, lowering on the horizon, gave it blood-red ribs. Date palms fringing the river swirled tousled heads to the mad drumbeat of the wind. Officer Abdul Rahim, reinstated by special request of Inspector Chafik, leaned against the blast as be crossed Rustan Higidar to the house of Zakir Faris.

"Open!" he shouted, hammering on the door. "We have him, sir — that one on the stair, sir! Open!"

The man who rushed out, leaving the door wide, was part of the storm. He screamed with the wind that whipped his thinning hair like the fronds of the palms and waved the gun which Chafik had given him. "Where?" he shouted. "Fools!" he yelled.

"Here! Up the road!" said the constable, and ran with the raving man at his heels.

Inspector Chafik left a discreetly parked car and entered the house. The dust on the stairs was refreshed by the storm and the Inspector, who was wearing new shoes, walked firmly to leave sharp impressions. When he reached the landing he turned and bowed, then went on to the upper floor; he broke the seal on the door of the unoccupied room and entered.

Hands folded, head lowered, he prayed — and waited.

He heard Zakir Faris come back. The high voice, fragmented by the wind, ranted, "You drag me out for nothing in such a storm! A man — a little man! — no man! — leave me! Go away! Go!" There was a soothing reply from Constable Rahim, another shout of "Gct out!" from Zakir Faris, and then the flapping of his slippered feet, the stomp of his favored left leg, as he climbed the stairs.

And then the howl —

"Who is here? *What* is here?"

And the voice of Constable Rahim, "Sir — sir — do you see the footprints on the stairs? That man —"

"He isn't here!"

"That small dark man with the scar on his face —" persisted the constable.

Inspector Chafik found time to say to himself, "Oh, what an excellent policeman I have here!" Then he began to walk up and down the attic-smelling room, stamping like a guardsman at the gate of Buckingham Palace.

When Zakir Faris burst in, Chafik wheeled, halted, and looked up at the yellow shell of a hornet's nest dangling from the rafters. "Poor creatures, they worked hard and then had to abandon their home. Why?" he asked, and fumbled for a cigarette.

Zakir Faris stood less than twelve feet away, a gray-faced man, his eyes staring, his nose an eagle's beak. The gun nestled confidently in his hand; he was no stranger to the weapon. "Who are you?" he asked quietly. Then he screamed, "*Who are you?*"

"The man on the stair who wasn't there," answered Inspector Chafik. "Not your nephew," he added. Then he said, "Please, Mr. Faris, try and understand. I know you worked on the susceptibility of a junior constable under my command. You made him your gun. He killed the man who stood between you and a fortune. An insane plan — the Law will take this into consideration. But please, Mr. Faris, confess!"

He extended his hands, palms upward, and offered them cupped with compassion.

Zakir Faris turned down the corners of his thin mouth.

The Inspector looked into the blue steel eye of the gun. He thought of his wife and his son; in that flashing second another level of mind registered the crumbling plaster on the wall near the hornet's nest, and he remembered such a patch on his son's room. *Always tomorrow, Chafik*, he said to himself. *Tomorrow, you said, you'd fix it. And now there may be no tomorrow*, he said as he watched Zakir Faris tighten his finger on the trigger.

Constable Abdul Rahim fired from the doorway and the corpse dropped at Chafik's feet. The bullet from Zakir Faris' gun made a star in the crumbling plaster an inch from the Inspector's head.

Drawing breath, Chafik said to the young officer, "You killed the right man this time."

He was still struggling with his cigarette when Sergeant Abdullah emerged and offered a match shielded in the cobra-hood of his hand. "It is apparent this individual tried to kill you," he said in an official voice as he looked from the corpse to the scarred wall.

"Yes, Abdullah."

"But was it necessary to provide him with a loaded gun?"

"Yes, Abdullah — for otherwise how would we have evidence to satisfy the Director that this policeman saved my life?"

Inspector Chafik patted Constable Rahim's arm and went home.

THE INSPECTOR CHAFIK J. CHAFIK STORIES

by Charles B. Child

The Chafik stories were first published in Collier's *in the United States and often reprinted in* Ellery Queen's Mystery Magazine *(frequently under a different title). When* Collier's *ceased publication in January 1957, the final four stories appeared only in EQMM. The first British publication was in* John Bull. *Thanks to B.A. Pike, we include many of the* John Bull *appearances but not all the Chafik stories in that magazine have yet been located.*

"The Inspector Is Discreet," *Collier's*, June 21, 1947; collected in *The Sleuth of Baghdad*

"Inspector Chafik Closes the Case," *Collier's*, July 19, 1947 (*John Bull*, June 5, 1948, as "The Inspector Closes the Case"); collected in *The Sleuth of Baghdad*

"Death Is a Gentleman," *Collier's*, September 6, 1947 (*John Bull*, May 15, 1948, as "The Devil Is a Gentleman"; *Ellery Queen's Mystery Magazine*, hereafter, *EQMM*, 6/48)

"The Inspector Picks the Winner," *Collier's*, November 8, 1947 (*John Bull*, July 3, 1948, as "The Inspector Picks a Winner")

"Satan Had Another Name," *Collier's*, January 24, 1948 (*John Bull*, July 31, 1948; *EQMM*, 5/52)

"Blessed Are the Merciful," *Collier's*, March 6, 1948 (*John Bull*, September 11, 1948)

"Death Had a Voice," *Collier's*, June 26, 1948 (*John Bull*, October 9, 1948; *EQMM*, 9/52)

"The Inspector Had a Wife," *Collier's*, August 21, 1948 (*John Bull*, December 11, 1948; *EQMM*, 12/52); collected in *The Sleuth of Baghdad*

"Death Had Strange Hands," *Collier's*, September 25, 1948 (*John Bull*, November 6, 1948; *EQMM*, 2/65, as "Do Not Choose Death")

"The Sheik It Was Who Died," *Collier's*, December 11, 1948 (*John Bull*, February 12, 1948; *EQMM*, 3/53)

"The Inspector Had a Habit," *Collier's*, March 26, 1949 (*John Bull*, July 2, 1949); collected in *The Sleuth of Baghdad*

"Then There Was Light," *Collier's*, August 6, 1949 (*John Bull*, December 31, 1949)

"One Came Back," *Collier's*, October 29, 1949 (*John Bull*, March 11, 1950, as "The Cat Had One Master")

"He Had a Little Shadow," *Collier's*, January 14, 1950 (*John Bull*, July 28, 1951, as "The Little Shadow"; *EQMM*, 5/53); collected in *The Sleuth of Baghdad*

"A Quality of Mercy," *Collier's*, March 11, 1950 (*John Bull*, November 11, 1950; *EQMM*, 2/67)

"All the Birds of the Air," *Collier's*, June 17, 1950 (*EQMM*, 9/53); collected in *The Sleuth of Baghdad*

"The Long, Thin Man," *Collier's*, September 16, 1950 (*EQMM*, 7/54)

"The One Behind Him," *Collier's*, January 13, 1951

"Violets for a Lady," *Collier's*, June 2, 1951

"There Is a Man in Hiding," *Collier's*, September 29, 1951 (*EQMM*, 11/54, as "The Army of Little Ears"); collected in *The Sleuth of Baghdad*

"Death Danced in Baghdad," *Collier's*, April 19, 1952 (*John Bull*, July 12, 1952; *EQMM*, 3/55, as "The Face of the Assassin")

"Death in the Fourth Dimension," *Collier's*, September 27, 1952; collected in *The Sleuth of Baghdad*

"The Web Caught the Spider," *Collier's*, November 29, 1952 (*John Bull*, May 23, 1953, as "His Excellency's Wife"; *EQMM*, 11/55, as "The Cockroaches of Baghdad")

"Death Was the Tempter," *Collier's*, July 18, 1953 (*EQMM*, 7/56, as "Murder Weaves a Pattern"; *John Bull*, December 19, 1953, as "Husband of the Lady Alicia")

"Death Had a Birthday," *Collier's*, November 13, 1953 (*EQMM*, 12/56, as "The Lady of Good Deeds"; *Mystery Digest*, January 1959, as "Queen of the Wretched"); collected in *The Sleuth of Baghdad*

"Death Was a Wedding Guest," *Collier's*, November 26, 1954 (*John Bull*, September 24, 1955, as "Murder on the Wedding Eve"; *EQMM*, 5/61); collected in *The Sleuth of Baghdad*

"The Invisible Killer," *Collier's*, January 21, 1955 (*EQMM*, 12/61, as "The Thumbless Man"); collected in *The Sleuth of Baghdad*

"Royal Theft," *Collier's*, April 29, 1955 (*John Bull*, December 24, 1955; *EQMM*, 1/63, as "The Holy-Day Crimes"); collected in *The Sleuth of Baghdad*

"Revenge of the Bedouin," *Collier's*, November 25, 1955 (*EQMM*, 7/62, as "The Caller After Death")

"Death Starts a Rumor," *Collier's*, June 22, 1956 (*EQMM*, 11/60, as "The Chicken Feather of Rumor"); collected in *The Sleuth of Baghdad*

"A Time to Mourn," *EQMM*, 4/57

"A Lesson in Firearms," *EQMM*, 12/65

"The Dwelling Place of the Proud," *EQMM*, 10/66

"The Man Who Wasn't There," *EQMM*, 4/69; collected in *The Sleuth of Baghdad*

Super-Detective Library All in Pictures, Amalgamated Press, London. *These are booklets with the stories in comic-strip form. They are based on Charles B. Child's stories, but they do not name him anywhere; nor do they include the names of the adapter or the illustrator. They are undated, but Jack Adrian has provided the following dates.*

No. 47: "Baghdad Manhunt," February 1955.

No. 52: "Who Killed the Ghost?" April 1955.

No. 71: "Mystery in Baghdad," January 1956 (contains "The Little Shadow" and "A Ghost Walks in Baghdad")

No. 87: "Inspector Chafik Investigates," September 1956 (contains "The Mystery of the Missing Merchant" and "The Case of the Frightened Man")

The Sleuth of Baghdad

The Sleuth of Baghdad: The Inspector Chafik Stories by Charles B. Child is set in 11-point Perpetua font and printed on 60 pound natural shade opaque acid-free paper. The cover painting is by Carol Heyer and the Lost Classics design is by Deborah Miller. *The Sleuth of Baghdad: The Inspector Chafik Stories* was published in June 2002 by Crippen & Landru, Publishers, Norfolk, Virginia.

CRIPPEN & LANDRU LOST CLASSICS

Crippen & Landru has announced a new series of new short story collections by great authors of the past who specialized in traditional mysteries. All first editions, each book collects stories from crumbling pulp, digest, and slick magazines, and from collectors and the estates of the authors. Each is published in cloth and trade softcover.

The following books are in print or in press:

> Peter Godfrey, *The Newtonian Egg and Other Cases of Rolf le Roux*
> Craig Rice, *Murder, Mystery and Malone*, edited by Jeffrey A. Marks
> Charles B. Child, *The Sleuth of Baghdad: The Inspector Chafik Stories*

The following are in preparation:

> Stuart Palmer, *Hildegarde Withers: Uncollected Riddles*, introduction by Mrs. Stuart Palmer
> Joseph Commings, *Banner Crimes*, edited by Robert Adey
> William Campbell Gault, *Marksman and Other Stories*, edited by Bill Pronzini
> Gerald Kersh, *Karmesin: The World's Greatest Crook — Or Most Outrageous Liar*, edited by Paul Duncan
> Christianna Brand, *The Spotted Cat and Other Mysteries from the Casebook of Inspector Cockrill*, edited by Tony Medawar
> Margaret Millar, *The Couple Next Door: Collected Short Mysteries*, edited by Tom Nolan
> William L. DeAndrea, *Murder — All Kinds*, introduction by Jane Haddam